AS THE CROW FLIES

Elaine was born in Tonbridge, Kent, where she still lives today with her husband and two children. Living very close to Starvecrow Hill and Wood, she is within hearing distance of the constant reminder that crows are in residence there and probably have been for hundreds of years. She works at Tonbridge School as an administrator.

Elaine Venus

AS THE CROW FLIES

Olympia Publishers
London

www.olympiapublishers.com
OLYMPIA PAPERBACK EDITION

A CIP catalogue record for this title is
available from the British Library.

ISBN: 978-1-84897-562-0

(Olympia Publishers is part of Ashwell Publishing Ltd)

This is a work of fiction.
All names, characters – apart from the obvious historical figures –places and
incidents in this publication originate from the writer's imagination. Any
resemblance to actual persons, living or dead, is purely coincidental.

Published in 2015

Olympia Publishers
60 Cannon Street
London
EC4N 6NP

Printed in Great Britain

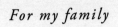

For my family

Acknowledgements

Firstly I would like to thank Jeanette, a colleague at Tonbridge School, who convinced me that I *could* write a novel alongside work and family commitments. Well, Jeanette, here it is, six years on!

My thanks and appreciation also go to Beverley, the school's librarian for her interest, and who kindly allowed my access to some very helpful books, and Patricia, the personnel manager, also for her interest, as well as her help and encouragement.

My dear friend, Pat, a librarian at Tonbridge North Library, was my first reader, reading every chapter as and when I finished them. She has given me her unstinting support and urged me on when I needed that push to never give up until those two little words, THE END, were written on the page. Thank you so very much, Pat.

Lastly, my gratitude goes to my father and mother, Kenneth and Valerie Barth, for their unwavering faith in my ability (and the book), and my husband, Paul, who cut out Olympia Publishers' advert for submissions and passed it to me, telling me to 'go for it. You won't know unless you try.'

One is for bad news, two is for mirth.
Three is a wedding, four for a birth.
Five is for riches, six is a thief,
Seven a journey, eight is for grief.
Nine is a secret, ten is for sorrow,
Eleven is love and twelve is joy on the morrow.

September 1272

The warm rays of the sun had already burnt off the last of the early morning mist. It had been a very dry, hot summer but now, as autumn approached, it was a tolerably warm and pleasant heat that filled the air. It was promising to be another fine day, one of those days when you felt glad to be alive, he thought. He was certainly *lucky* to be alive, he knew that much.

He inhaled deeply. The clean, crisp, fresh air seared through his nostrils. It smelt so good after the rancid, gut-retching odours that had assailed his nostrils on the battlefield.

The Infidel and Crusaders had fought with equal savagery. All the pent-up emotions from years of fighting; the anger, frustration and retribution had made even the meekest of men ruthless, mindless killers. Kill or be killed. The fundamental instinct to survive had been paramount.

He, Sir Guy Guiscard, a knight of the King's Realm was one of the fortunate ones. He had survived and was now on his way home.

He had set sail from Dover in 1270 with Prince Edward to join the eighth crusade. It had been launched in 1267 by Edward's uncle, Louis IX of France, to expel the Infidel Muslims from Palestine. On campaign, Louis had died of plague, and although his successor had been unconcerned with continuing the quest, Edward decided to carry on.

They arrived at Acre in 1271, but once there, a year had been wasted by squabbles between the various Christian armies. Edward, finally deciding to withdraw, left Palestine and started to make his long, slow journey home. Too slow for his liking; he was in a hurry. He had been away from home for nearly three years and did not want to delay his return any longer than was necessary. He had requested, and been granted, permission to return ahead of the royal entourage and had landed at Winchelsea early yesterday.

On the road he had met a woodsman who advised him to take an
alternative route if possible as there had been a spate of robberies
recently. Travellers were being waylaid on the Castle Hill descent
into Tonbridge. Fortunately, being a local man, he knew of an old
track that cut through the Wealden Forest and out onto the quarry
road. He would travel down to Tonbridge that way. It would take
a little longer, but at least he would arrive at his destination safely.
What irony, he thought, that after all he had survived, he could end
up in a ditch with his throat cut just a few miles from home.

He nudged his destrier forward into the vast, dense woodland of
the High Weald and followed a rutted track just wide enough for a
man and his horse. The trees on either side of him formed a canopy
way above his head, making it appear as though he were travelling
through a tunnel. As he carried on deeper, it became quite dark and
gloomy considering it was a bright, clear morning. What little light
that did filter through the canopy dappled the trees and track in
front of him. The further he went in, the more uneasy and
vulnerable he felt. Few would risk penetrating the forest alone and
he decided that maybe he had been a little too hasty to dismiss his
squire, Adam, to travel on his own. He pulled up his horse to listen
and scan the surrounding woodland. The only sounds that could be
heard were the buzz of insects, the breeze gently rustling through

the trees and a lone blackbird singing its shrill, solitary song. At that moment a rabbit broke cover from the undergrowth and bolted across the track in front of them. Spooked, his horse reared up onto its hind legs. This took him completely by surprise, and as he was only holding onto the reins with one hand, made him topple backwards. He swore under his breath and only saved himself from being unseated by snatching at the reins with both hands and gripping tightly to his horse's flanks with both knees and thighs. He managed to hang on until it came back to rest on all fours. It took a moment or two for horse and rider to recover. That had been a close call. He could have fallen heavily and injured himself, he thought.

'Then where would we have been, eh, Felix?' he said aloud.

An unsettled Felix whickered and pranced in a circle. He seemed to be as eager as his master to be away from this place and, when spurred on, he turned and at a canter headed for the bright, clear blue sky that could be seen at the end of the leafy tunnel.

Emerging from the forest, they crossed a shallow stream, cantered along a ridge and then travelled down to skirt a smaller wood. The track then took them back up again from where, continuing to follow the line of trees, he could look down into the quarry and see the outcrop of yellow sandstone below him. He reached the top of the quarry road and drew rein to gaze down on the Medway Vale opening up before him.

From this high ground the contours of the land showed up clearly, and with his eyes he followed the course of the River Medway. His gaze rested on the castle, which stood tall and imposing, the sun glimmering off the yellow sandstone walls. It loomed over the bridge, which spanned the river and the small township of Tonbridge. Beyond the town, where the ground started to rise again, he could see where forest and scrubland were gradually being cleared to make way for sheep and arable land. In front of the town wall, the river was busy with many boats docked at the wharf-side bringing in supplies, and no doubt a few luxury goods for the Lord and his Lady.

The castle was still held by the family of the man who had originally been entrusted with it, Lord Richard Fitzgilbert of Brionne. He had been rewarded for his loyal service at the Battle of Hastings with a grant of land and castles, one at Tonbridge and the other at Clare, in the county of Suffolk.

There followed a succession of Richards and Gilberts, as was the fashion to name sons after fathers, until the current Earl, Gilbert de Clare, took ownership. He became Earl of Gloucester in 1262 when his father, Richard, the third Earl, had died. Gilbert, known as the 'Red Earl' because of his fox-red hair, inherited his father's lands and title and the family were still residing and flourishing at the castle today.

Carried on the breeze, the sound of a tolling bell could be heard and the faint tapping of a blacksmiths hammer hitting its anvil. He heard a shout, laughter, a dog's bark. He kicked Felix forward and started the gradual descent down to Tonbridge. It came to mind why this was called Hangman's Hill when he passed a gibbet by the side of the road. Here hung the desiccated remains of somebody; he could not say an unfortunate as he did not know what the man's crime had been. He could have been a murderer, an outlaw or just a common petty thief but, nonetheless, the punishment had been the same. The blackened limbs hung in rags and empty sockets stared where eyes had once been, plucked out by hungry birds and eaten by maggots that were now erupting from other parts of the decaying flesh. Guy looked away in disgust. He did not wish to be reminded of scenes he had left way behind him in the Holy Land.

Thankfully the summer had been a dry one so the main river and its many tributaries that crisscrossed the valley floor had not flooded. This was a very damp, wet and marshy area where the sticky clay soil made cultivation and habitation almost impossible. The only dwelling this side of the river was the Priory of St Mary Magdalene,[1] inhabited by the Augustinian order of the Black Canons and was a place where many a traveller had sought shelter and hospitality when the rivers had flooded and made the way impassable to the town and beyond.

'Good morning,' called a black clad figure opening the large oak door in the priory's outer wall. 'On your way home, Sir Knight?'

'Aye, that I am, and more than glad of it.'

'God speed you on your journey,' the Canon called after him.

Yes, not far now, he thought.

Before he reached the main river crossing he had to negotiate four separate streams that cut across the main road. Broken wattle fencing, used for laying over muddy or flooded stretches, lay discarded, made redundant by the dry weather, and large flat stepping stones were strategically placed in the waters to enable those on foot an almost wet-free passage across. This, of course, would greatly depend on the current weather conditions. At this moment in time the waters were quite shallow and, being on horseback, did not pose any problem at all. The main river though, being much wider and deeper, was a very different matter.

A river crossing point had always been here at Tonbridge. People in the past would probably have been ferried across by raft. Being

---

[1]Buried in the foundations of the railway track and the old Goods Yard between Vale Road and Priory Road – now car parks.

on the main route to London, it had become very important to first the Romans and then the Normans, and thus a bridge had been built to accommodate the ever growing traffic. This had been constructed of solid oak, the tree that grew in abundance in the Kent forests.

The stone castle that guarded the river crossing had originally started life as a timber fortress over two hundred years ago at the time of the Norman Conquest, to secure and protect the Normans from a potentially hostile Saxon population. Over time a tolerant co-existence had been established, so much so that many a Norman had married into a Saxon family, as his own ancestors had done.

His father, Sir Robert Guiscard, had married his mother Matilda Wardle who came from Saxon nobility, born and bred in the manor of Soar in Plaxtol. He, also being a knight of the King's Realm, had sworn his allegiance to King Henry III when they were both young men of twenty years. Since then, he had been a fine soldier, a good and faithful friend, and loyal supporter of the King. On his marriage to Matilda, the King had shown his gratitude by granting him land located to the north of Tonbridge.

The river also acted as a natural barrier in front of the town. Water from it was channelled around the castle and keep via a deep fosse to form a defensive moat.

The only admittance to the Gatehouse was by way of the Castle Barbican,[2] an outer fortification, and a drawbridge at the north front of the building.

Looking across to his left, he could see the staircases in the south curtain wall that gave access to and from the river and the living quarters up in the castle's inner bailey.

---

[2] On the site of the Old Fire Station.

Looking up, a man-at-arms was stationed on the corner bastion, which commanded the approach to the bridge and town. The family standard flying from the gatehouse battlements confirmed Lord Gilbert de Clare, known to be a frequently absent Lord, was at this present time in residence.

The bridge's arched barbican and adjoining wall running east was an added defence for the town and from here men-at-arms could be seen patrolling the fighting platform. The wall ended with another bastion and continued round to enclose the entire town. Running alongside this was a fosse also filled with water channelled from the river.

Guy clattered over the bridge.

He was waved through the archway and made his way to the guardroom. Here he was asked his business and requested to relinquish his sword and belt, along with any other weaponry he might have on his person. This was compulsory for everyone, even a knight, who wished to gain entrance to the town. This was also an opportune time for him to divest himself of his heavy and uncomfortably hot hauberk and tabard. These would all be returned, ready and waiting for his collection at the Horse Gatehouse[3] at the north end of town, on the point of his departure.

---

[3] Bordyke – Running from the Ivy House towards Lansdowne Road.

The noise was very apparent after the quietness of the countryside. Tonbridge was normally a relatively quiet town, but it was market day and he found himself being pushed and jostled by the crowds. While some were here to live it up boisterously in the taverns, others were here to meet up with friends for a good gossip and an exchange of news. Whole families were out browsing the stalls and enjoying the sunshine. There were peasants dressed in the light greys and browns of the poorer classes, and elegantly dressed merchants, gentlemen and their wives, the sunlight showing off the rich and vibrant reds, yellows and blues of their garments. There was the chatter and laughter of people conversing and bartering in both French and English. Street vendors with trays full of pies, pig's trotters and ribs of beef were shouting their wares. A black-robed Augustinian monk with a crucifix and rosary hanging from his girdle preached to a handful of people outside a tavern about the evils of drink. Horse-drawn carts, ponies and packhorses ambled through the town towards the market place, laden with goods and guided by peasants from local farms and villages. He could hear a commotion. A handcart full of apples had lost a wheel, spilling its contents all over the road. While the owner stood swearing and cursing his broken axle, his young companion ran around trying desperately to retrieve the escaping apples before they were kicked further afield or trodden on. At the same time, a passing farmer was trying unsuccessfully to steer his herd of goats up the main road. It did not help matters when the goats, spying the apples, went charging off in all directions to gobble up as many as they could. They got a whack on the backside with a stout stick for their trouble. Seeing his precious harvest being plundered evoked further curses from the cart owner. Tempers were running high and would probably lead to a few fists flying, he did not doubt. Merchants, tradesmen, farmers and villagers from miles around made the journey into town, to the market cross that centered the widest part of the main street to sell and purchase goods. Many of the stalls sold local produce and craftsmen sold everything from belts, woven baskets and wooden storage boxes to milking stools. An ironmaster's wife was selling his ironware – cooking pots, fire backs, nails and harness fittings. There were a handful of stalls selling more exotic wares such as fine linen, spices, perfume and jewellery. This showed the proximity of the town to the main trade route from the coast up to London. A farrier at his forge was doing a fine trade. A queue of horses were tethered to a hitching bar waiting patiently to be re-shod. Livestock were being herded up the back lane[4] behind the market cross. The lane led to the Castle Barbican and the Shambles,[5] a very poor area of town and a place where animals were sold and kept prior to slaughter, or held in holding pens before continuing their journey with their new owners. A tannery was also located here, unfortunately not relegated far enough away from the centre of town to stop the obnoxious smell permeating the air. He spied the piss-pots of human urine on the corner of the lane entrance. The contents of these would be collected and mixed in

---

[4] Castle Street.
[5] Original Cattle Market site, old Saturday Market – now housing.

large stone tanks with dung, bird droppings and animal brains. The tanner, or more likely his apprentice, would soak the dried stiff and dirty animal hides in the noxious solution before kneading them with his bare feet until they became supple. It took a person with a strong disposition to be in that odiferous trade, he thought, and wrinkled his nose in disgust. He needed a drink.

He dismounted, headed for the tavern[6] and led Felix round to the rear of the building where he could see a young boy mucking out the stables.

'Good morning young man,' he called.

The lad looked up from his task. 'Mornin', sir,' he replied cheerfully enough.

'Allow me to introduce Felix here. Could you please relieve him of his burden and give him some food and refreshment?'

'Aye, I can do that for you, sir.'

Guy tossed the lad a silver penny. The lad could not believe his eyes, or his luck.

'Thank you, sir,' he said as he caught it expertly with one grimy hand.

He swiftly deposited it down the back of his shoe in case the gentleman had made a mistake. If no mistake, this was very generous indeed. It had been worth getting up this morning after all.

'I shall be inside partaking in your landlady's excellent ale.'

Once stripped of his bridle and saddle, his master's shield, helmet, bedroll and cloak, Felix was quite happy to be led to a clean, dry stall where fresh straw had been laid. There was a trough of fresh

---

[6] On the site of Ye Olde Chequers Inn.

water, a net of hay and a nose bag hanging on a hook, just waiting to be filled with oats for him.

Ascending the well-worn stone steps and pushing open the heavy oak door, Guy could tell by the noise that the tavern was busy. A delicious aroma of pottage wafted around him. It made his mouth water, but he was only to quench his thirst here. He had finished his food rations on the road only this morning so he was not that hungry. He would wait until he got home before he ate again. Mistress Ralf's food was renowned for being tasty and wholesome, and her ale was hailed as the best for miles around. This was not only an alehouse; accommodation was also available and although her rooms were basic, they were very clean. But she would not let just anybody stay. There were plenty of not-so-particular lodging houses to be found in the town for the not-so-particular traveller and many an expectant guest would be scrutinised first to make sure they were well within her requirements before she would let them a bed. This was most appreciated by the more fastidious customer, as more often than not, if it were busy, would find themselves sharing a room, or even a bed for the night!

He jostled his way into the taproom, which was packed to almost overflowing. Raucous laughter erupted from one trestle table in the corner where a group of off-duty soldiers, minus their helmets and weaponry, sat huddled around. Other patrons included an assortment of merchants and carters. He was just thinking that he had not seen anyone he knew yet when, craning his neck to get a good look around, his eyes rested on two of the occupants. He recognised his good friend Sir Hugh Breton, the town's sheriff, and his deputy, Percy Ralston. They were seated over in the farthest corner and had positioned themselves in such a way that they could get full view of the room and doorway. At ease within each other's company, they sat in silence, seeing no reason for idle chatter. They were obviously on a mission. Percy Ralston lifted a mug of ale to his lips and scoured the room. His eyes passed over the newcomer's face and slid back again in a double take. Their eyes met and Ralston's widened in recognition. He stopped mid-gulp and gave a curt nod of acknowledgement whilst at the same time nudging his companion. The sheriff looked up, saw Guy and, in delighted surprise, got to his feet and headed towards him.

'Guy, you are back at last. It is good to see you!'

His grey-green eyes were bright and sharp, and his grip was firm as he grasped Guy's forearm in greeting.

'Thank you, Sir Hugh,' replied a beaming Guy. 'You don't know how good it is to see you too.'

They stood back and regarded each other. Although he looked tired, leaner, and a little rough around the edges, nothing that a good shave and haircut would not put right, Guy looked particularly well considering where he'd been for the last three years, thought the sheriff. If lucky enough to return home at all, many had been left maimed or disfigured and changed beyond all recognition. Guy also perused his friend who had put on weight since he had last seen him. His gaze lingered on the protruding paunch, supported by a taut and straining belt buckle. The look was not lost on Sir Hugh who drew himself up sharply and inhaled deeply to hold himself in.

'I know, I can't do a thing with it I'm afraid. My only excuse is my age!' he laughed, patting his tightened stomach and not in the least offended.

The words ended with a gasp as he was forced to breathe out, his stomach coming back to rest on the belt buckle once more. They both laughed. Sir Hugh's tanned face was relatively unlined, and apart from the flecks of grey beginning to appear in his dark hair and beard and the few extra pounds, there was very little to show that this dear friend was on the threshold of middle age. Guy placed an affectionate hand upon his shoulder.

Guy had always greatly admired this man. He was a man of plain speaking, who did not suffer fools gladly. Sheriffs were notorious for their greed and dishonesty, but not this one. He was highly respected and known far and wide for his efficiency and fairness.

After delivering Guy a bracing slap on the back and inviting him to join them, Sir Hugh called to Mistress Ralf for another mug and a jug of ale to be brought over. They made their way back to the corner of the room. As they approached the table Percy Ralston stood up. He was a lanky, ungainly Saxon who stood awkwardly, trying unsuccessfully to disguise his great height. He grasped Guy's hand in greeting.

'Good day, sir.'

'Good day to you, Percy. Glad to see you're as vigilant as ever!'

'Case of 'avin to be, sir. You 'ave to watch your back round 'ere,' Ralston replied, swivelling his eyes about the room.

Guy knew this to be true in Percy's case.

Alys Ralf brought over another mug and a jug of ale for Guy, and a basket of freshly baked mutton pasties, which she placed at the centre of the rough oak trestle.

'There you are gentlemen, on the 'ouse these be. Big, strong, 'ansome men like you need regular sustenance to keep 'em going, eh?'

Sir Hugh cleared his throat.

'Uh, yes… Well, thank you, Alys… We will enjoy those,' he replied, reddening slightly.

He was embarrassed by her boldness but his bluster did not trouble Alys in any way. She stood with her hands on her wide ample hips, her bodice revealing her equally ample bosom. Nibbling her lower lip, she made eyes at Percy. Just as she was beginning to think he was more interested in the basket of pasties than her, he looked up. She caught his eye and fixed his gaze for a couple of seconds. She then winked at him, turned, and with a very slow, seductive sway flounced off, calling a greeting as she went to two merchants who had just entered the taproom.

'Good morning, gentlemen. What can I get you?' she called.

Knowing Percy would still be watching her, she turned and winked at him once more. Guy could not help but smile to himself as he watched Percy's face. With his eyes agog and mouth drooping open, he was nigh on salivating as his gaze followed Alys' voluptuous frame across the room. When he realised Guy was watching him, he snapped his mouth shut and quickly averted his attention back to the basket of pasties. Reaching for one, he grabbed it and sat down abruptly.

Percy had come from a very poor family who had lived in a hovel just outside the town. His parents were dead. Both had died of the coughing disease when he was a young boy, brought on by years of living in the damp and mist that came up from the river. Due mainly to malnourishment, Percy had never been a strong lad, but having to fend for himself had managed to keep reasonably fed by means of begging, hunting and, if necessary, poaching. He found casual work wherever he could and he made sure he slept anywhere other than near the river. If he was lucky a bed for the night would have been available with the job, if not, he would sleep rough, camping out in the woods in summer and in barns and stables in winter. Some landowners and farmers were accommodating enough, but there had been occasions when he'd had to make a run for it, especially if he had been poaching on the land. Unfortunately he became involved with a band of local thieves and vagabonds and progressed into petty crime. Percy and his colleagues had always evaded capture until one night, after a particularly ambitious operation to steal sheep from the holding pens outside the castle barbican, Percy had been caught. His fellow miscreants had managed to escape but not without leaving behind a dead constable. Percy knew he was in deep trouble. The sheriff at the time had been Sir Hugh's father who, taking into consideration Percy's young age, had offered him clemency if he revealed names of the other gang members. Percy realised that if he did what the sheriff asked, he might as well put the noose around his own neck, so as part of the bargain, he wanted protection. This was granted and he was given a job as a stable boy. As a further safeguard, for he could potentially become a target for the families and friends of the men he had condemned to the gibbet, accommodation was also made available to him within the castle walls. Percy soon became a great asset to the sheriff. He was elevated to constable and eventually promoted to deputy. Sir Hugh had since taken over as sheriff from his ageing father and although they argued and bickered, much like an old married couple, he and Percy worked well together and were both wholly committed to upholding law and order in their jurisdiction. But even though many years had passed, Percy knew there were people still out there with long memories and who, given half a chance, would not hesitate to stab him in the back. Hence his need for constant awareness.

Guy poured himself a drink and downed it in one draught.

'That went down well,' observed Sir Hugh.

'It certainly did,' replied Guy, replenishing his mug.

He had ridden a long and dusty road and there was nothing like a long cool draught of ale to soothe a parched throat.

His thirst sufficiently slaked, he turned to his companions.

'Now, what's afoot?'

Sir Hugh and Percy glanced at each other, but neither spoke.

'Come on gentleman, I have known you both long enough to know you do not frequent taverns for the pleasure of it. There must be a reason why you are here. You're looking for someone, are you not?'

Sir Hugh had to smile to himself. Not much got past Guy; he was a very intuitive and articulate young man.

He cleared his throat and leaned forward.

'Yes we are. More than one person in fact. There has been a major increase of robberies in the area of late, most to the south and on the outskirts of the forest.'

'Yes, I'd been warned on my journey here,' put in Guy.

'Some incidents have been more violent than others, but all the victims tell of being jumped on from behind and hit over the head so swiftly that they did not have a chance to see the perpetrators. There have been many victims. To name but a few, one was a merchant from Robertsbridge who was set upon on Castle Hill and thrown into a ditch. He may well have perished there had he not been found by a travelling peddler family and taken to the priory to recover. Another was a knight and his squire. They managed to get themselves to the castle, where they have now recovered sufficiently enough to continue their journey. All were left alive, although barely in some cases. All were stripped of their valuables, and every horse was taken. But there was an exception for our latest victim, I'm afraid – the unfortunate warden of the forest. He was found dead by one of the foresters and his page, crammed into the hollow of an old decaying oak tree; very undignified, I must say, with the stump of a broken willow shaft sticking out from between his shoulderblades.'

'Forest wardens have never been popular. He would not be the first, and possibly not the last, to take an arrow in the back,' pointed out Guy.

'Aye, they're all scheming, grasping swine...' grumbled Percy, taking a swig of ale and wiping his mouth with the back of his hand.

Forest officials were another bad lot, known for their greed and corruption and taking full advantage of their position.

'Not all, Percy. Hubert Green was a good man', the sheriff said sadly. 'He was honest and reliable... *and* he was not killed for his purse. That was still on his person... or for his horse for that matter. That was recovered, found roaming nearby. No, he was murdered. It seems to me that someone wanted him out of the way and tried to hide his disappearance for as long as possible. The offending arrow was very crudely made by the way, the sort an outlaw would make himself.'

Guy thought for a while.

'Is there a clue as to who these villains might be?' he asked.

'None whatsoever,' answered Sir Hugh with a deep sigh and a shake of his head.

'And what about the other foresters? Have they seen anything?'

'They say not. They have been liaising with us and De Clare's men and are scouring the roads and forest from dawn until dusk. So far the wily bunch have managed to elude us, but then the Wealden is so vast an entire army could remain there undetected. De Clare is not happy. He says that the powers that be will undoubtedly pass judgement on his ability, or rather his inability, to bring the situation under control and, of course, the King will need to know about the demise of one of his appointed wardens. So he has demanded that we apprehend these scoundrels as soon as possible, and knowing this to be the most popular tavern for traveller's passing through, we thought it a better place than any to try and glean any information. We have already learnt from Alys that a stranger was in here only the other day who looked of dubious character. She said he seemed to be waiting for someone and had a shifty alertness about him, but he did not speak to anyone and eventually left alone.'

'Well, I still reckon they be local,' muttered Percy, under his breath.

Sir Hugh tutted at this remark and gave him an irritable sidelong glance. This was obviously not the first time Percy had voiced this sentiment, and Guy deduced a difference of opinion here.

'Don't be ridiculous, man!'

Percy looked stung, but was not to be put off.

'Ow else 'ave they managed to evade us then?' he challenged, shrugging his shoulders questionably.

Sir Hugh opened his mouth to speak but closed it again when Percy continued.

'What I'm saying is, they seem familiar 'nough with the area to stay out of capture's way.'

'And what have I explained to you before?' pointed out Sir Hugh. 'Frankpledge. That should have put paid to that.'

Percy shrugged and folded his arms.

'Maybe so,' he said nonchalantly looking away, but he was not to be convinced.

The frankpledge system ensured that every male between the ages of twelve and sixty living in a hamlet, village or street, became a member of a tithing. Each member must swear to uphold the law and each group had a chief tithing-man. His position was of great importance in the community as he was expected to make sure that his tithing was complete and that all its members observed the law. If anyone should break it, or a stranger was seen in the area where a crime had been committed, it was the responsibility of all to report or deliver that person to the sheriff. If this was not upheld, the group could be fined very heavily.

'There may not have been any reports of strangers in the area, but that does not mean to say they are not there, just successfully keeping well out of the way. My guess is they are hiding out deep in the forest,' countered Sir Hugh.

'You might both be right. They could be strangers receiving local help,' put in Guy.

'Um, that is possible.'

They bandied the issues back and forth for a time, but with no solid facts it became a pointless exercise.

'Mark my words, there's something brewing in the forest and it's not ale, that's for sure,' was Percy's last word on the matter.

'To travel at this particular time is more dangerous than it has ever been, and my main concern is for the heedless and the unaware,' was the sheriff's.

That they all agreed on.

Percy, still keeping a watchful eye on the taproom door, took the opportunity to refill his mug and grab yet another pasty from the basket. He leaned back against the wall and stretched out his long, gangly legs. After swallowing a large mouthful of pasty followed by a long draught of ale, he let out a very loud, resounding belch and had to apologise, shamefaced, after receiving a withering, reproachful look from the sheriff.

They sat in silence, contemplating for a while. Guy's gaze wandered around the popular taproom. It was long, spacious and open to the roof beams high in the thatch above. A fresh carpet of rushes had been strewn over the beaten down, hard-packed earth floor. No fire was lit in the large hearth set in the wall on this warm autumn day, but two dogs still lay before it, their legs entwined and twitching, sprawled out under a long wooden bench. The smell of onions drifted in from the back kitchen and the sound of a cooking pot clattering to the floor could be heard above the incessant chatter. Shafts of sunlight poured in through the high, open wooden shutters, catching the dancing dust motes in the air and reflecting off the odd piece of gold jewellery worn by the few more affluent customers. The off-duty soldiers were starting to get rowdy and boisterous and he surmised there would be a few thick heads in the garrison on the morrow. Merchants on the next table sat with their heads together, avidly discussing the price of cloth. Some patrons bemoaned their losses so far, while others proudly showed off their bargains of the day. He could hear the easy banter of a group of young men and their teasing and cajoling of a pretty young serving maid who had to squeeze past them to deliver a jug of ale and a platter of food. She turned pink and kept her eyes lowered as she was forced to return back the same way she had come.

Here, for one day a week only, was a hubbub of activity. This was the place to come to discuss commerce and politics, to gossip, have fun and relax.

His attention was brought back by the ever-famished Percy, reaching out to take yet another pasty. Sir Hugh, seeing it to be the last one, quickly snatched the basket from his reach and offered it over to Guy.

'Pasty?'

'No, thank you very much. I'm looking forward to eating my midday meal with my father. We shall have much to catch up on.'

'Aye, that you will,' said Sir Hugh.

'If you don't mind gentlemen, I shall take my leave now,' said Guy, as the mention of his father made him impatient to be on his way.

He downed the last of his ale and they all stood to say their farewells.

'Goodbye to you, Sir Hugh, Percy. Let us hope you have heard the last of these scoundrels, whoever they are. Please take care, and Percy, watch your back.'

'Aye, that I will, sir.'

Guy and Sir Hugh embraced briefly.

'Send my good wishes to your father, and tell him I hope to see him soon.'

With that, Guy nodded to each of them in turn, turned on his heel, and weaving his way through the crowded taproom, headed for the door and out into the late morning sunshine.

He collected a well fed and watered Felix from the stables and headed north out of town.

He donned his hauberk and rode with his sword once again belted to his hip. For extra protection a mace was close to hand, wound around his pommel. He was not about to take any chances.

He was waved through the Horse Gate entrance by the gatekeeper who was enjoying a well-deserved rest in the warmth of the sun. He did not bother to get up; he'd been awake since dawn giving admittance to the busy traffic making its way through to market. It was going to be a long day too by the time the finalising of business deals and the sealing of them with a drink or two had been done. It would probably be well into the night before he got to his bed again.

Guy rode up Dry Hill where he passed another tavern opposite the London road junction. The building had seen better days and its patrons, some of whom loitered outside, were a bunch of unpleasant wastrels. One in particular who was so drunk he could barely stand, shouted something incoherent to him as he passed. Guy raised his hand in return, even though he guessed what had been said was more likely to have been an insult rather than a greeting.

Open heath and scrubland sprawled away to the east and to the west and from the main road many well-trodden paths radiated out in different directions, all were edged with heather and bracken flecked with yellow splashes of gorse.

Ahead, among a coppice of hazel trees, a herd of swine were foraging. Their guardian was a young peasant boy who was also gathering kindling wood. He stopped in his tracks to acknowledge the knight who thundered past on his magnificent white charger. The sun dazzled his eyes as it glinted off the silver hauberk and the gold silk tabard. The snarling, rampant red lion emblazoned on the front roared into his face as it passed by, and he instinctively took a step back. With a look of pure admiration and reverence on his face, he stood and watched as the wonderful spectacle disappeared in a cloud of dust into the distance. At that precise moment he decided, beyond any doubt, he was going to be a knight when he grew up.

Over the trees ahead, Guy could see the sails of the manorial windmill. The deeply rutted lane that led to it[7] was well used by the local community. He hailed a lone figure making his way with some difficulty up the track, pushing a handcart full of wheat sheaves to be ground into flour. The feudal lords had recognised the necessity for a mill and had made it obligatory for everyone to grind their grain there on payment of a fee. To grind one's own grain was a punishable offence. Although he could not see the mill itself, as it was a way round the bend in the lane, he could hear the huge stone turning. He guessed the horse would be doing most of the hard

---

[7] Uridge Road. There once stood a windmill here. Part of the lane still remains today, running between the houses and the Shell Petrol Station.

work today as there was only a whisper of a breeze to help turn the sails.

As Dry Hill became Spring Hill, the trees closed in around him once more, and the further away from town he travelled, the narrower the road became until in some places it was no wider than a track. This track had been used by the earliest of travellers and in relatively more recent times the Romans had used it to transport iron from the Weald up to North Kent.[8] The Romans had long since gone and the track that would have been maintained with ironstone and flint fragments was now covered with earth and leaf mould, and once again consigned to being used by only the most errant of travellers. Meadowsweet and shepherd's purse grew in the grass margins of the track, which now wound its way through dense woodland. In some places the trees grew sparse, and beyond these, glimpses of meadow, pasture and other woodland could be seen.

The ancient hedgerows of hawthorn, dogwood and elder, entwined with honeysuckle and dog rose were abound with bright red and black clusters of berries and hips. The bramble with its beguiling pink and white flowers and plump black fruit, a distraction from its arching prickly stems, snatched at Felix's tail as they passed. A resident blackbird and a mistle thrush, guarding their own berry-bearing bush, were taking advantage of the autumn bonanza.

---

[8] Route traced from Cross-in-Hand, Sussex, through Tonbridge and Shipbourne to Wrotham. The ancient track ran parallel with Shipbourne Road; part of its course is marked by a wooden fence in the wooded verge running alongside Rowan Shaw.

The gradual incline from Tonbridge levelled out onto flat, open land and from here a clear view of the surrounding enclosures were visible. The Ridgeway ran east and above this sat The Cage enclosure, set with many beeches and oaks, and where hundreds of deer and boar roamed. He was sure many a father with hungry mouths to feed would risk the occasional foray onto the King's property here. The same could be said for The Postern, another enclosure, which lay further east, running below the ridge.

In front of him, the North Frith Forest was evident, and looking northwest, stretching from Starvecrow Hill where his father's estate lay, to Dachurst,[9] he could see breaks in the forest being cleared for more farmland.

He spurred Felix on and as he rode along the dry, dusty track listening to the twittering of birdsong, he slowed him down to a walking pace. Eventually the gentle gait and soft plod of Felix's hooves, coupled with the heat of the day's sun on his back, made Guy relax into the saddle. His mind started to wander and he thought back to his childhood.

It had been a very happy one. He knew nothing of his mother, only what his father had told him. She had died in childbirth when he was two years old, along with a second son. He dreamed of her at times. In his dreams she was beautiful, highborn, and her eyes were soft and kind. His father had spent as much time as possible with him when not at court or on campaign. They both shared a delight in hunting and hawking, but rather than live a life of idleness and indulgence, they spent a great deal of their time organising and helping out on the estate. He recalled the long, heady, sun-drenched days of many summers playing with the tenants' children, in particular Ben and Lucie. The surrounding

---

[9] Hildenborough.

meadows, fields and woodland had been their playground. The border stream, which trickled in some places and flowed deeper in others, had given them endless days of pleasure when hot and sticky from playing hide and seek or jumping corn stooks, they would paddle barefoot in the cold refreshing water to cool themselves. He remembered them all sitting on the bank, fishing for that elusive giant pike his father had said lurked deep within the dark recesses of the weed beds. Of course it never materialised, and they never got so much as a glimpse of it. Was that because they were bad fishermen or because it never really existed? His father always insisted it had. They played for hours, forgetting the time until a grown-up ventured out to find them when it was getting near supper and bedtime. Nan, his old nurse, had looked after him from babe in arms to a boy of seven, when he had left to be a page to his father's younger brother, Hugo, in Normandy. He had returned fully fledged at fourteen and had been devastated to learn that Nan had passed away and Ben had left to become a lay brother at the nearby Dene Abbey. He was fortunate enough to be taken into the royal household to undergo his squire training and then to be heralded into manhood by being knighted at the age of twenty-one. He still had the same cloak, shield and sword belt that had been presented to him at his knighting. The cloak was of Flemish weave, the colour deepest blue, and it had so much material it covered him from sable collar down to hem in a great swathe of cloth. It was now looking a little worse for wear and a mere shadow of its former glory, but considering how it had been used over the years, no wonder of it, he thought. He had used it to sleep in, rolled up on hard ground as well as soft pallet and, on occasion, not only was it used as a horse blanket for Felix, it had also been made into a makeshift awning to keep the elements at bay. It was now rolled up and stuffed under his shield hanging from his saddle. His shield had also been battered and dinted over the years, making it difficult to discern the black spread-winged crow at its centre with the family motto "Comme de Trouve" – AS I FIND – inscribed beneath it.

The landscape started to descend slightly and soon he would pass through rowan shaw and come to the banks of the stream he had played in as a child. Looking through the trees to his left, he could see the border meadow with its many willows[10] that lined the same stream. Felix gingerly stepped down the steep bank into the shallow ford and dipped his muzzle to drink before climbing up the opposite bank. Guy reined him in and sat for a brief moment taking in the sights, scents and sounds. He closed his eyes and drew a long, deep, savouring breath. His nostrils took in the familiar earthy, fusty smell of the damp surrounding woodland. A faint breeze drifted across from the meadow bearing with it the smell of meadow grass intermingled with the scent of wild poppies, ox-eye daisies and the buttercups that grew there. He could hear the burble of water as it cascaded and swirled over rocks further downstream. The habitual sound of crows cawing could be heard as they flew, circling high above the canopy.

No matter how far and wide he had travelled in his thirty three years, nowhere compared to this place. His heart pounded in his chest with mounting excitement.

He had been a restless young man, intent on adventure and excitement, impatient to be away at court with all its intrigue, and eager to gallop onto the battlefield as a fearless warrior. Well, he had certainly got his fair share of all that, he thought sardonically. Dear God, he had seen enough bloodshed to last him a lifetime. He was loyal to King and country, rightly so, and always would be, but he

---

[10] Willow Lea.

was weary of being at the King and his son's beck and call, and life at court was getting tiresome as well as risky of late. Many a conspirator would stab you in the back if they thought it would benefit their cause.

He now had a longing to settle down and take some direction in his life. Maybe it was time to take a wife and have children? He'd had his dalliances at court. He smiled to himself as he remembered Jayne, a very sweet and accommodating girl. Angelique, a lady of the Queen's bedchamber, had also been obliging and pleasant enough company, although she did have a tendency to cling. And then there had been the exotic, sultry Serena in Palestine. What a lithesome and passionate bed mate she had been. An exceptionally fiery one too! He often had to dodge low flying objects and even a dagger pointing at a very delicate part of his anatomy if he so much as looked at another female. Oh yes, he certainly was lucky to make it back all in one piece! He smiled to himself. But dalliances were all they had been.

A disturbance in the branches above made Guy jump from his reverie. Two crows were squabbling over a morsel of carrion. He rubbed and patted Felix's neck.

'Almost there, boy.'

He was at the bottom of Starvecrow Hill and only a stone's throw away from home.

On reaching the entrance of the lane, he turned into it and there, in front of him, stood Starvecrow Manor. He felt as he imagined he would feel when he came face to face with it again, elation mingled with some relief. On crusade he had often pondered that he might never see it again, but that had only made him more determined.

It stood in a clearing of trees with the lane skirting it to continue onto the estate and tenants' homes. The outbuildings consisted of a large stable and pig pen, a wood hut and a small dairy. A well stood in the centre of the yard.

At his approach, a dog barked and out of the stable bounded a very large grey wolfhound, wagging his tail furiously. It gambolled excitedly around Felix and when Guy dismounted, stood up on its hind legs to rest its massive paws on his shoulders, nearly knocking him off balance.

'Angus!'

Ruffling and fondling the soft downy ears, Guy buried his face into the rough shaggy neck, taking in the familiar warm, comforting aroma of his dear, faithful old friend.

'Angus, have I missed you so. What a welcome!'

The door to the undercroft opened and out stepped Matthew the manservant, closely followed by his young son, Tom. They hurried towards him.

Matthew stopped and bowed.

'Welcome home, sir!'

It was evident by the massive smile on his face that he was really pleased to see him.

'Thank you Matthew. It's good to see you and… my word!' he said in mock astonishment, 'is this the same young man I last saw standing on this very spot, holding tightly to his mother's hand when I departed? My, you have grown!' exclaimed Guy, bending down to make level eye contact with the lad and chucking him under the chin.

Tom looked back shyly and giggled, a forefinger finding its way into the corner of this mouth where the remains of a meal could be seen smudged around it. He liked this man as he recalled, and could just remember waving farewell to him. It seemed a long time ago now.

Guy straightened up and laughed.

'I apologise. There is evidence to suggest that I have interrupted your meal!'

'No, do not worry, sir, we had just finished. Alisoun is now preparing your father's. You are just in time to join him. Please, let me take Felix from you. You will no doubt be eager to see Sir Robert and freshen up. I will arrange for hot water to be sent to your chamber. You will find Sir Robert in the solar.'

'Thank you, Matthew.'

After Matthew had helped to divest him of his weaponry, hauberk and gambeson, leaving him only in hose and undershirt, Guy strode over towards the outer stone steps that led up to the solar. Angus bounded after him.

'Stay, Angus,' Guy commanded at the bottom of the steps before he took them two at a time to reach the heavy oak door.

Before entering he quickly raked a hand through his dusty, unruly hair.

It took a while for his eyes to become accustomed to the dimness within after the brightness of outside. A fire had been lit, which surprised him. He did not think that the present warm weather warranted a fire. The room was stifling.

Sitting in front of it, he could make out a figure. He sat as close as was possible to the fireplace, despite the fact that he had a fur wrap draped around his shoulders. On approaching, Guy realised it was his father, who was trying desperately to stand.

'Guy?'

'Father!'

Guy rushed forwards just in time to catch his father before he toppled over, hugging him to his chest as arms clasped around him.

Sir Robert thankfully leant and clung to his son. He thought his legs were about to give way.

'Sit down, Father.'

Guy lowered him gently back into the chair. His father sat back with an exhale of breath, clutching the arm rests.

'Is it really you?'

'Yes, Father, it is.'

It was a shock to see his son standing in the doorway. He thought at first it was an apparition, his mind playing tricks on him. He had been so desperate to have him home again.

It was immediately apparent that his father was not well. He sounded exhausted and his breathing was very shallow. Even in the dimness of the hall, Guy could see there was not a trace of colour in his face. He had never seen him looking so frail and defenceless.

'Father, you are not well. What ails you?'

'I have had a chill of late, which has left me with a fever and a persistent cough,' was the rasping reply.

He held out a weak and tremulous hand to grasp Guy's.

'Do not concern yourself, it will pass.'

Of course he was concerned! He could see that during his long absence, the lone responsibility of running the estate had been too much of a burden for his father, and had taken a considerable toll.

Sir Robert saw Guy's worried frown and to avert any more questions, for the time being at least, said, 'Come, sit with me. We have much to talk about.'

Guy sank into the duplicate chair next to his fathers. The heat from the fire made him uncomfortable. He was travel-weary, sweat-sodden and grimy from his long journey, and it all added to his discomfort. He really needed to wash the dirt from his face, freshen up and change his clothes before he settled down. As if on cue, a sound from the far side of the room made him turn to see Alisoun appear at the top of the undercroft stairs, carrying a large pitcher of water. She was a handsome looking woman with a warm smile and nature to match. She could turn her hand to most tasks, outside as well as within, and she was a marvellous cook. She had always lived on the estate, her family being tenant farmers, and she had wed Matthew, the son of old Matthew, known as 'Old Matt' so as not to muddle the two. Old Matt had been Sir Robert's manservant before he became too advanced in years to undertake the more strenuous chores needed to serve a master and his household, although he still made himself useful around the place doing whatever he could manage. The family lived together in the undercroft and between them looked after the household diligently. Nothing was too much trouble, a grumble never to be heard.

'I will take this to your chamber, sir.'

'Thank you Alisoun.'

Guy stood, and turning to his father said, 'Father, I will not subject you to the consequence many miles of travel emanates. By your leave, I will quickly wash and change so we can settle down and enjoy a leisurely meal together.'

'Yes Guy, very well,' replied his father.

The aroma of horse and human sweat had just started to waft around Sir Robert's nostrils so he thought it a very good idea. It caught at the back of his throat and he started to cough. He lifted a linen napkin to his nose and mouth.

As Guy headed for his chamber, Sir Robert tried very hard to suppress his coughing. He did not want Guy to know at what extent it was affecting him and he kept it at bay for as long as was possible. He waited until he thought him out of earshot, running up the stairs. The lack of air to his lungs was becoming unbearable and the urge to cough overpowered him. He desperately needed air and inhaled deeply. This brought forth a surge of coughing, which at first started quite quietly but grew quickly and violently into a crescendo of prolonged racking coughs. They eventually petered out, leaving Sir Robert feeling completely drained, exhausted of all strength and slumped in his chair trying to regain his breath. Beads of sweat sat on his forehead. His ribcage felt as if an army of daggers had been stabbed into it. Reclining to rest his head on the chair back, he took the napkin away from his mouth and looked at it. He saw the telltale signs of bright red blood, stark against the pure white linen. It was as he had suspected, and now he knew for definite. This was not just an ordinary or prolonged cough. This was going to be an unrelenting, persistent, unflagging and tireless cough. This was a cough that was waging an attack on his lungs and ultimately in pursuit of his life. He stared into the fire with the realisation that his time was limited and there was absolutely nothing he could do about it. After a while he roused himself from the desolate thoughts that could so easily overwhelm him. He must try to conceal his predicament from his son. He had worried so over the last three years. He'd had no idea how long Guy would be gone and had spent his absence alternating between optimism and despair. His life and been on hold, wondering whether he would ever see him again. He had never stopped praying for him and had been an avid listener for any news that could be gleaned from court or the castle as to how the campaign was going. But now, thank God, he had his son back and he was going to make the most of what little time they had left together. He was not dead yet, and if he had anything to do with it he was not going to yield that easily. He convinced himself he would feel better now that Guy was home.

'Yes,' he hissed into the fire, thumping his clenched fist on the arm of the chair. 'I must pull myself together, regain my strength and take a turn for the better!'

*

And he did.

Over the next sennight there was a marked improvement in Sir Robert's health. Everybody could see it. Matthew, Alisoun, Old Matt, they all commented on it. Guy thought it was as his father had said on his arrival, it was just a cough and it would pass. His ill health of late had been put down to worrying about and missing his son.

He woke to the familiar sound of cawing crows.

The early morning sun shone through the casement window, bathing his chamber with a warm, rosy glow. Lately he allowed himself the luxury of lying in for a while to fully wake up and gather his thoughts. This was bliss indeed, he decided, as he stretched out his limbs to all four corners of the bed.

He was settling back into life at the manor with ease, and was happy to be kept occupied helping on the estate. His father had overlooked the need for a bailiff years ago when his months, sometimes years, of absence whilst on king's business were depleted. Sir Robert managed the accounts himself, and with the help of Grainger the reeve, everything ran smoothly enough.

Wheat, oats and barley were the main crops grown on the estate, although just enough for themselves, their tenants and their nearest neighbour, the Abbey. Six large orchards produced apples, they had a small herd of cattle, a couple of oxen, a few pigs that were kept for bacon, and chickens roamed the yard. The tenants cultivated vegetables and fruit on their own land, which they consumed themselves, and the manor house had its own garden and vegetable plots. The main source of income, which kept father and son in comfortable security, came from the rearing and selling of sheep for their meat and wool.

The tenants were overjoyed to have Guy back and even more so to see Sir Robert out riding with him on many occasions. Guy was pleased to see the improvement in his father's health. Being out in the fresh air had taken the pallor away from his flesh, and the dark circles around his eyes were becoming less prominent, though he did tire rather quickly. But he knew his limitations and would excuse himself to return to the manor house and rest awhile.

They had received an invitation from Whitelawne yesterday. Lord Charles de Coulances had heard Guy was home, and requested they both visit today for dinner. The invitation was duly accepted.

In the meantime there was work to be done. He was to help move their flock to a new pasture. He jumped out of bed to wash and dress. He took from his coffer a clean linen shirt and a pair of braies. His work clothes, a tunic of green linen and a pair of woollen hose, lay over a chair where they had been discarded the night before. Fresh air and hard labour was certainly a recipe to hasten his retirement to bed at night. He pulled on a pair of heavy-duty black leather boots.

Downstairs, Alisoun had laid a breakfast of wheaten bread, cheese, smoked pork and a mug of ale. He ate alone. He had advised his father the night before to rise a little later as he had tired himself yesterday and they were to visit Whitelawne today.

On finishing his fast, he took a light woollen cloak hanging from a hook on the wall and swung it around his shoulders, sure in the probability it would be cast off by mid-morning. He opened the heavy oak door, ran down the stone steps and made his way to the stable, where he was greeted by an excited Angus and where Matthew stood with Felix at the ready.

*

The morning did herald in another glorious day, the sky clear and blue.

Late morning, father and son made their way up Starvecrow Hill. At the top, the road branched off in three directions. Running straight on, it cut through the North Frith Forest onto Plaxtol. The road east wound its way alongside the forest towards Hadlow, by way of Pittswood. They continued around the sharp bend and headed west to the small hamlet of Shipbourne and Whitelawne. The road ran along a ridge with the forest fringe being on their right. After passing Dene Abbey and emerging from the trees, they could look across to the left and survey their land and the continuing landscape sweeping down to the Medway Vale and up again to the Wealden Forest far in the distance. As it nestled way down amongst the trees, the township of Tonbridge could not be seen. They travelled up Stumble Hill, past Shipbourne's tiny church and onto the Whitelawne Estate.

Sir Robert looked splendid in a deep burgundy velvet tunic embroidered with gold thread, and hose in a slightly lighter shade. A cloak of rich red wool was secured around his shoulders by a large round gold pin, set with a deep red garnet. For as long as Guy could remember, the pin had been in his father's possession.

In his sixty-fifth year, Sir Robert was still a very distinguished and handsome man, even though his dark hair, once thick and glossy, was thinning and greying now. He had never worn a beard, preferring to be clean shaven. He still had a fine set of pearly white teeth, which he showed off readily in a wide, warm smile and his eyes were a rich, dark brown laced with dark lashes. He was quite tall and held himself well with a broad-shouldered frame, though he was not of such a robust build as he once was.

Guy wore a dark green linen tunic etched with embroidery of light green thread. His hose were also of a lighter green, and he wore his best soft brown kid boots. Having a fairer complexion than his father pointed to his mixed ancestry, in spite of his Norman name. The flaxen hair of infancy had gradually darkened through boyhood and was now a very light brown, but the searing rays of the desert sun had streaked it with gold. It was curly like his mother's hair had been, and he had inherited her green eyes. His features and build were like his father's though, and he was very much his father's son in more ways than one, it had been said.

The journey did not take them too long at all, and before they knew it, they were riding into the courtyard of the great house. Whitelawne had many hundreds of acres. It was the largest estate for miles around and the manor house was very grand. William must have been very grateful indeed to have bestowed this massive amount of land, Guy mused.

There was much activity as they came into the courtyard. Two young stable lads came running out to meet them. Sir Robert's chestnut mare was caught by the bridle and steadied while he dismounted.

'Thank you, young man.'

The boy, a skinny feeble lad, barely looked up to acknowledge Sir Robert as he led his horse away to the stable. The other lad was slightly bigger but just as puny. Holding onto Felix, he stood staring down at the ground with a sullen expression on his face.

'Thank you,' said Guy whose politeness was repaid with a quick sidelong glance dripping with contempt.

Guy gave his father a quizzical look to which a shrug of the shoulders was his reply.

They were greeted by a manservant who appeared from the main doorway. He was a wiry, nervous looking man who hopped from one foot to the other, wringing his hands together.

'Good day, gentlemen, please follow me,' he said as he led them into the hallway.

Guy knew from previous visits that the great hall was through the door to the right, but the servant opened the left hand door and stood back for their admittance. They stood for a moment allowing their eyes to adjust to the muted light after the brightness of the courtyard. The room was very opulent. Lavish tapestries of many colours lined all four walls, giving the large room an affluent but cosy feel. The floor was laid with fresh rushes and bowls of herbs, and lavender had been placed on the window sills. Chair backs and coffers were inlaid with brightly coloured gemstones and covered with thick sumptuous cushions. A large oak table in the centre of the room was laid with wine goblets made of thick Flemish glass and matching horn-handled knives and spoons. Above the great fireplace two crossed swords and a shield baring the De Coulances' crest radiated out its brilliant colours as shafts of rainbow coloured light slanted down through the stain glass window. Ornate wrought iron braziers stood in the farthest corners from the fireplace in readiness for the chillier evenings and intricately patterned iron sconces lined the walls. A door in the far corner of the room opened and in swept Lord Charles and Lady Isabelle in all their glory. They both sparkled like jewel-encrusted trinket boxes, their robes adorned with brooches, their fingers dripping with gemstones. In comparison, Guy and his father felt very frugally attired.

'Good day, gentlemen. Please, make yourselves at home,' bellowed Lord Charles.

He was an enormous, heavily built man with an equally enormous voice. His face was a florid red that suggested too much good living with little abstinence. He stood legs apart, hands on hips surveying the room.

'Have you a drink? No? Drake, come on man, get our guests a drink!'

The manservant had already made his way over to the massive, elaborately carved wooden sideboard and was halfway through pouring wine into goblets. The sound of his master's raised voice made him jump and the hand holding the flagon shook so that some of the liquid spilt onto the silver tray. With a quick, furtive glance in Lady Isabelle's direction, he swiftly took a napkin and wiped the spillage. She had not noticed, thank goodness.

Greetings were exchanged and Lord Charles made apologies on behalf of his two absent sons who were on a hunting trip.

Lady Isabelle went to each of her guests in turn, offering her tiny delicate hand accompanying a pained smile. To the eye she was a very small, contained woman, but there was nothing fragile or flimsy about her. She walked and stood ramrod straight and she ran her household with identical rigidity. Woe betide anyone who disobeyed or crossed her. Her harsh, pointed features were exaggerated by her long straight black hair, which was pulled back severely from her forehead and covered with a fine silk veil and circlet. She had a pointed, aggressive chin and her shrew-like beady eyes darted everywhere and, usually, did not miss a trick. The habit of pursing her thin lips had etched lines around her mouth, and she gave off an aura of cold aloofness and indifference.

'Good day, Sir Robert, Guy. It has been a while.'

Sir Robert took the outstretched hand, raised it to his lips and lowered it again.

'Good day, my lady. Yes it has. The estate has taken up much of my time of late, and as you know, Guy has just returned from the Holy Land.'

Isabelle turned her imperious gaze upon Guy and swept it over him from head to toe.

'Yes, so I understand,' she said offering her hand to him.

Guy took it and, lowering his eyes, gave a short, sharp bow.

'Lady Isabelle.'

She opened her mouth as if to speak again, but after the briefest pause she seemed to think better of it and turned away. Taking a goblet from the proffered tray, she sat down abruptly, leaving her guests in no doubt that was the end of any conversation on her part.

The air started to feel somewhat chilly and Guy shivered, wondering how the afternoon would fare.

Lord Charles was a prolific talker, which, at this moment in time, was a godsend as it made up for his wife's lack of enthusiasm. He seemed genuinely interested in the campaign abroad, and by the time they sat down to their meal, the atmosphere had thawed a little, although Lady Isabelle was still more apt to listening rather than joining in their discourse.

The wines were of the best quality. The white must have been stored somewhere cool prior to serving as it was pleasantly chilled, and the red, as Lord Charles informed them, was King Henry's favourite, 'made from the Loire Valley red grape Pineau d'Aunis, which he introduced to England, did you know?'

The food was delicious and plentiful. An abundance of mouth-watering dishes, which Guy had only ever seen the like of at court, kept coming. Course after course, it seemed never ending.

First duck terrine, then white fish in a white wine sauce flavoured with onions and spices, followed by a poultry course, which consisted of a fat, succulent goose, pheasant in red wine sauce and a selection of smaller birds such as partridge, woodcock and pigeon. Venison and wild boar finished the main courses. During the poultry course, Guy decided he ought to slow down and started to only pick at what was placed before him. If he was not careful there was a real danger he would disgrace himself at the table from overeating. The sweet course, a light creamy pudding sprinkled with almonds and nutmeg, made a welcome change. Preserved fruit ended the banquet.

Guy was thankful to take his last mouthful. He wiped his mouth on a napkin and sat back with a sigh, more from relief rather than contentment.

Like himself, his father and Lady Isabelle had only picked at their food, but Lord Charles had ploughed through each and every dish with great relish.

No wonder he was the size he was, Guy reflected.

Through the course of the meal, the gentlemen exchanged their knowledge and experience, which Lord Charles freely admitted in his case was very limited, of the sheep and wool trade. Last winter had been long and bitter, one of the worst seen for many a year, but that had the advantage of producing thicker, better quality fleeces.

'Plenty of snow in winter means a good fleece in summer,' pointed out Lord Charles, who was pleased he knew that much at least.

'Aye, that is true enough,' agreed Sir Robert.

Both admitted to getting a good price for their wool this season, though they did not divulge exactly how much. They also debated how the huge task of head-counting their flocks could best be executed. Charles left this, like so many other tasks, to his reeve and bailiff to organise. All he knew was that it 'took a good few days and the damned things led them a merry dance, I can tell you!' he guffawed.

Giving a polite period of time after the meal, Lady Isabelle excused herself from the table, but not before instructing Drake, who stood behind his master throughout the meal, to clear it. They all stood, and Sir Robert and Guy bowed to their hostess.

'Thank you for the excellent repast, madam.'

She nodded her head in acknowledgment of the compliment.

'Gentlemen,' was her only stiff reply, and she left the room.

Drake employed the services of others to help with the task so as to undertake it quickly, effectively and with as little fuss as possible.

A succession of servants filed into the room. They were a bedraggled looking bunch, all of different ages, ranging from the young to the very old. Watching them, Guy quickly came to the conclusion that they were less than enthusiastic in their duties. They appeared in a trance-like state, staring straight ahead and looking neither left nor right. They resembled puppets on strings, their movements being controlled by some hidden entity.

One in particular, a girl no older than sixteen, he guessed, caught his attention. She stood out by the way that she walked which was quite unlike the usual maidservants scamper. She had poise and held her head high. At first glance, what would seem to be a haughty or even arrogant expression on her very pretty face was, in fact, a proud and confident one. She did not appear to be as undernourished as her contemporaries, nor was her complexion as pallid. She boldly glanced Guy's way and saw him looking at her. She studied him with her sapphire blue eyes and then held his gaze longer perhaps than was fitting for a servant. She held it long enough for him to realise it was intentional and leaving him in no doubt that she was trying to convey a message to him. Before he had time to reflect on this, she had looked away, picked up a dish from the table, turned and was gone, disappearing behind a screen placed before a doorway, which led to the kitchens.

The encounter unnerved him and he thought back to the two puny, glowering stable boys. There was certainly a distinct air of dejection and despondency amongst the servants here. Something was wrong; he felt it. He was brought back to the moment by a flagon of wine being placed before him. Lord Charles had refilled his goblet and was gesturing for his guests to do the same. Guy had had enough wine, but he poured himself a small amount to be sociable and passed the flagon onto his father who held up a hand in refusal.

'What news at court? I did hear a rumour Henry is not well,' boomed Lord Charles. 'Here's hoping Edward does not loiter; he might be needed far sooner than he thinks.'

Sir Robert drank down the last of his wine.

'What you heard is true. Henry has taken to his bed. Let us hope it is nothing too serious, but when God does eventually choose to take him from us, it could not be a better time for Edward. He is lucky insomuch as the country is at its most prosperous and united right now, and he will be a most welcomed successor. This can only be attributed to his father. For all that might be said of Henry's downfalls, he has redeemed himself as a ruler. After all, we cannot all be great warriors, and he has spent far too much of his reign fighting the barons and trying to re-establish control in France. At present we are at peace, and by his patronising the arts and education, we have seen a great advance in such things.'

'Yes, that is true, and you are right regarding our prosperity. You and I cannot complain, eh? We have certainly done all right for ourselves, have we not?' laughed Lord Charles, indicating the extravagant surroundings with a flourish of his plump, beringed hand and looking very satisfied with himself.

A look of distaste passed over Sir Robert's face. He wondered, not for the first time, why he counted this pompous, overbearing man a friend.

'Yes, and our good fortune,' he retorted, indicating Guy and himself, 'has not been achieved without hard work and an equal desire on both sides to attain a favourable way of life for all.'

Both men regarded each other across the table. It was not a hostile exchange, but there was a distinct change in the atmosphere. Guy groaned inwardly. He knew it would not be long before the usual topic reared its ugly head again. One would bait, that would normally be Lord Charles, and the other would bite and, as Guy had witnessed on previous occasions, the debate would always become quite heated.

Although both families had inherited from an invading force, Sir Robert felt vindicated from his ancestors' plundering and ill-gotten gains by the way in which he looked after, and worked together with his tenants, for each to regain some honour, dignity and respect. Lord Charles, however, ran Whitelawne very differently. He was severe, inflexible and ran a very tight ship. Both would argue what level of consideration should be afforded their respective working tenants, and this had always been a bone of contention between them. Sir Robert reproached Lord Charles, told him he should be more lenient as it did not bode well for present or future relations, and Lord Charles scoffed that Sir Robert gave too much precedence to his.

The remark had not gone unheeded.

'You have always taken too much upon yourself, Robert. You know I think it unwise to rub shoulders with serfs. They will take advantage and get ideas above their station,' said Lord Charles in a disdainful tone, reaching over to refill his goblet.

'But we have their loyalty and I will not forsake that to appease anyone who thinks it acceptable to govern over an oppressed and downtrodden workforce!'

Sir Robert was not antagonistic by nature, but the same argument time and time again was becoming tiresome.

Lord Charles deemed it worthy to look offended and defended himself.

'But we need to keep them subdued or they will rise up and avenge themselves!'

'If they were treated with a little more respect, that situation would never arise,' was the blunt reply.

'Don't you believe it!' roared back Lord Charles. 'They will forever be uncivil, deceitful and conniving!'

He slammed a hand violently down on the table, an unexpected gesture that made his guests start, and it became obvious that Lord Charles had overindulged with the wine. His face was flushed and the broken purple veins stood out on his cheeks.

'I will give you a case in point!' he said, visibly becoming irate now.

'We have just had to throw a troublesome rabble rouser off the estate. A reprobate who's been stirring things up with the peasantry! You know him,' he said, jabbing a forefinger in the air at Guy.

'Uh... Turner, yes, William Turner, that's his name! We sent him packing when he had the audacity to attack the reeve! He is an agitator and a miscreant and I will not have it, the insolent pup!'

Guy showed his surprise. Will, as he had always addressed him, and his brother Jack were known to him and his father. Occasionally they had helped out on Starvecrow when extra hands were needed, and were especially adept at sheep shearing. He knew they had been a little troublesome in the past, although probably no more than any other youngsters with their pranks and minor misdemeanours, but they were likeable, well-meaning lads and he could not imagine Will being involved in anything quite so ugly. Although such behaviour could not be condoned, something must have happened to make him lose his way. This certainly did not sound like the young man he knew before he went away, but then he had been gone awhile and circumstances change, and circumstances can change people. He supposed he must keep an open mind on this.

Whatever had happened between Lord Charles and his tenants had obviously upset him greatly, and feelings lying just below the surface always had a tendency to be unleashed when too much wine had been consumed.

'Calm down, Charles. Do not distress yourself so, it is not good for your wellbeing,' put in Sir Robert, who looked genuinely concerned for his host, who was so agitated his face had turned quite puce in colour.

Lord Charles could see his guests were becoming alarmed by his tirade and he composed himself.

'Please forgive me, gentlemen,' he blustered. 'Come, let us not spoil the afternoon with our differences. I propose we agree to disagree and not trouble ourselves any further with the subject.'

He alone raised a glass and took a large gulp of wine.

Through the open window the sound of horses' hooves could be heard clattering into the courtyard. A shout went out and an abrupt order was given, although what was said was lost in the melee. There followed a commotion, which involved many scampering feet and raised voices.

'Sounds like the hunting party are back early,' slurred Lord Charles, thankful for the timely interruption.

He felt uncomfortable about his altercation a moment ago, embarrassed that he had allowed himself to lose his temper in front of his guests. It was one thing to lose it with his servants, but it was totally bad practice to do so in front of company.

It soon became apparent that something was amiss in the courtyard. Normally a few curt orders were barked at the grooms and stable lads. This would shortly be followed by the heavy footfalls of his sons as they entered the manor house, impatient to quench their thirst and eager to recount their days of sport to their father.

But not so today.

There still ensued what could only be described as pandemonium outside.

A puzzled frown crossed Lord Charles' face. He stood and made his way to the open casement window. He was a little unsteady on his feet, but he rested his hands on the sill and tiptoed slightly to enable himself to see outside into the courtyard. His upper body and head ducked and weaved about, and he was obviously trying to see through the confusion. He suddenly stopped and gasped.

'What the devil?'

At that moment his younger son Richard appeared, skidding to a halt in the doorway.

'Father, there has been a terrible accident! I fear Geoffrey is dead!'

Lord Charles turned to face his son. Whatever he had seen outside had made the colour drain completely from his face. His high colour had gone. It was now replaced with a white and shiny waxen hue. His mouth dropped open as if to speak, but no sound came. Instead he put his hand to it and retched. He looked on the verge of collapse and in his haste to get to him, Guy toppled his chair over to catch him just as his legs buckled beneath him. Sir Robert helped to secure him in a chair.

While Sir Robert stayed with Lord Charles, Guy stepped back outside with Richard.

All the horses had been stabled and there was nobody to be seen in the courtyard. The noise and confusion of what could only have been a few moments ago had now descended into an eerie silence.

They made their way to an empty stall. Inside, upon a pallet, lay Geoffrey. His eyes were still wide open and his hands lay, palms up, by his side. Richard knelt down by his brother and closed the lids down over his staring, lifeless eyes. He now looked as though he were in slumber except that, on closer examination, a tiny knife wound could be seen. An accident my foot, thought Guy. A blade had been driven cleanly through his heart.

Guy sat in a small leafy rose arbour at the rear of the manor house overlooking the garden, with Angus stretched out at his feet. The sun was warm on his face and a pleasant breeze wafted the scent of clean, damp earth towards him. The birds were singing and he watched as a pair of tiny blue butterflies dizzied about a lavender bush.

It was a peaceful garden surrounded by trees, which gave plenty of protection from the wind. The paths that wound their way through it were attractively edged with flowers. Lilies, pansies and poppies in the height of summer, with scented stocks, lavender and daisies continuing into autumn. Flowers and herbs grew together in beds bordered with low wattle fencing. Thyme, rosemary, wormwood, yarrow and sage all grew in abundance. They cultivated turnips, cabbages, onions, peas and beans in a separate vegetable garden, which Alisoun was at work in now, weeding, hoeing, and picking and pulling a selection for their dinner. Young Tom was kneeling in his own small patch, diligently weeding with a hand trowel. He looked up to see Guy watching him and waved, giving him one of his shy, sweet dimply smiles. It gladdened Guy's heart to see this tranquil scene of domesticity before him and to see them looking happy and content.

The events of yesterday had shaken him more than he would like to admit. That morning they had received a visit from Sir Hugh and Percy, who had been with the coroner, first up in the forest to the scene of Geoffrey's demise, and then back to Whitelawne for an inquest. They sat where he was now sitting alone as his father, admitting to not feeling very well today, had returned to the house.

The hunting party had stayed at Horns Lodge, a timber-framed hunting lodge deep within the forest. During a chase a second boar had been routed, separating Geoffrey from the main party when he rode off in hot pursuit. When they found him they at first thought the horse had stumbled or thrown him, but on closer inspection, his plight soon became apparent.

'The coroner reached a verdict of murder by person or persons unknown,' declared Sir Hugh.

'He thought there was more than one person involved?' questioned Guy.

'Trampled areas of undergrowth and broken greenery suggested more than one person had lain in wait.'

'But what were the chances of the hunt passing anywhere near them, let alone Geoffrey being on his own? Were they intent on him in particular? Any one of the party could have become separated from the rest. It seemed rather a hit and miss affair.'

'Yes, I agree, but I am in no doubt they meant to kill somebody, whether Geoffrey was the intended victim or not.'

'How is Charles?' enquired Sir Robert.

'Not good, I'm afraid, as you can well imagine.'

Guy spoke of their observations on the previous day's visit and how the sight of the unkempt and sullen servants had concerned them. He kept to himself the matter of the girl, whose eyes he could still see burning into his when he tried to sleep last night.

'I heard the family were hard task masters, but I did not realise they neglected the welfare of their servants,' said Sir Hugh.

'To the extent that was evident, neither did we,' informed Guy ruefully, glancing at his father who was shaking his head with disappointment.

'I have been informed by a very reliable source,' carried on Sir Hugh, 'that Lord Charles has been persuaded by his sons to enclose the village lands. This has caused much unrest amongst his tenants and certainly made the family very unpopular. Lady Isabelle has confessed to me she feared they would all be murdered in their beds one night and Richard, well, he is like a frightened pup, fretting he might suffer the same fate as his brother.'

Percy, sitting someway off from the others and thoroughly engrossed in a platter of salt beef, suddenly roused himself.

'Aye, an' 'e be right to fret an' all I reckon. That miserable lot up there are toastin' their good fortune,' he shouted through a mouthful of bread, spraying crumbs in every direction.

He made Sir Hugh start. He had forgotten Percy was sitting behind him.

'Saints on earth, Percy, do you have to shout so?'

'Sorry,' apologised Percy.

By the grimace on his face he had just tried to swallow more than he could manage comfortably and, thumping a clenched fist between his ribcage, had to gulp down a few large swigs of cider to help it on its way. Once the offending blockage was dislodged, he was able to continue.

'When I spoke to the servants, they were as 'appy as pig's in muck 'bout what's 'appened. They 'ated Geoffrey, said 'e was a bully. In fact, they 'ated all of 'em. One even went as far as to say that 'e wouldn't piss on any of 'em if they be on fire.'

Sir Hugh nearly choked on his cider.

'That's enough of that sort of talk, thank you, Percy,' he spluttered testily.

Not only did his deputy shovel food into his mouth as if it might be the last meal he would ever consume, his language also took a lot to be desired.

Guy had to grin to himself. You could always trust Percy to tell it how it was.

'I were only repeatin' what I'd bin told,' said a hurt deputy.

'Oh, an' I also found out,' he added as an afterthought, 'William Turner was sweet on one o' the girls who worked in the big 'ouse an' wanted t' wed 'er, 'cept there was an objection – not from 'er family, mind, but from the De Coulances. There was a hell of a to-do apparently. They threw 'im off the estate an' then Jack, his brother, followed.'

This remark got an immediate response from Guy.

'Which girl? Did you get her name? What does she look like?'

Percy considered for a moment.

'Uh… dark 'aired with a pretty face… aye, bonny lass… can't rightly rec'lec 'er name though.'

'Typical,' quipped Sir Hugh, raising his eyes skyward.

Guy instinctively knew to which girl he referred. He could still feel her eyes right now boring into his skull.

'Of course!' It hit him like a thunderbolt.

'He jumped up abruptly and slammed his fist down on the table, again giving reason for Sir Hugh to look alarmed.

'That is what she was trying to convey to me – for me to help and… yes, that's it!'

They all stared at him, waiting for an explanation. He looked from one blank face to another. No, he decided, they would think him fanciful. It was not really something they needed to know anyway.

'Thank you, Percy, for that piece of information, it could be most helpful.'

'Aye. Who's to say what a man might do when thwarted in love?'

'Exactly so. Maybe his rebellious behaviour of late was in retaliation for the denial of his heart's desire? Strange they should be refused marriage, though. The lord of the manor does not normally decide who marries who amongst his tenants?' disputed Guy.

'Come on, Guy, you know as well as I do, the De Coulances make up their own rules and can change them with a turn of a coin if it meant they would benefit all the more,' said Sir Robert.

'As I see it, anyone could have wanted to take revenge on Geoffrey, or even Richard for that matter if it had been his misfortune to be found alone. But is it only the tenants and William Turner who are aggrieved? The brothers have made many enemies over the years. They have been spoilt and indulged, used to getting their own way and taking what they want, when they want,' said Sir Hugh.

There was an 'aye' of agreement from all seated around the table.

Geoffrey and Richard had caused plenty of chaos with their wild and unruly ways, and from a very early age Guy had made a concerted effort to distance himself from them and their fellow revellers, all offspring of the neighbouring ruling classes.

'I should think there are quite a few local families who could attest to having offspring begat by one or other brother after one of their drunken sorties,' conceded Sir Robert, his face twisted with distaste.

'Aye, they have always been bad business,' remarked Sir Hugh, shaking his head. 'Now, let's look at the facts we have,' he continued, settling himself forward on his elbows. 'We know William Turner was thrown off Whitelawne for violence and encouraging unrest. We also now know he was refused permission to marry. Why, we may well ask, and did this prompt his behaviour? I suspect it did, and that he has one great big grudge to settle with the De Coulances. We need to think seriously whether he is linked to the murder. Could William and Jack be hiding out up in the forest, and did they take the opportunity to murder Geoffrey yesterday?'

Sir Hugh looked from one to the other. All of them realised that could well be the case.

'I think a visit to Will's parents is necessary,' said Guy.

He felt some sensitivity might be needed here, and because he had some acquaintance with the brothers, thought it best he undertake the task.

Sir Hugh stood up to leave.

'Thank you, Guy. Now, with regard to the situation on our highways. I have my men positioned each day at different locations on the main routes in and out of Tonbridge, but still no one has been apprehended...' He gazed at all seated around him. 'And I must finish by imparting to you another matter that has been brought to my attention. Lady Isabelle informed me this morning that Geoffrey's wife, who is blissfully unaware of her husband's fate, is at this moment en route from Suffolk, accompanying Richard's young betrothed. She does not know their exact location but, if the journey is running to schedule, they should be quite close to home.

I intend to send a party out to escort them back. All things considered, my immediate concern is for their safety.'

'Yes, and let's hope they have a substantial escort themselves,' interjected Guy.

Guy decided to travel the back way, through the forest onto Whitelawne. The fewer people who saw him the better. He rode through the fringes of the forest, just far enough in to avoid the dense impenetrable populace of coniferous trees, which could stretch deep and dark for miles. The woodland tracks were alive with colour. The red and the white campion, the yellow of the celandine and the pink herb robert, all nodded a cheerful welcome in the soft breeze. The surrounding hazel, beech and oak were taking on their autumn colours, their ripened fruits dropping onto the woodland floor, ready to be gobbled up by the foraging swine who would stray into the woodland on their quest to find and devour the sweet, wholesome delights. A narrow track ran uphill to emerge high up on the common and rough pastureland on the edge of Whitelawne, which was used by its tenants to graze their animals. He could look down from here onto the huddle of dwellings where the tenants lived. Beyond them he could see the stream, which continued through to border their own land. He and Felix slowly meandered down between the gorse and bracken, disturbing the occasional sheep. Rabbits zipped about in the undergrowth. A woodpecker whooped as it flew across in front of them, dipping up and down to disappear into the forest behind.

He could hear the incessant trilling of a skylark as it flew high, way up into the blue heavens. As he shaded his eyes to locate the minute speck of sound, it stopped and the bird plummeted back to earth and was lost amid the grasses of the pasture.

Guy dismounted when he reached the village and led Felix up the worn grass and dry mud track that ran central between the two rows of huts, looking for any sign of life. Smoke eddied from gaps in the reed thatched roofs, which were in varying states of dilapidation, making it evident somebody was at home, although the majority, he guessed, would be out tending their strips of land or working for the manor. A flea-ridden bitch watching over her young offspring cavorting and tumbling together a short distance away from her, lazed against a sheep fold. She watched Guy's progress intently, all the while scratching behind her ear with her back leg, but she decided she was too tired and hungry to be bothered with harassing this approaching stranger, so she let him be. A way in the distance, two small children sat playing with stones in the dry, dusty earth, and an old man sat in the shade of a tree whittling a piece of wood. He looked up and nodded a greeting.

Guy was about to make his way over to him when a voice behind him said, 'Can I help you?'

He turned to find a middle-aged woman standing in a doorway. She wore a ragged but clean brown woollen gown with a dark grey shawl wound around her head and neck. Wisps of grey hair escaped to frame a well-worn and lined face.

'Good day to you, madam. I certainly hope so. I am looking for the Turner's abode. I am Guy Guis—'

'I know who you are,' she interrupted abruptly, her eyes never wavering from his face.

'It's regarding their son, William.'

There was the tiniest flicker in her tired looking eyes. She lifted her chin slightly but still stared intently into Guy's face.

'Well, you found us.'

When she still did not move, Guy continued, 'I need to know what happened here on Whitelawne, and because I cannot speak to your son personally, I thought you would have a vested interest in sharing with me your version of events.'

Only then, her eyes dropping from his face did she stand back conceding, 'You had best come in then.'

Leaving Felix tethered to an alder tree next to a water trough, he made his way to the hut.

He had to step down into the sturdy-framed wattle and daub building. The beaten earth floor had been swept so often over the years it was now lower than the ground outside. The only tiny window had an animal hide shutter rolled up to allow as much light as possible into the dark interior, which, though sparse of any furniture, was very neat and clean. A small hearth was at its centre, the stones laid in a circle with bracken, kindling and small twigs sitting within it, waiting to be lit. A blackened pot hung from a tripod above it. Wooden planks served as shelves and a couple of three-legged stools sat next to a low small wooden table. Sleeping quarters were screened off in each corner. It must have been very cramped indeed when it was shared by four adults.

Mrs Turner was not alone. She was leaning over, speaking quietly to someone propped up on a pallet of straw in one of the corners. When she turned, she kept a reassuring hand on his shoulder.

'This is my husband, John, who I am afraid is not well enough to stand and welcome you. We hope you don't mind.'

'No, of course I do not mind,' said Guy, walking over to the invalid. 'Please do not worry yourselves.'

He looked down at John Turner. The skin on his face was pitted and scarred by some childhood pox, and he too looked tired and drawn and most likely old before his time. His dark eyes stared out from sunken sockets, the black smudges beneath them emphasized by the dim light.

'Good day to you, Mr Turner.'

John Turner lifted a quivering hand in greeting. 'And a good day to you, sir,' he replied with a gentle courtesy.

Mrs Turner pulled over a stool and gestured for Guy to sit. She seated herself close by her husband and folded her arms defensibly.

Both John and Ruth Turner had been born and bred on this land surrounded by green hills and forest. Their ancestors had settled here many generations ago and it may well have belonged to them long before the Normans had procured it.

'I am sorry to see you abed. What ails you?' asked Guy, once he had seated himself.

'He is bone weary and heartsick,' spat out Ruth before her husband could reply, 'and weak through lack of any nourishment. The whole village is starving and what little food there is goes to the children.'

'You are all going hungry?' queried Guy, leaning forward, concern etched on his face.

'Aye, we are. They're trying to starve us out,' was the curt reply.

'But how, and why, are they doing that?'

'Well, firstly they made sure there was no gleaning left for us at harvest time and now our rents have been put up and...'

'Hush, Ruth,' interrupted John, placing a calming hand over hers.

73

'Let me, please.'

'Aye, very well…' said Ruth begrudgingly, 'but it's since those sons of his poked their noses in,' she managed to get in, jerking her head in the direction of the big house, before allowing her husband to continue.

John was a humble, unassuming man who had spent his life doing other men's bidding and had never lost his patience, or his dignity.

'Our manor lord has put up our rents for a much shorter lease, and now he be looking to withdraw some of our old, traditional rights – though he don't see them as rights, he calls 'em privileges. In the past the woodward would turn a blind eye to the poaching of the odd fish or the snaring of a rabbit or two, but now they've threatened to come down hard on offenders. We've been threatened with being thrown off the estate, or worse, gaol. What little food we do have we're trying to make last, but it's coming to season's end for vegetables. Now he plans to close off the common land to us and take back the few fields we have. What he be doing is trying to claw back as much land as possible, for sheep most probably.'

No wonder the tenants felt aggrieved and frightened, thought Guy. They needed the common land for grazing their beasts and gathering firewood. Their livestock had always been a safeguard against hunger in winter, and wood, kindling and brushwood was a necessity for cooking and warmth. To have this denied them, plus the inability to grow their own crops and vegetables, would be disastrous and could eventually force them off the land altogether, with only the parish for support. It was true these people would never be wealthy but they seldom feared or faced such abject poverty. They have found themselves without wheat for bread, they dare not risk poaching for fear of punishment, and their meagre strips of vegetables were all that stood between them and starvation. Added to that, there was nothing more guaranteed to lower the spirits than uncertainty about the future. No wonder everybody looked so dismal and dejected.

Realisation of these people's plight suddenly dawned on him. He scooped his hands through his hair and exhaled deeply, puffing out his cheeks.

'This is a dreadful situation,' he responded, shaking his head.

'Aye,' John sighed, 'but it's no fault of yours.'

Guy's remark bought Ruth's eyes up to his face.

'Yes, why should you care?' she demanded coldly.

'Because I do, and you all deserve better.'

She continued to look him in the eye but did not smile.

'If he goes along with these plans, it will not only finish off the likes of us, it will break the heart of Whitelawne.'

In a barely audible whisper and with her voice faltering, she added, 'Just like he broke ours when he kicked our William out and Jack followed close behind.' She swallowed hard and set her lips in a tight line, trying desperately to collect herself. Guy, witnessing the pain and sorrow etched on this woman's face, decided she would have been pretty once, before the drudgery of the repetitive hard work year in, year out, had taken its toll.

'Yes, about William,' he coaxed, 'can you tell me what happened?'

'Aye, I will,' replied John.

He could see his wife was fighting to compose herself, and she would not want to break down in front of this gentleman.

'Our William wanted to marry his sweetheart, Joanne. They'd known each other since they were little'uns and there was nobody else for either of 'em. Anyways, her ladyship took Joanne on at the big house. William would go up to meet her when he could and sometimes – only occasionally, mind – Joanne would visit home, but that all changed after a while. She stopped coming and whenever William tried to see her, he was sent away. Finally our suspicions were settled when gossip got to William's ears that she was being ill-used. When he found out, he went mad. It was Geoffrey by all accounts, and all of 'em up at the house knew about it. They had allowed their precious son have his way with no regard for her or our boy. Joanne had tried to hide her plight and was devastated when she knew William had found out. She thought he would not want her any more, being soiled goods and all that. But he wouldn't abandon her. We and her family have tried to get her back, offering to pay more than the usual fine even though we knew it would finish us, but they would have none of it. He went off the rails then, William did, causing no end of trouble. What with that business and the way things were going to change on the estate, well, he wanted us all to make a stand. Most were afraid to do so, and in truth it did us no favours anyway, only made the situation worse. After all, they hold the upper hand, don't they? The reeve stopped him one day, for his own good, mind, from making a run at Geoffrey when he passed by on his horse. William didn't take too kindly to that and hit 'im. That were the end for our boy. He were thrown out. Wasn't long afore Jack followed. He couldn't stay here wondering what was happening to his brother.'

John's sunken eyes looked across at Guy. Wearily resting his head back on the straw-filled pillow he finished. 'So there you have it, that's the story.'

Getting up to fetch her husband a mug of ale, Ruth added, 'And we haven't seen 'ide nor 'air of 'em since, we don't know where they be. I know one thing for sure though, I'm not sorry about the killing. Good riddance to him, that's what I say. Good riddance to bad rubbish.'

She offered Guy a mug.

'Sorry 'tis weak but all we have.'

'No thank you, I am not thirsty enough to take the last of your ale.'

'You are a good man, sir. 'Tis a pity others aren't the same.'

'Aye,' agreed John, 'you and your father have always been good and fair. Our boys always enjoyed working for you.'

Guy was positively outraged by what he had just heard and could not speak for a moment, but he nodded in acknowledgement of the compliment. These were decent, honest, hardworking people, and none of them deserved to be treated so. Geoffrey's behaviour had been absolutely disgraceful, unforgivable. What had he been thinking of? It was a classic case of abusing one's authority and the whole family ought to be ashamed of themselves. Who would blame the tenants if they had become rebellious? Who would deny William his dudgeon and frustration at his fellow workers reticence, who, in turn, were worried of reprisals? The De Coulances would then get their own way, and being tenant-free, would be able to do whatever they planned to do with the repossessed land. He knew these people would need help soon; winter was not far off. He would talk to his father; maybe there was the possibility of supplementing their food shortage? Maybe he could talk to Lord Charles and make him change his mind.

As Ruth fussed around her husband, taking the mug from him and making him as comfortable as she could, Guy took the opportunity to sit quietly and deliberate. By the time they had settled down again, he had come to a decision.

'Thank you for enlightening me. If I had known the situation, I would have come sooner. Allow me to reassure you that my father and I will do whatever we can to help you and your fellow tenants. I am sure my father will speak with Lord Charles to try and dissuade him from these new proposals. I will also expect young Joanne to be back with her family again very soon.'

He knew he was sticking his neck out making this last promise, but he had to try and rescue her at least, even though Geoffrey could not abuse her any more. There was a gasp from Ruth as they both stood up at the same time. She stepped towards him and encased his hand with her own in an outburst of gratitude.

'Thank you, sir. You are our saviour and truly a good man. God bless you!' she cried.

John nodded his head in approval. 'Thank you, sir,' he muttered.

Guy thought it best not to question them further about William and Jack. Their whereabouts would probably be resolved in time anyway. Even if they were guilty of any crime, it did not mean he should ignore the dilemma these people had found themselves in.

'I will take my leave now and I will make sure flour and other supplies get here as soon as possible.'

'God bless, and thank you again, sir,' John called after Guy as he stepped out of the door.

*

On the way home Guy took a detour to a small alehouse at the top of Starvecrow Hill. It was located on the road to Hadlow just off the main track in a woodland clearing. Its low stone walls supported a huge thatched roof. Above the door there hung a piece of wood with "The Starveling Crow" crudely etched on it. The proprietors, his friend Ewen and his wife Gwen, had not always kept it as an alehouse. Originally they had just reared pigs, but what had started as the occasional offer of Gwen's homemade ale to passing travellers soon became a popular, money-making business. They had also discovered that if they fed the mash and any leftover stale and undrinkable brew to the pigs, it improved the flavour of their meat, making them very sought-after indeed.

Gwen brewed two ales. One was a rather indifferent brew with not much alcoholic content, but it was cool and pleasant, enough to refresh the travel-weary without befuddling their wits, which were much needed on the precarious roads. The other, being left to ferment longer, was a much stronger ale. An extra secret ingredient was also added. This 'special brew' was served on request, and drunk only by the local community... and Ewen.

Guy often dropped in to see Ewen. He was a cordial, friendly enough fellow and Guy liked him well, but because of his insistence to take a drink with almost every customer, he often ended up a little worse for wear, making it impossible sometimes to get much sense out of him, but Guy was in luck this late afternoon. Obviously not many people had passed through today, so Ewen was more lucid than usual. He had still had a few though, which was evident as Guy watched him lurching around the yard trying to round up his pigs for the night, 'else they'd end up a tasty treat on many a table!' he called back at him.

He made a lunge for a massive pink and black sow who was hellbent on making a break for the woods, only to stumble headfirst into a feeding trough, with the sow squealing in triumph as she disappeared into the growing gloom of the woods.

'Damn!'

He sat round on the hard, dusty ground, brushing off the knees of his hose.

'Oh well, if I can't catch her, nobody else will.'

'I would not wager on it,' laughed Guy, giving him a helping hand to his feet.

Out from the small single taproom door bustled a cross and irritable looking Gwen, cloth and mug in hand.

'What's all the rumpus?' she enquired.

'That blasted pig got away again. I swear it's got eyes in its backside!'

'Ha! If it had no eyes at all it would still manage to sidestep you. You're too slow and you couldn't do anything quietly, not even if your life depended on it!'

With her flushed pink cheeks, she turned her head where golden curls strayed from her white linen coif, to identify her husband's companion.

'Guy,' she acknowledged curtly with a nod, and flounced off back to clearing up inside calling after her. 'Hurry up, it'll be dark soon!'

Ewen gave a sheepish shrug.

'Here, I'll give you a hand,' offered Guy, feeling a touch of sympathy for his friend.

It did not take long to pen the remaining pigs. The escapee would have to take its chances in the woods tonight.

'A drink?' asked Ewen.

'Thank you. It will have to be a quick one though; daylight is fading fast.'

They sat outside at a trestle table, the early autumn chill starting to settle in around them. As they talked, their warm breath mingled with the cold air, sending wispy clouds up into the atmosphere. Guy had retrieved his trusty cloak from under Felix's saddle and pulled it further around his shoulders.

'Bad business up at the house, then? Still, he got what he deserved I hear,' said Ewen.

'That seems to be the general consensus,' replied Guy.

As the alehouse accommodated a steady stream of travellers and regular customers who lived thereabouts, Guy knew the gossip picked up from there could sometimes be of considerable value.

'Heard anything of who the culprits might be?' he asked, after a sip of ale.

'Well, that's anyone's guess. He was not very popular, was he?'

'No, he was not, and neither are the rest of the family. Let me know will you if you see or hear anything,' asked Guy, finishing off his drink.

'Aye, that I will. I shall keep my ears pricked and my eyes open,' slurred Ewen, pouring himself another drink from a nearby jug.

*

It was dusk by the time Guy made his way home down the hill, the darkening sky grey against the solid black of the woods. A fox barked in the distance and the trees whispered softly in the wind. As he turned into the lane, Felix shied suddenly and stopped in his tracks. He whinnied gently, trampling the ground and showing a reluctance to go on. Guy stilled him and sat quietly, straining his ears to listen into the darkness. He felt uneasy, his heart pounded in his chest and he placed a hand on the hilt of his broadsword.

'Who's there?' he called into the darkness.

He could hear nothing but the faint whisper of the wind soughing through the trees.

After reassuring himself nothing was amiss, he gently patted Felix's neck and persuaded him forward.

Felix responded abruptly with a short, sharp snort and, with a flick of his tail, leapt forward into a trot. He was suddenly keen to be within the sanctuary of his stable with its bed of warm, clean straw. Hopefully a manger of hay would be waiting for him.

Back up the lane, a figure emerged from the shadow of the trees. He stood watching the receding backs of horse and rider. Lifting his hood, he pulled it down well over his head, concealing his face within its deep, dark folds, and as silently as a cat stalking its prey, he turned and slipped away.

The covered wain swayed and bumped over the rutted track, the occupants not knowing which way the uncomfortable vehicle would lurch next. Having rested the night at Eynsford Castle, made welcome by the Eynsford family who were friends of the De Clares and the De Coulances, they had resumed their journey early that morning. It became warmer as the morning wore on, and by midday, it was evident by the damp heat and the stillness of the air that a storm was brewing. The fur rugs had long since been discarded and because of the close proximity of the four women within the wain, the stifling heat had become unbearable. Lucie wiped the perspiration that trickled down the back of her neck with a linen kerchief and leant forward to open the canopy as far back as she could to enable as much air as possible to enter their diminutive space. Behind and in front of them rode their escort, comprising of four De Clare men at arms wearing the yellow surcoats displaying the scarlet chevrons of Clare, and two grooms, one from each household. If she had her way she would be out on the open road, riding pillion with one of them or sitting with the driver, but her mistress would have the vapours at the merest suggestion. Lady Eleanor rested her head back against a cushion, fanning herself with an ornately decorated calfskin fan. She expelled a long drawn out breath.

'Thank goodness we are nearing the end of this infernal journey. Lucie, make up a tincture for my head; it throbs so and I need to sleep a while to escape this incessant lurching and rumbling!'

Lucie reached into a small silk purse and pulled out a phial of poppy syrup. She preceded to mix into a goblet a couple of drops with a little wine from a flask. Taking the offered drink, Eleanor downed the mixture in one gulp and sat back again, closing her eyes and continuing to fan herself. It was not long before the concoction had the desired effect. Her hand gradually became heavier, eventually coming to rest in her lap. As she drifted into sleep, her mouth lolled open slightly. She was oblivious now to the movement of the wain.

Their charge, the fifteen-year-old Heloise sat huddled in the far corner, looking and probably feeling very sorry for herself. If the truth were known, she most certainly felt frightened too. She was so young, thought Lucie, watching her. To be taken from her home and family at such a young age, brought miles away to an unknown household to be married to a virtual stranger, twice her age, was cruel indeed. She was a sweet girl and did not deserve her fate. Her nurse, Nell, sat beside her talking gently and soothingly trying to rouse her from her melancholy. Being Richard de Coulances' wife would not be an undertaking envied by most females that knew him, young or even of a more mature age. Lucie had been fortunate. She had been a little older than Heloise when she had married, and it had been a love match. Until her beloved Owen had been prematurely taken from her, their attachment had been very satisfactory, their love and affection for each other reciprocated.

Unfortunately she had not borne any children by him, which did grieve her greatly, but it was not meant to be.

The thunder that had rumbled in the distance most of the morning had moved closer and was now almost upon them. A strange half-light descended as the sky darkened. A sudden squall sent swarms of leaves swirling around the wain and track behind them. The swift change in weather chilled the sweat on Lucie's neck, but the air still felt heavy. Large spats of rain started to drum down upon the canopy above their heads and as it became more persistent, the squall carried drops of it into the wain, leaving her no choice but to close the canopy, and move back deeper into its confines.

After the initial burst of heavy rain, thunder and lightning, they sat in the semi-darkness listening to a now softer pitter-patter and more distant rumblings. Lady Eleanor could once again be heard snoring softly as she carried on sleeping, unaware of the storm that had now passed over. Lucie once again drew open the canopy and the air that was now rain-fresh, blew through the opening. One of the grooms splashed up to the back of the wain. He was heavily cloaked against the fierce downpour, his face partly obscured by his hood.

'Not far now, mistress. We are just beginning to descend Oldbury Hill. We should easily make Whitelawne before nightfall.'

'Thank you, Roger,' answered Lucie as he fell behind and took his place again with the rest of the escort.

She could hear the guards mumbling about the foul weather and was thankful now for the wain that had at least kept them dry.

The early afternoon saw the sun peeping through the clouds and it soon became warm enough to dry off the horses and riders. They had started to steam slightly, she noticed. With the sun, their mood lightened too. She heard them talking and laughing together as they lumbered along. Thankfully, the rain had not lasted long enough to sodden the track.

They continued on what seemed to be an interminable journey, this last stage dragging on endlessly. Maybe if they had been able to see more of the surrounding landscape, the trek would have been a little more interesting, but not much was visible from the rear of the vehicle, the canopy obstructing their view left and right. Sometimes the track ran straight, keeping to the line of the old Roman road, but then it would wander away over the curving contours of the land among trees and gently sloping hills. Even though the jerking and bumping of the wain had made it impossible to relax, Lucie and her companions soon began to feel heavy-lidded with fatigue. Lucie was almost on the point of drifting off to sleep when one of the wheels must have rolled down into a particularly deep rut, making the wain lurch and tip dangerously to one side, the jolt making the horses rear to a sudden standstill. The occupants found themselves and its entire contents in a heap in the corner, with Lady Eleanor having the misfortune of finding herself at the bottom of the pile. Panic and uproar ensued, all trying to scrabble off the abruptly woken Eleanor, but finding it impossible to do so with the cart leaning at such a precarious angle.

'What's going on, what's happening? Get off me, girl!' she screamed.

With an almighty shove, she tried to push the young Heloise off her, but to no avail, as the nurse was on top of her and Lucie was on top of the nurse, their arms and legs flaying in all directions. Luckily the vehicle was stuck fast, as all the movement and commotion could easily have sent it further over, causing serious injury to the occupants and the horses still in their harness.

Suddenly a hand appeared and grabbed Lucie's forearm, pulling her clear of the affray. She then felt herself being lifted out of the wain, carried clear and placed on a fallen tree trunk by the side of the road. Nell and Heloise soon followed, each being carried by a member of the escort. One of the grooms stood holding and calming the horses, while the driver sat for a while rubbing a sore head, where he had been fully pitched from his seat to land in the road. Eleanor was not going to be rescued so readily or as quietly, it seemed.

'Get your hands off me! Leave me be!' was the vigorous retort heard coming from the back of the wain. 'I can manage without your help thank you very much!'

The guard reappeared, straightening his helmet and looking appropriately chastened, although a faint smile could be detected on his lips. Then Eleanor appeared, headfirst on her hands and knees, her face ablaze with indignation. In her haste she almost toppled into the road, but managed to scramble out safely, not without first showing a great deal more of her legs than she would have wished the onlookers to see. She huffed and puffed as she lifted the hem of her surcoat clear of a muddy puddle and tiptoed across the furrows to join the others.

'I hope this does not delay our journey too much,' she growled ill-temperedly, throwing herself down next to Lucie.

'I hope not too, my lady,' replied Lucie.

They did not want to find themselves still on the road at nightfall and anyway, she was starting to feel hungry. They had eaten what food had been given to them that morning. She gazed around apprehensively. Save for the creaking of the wain and the chinking of harness as the guards laboured to reinstate their transport back on the road, it was eerily quiet. The very stillness of the forest worried her. Where were the woodsmen, the charcoal burners and swineherds? Come to think of it, it had been a while since they had set eyes on anybody at all. A sense of disquiet and foreboding suddenly overcame her and she had the distinct feeling of being watched. She peered into the surrounding woodland, straining her eyes to see if anything or anyone were hiding there. Her attention was taken by the young charge.

'Are we nearly there?' asked Heloise, tugging at her sleeve, her blue eyes looking at her beseechingly. They were red-rimmed with exhaustion and she bit her lower lip nervously.

'Yes, we are almost there, Heloise. Do not worry yourself.'

Lucie pushed away a stray strand of hair from Heloise's eyes and patted her hand reassuringly. She wished that she herself felt as assured as she sounded.

'Stop whining, girl; we're all in the same cart!' barked Eleanor, who was becoming all the more irritable.

Heloise swallowed hard, and for a moment looked as though she might cry, but with a palpable effort, pulled herself together.

'Good girl,' whispered Lucie, catching hold of her hand and squeezing it gently.

The girl made an effort to smile, but Lucie could tell by her white face and trembling chin that she was frightened and regretted ever starting this journey. Not that she would have had a choice in the matter, she thought. A cry of 'whoa' went up as the wain was successfully righted and the grooms struggled to hold the horses steady. On inspection, and to the relief of all, there was no damage done to vehicle or beast. Before the journey commenced, the escort refreshed themselves with a drink from their leather travelling costrels. Two of the guards wandered off to relieve themselves in nearby bushes. As the ladies were making their way tentatively over the ruts back to the wain, a sudden yell of warning made them stop and look up, to see one of the guards running as fast as he could back from the bushes, clutching the drawstring of his hose, which were rucked up around his buttocks and hampering his flight. Behind him, out of a copse of trees a hundred yards away, four men on horseback galloped down upon them. These were followed by at least another four on foot. They were a motley, villainous-looking bunch, all carrying weapons, ranging from daggers, cudgels, longbows and pikes. The guards were taken completely by surprise. One threw down his costrel and, with the riders almost upon him, made a leap for his horse. Before he had the chance to sit down in the saddle and draw a sword to defend himself, a pike pierced the centre of his chest. When his assailant pulled it out again he crumpled, dropping his sword and, with an expression of utter astonishment on his face, toppled off his mount, hitting the ground hard. Blood trickled from his mouth, his eyes stared, the life already gone from them. The guard who had shouted the warning could be seen spread-eagled, face down in the road with a feathered shaft protruding from his back. In the following turmoil and panic, Roger, on seeing his companions being cut down one by one, managed to reach the women and draw his sword. He turned his horse to face the enemy, intent on protecting them. The women were so petrified they were rooted to the spot. The attack was executed so swiftly and with such ferocity that they were rendered incapable of doing anything. Two of the footpads, their faces covered, turned their attention from the blood-soaked torso of the driver lying on the ground to the group of women and their protector. On realising their intention as they bore down on them, weapons in hand, Lucie suddenly roused herself into action. She grabbed hold of Heloise's hand to make a run for the woods. It was their only chance. There was resistance for a second or two from

Heloise, as she was still in the same state of paralysis Lucie had been in a few seconds ago, but she pulled her arm roughly and shouted at her harshly.

'Run! Run as fast as you can!'

A long drawn out howl escaped from Heloise. It surged up from somewhere deep within her, and the fear, stifled by the survival instinct, spurred the girl into flight. They both ran together, crashing through the undergrowth, not caring in which direction they went as long as they put as much distance as possible between themselves and the carnage behind them. In the commotion, Lucie heard an ear piercing scream. She could not tell if anyone had given chase, but she most certainly was not going to waste a second in stopping to investigate. All she could hear was the foliage zipping past her ears, her rasping breath and the pounding of her heart. As they ran deeper and deeper into the woods, driven on by pure terror, the undergrowth began to thicken, and where the sun had not been able to penetrate the canopy, was still wet from the storm. Branches and twigs pulled at their clothing as if intent on slowing their progress, but they launched themselves through the dense, tangled undergrowth, protecting their faces and eyes with the crooks of their arms against the sharp twigs and whipping saplings. They had to stop at one point, snared by brambles. Their clothes were soaked through and ripped to shreds, and Heloise's soft calfskin slippers were covered in mud. They moved on, more slowly now. How far they had travelled and for how long they could not judge, but the further they penetrated the woods, the darker it became. The daylight was starting to fade. Through sheer exhaustion, Lucie eventually stopped. She had to forcefully restrain Heloise by grabbing both her upper arms and shaking her until she understood they were not being pursued.

'Stop, Heloise! Now! We are safe.'

Lucie's breath burned in her chest and her limbs felt like they were on fire. Heloise, exhausted, out of breath, her hair tangled and wild, had stopped, but her eyes darted about frantically. It was evident a branch had whipped across her left cheek, leaving a nasty welt, which was already turning a livid black and blue. Brambles had ripped open her bodice, leaving a crisscross of angry scratches enlaced with tiny droplets of blood on her bare chest and shoulder. They both had scratches up their forearms where they had raised them to protect their faces. Heloise looked like a mad woman, and hysteria could be detected edging into her voice.

'We can't stop here. What are we to do tonight? It is getting dark, we cannot stay in the woods!'

Lucie knew they were in a desperate situation, but she did not want to panic the girl any more than she already was. She did not relish the idea either, but she would have to remain calm for the child's sake. She grabbed her shoulders and pulled her into an embrace, folding her arms around her gently and stroking her hair. Heloise gave herself up willingly and clung to Lucie, burying her face into her chest.

'Hush now, it will be all right,' she crooned. 'We will search for somewhere dry to rest. Maybe we will find a hollowed-out tree where we can shelter for the night. I used to sleep outside often when I was your age, you know. Do not worry, we will find somewhere warm and dry and we will be safe.' Her voice was strong, which comforted Heloise.

Thankfully, they did find somewhere before it grew dark. A causeway of rock, lined on either side with trees and undergrowth, revealed a number of small niches and hollows underneath. One of these, carpeted with a thick layer of warm, dry leaves and having a ceiling sufficiently wide and deep enough to offer protection from the dank night air, which would soon descend upon them, made a perfect haven, and although they lay awake well into the early hours, they passed an adequately comfortable night.

It took a long while for Heloise to calm down, but eventually, with a lot of gentle persuasion, she finally succumbed to Lucie's earnest requests to rest and ease her agitation. Lucie had on her person the phial of poppy syrup made from the seeds of the white eastern poppy, but would only use it as a last resort. Although it would help Heloise sleep, without any food in her stomach, it might render her very groggy and unsteady in the morning, and tomorrow they would need to gather as much strength and resolve as they could.

It was a clear night with enough moonlight to outline the shapes of the trees that shivered in the light wind. Apart from something skittering through the leaves and undergrowth outside their refuge, all was still.

As they lay huddled together, Heloise laying across Lucie's lap under her cloak to keep warm, the latter recounted her childhood in an attempt to take their minds off the horrors of the day and their predicament.

She told of being raised on a manor, somewhere not far from here she thought, which the tenants, she and family included, thought a privilege to live. They were fortunate enough to have the most kindly, fair and honest master ever and they had that much respect, and held him in such high regard, that they would all, young or old, follow him to the ends of the earth if necessary. Admittedly they all had to work hard but the rewards had been plentiful. On saint's days and at harvest time she remembered gathering on the greensward by the huge tithe barn to celebrate.

They would eat, dance and be merry, some getting very drunk in the process. She smiled to herself remembering the antics of the young boys who had their first taste of Widow Mooney's cider. Not a birthday would pass without a celebration of some sort. They were always joined by the master and his son, if and whenever they were home from business, court or the latest campaign. It had been on one of these occasions that she had first set eyes on Owen she thought wistfully, who, although lived and worked on the adjoining manor, had cousins on theirs.

Her father had been a shepherd. As far back as she could remember she and her brother Benjamin had always helped at lambing time, and when they were older they had gripped the fat summer sheep between their knees and fleeced them expertly. She had not lied when she told Heloise that she had often slept out of doors at night. If the flock had been interfered with and scattered by man or beast, many a time they would go with their father to seek them out. Sometimes miles would be covered in their search, making it impossible to get home before nightfall. They always took a bed roll each and provisions just in case.

Her mother helped tend the land as well as look after their own small plot enclosed around their dwelling, together with a handful of hens, usually a pig and always a cow. Lucie helped her with the milking and churning and the general chores. Her mother was also known for her knowledge of ailments and remedies, which always brought their neighbours knocking at the door. No matter what time of day or night, they always received a sympathetic, obliging welcome. This knowledge, or gift, as her mother preferred to call it, had been passed onto her. She had to stop talking here; a lump was forming in her throat. This was the gift that made her indispensable to the De Coulances family, she thought bitterly. She shook her head to dispel them from it. She did not want to sully her precious memories of a loving family and decent, honest people with the likes of them. Her parents had long since passed away and she seldom saw her brother, who was now a lay brother at Dene Abbey. She gave a deep sigh and swallowed, trying to chase away the tears that were threatening to fall. What she would give to once again run with Ben and Guy in the woods and meadows of her childhood, to see and speak to her mother and father, to spend a warm summer's evening dancing with Owen on the greensward by the barn, with a table fit to bursting with food and drink.

The hoot of an owl in the branches above broke into her thoughts. She looked down to find Heloise asleep, her deep, steady breathing reverberating softly around their sanctum. She settled herself down, moving carefully so as not to disturb her, drawing the cloak up over them both to keep out the night's damp chill. Finally, before sleep eventually claimed her, she looked ahead to the morrow, which she knew was going to be a very long day indeed.

What I do on my own land is my business!' roared Lord Charles, banging his empty goblet down and squaring up to Sir Robert across the table.

'It will be the talk of the alehouses for no more than a sennight, and then it will be forgotten!'

'I do not think so. By putting the livelihoods of so many men, women and children at stake, you will be pilloried. See sense, man! You cannot discard them like you throw a gnawed bone to your dogs! You have responsibilities towards these people – and anyway, who will tend to your land and livestock?'

At this point Lord Charles hastily dismissed Drake, ushering him out of the room. In his haste to do so, he even held the door open for him to leave and closed it behind him.

'I will pay wages to casual workers as and when I need them,' he answered, making his way back to the table.

'That is a ridiculous idea; it defeats your objective. You would need to employ them all year round!'

'Ah, but I would not need to supply their families with a roof over their heads and put food in their mouths, would I?'

'It is questionable whether you are doing that as you should now!'

If he thought he looked after and provided his tenants with an acceptable level of living, he must be either delusional or downright heartless, thought Sir Robert in baffled astonishment. The sight of the sorry-looking hovels and the grateful smiles on the thin, haggard faces that had greeted him today as he had ridden in with the supply cart, had appalled him. How could this man justify their living conditions as acceptable?

'So, that is what this is all about, is it? Getting them off your land?'

At Sir Robert's last statement, Lord Charles' face had reddened all the more. Whether this was from guilt or anger, Sir Robert could not tell.

'Yes, it is,' he conceded through tight lips. 'Things need to change. We cannot carry on being their keepers. They need to make their own way, not be mollycoddled by us.'

'Mollycoddled!' spluttered Sir Robert.

Why on earth was he bothering to try and convince this man that he was heading for not only his own ruination but the end of a way of life that, if conducted fairly and in an unbiased manner, could be beneficial to all, himself as well as his tenants?

'How can you say these people are mollycoddled? They are forced to work for and be at the mercy of their masters, some good, and some bad. And may I say, you, sir, are of the latter category. You cannot beget loyalty with bullying and fear!'

'How dare you talk to me like that? Do not come here with your nasty accusations! That is a grossly unfair assumption and one that I demand you take back!'

'I will not, and I suggest you think again about your plans or I can see you ending up in the same predicament as your son!'

Both men had been stalking about the room, each in anger. Lord Charles stopped in his tracks and glowered over at his assailant.

'Are you suggesting Geoffrey's fate had something to do with the way we manage this estate?'

'I am saying that you do not need any more enemies than you and your family already have!'

Lord Charles seemed taken aback by this remark.

'What do you mean, enemies?' he said incredulously.

Was he really that oblivious to the level of hostility aimed towards his family? Was he that thick-skinned that it needed spelling out?

'Enemies. Um, now, let me see.'

Tapping his chin with his forefinger, Sir Robert raised his eyes to the ceiling as if deep in thought.

'Opponents of an oppressor comes to mind. Hostile persons intent on destroying others is another. Oh, and of course, not to forget to mention those who might stab someone through the heart. They cannot be discounted either!'

Lord Charles did not appreciate Sir Robert's sarcasm one little bit.

'Do not be flippant. It does not suit you.'

Sir Robert carried on, this reproof of little consequence.

'Enemies? Well, firstly, I am not suggesting they are your enemies as yet, but if you persist with these plans of yours, your tenants could very soon well be. Secondly, the free rein given to a family member to use a certain young lady in your employ as he wished, resulting in the exile of her sweetheart, might not have done you any favours either. Ah, what else…'

'All right, all right, stop!' shouted Lord Charles, holding up a placatory hand.

He sat down heavily on a nearby chair.

'He was evicted for violence against the reeve. We do not tolerate violence here. Do you condone that sort of behaviour, then?'

'No, I do not, but more importantly, is it acceptable to stand by and condone the abuse of a young girl?'

'The girl was—is—my wife's responsibility, not mine,' said Lord Charles sulkily.

'Does that make it right to turn a blind eye? Do not pass the buck, sir. She is ultimately the responsibility of all once under their roof!'

Lord Charles deigned to look uncomfortable at this and was unable to look his compeer in the eye.

'Sit down, Robert, let's not fight any more,' he said wearily as he went to pour another drink from the flagon.

He was tired of trying to defend himself and he had admitted to himself, deep down, he knew, that his families' misdeeds had probably culminated in the death of his eldest son.

Sir Robert realised there was nothing more he could say; it was up to Charles now to search his own conscience.

In a softer voice, he said, 'Charles, over the many years I have known you, I have come to realise that you are a man who can easily be charmed and persuaded into believing others' conceptions and beliefs are honourable and just.'

Lord Charles tried to interrupt here, but he held up his hand to still him.

'Let me finish. I do not say this as a criticism, only as an observation. It only shows your desire to please and be acknowledged. Unfortunately, sometimes these ideals can be flawed and unfitting, which, I think, in some circumstances you recognise, but find it hard once committed to retract your support. It is not too late to drop these proposals. You will not lose face because of it; in fact, it would only act as being more favourable towards you. Just remember that your decision either way will determine the future for everyone, your tenants and your family alike. You need to think on this, if only for your own salvation.'

Lord Charles sat staring into space, his expression unfathomable. Was he feeling penitent or stubborn? There was no way of telling, and Sir Robert quickly came to the conclusion that he was not about to impart a decision any time soon.

'I will take my leave of you now, Charles, but not before requesting the release of the young Joanne from your wife's service.'

Although it lacked a woman's touch, the solar was comfortable enough. Matting covered the oak-panelled floor instead of the usual rushes, and this main room stretched high up to the exposed rafters of the roof. A large oak table sat in the centre, and a raised dais ran along the east and north side of the room. This accommodated a very large aumbry displaying the family's few pieces of silverware, and where a pair of oak settles sat beneath the two huge arched windows. The wooden shutters had yet to be closed against the chill of the evening. Tapestries depicting autumn hunting scenes in shades of green, brown, red and gold lined the stone walls. These, together with the tallow dips hung in sconces around the walls, created a warm, homely atmosphere. Tapestry-covered screens, which helped to block out the draughts, were placed about the room, one being at the top of the stairs which led down to the undercroft, another in the far corner in front of the stairs leading up to the bed chambers. Behind him on the south wall, an ornately carved wooden screen stood before the oak door that opened onto the outside stone steps. A large stone fireplace was located on the west wall. Guy sat in front of this in one of the matching chairs, with Angus in his usual position, sprawled at his feet.

This evening, Guy and his father had enjoyed a hearty meal of spit-roasted duck, onions, turnips and beans, or rather he had. His father had little appetite and had only picked at his food and pushed it around his plate. Guy had not failed to notice his father's despondent mood, and, trying to lift his spirits, had opened a bottle of his favourite red wine, breaking the wax seal and pouring them each a generous measure.

'Come, Father, let us drink to your achievements today. There are many families tonight who have you to thank for their full stomachs, and one family in particular who is more than grateful to have their daughter back once again under their roof.'

Sir Robert made an effort, for Guy's sake, to dispel the heaviness he felt in his heart. For all he had achieved today, he did not feel a desire to celebrate. He wished there had not been a cause for intervention in the first place, and he had been deeply saddened by Charles' decline into ignominious apathy. He took a sip of wine. Maybe he did have a reason to feel a little more optimistic, he thought, and at least Charles had agreed to release the girl. He had also promised to think again about the new proposals for the estate, and had seemed somewhat contrite when he had left him that afternoon.

'Yes, let us raise a glass to common sense and hope it will prevail and put an end to the nonsense of recent days.'

Guy concluded his father's mood was a result of these events and hoped it would soon pass. He was increasingly worried for his health as it seemed to have taken a downturn of late where it had significantly improved for a while. He had started to look overly tired and pale again, had become withdrawn and spent more time alone, retiring much earlier to bed at night. He got the impression that he was trying to avoid his company as much as possible.

'How are you, Father?' he enquired, watching his face intently. 'Do you feel up to making the journey into Tonbridge tomorrow? You need not accompany me if you prefer not to.'

It was market day and they planned to help Grainger the reeve and Joseph the shepherd drive fifty head of sheep into town to sell, and meet with Godfrey Bartholomew, their business partner in wool-exporting.

'Of course I feel up to the journey! I am looking forward to a day in town and a bit of haggling over fleece prices!'

Guy did not expect to hear any different from his father, even though his demeanour contradicted his response. He accepted his reply without dispute, even though he was not convinced. He knew from experience that to harry his father would only serve to make him more stubborn and uncommunicative. A log shifted in the fire, sending cascades of sparks up the chimney and startling Guy from his reflection. Sir Robert had since retired to bed as an early start was intended in the morning. He looked down to find a pair of dark eyes staring adoringly up at him. Angus had rested his chin upon his master's outstretched leg, hoping for a show of affection. Guy, not wanting to disappoint, fondled a soft silky ear. With his other hand he rubbed his own chin and, in contrast, felt the harsh prickly stubble of a beard.

'Time for a shave, I think. Come, Angus, let us pay a visit downstairs.'

Down in the undercroft, Old Matt sat by the fire cleaning his boots. He looked up to acknowledge Guy.

'Evenin,' he said, with a nod and a toothless smile.

Angus loped over to the hearth to join him, settling down beside the log basket. Matthew sat at the table mending a bridle, while Alisoun stood kneading bread ready for baking the next morning.

On the other side of the fireplace, a ladder led up to the open-fronted sleeping loft. Guy guessed that Tom was already abed, tucked up on his straw palliase. More often than not he found himself coming down here in the evenings in search of company. He was always made to feel most welcome and it was hugely preferable to sitting alone upstairs. Alisoun fetched him an earthenware bowl filled with warm water, taken from a pot hanging over the fire. She reached into a cubby-hole by the hearthside and passed him a small knife, kept honed by a whetstone for the very purpose he was about to use it for. Through a thin lather of sheep tallow soap, he rasped the knife carefully over his face, chin and neck, finishing off by rinsing his face in the water and wiping it dry with a square piece of linen. Stepping behind a plain, rather crudely made wooden screen, he opened the door, which led to the back garden to rid himself of the now cold scummy water. The evening felt fresh after the day's storm and he stood for a while, deeply breathing in the wonderfully clean air. Turning to go back inside, something – a shadow or a movement in the corner of his vision – made him stop. It had been by the lean-to where Alisoun stored her garden tools, and Matthew his axes and scythe. He was sure he had seen something but could see nothing now. His ears alert for any sound, he called out sharply.

'Who is there?'

There was no reply, no sound except the distant hoot of an owl. Angus appeared at his side and sat on his haunches. He growled low in his throat, but stayed where he was, so close to his master that he pressed against his leg. The hairs on the back of Guys neck stood on end. He recalled the night, a while ago now, when he'd encountered the same feeling up the lane, when Felix had been unsettled. He shivered. Returning inside, he pulled the door tight shut and secured it. Crossing over the rush-strewn floor to the corner just beyond a window, he placed the bowl back upon the dresser. Alisoun, who had finished her dough kneading and was now laying out a tray of pasties for supper, along with a jug of ale, saw the troubled frown on his face.

'Is everything all right?'

'Uh, yes… Yes, everything's fine.'

As he turned from her to make his way over to the table to converse with Matthew, she placed a restraining hand lightly on his arm. She kept her voice low.

'Actually, sir, I need to talk with you regarding a rather pressing matter.'

Guy met her gaze and by her expression knew that something was amiss.

'What is it, Alisoun?' he asked apprehensively.

She looked furtively behind her. Although her husband was engrossed in his work, and her father-in-law nodding by the fire, she worried they might overhear what she had to say. She felt Guy ought to be told first before it was shared with the rest of the household. Still keeping her voice low and looking at him intently, she said, 'I think you should make your way upstairs. I will follow you up with a supper tray.'

Guy went to intercede 'But—'

Alisoun once again placed a hand on his arm. 'Please, Guy.'

He recognised the demand to obey.

Alisoun was sorry she had blurted it out there and then, and felt wretched for leaving Guy in suspense, but she thought it best he was told in private. She needed to be relieved of this burden she had kept to herself for so long. After placing supper on the undercroft table, she made her way upstairs to Guy. As she came to the top of the stairs and stepped out from behind the screen, she found him pacing the floor. She quickly put the tray on the table; she would not prolong his agony any longer.

'Please, sit down, Guy.'

Guy reluctantly strode over to the fireside and sat down, indicating for Alisoun to do the same. She sat on the edge of the opposite fireside chair, her hands clasped together in her lap. Her very body language intensified Guy's anxiety.

'I will get straight to the point…'

'Yes, please do.'

Alisoun closed her eyes and took a deep breath.

'The master is ill, but he wants to keep it from you. I have known for a while now, but am forbidden to tell you. The thing is, I cannot keep it to myself any longer. I thought it best you should know, even if it provokes the master's displeasure.'

'I myself have had cause to worry about my father's health of late. He seemed to be on the mend for a while, but once again is tired and distracted.'

Alisoun realised then what she had suspected all along; Guy had no inkling of the seriousness of his father's condition.

'I have to tell you, Guy, that I have seen him coughing up blood.'

Guy sat stunned, staring into her face. He felt he had been kicked in the stomach.

Understanding slowly began to seep into his mind. He knew his father still coughed, but he had not the slightest clue as to the gravity of the situation.

'You need to know so that he gets the rest he needs instead of pretending all is well and continuing about his business. I am sorry for disobeying the master, and also for keeping it from you for so long. I have been at my wit's end knowing this dreadful secret and not being able to share it!'

Alisoun's eyes brimmed with tears.

'Have you not noticed how he coughs? Have you not heard him in the night, or when he thinks nobody is near enough to hear? He has a pallor that is not natural for a man who spends time out of doors. The damp got into his lungs last winter but he did not have the time or the opportunity to rest and recuperate. No sooner was he settled by the fire, when someone would need his help, or something required his attention.'

She shook her head and looked away from him, trying unsuccessfully to stop the tears from falling.

Although Guy felt adrift and a little discomforted faced with a weeping woman, he could not ignore Alisoun's distress. He stood and went to her. Standing at her chair side, he slipped his arm about her shoulders.

'Do not distress yourself, Alisoun, you were right to tell me.'

They sat and stood in mutual misery for a few moments. Guy then took great pains to reassure Alisoun that she had done the right thing and that he would not divulge her betrayal of trust. Together they needed to be more attentive and persuade the master to rest.

Eventually, Alisoun wiped her eyes with the hem of her apron and tucked her escaping dark hair back under her cap.

'I had better go down to finish off. They will wonder where I have got to,' she sniffed, nodding her head in the direction of the stairs.

'Yes, you had. Goodnight, Alisoun. I will see you in the morning and thank you,' replied Guy reassuringly.

As she left the solar, he made his way over to the table and poured himself a drink.

On returning to the hearthside, he sat down heavily in his chair and, as was his habit, raked his fingers through his hair.

And there he sat well into the night, staring sombrely into the fire, trying to fully digest the devastating news he had just heard.

They were on their way by the seventh hour the following morning, the mist still lying low over the fields. They left young Tom and Angus at the end of the lane, the latter looking on forlornly. Although he was very well behaved with their own flocks, he could not be trusted out and about with others. Due to his exuberant nature, he was always apt to get overexcited, especially on a day out, and the desire to run amok might be too tempting for him. Both on foot, Joseph the shepherd led the flock, with Grainger at the rear. On horseback, Guy and his father took up positions on either side as they drove the sheep down to the bottom of Starvecrow Hill and forded the stream. If they made good time, they should enter Tonbridge just within the hour but that would depend entirely on what other traffic they might encounter on the way. Guy had tried to dissuade his father from joining the expedition, but to no avail. He was immovable in his intent. As Guy was slightly behind and opposite his father, he was able to overtly scrutinise him without his knowledge. He did look unwell again, the pale grey pallor had returned to his face and he looked much leaner. He wondered how he had missed the signs, but realised his father had been very adroit in concealing his condition. That he had been avoiding his company of late was testament to his determination, but only time would tell how much longer he could keep it hidden. Guy knew that this disease, phthisis – or consumption, as it was better known – attacked the lungs, resulting in their wasting and destruction to be coughed up by the sufferer, with only rest and fresh air giving some short-term relief before it truly took a hold. Guy could not know what stage the disease was at, but his intention was to pay more attention from now on and try to gauge its progression. Luckily the storm of yesterday had dampened down the earth so they were not plagued with the usual dust kicked up by the many pairs of hooves, but he did notice his father had a kerchief tied around his neck, ready to pull up over his nose and mouth if necessary.

As they travelled, Guy kept a close eye on the surrounding woodland, his right hand covering the hilt of his broadsword. One could not be sure, but he doubted very much they would be attacked for fifty head of sheep. They would make a quick getaway nigh on impossible and they were too numerous to hide easily. Movement in the bushes to the left caught his eye. Within a split second, he had pulled up Felix and unsheathed his sword as a pheasant, showing its agitation at being disturbed, flew straight at him with a heart stopping 'krook-kook' and a flap of wings, just skimming his head. Sir Robert and Grainger jumped in alarm. Then it was gone, leaving them grinning in amusement at the way it had startled them all. Sir Robert called over.

'Son, you are too quick to draw your sword!'

Guy, feeling a little foolish, defended his actions.

'I do not think you realise, Father, the danger we face on our highways at present and we need to stay alert.'

'Aye, for we might be set upon by a flock of pheasants!' his father replied, laughing at his own jest.

Guy good-naturedly laughed with him, but hoped his father's humour was not an indication of a careless attitude towards the true dangers that might lurk hereabouts. He would be in trouble if it were.

The rest of the journey continued without further incident. As they drew nearer Tonbridge a steady stream of traffic built up, slowing their progress somewhat, not that it mattered. All were in cordial spirits, calling greetings to each other and making merry banter along the way. Merchants on horseback, accompanied by servants and carts loaded with goods, seemed to appear from nowhere. The miller and his wife turned out from their lane with a cart full of freshly baked loaves and pasties to sell. A small herd of cattle cutting across through The Slype[11] held up the procession as they were steered into the gathering throng. Country folk on foot, some alone, others in family groups carrying baskets of vegetables, eggs and a variety of crafts, stepped out from the many pathways on the open heath to converge onto the main road into town. London Road, the busiest road in the southeast of England, had its own constant trickle of traffic. A newly fashionable horse-drawn carriage bearing lords and ladies merged in with them. They had the protection of an escort carrying pikes and swords. Very sensible in the circumstances, thought Guy. A procession of horse and carts, herdsmen, sheep and goats and more folk followed.

They descended Dry Hill. Sir Robert and Guy headed for the Horse Gate, where the huge oak iron studded doors stood wide open. Grainger and Joseph continued to herd the flock round to the Postern Gate, which regulated entry across the fosse from the east and for those on foot with livestock, and where different tolls would be paid. Sir Robert and Guy made their way to the bridge

---

[11] Yardley Park Road.

that straddled the filthy, foul-smelling waters of the fosse. Their nostrils were invaded by the stench of the refuse. Broken pottery, animal bones, rotting meat and human faeces, which lay strewn on the banks and in the water, was brought out from the town in barrel loads and dumped there. On the wall either side of the gatehouse stood sentries keeping a watchful eye on the proceedings. They both hastened across the wooden bridge and made for the gatehouse keeper and his son, who took their money and waved them through. They then made their way down the main street to the end of Swan Lane[12] opposite the market cross, to await Grainger and Joseph. Most streets in the town were of hard packed earth, but the market cross area was roughly paved, with a central gutter running down to the river. Again, sewage and all other manner of rubbish was thrown here, and this, together with the smell of the castle's latrine outlet, which emptied out into the moat, nearby, could be unbearable if not flushed away regularly. The main river supplied the castle moat but its water level could be difficult to maintain in dry weather. To ensure an adequate level that would enable the refuse and human waste to be flushed out, an elaborate system of dykes and sluices had been constructed running north up the river for two miles.

On this market day, Guy noticed there were more guards than usual patrolling the town, all in pairs, some looking watchful, others unenthusiastic and miserable, slouching against walls and leaning upon their pikes. There was plenty of pushing and jostling as people struggled past peddlers with handcarts, porters with huge bundles, and herds of animals, all making their way into the centre of town. Managing to keep the flock together they negotiated the assembling

---

[12] East Street.

market stalls and the gutter, which was reasonably clear after the downpour of yesterday.

They made their way up the back lane behind the market cross to the Shambles, where the buying and selling of livestock took place. A slaughter house and an alehouse were also located here, and for some there was really no reason at all to venture away from the site. Guy and his father waited for their animals to be secured into pens, before handing Grainger a coin and telling him and Joseph to get themselves something to eat at The Bear and Ragged Staff and to tell any interested parties that they would return in time for the auction. It was their intention to break their fast with Godfrey Bartholomew at mistress Ralf's establishment, The Chequers.

*

Godfrey Bartholomew was a burgess, one of many that ran the town's administration. He was a merchant of some substance and a free man who had bought out his knight-service some years ago. He had his fingers in many pies and was both powerful and influential. He looked every inch the model citizen in his meticulously laundered long light grey tunic, with a light surcoat of dark grey linen.

A heavy gold chain ending with a golden sheep medallion, the emblem of his guild, hung around his neck and rested on his substantial paunch. He was a burly man in his late forties with a short, thick neck, who was used to good living and had a waistline to show for it. He had a mop of brown hair and a full moustache, both flecked with grey, and a face like a bullfrog. A long jagged scar ran down from his left eye to his jawbone. This had been sustained in the service of the King during the Baron's War some ten years earlier, when he had been much fitter and leaner. He and Sir Robert often exchanged memories of campaigns long past, but today he was more interested in affairs a little closer to home. Upon finishing their own business, and replete with Alys' robust breakfast of oat gruel, salted bacon and eggs, served with freshly baked bread, washed down with a satisfying quantity of best ale, Bartholomew leaned back from the trestle and wiped his mouth on a napkin held in his fat, stubby fingers. He spoke of his concern at the escalation of lawlessness in the town and how a horse fair held on Swanmeade, one of the town's outfields, over the last two days had generated a lot of trouble. Local, and merchants further afield, had joined in the usual scrabble for business and the town had become immersed in a fervour of buying and selling. Almost every available bed in the town had been taken, and the taverns and alehouses had been overflowing with drinkers and drunken revelry.

Hence the extra guards, thought Guy, but then there was always trouble when a horse fair came to town.

'And we all know the forests and roads are now overrun with outlaws. It really is getting out of hand! How can we go about our business in safety?'

He turned up his hands in a gesture of helplessness and continued to bluster on.

'And De Clare's cleared off to Suffolk, taking most of the garrison with him! Still, what more can we expect from him? Any sniff of trouble and he's off. Too preoccupied looking after his own interests, no doubt! Only yesterday I heard of Geoffrey de Coulances' fate, and then this morning I hear his wife has probably fared no better, herself and her escort set upon somewhere up near Ightham! We – that being myself and the town's council – paid a visit to Breton yesterday to voice our concerns. We told him that if it continues, some action must be taken. He must be persuaded to send troops against them!'

On hearing this last piece of distressing news, Guy decided that after business was done, he too would pay a visit to the castle and Sheriff Breton.

Identified by an armband bearing the Guiscard family crest, and with Felix's brow band and breast strap bearing the same, Guy was granted entry through the barbican, an outer stone fortification, by a sentinel who pulled himself up sharply to attention when he saw his approach. This took him into the outer bailey, where the garrison would practice their fighting skills and the knights their horsemanship in the tiltyard. All was quiet. Most of the garrison, the knights and their squires, grooms and servants, had all vacated the castle with Lord de Clare, either to travel with him or to return to their own estates. He could see a few off-duty soldiers enjoying a game of dice on the now dry again and dusty ground. These were the skeleton force left behind to watch over the town's approaches and the gatehouse. A muddle of huts and shacks, together with stables, forges and store sheds, turned this outer bailey into a small village, where many of the garrison and some of their family members lived. He looked over to the wooden shacks clustered around the bailey wall, where a group of small children squealed in delight. They were playing Hoodman Blind and trying to avoid the outstretched fumbling hands of the 'hoodman', who lurched and grabbed at them, his hooded jerkin turned back to front. Their mothers sat around a fire, preparing food whilst gossiping with the redundant washerwomen. From the forge on the far side of the bailey, he heard the sound of hammering and the hiss of a horseshoe being dunked into cold water. The acrid smell of hot metal and burning horn filled the air. It had been less than a decade since the castle had seen any military action and was hardly used as a fortress these days, but more the home of a lord, a garrison of soldiers and the administrative office of the sheriff.

In 1262, the current earl Gilbert de Clare, or 'The Red Earl', had supported Simon de Montfort in a rebellion against King Henry III. He had joined what he thought to be the strongest side, but unfortunately that had been a serious error of judgment, as two years later Henry seized Tonbridge town and castle. The King's luck ran out though when he was defeated at Lewes by the barons led by Montfort and assisted by Gilbert. Always looking out for himself and being the turn-cloak that people said he was, Gilbert de Clare switched his allegiance back to Henry when he became alarmed by Montfort's plan to ally with the Welsh. Reconciled with Henry, Gilbert joined forces with the army led by the King's son, Prince Edward. They defeated and killed Montfort but, by then, Gilbert's loyalty was suspect. He regained his castle, but the reward came with a reputation for duplicity and fickleness. Feeling thoroughly humiliated at the seizure of his castle, Gilbert decided to build a gatehouse so strong he would never suffer the same indignity again.

Approaching from the north and front of the castle, and looking up at the magnificent five-storey yellow sandstone fortress, Guy never ceased to be impressed by its sheer size and grandeur. The walls were supported by angled spurs, which reached deep into the ground and these, together with the high earth bank, made it well-nigh impregnable. The gatehouse was joined to the keep by a curtain wall, or stone corridor, through which the occupants could retreat to the keep if necessary. The enemy would need to negotiate the moat, drawbridge and a series of portcullises, murder holes, and two pairs of strong gates before gaining entry into the inner bailey.

Today, in these times of peace, the drawbridge was lowered and the portcullis up. Guy made his way through the gatehouse, passing the guardroom and armoury on either side of him. A larger, more substantial armoury could be found in the keep. He dismounted and passed Felix's reins to a waiting valet, as no grooms were available. Around the inside of the curtain wall stood more sheds, stables, and storerooms. He walked back to the gatehouse. Within the armoury chamber to his right, an old armourer sat at his bench, repairing a mail shirt. His tools lay close to hand alongside wooden bowls containing hundreds of shiny mail links and tiny rivets the size of pinheads. He was diligently inserting new links and closing each one by hammering in a rivet. The new rings were a shade darker than the old ones, and the knights that fought the hardest could always be identified by the flecked patches of repair on their hauberks. More chainmail coats wrapped in oiled cloth to prevent rusting hung in the corner, and swords and spearheads were kept in barrels of sawdust for the same reason. Bundles of bow staves and bowstrings hung from wooden shelving, the bows not strung until needed, and rows of helmets sat waiting in readiness. Guy ducked his head through the door to his left, taking him into the guardroom. Two guards enjoying a late breakfast sprung to attention and, upon Guy's enquiry, sent him up the narrow spiral stone staircase in the far corner to the west chamber on the first floor, and Sir Hugh's office and living quarters.

Sir Hugh's clerk was the first to greet him. He sat in the corner on a high stool, hunched over his desk. He was a wizened little old man with humped shoulders, probably due to years of labouring over his writing. He had a thin, pinched face, with a long pointed nose and a receding chin. His looks were further marred by a squint that he turned on Guy, accompanied by a tight-lipped smile. Without saying a word, he raised his hand, his ink-blackened fingers holding a quill pen. Ink proceeded to run down his wrist. He quickly lowered his hand again to dip it into a stone ink phial, and the steady scratch of his quill continued.

Sir Hugh looked tired. He had been kept busy with a number of incidents, mostly related to the horse fair yesterday. Drunken brawls had broken out in the many crowded alehouses and taverns. One, at The Bear and Ragged Staff, had resulted in a man being beaten and kicked to within an inch of his life, and many more being injured. The night before, a visiting merchant had been stabbed and robbed of his silver in a dark alleyway and had died after he was carried off to the infirmary at the Priory of St Mary Magdalene.

'Quite what he had been doing there was questionable, but nonetheless, a dastardly crime indeed,' said an indignant Sir Hugh.

Although all incomers were, or should be, searched for weapons, some were still going undetected.

'Either they were very well hidden or the guards are not being diligent enough in their duties. Hugo had to have a word with the idle dawdlers yesterday. Oh, and this is interesting. You remember the merchant from Robertsbridge who was set upon on Castle Hill and robbed of everything including his horse? Yes, well, while he was still recovering at home, he sent his manservant to the fair to buy a replacement and, lo and behold, his own palfrey was on sale there! The servant recognised it and confronted the trader. Needless to say, the man denied any wrongdoing, saying he had bought it fair and square from a horse dealer and was selling it on. At a profit, no doubt. As the manservant was about to call over a constable, he tried to make a run for it but was chased and restrained, and we now have him locked in the cage with all the other drunks and varlets. He won't talk, but the manservant is adamant it was his master's horse.'

'Surely though if he knew where the horse had come from, he would not have tried to sell it so close to home?' questioned Guy. 'He'd either be very stupid, or desperate.'

'Exactly,' said Sir Hugh, nodding in agreement.

'If what the manservant says is true – and there is no reason to doubt him – we need the ambitious tradesman to identify the horse dealer, who may well have been involved in the initial robberies or, at least, been the receiver of stolen goods. Either way, we need to know how he acquired the palfrey. In every robbery the horses have never been retrieved, which means somebody somewhere must have them.'

Guy sat down on the edge of Sir Hugh's table and poured himself a mug of ale.

'If you can get the trader to talk, we might be a step closer to finding the culprits of all this villainy. Talking of which, I hear you had a deputation yesterday?'

A look of unease passed over Sir Hugh's face.

'Yes, they came to see me directly to express their dissatisfaction. They want some explanations, and some action. As if I haven't got enough to contend with without them breathing down my neck! I understand their concerns, and of course the situation needs to be brought under control, but I do not know which way to turn at present. With all the added upheavals of the last two days it has not left me much time to concentrate on anything in particular.'

Guy felt some sympathy for his friend, but Bartholomew was right, Sir Hugh had to get a grip, and show he was in command of the situation before people's patience and regard were lost. He broached the most recent developments.

'Your concerns for Lady Eleanor were not without foundation after all.'

Sir Hugh got up from his chair and walked over to the arrow slit window where he stood with his back to Guy, looking over the outer bailey.

So, Bartholomew had already told him the news.

'Yes, what a dreadful business. I was too late sending out the escort, unfortunately,' he said, shaking his head.

He turned and made his way wearily back to his chair and sat down.

He picked up his seal and tapped it absent-mindedly on the table. The sun shining through the narrow arrow slit opening caught the disturbed dust motes dancing around the chamber. Piles of papers and scrolls of manuscripts lined the walls of the dim chamber. He kept meticulous records of all incidents in his jurisdiction with the aid of his clerk, both of them sometimes working well into the night.

'It was the escort who found them. An older woman, who we think was a servant, four guards, one groom and a driver were all butchered. Not a pretty sight. It was the buzzards that first drew their attention to what looked like bundles of rags lying in the road. They found another groom barely alive, who was taken into the Abbey on passing but might not live to tell the tale. Lady Eleanor and the young betrothed were nowhere to be seen. We don't know whether they were taken or if they managed to escape. I don't think much of their chances if they've been out in the forest all night. The victims, or should I say, the remains of the victims, have been brought back here, transported in the wain the women had been travelling in. The escort had to hitch two of their own horses for the purpose, as again all others had been taken.'

Sir Hugh turned questioning red-rimmed eyes upon Guy.

'Do you think it a deliberate act or purely coincidental that another De Coulances has been attacked?'

'There are coincidences that need explanation, but something tells me there is more to this than meets the eye. If you're thinking the Turner brothers are involved, remember all the evidence against them is circumstantial. That they might be running with outlaws, terrorising and robbing indiscriminately, their ultimate goal being to reap revenge at any opportune moment on members of the family, would be an all too easy conclusion.'

'I trust your judgement, Guy and, at present, I reserve my own but we do need to find the culprits in all this, and soon.'

Sir Hugh, suddenly intent on a path of action, jumped up from his chair.

'I will get Percy to follow up the stolen palfrey; he'll get the scoundrel to talk. In the meantime I will go to Dene Abbey to see what I can find out from the groom... if he is still alive.'

'If you can wait while I speak with my father, I will accompany you.'

'That would be most appreciated,' replied Sir Hugh.

Guy watched as the sheriff strode away, his bearing determined again and he hoped, prayed, that William and Jack Turner were not involved in all this mess, as he did not want to think that he might just have squandered his good name on defending guilty men.

Dene Abbey was set back from the road, occupying a stretch of land reaching down to the borders of Starvecrow Manor. The Abbey, founded by the De Clare family nearly a hundred years earlier, was inhabited by Cistercian nuns or "white ladies" as they were better known on account of their flowing white robes. There were twenty nuns in residence at this particular time, and all stayed within its walls to follow a life of prayer. This was in contrast to the Black Canons of Tonbridge who regularly went out preaching in the town.

Like many abbeys and convents built outside a town's defences, it had to provide its own security, and was protected by a very high stone wall. The only entrance was through a heavy iron-studded door with a small grille to enable its inmates to identify visitors before granting them entry. As an added precaution, a lookout platform housed in the bell tower and accessible by an outside flight of wooden steps, made it possible to survey the outer approach and surrounding area. The buildings stood around two separate yards, with the chapel and cloister leading to the Abbesses' chambers at its centre. The nuns' dormitories, refectory and the infirmary lay to the west, while the lay brothers had a similar set of buildings to the east. Lay brothers were the Cistercian's workforce. These were men and youths who laboured on the land and carried out all construction and maintenance work on the buildings, for their bed and board and a small wage. A two-storey hall with accommodation for guests upstairs, with servants and lesser mortals quarters downstairs, stood to the south. To the north of the compound, a muddle of kitchens, pantries and store houses stood overlooking neat vegetable plots and a small orchard of fruit trees and bushes. There was a stable and a barn, an enclosure for pigs, a cow-byre and a couple of fields for their small herd to graze.

On approaching the door, the sheriff took a cudgel from his belt and rapped it hard several times on the grille. After hearing the approaching scuffle of running feet, the small wooden shutter behind the grille snapped back to reveal a pair of dark, enquiring eyes, which darted back and forth to each visitor in turn.

'Good day, brother. Please bid the Sheriff of Tonbridge and your good neighbour, Sir Guy Guiscard, entry. We wish to be granted permission by your Abbess to speak with the unfortunate brought here yesterday.'

The shutter quickly snapped closed again, and after the sound of a large wooden bolster being removed from the other side of the door, and iron bolts being drawn back, one half of the door was swung open by the young porter. After lashing their horses to a hitching bar, he escorted them across the courtyard towards the Abbesses' chambers. The heavy footfall of the visitors' stout riding boots and the ringing of their spurs were in complete contrast to the soft slap of leather sandals upon the flagstones as they made their way past the chapel, and through the cloister towards a door at the far end. On reaching the door, the youth climbed a couple of steps to knock firmly on it, before descending them again. Turning, he smiled at Guy before retracing his steps back through the cloister, leaving them to await attention. After a moment, the door opened to reveal a woman dressed in the white habit of a Cistercian nun. Her hair was hidden under a head veil, and her throat swathed up over the chin in a linen gorget. A wooden crucifix hung from her braided belt. Her long, pale, serene face looked down at them impassively. Sir Hugh once again introduced himself and Guy, even though the nun must have recognised his companion as their neighbour and benefactor who supplied the flour for their daily bread. He repeated the reason for their visit. She bade them enter into a very narrow vestibule, which had only a plain wooden bench resting against the back wall and a small wooden crucifix hanging from it. She finally spoke to them in soft dulcet tones, as she motioned for them to sit.

'Please wait here. I will let the Abbess know you wish to speak with her.'

She turned and glided silently out of the room.

Sir Hugh gave Guy a bemused smile.

'Few could live such a simple existence,' he whispered, his gaze wandering about the stark room.

'Monastic life could have its benefits,' replied Guy wryly.

'It may be austere, but there is safety behind these walls, and aspiring hope for humanity outside of them.'

Feeling a shade embarrassed now at his comment, Sir Hugh nodded in assent, a grunt escaping from his throat.

They waited for a few more minutes in silence. Where the sheriff felt slightly uncomfortable being here, Guy felt the complete opposite. He soaked up the calm, placid atmosphere. A sense of peace and tranquillity had always enveloped him when he entered the abbey's confines, even when he was a young boy helping their old reeve, Randal, deliver supplies. If he were honest, he always did have a propensity for the monastic life but that had been impossible of course, not only due to his lineage but also his father's expectations of him. He remembered feeling a jot jealous of the opportunity afforded his childhood friend Ben, to enter here into this community when he himself had departed to undertake his squireship. He had not seen Ben since well before his departure to the Holy Land. He should really seek him out before he left today. Yes, he supposed, life could have been very different, although he should not complain – his had been full of privilege and liberty. He only wished he had not had to endure the atrocities he had seen, or even worse, been part of, during his years of campaigning. Atrocities he would rather not witness again…

The nun reappeared and bade them follow her.

'Abbess Margaret will see you now.'

The two men followed the white flowing figure through an open archway in the far corner of the vestibule and up a short corridor. Upon reaching a door to the left, she stopped and tapped on it, after which a terse 'enter' was heard. The Abbess' office was also very sparsely furnished, with just a small table at its centre encircled by four stools and the only adornment, again, being a wooden cross fixed to the wall, albeit larger than the one in the vestibule. Upon the table sat a pile of leather-bound books, an inkpot and quill. One of the books lay open to reveal columns of neatly written words and figures. The Abbess had obviously been in the middle of her book keeping. She stood facing them beside the table, her arms crossed in front of her, hands hidden up each sleeve of her habit. She was a small, amiable looking woman with soft, moon-like features, and Guy knew that her sometimes curt, abrupt voice belied her softer qualities.

Sir Hugh and Guy gave her a stiff bow of greeting, to which she replied with a slight nod and a warm smile.

'Good day to you, gentlemen. Guy, it's good to see you again so soon, although I wish it were in different circumstances.'

A couple of days ago Guy had personally delivered the latest supply of flour to the abbey.

'I too, Abbess Margaret. It is a gruesome business indeed that brings us here, but a necessary one. We need to speak with the injured man to glean any information he may have about the attack leading to the deaths of his fellow companions and the disappearance of two individuals, Lady Eleanor being one of them.'

'So I understand. What an unpleasant business. This troop of outlaws are utterly ruthless, it seems.'

'The viciousness of this crime makes it all the more crucial that we find the culprits,' put in Sir Hugh.

'This latest incident was a deliberate quest to kill, and we must assume that as we only have one dead female, Lady Eleanor and the young bride-to-be were either kidnapped or had managed to escape.'

Abbess Margaret looked grave.

'Yes, about the dead female. I must tell you that Brother Benjamin is most distressed. As his sister is Lady Eleanor's maid, he thinks she was most certainly travelling with the party. The fact that a woman's body was recovered at the scene, which was not identified as Lady Eleanor or her young charge, has greatly concerned him, as it can only bring him to the conclusion that it must be that of his sister.'

Guy had pricked his ears up at the mention of the lay brother's name. A puzzled frown clouded his face.

'Benjamin? Do you mean Ben, and the woman in question being his sister, Lucie?'

'The same,' nodded Abbess Margaret.

Suddenly it dawned on the Abbess how tactless she had been. She had forgotten that Guy and Brother Benjamin were old friends and that Guy would also have known Lucie. The family had lived and worked on his father's estate.

'I am so sorry, Guy. How thoughtless of me to blurt it out so!'

Guy had turned a shade paler. He slumped down on one of the available stools. Abbess Margaret anxiously leaned across the table to touch his shoulder.

'Are you all right? Would you like a drink?'

She turned to the chaperone nun and asked her to fetch some wine or ale. No, Guy was not all right. He was confused and needed some clarification here.

The last he had heard, Lucie had married Owen and they lived in a tied cottage on the Whitelawne estate, where he was head herdsman. When and how had that situation changed?

'This has come as a great shock to me. Lady's maid, you say? Since when? And what about her husband, Owen?'

'Unfortunately he died, not two years since. He was charged and gorged by a rampaging bull. Leaving Lucie a widow, and with no source of income, she had no alternative but to take up Lady Eleanor's offer of a place with her. As you know, Lucie has a knowledge of herbs and healing, and her Ladyship did not want to lose her skills,' explained Abbess Margaret.

'Owen dead. Why had nobody told me of this?'

He looked up accusingly at Sir Hugh, who could only speak for himself when he replied, 'With all that has happened lately, it completely slipped my mind... And it all happened so, well, it seems so long ago now… but that is no excuse, Guy. I am sorry, I should have told you,' he blustered.

He could kick himself. He felt such a buffoon and he had not an inkling that Owen's wife had become lady's maid to Eleanor de Coulances.

'Here…'

He took the cup of wine from the returning nun and placed it on the table next to him.

Abbess Margaret spoke softly to Guy in a bid to mollify his obvious agitation.

'Nobody wants to be the bearer of bad news, and all probably supposed, or hoped, that somebody else had told you.'

Guy nodded.

'And I have not seen Ben since my return,' he said with a touch of his own guilt. 'Poor Ben, he must be beside himself.'

Sir Hugh cleared his throat.

'Can I just say that if it is any reassurance, I was led to believe that the cadaver was of a much older woman. After we have spoken to the survivor, we may have more of an idea as to her identity.'

'Yes, yes of course,' said Guy.

He gulped down a large mouthful of wine.

'We should not make any assumptions until we have spoken to this man. Come, we must make haste.'

He stood abruptly, a little too quickly, and swayed slightly, having to rest a hand on the table for a second or two to steady himself.

'Are you recovered sufficiently for this errand?' queried a concerned Abbess.

'Maybe the sheriff ought to speak with him alone?'

'No, I am quite recovered, thank you. Let us just hope the man is conscious and coherent. I think Ben should also be present at the interview. Can you arrange for him to be available, Abbess?'

'Of course.'

Without speaking, she pointedly looked at and nodded to her fellow nun who, on hearing the request, acknowledged her understanding and left the room to seek out the lay brother.

'Now, if you are ready gentleman, please follow me.'

*

Ben was hovering outside the infirmary. He had heard that the sheriff and Guy were on the premises, come to speak with the patient. Well, he hoped they have more success in that quarter than he'd had. He had been keen to speak with the man himself, but had been told in no uncertain terms by the formidable Sister Hilda to stay away until such time as she deemed the patient recovered enough to answer any questions. It might make a difference, though, now that the sheriff was wanting to speak with him, he guessed sulkily.

He spotted them approaching across the courtyard. The Abbess, Sheriff and Guy. His eyes locked with the latter's and they made their way towards each other to embrace briefly.

'I pray to God it is not her,' he said in a cracked whisper close to Guy's ear.

He knew it was a wicked thing to say because whoever it was, she was someone who did not deserve to die in the way that she had, and that she herself was a daughter, maybe a sister, or even a mother to someone, somewhere who would also desperately grieve her loss.

Guy, putting an arm about Ben's shoulders replied, 'I know. Come, let us find out once and for all.'

They walked through the infirmary door into a room that led onto a corridor, recessed either side and curtained off to make individual cubicles. To the right was a room where all the medicines were kept. Around three walls and upon rows of shelves, sat an assortment of pots and jars, containing salves, lotions, potions, and powders. On benches either side of the door sat bowls, strips of clean linen, pestles and mortars, and an array of dubious looking implements and knives. Bundles of herbs and flowers tied with hemp twine hung from the ceiling to dry, suspended from a wooden rail stretching from one end of the room to the other, their pungent aromas mingling together to fill the air with that distinctive smell of an apothecaries storeroom. Standing at the centre table was the infirmarian, the daunting Sister Hilda, wearing a full length white linen apron, with the wide sleeves of her habit rolled up to reveal a pair of strong, muscled arms. The others waited outside while the Abbess entered to speak with her. She looked up from her task. She was making a poultice of comfrey and lavender to draw out and relieve bruising. She made sure not to breathe too deeply as the ingredients in the mixture could make one feel quite light-headed and dizzy.

'I suppose they're here wanting to speak with our new patient,' she said gruffly.

'Yes, they are, Sister Hilda, and I hope you can accommodate them. They need some questions answered,' replied the Abbess bluntly.

She'd had to stand her ground with this sister on a number of occasions. Sister Hilda knew her craft well, and for the patients she nursed, their chances of recovery were raised considerably, but she would jealously guard them as if her own life depended upon it and could be quite stubborn at times by not allowing anyone near them if she thought it might be detrimental to their welfare. On this occasion though, if she was to prove unhelpful, the Abbess felt it would be necessary to overrule her. Due to the seriousness of the current situation, and the amount of people involved in this latest incident, if the patient was indeed conscious and coherent, the smallest amount of information, which he could give the sheriff, or even poor Brother Benjamin, would be better than nothing at all.

'But he's not in a fit state to talk,' grumbled Sister Hilda, churlishly.

'Well, I will be the judge of that,' replied the Abbess testily, gesturing her to lead the way.

With a distinct look of disapproval on her face, Sister Hilda passed between the expectant group standing outside, and led the way to a curtained-off cubicle, herself and the Abbess disappearing behind it. Moments later she reappeared again, and made her way over to them.

'You'll be pleased to know he's conscious, but he is in considerable pain and needs quiet and rest. You can talk to him briefly,' she commanded.

She looked at each of them in turn, waiting for a nod of understanding before she added, 'His name is Roger and he is a groom from Whitelawne.'

They walked towards the cubicle. Ben glanced at Guy apprehensively as he held back the curtain to give admittance, first to the sheriff, then Guy, with himself following. Abbess Margaret stood in her usual pose quietly at the bottom of the low bed. There was an audible gasp from Ben. This was understandable, after all;

he was the only one in the group who had never seen such physical injuries before.

Roger lay staring up at the ceiling, his face a kaleidoscope of colours, his features unrecognisable. One eye was completely closed, encased in a mound of swollen flesh. Through the other eye he could barely see anything. His face was so swollen there were no discerning features, all its contours blending together to look like one big puffball. His lips were so swollen they were smooth and taut; only a split was visible, through which he was desperately trying to breathe.

'Oh my,' said Ben, 'what a mess. He had obviously put up a brave fight.'

The groom's body had been beaten badly. He had two broken ribs wrapped tightly with bandages and a broken left tibia, the inner and thicker of the two bones below the knee. The break was bad. He had been dosed with syrup of white poppy before it had been set, but the pain had been that excruciating it had rendered him unconscious. The limb was now held rigid with an ash splint bound tightly to his leg with linen bandages soaked in egg albumen. It would only be a matter of time to see whether the leg would heal straight. The pain was now replaced by a dull throb and he felt feverish. His ribs hurt and the whole of his body ached from the pummelling it had received. Sir Hugh edged his way forward and sat on the only stool by his bedside.

'Roger,' he said gently, 'I am the Sheriff of Tonbridge. I do not wish to cause you any more distress, but I had hoped you could give me a few details of what happened yesterday.'

Roger stared up at the ceiling. There was no indication as to whether he had heard anybody speak. Sir Hugh carried on.

'Lady Eleanor and the young girl – what happened to them? Did they run off?'

Roger's lip's trembled slightly.

'Were they kidnapped by the outlaws?'

There was no response.

Just as they were all beginning to think this may be a fruitless exercise, a visible shudder ran through Roger's body, and his throat seemed to be trying to work.

Sir Hugh glanced back at Guy and tried again.

'Lady Eleanor – did they kidnap her?'

Roger's mouth contorted and a sound, half groan, half sigh escaped from his scarcely moving lips.

'Yes,' was the barely audible reply. He was obviously in a lot of pain, not able to move his head, and his tongue was most certainly swollen.

'The young girl – what happened to her? Can you remember?'

Roger seemed to be getting agitated. He managed to turn his head slightly, tentatively, towards the sheriff.

He said in a hoarse, cracked whisper, 'Ran...' He seemed to muster enough strength to repeat again, 'Ran... away... woods.'

Ben, who could not contain himself any longer, butted in.

'Lucie – what about Lucie, the maid?'

Roger's Adam's apple started to work up and down again. After taking in a noisy breath of air, another hardly distinct, barely audible, 'Ran....' could be heard.

Abbess Margaret was becoming anxious and Sir Hugh knew that their time with the groom was about to come to a close.

'Ran away, you say? How many women were there in the party, Roger? Three, four?'

'Four...'

'So Lucie was not the dead woman?'

With much effort, Roger slowly, painfully, rolled his head from side to side.

'Thank God,' whispered Ben.

The crows were being particularly raucous this morning. Guy's head ached. He had barely slept all night, tossing and turning for the most of it and listening for any sound coming from his father's chamber opposite. The brief periods he had slept had been shallow and fraught, but sometime in the early hours before dawn he must have slept fitfully because he'd had 'the' dream again. He did not have the dream often, only in times of anxiety and stress. It had frightened him as a young boy, but as he had grown older it had become more of a comfort to him.

He would be soaring high above the tree canopy, circling and searching the landscape below. Then he would spy her, a speck in the far distance. She would always be somewhere different and never in a place he recognised. She could be standing in a clearing surrounded by trees, or in a meadow full of flowers or even on an outcrop of rock. Although he could not remember his mother, he knew this to be her. The breeze, gently blowing her corn-yellow curls away from her beautiful face, would reveal her lips set in a soft welcoming smile. Willing him to her, he would swoop down, ever closer. Then her deep emerald green eyes would open up to him and, turning her head, she would gaze out into the far distance. He knew she was trying to lead him somewhere or show him something or someone, but however tantalisingly close he came to finding out, he would wake up, never quite managing to see where, what or who it was...

He had never revealed the dream to anyone, not even his father. This was his secret and precious time with his mother, and all the time he had the dream he would never forget her beauty.

And yes, he was anxious.

On his return from the abbey yesterday, Matthew had met him in the yard, a look of disquiet on his usually temperate features.

'I am sorry to have to tell you that the master has taken a turn for the worst. Alisoun and I have put him to bed.'

Before Guy even asked the question, he already knew the answer.

'His chest?'

'Aye, it is,' replied Matthew ruefully.

'I should not have allowed him to venture out today,' said a frantic Guy, cross with himself and now intent on being relieved of Felix as quickly as possible.

He hurried across the yard toward the solar steps, sending the chickens squawking in all directions. He should not have abandoned him that morning, either, he thought guiltily. He should have realised it would be too much for him. He ran up the stone steps two at a time and made light work of the stairs leading up to his father's bedchamber.

The room was almost dark, Alisoun had closed the shutters. She was standing over Sir Robert, tending to his covers. At the sound of his entrance she looked round and quickly placed a finger to her lips to quell any utterance that might be on his. Guy walked quietly to the bedside to peer down at his quiescent father. He lay propped up against a number of bolsters and pillows, his face pale and drawn.

He was asleep, though Guy suspected not a restful one. His breathing was very shallow and laboured. It lacked the deep fathomless breathing only a restorative sleep would bring. Alisoun gestured for them to leave the bedside. Outside the chamber she spoke in hushed tones.

'Matthew and I found him collapsed in the solar. He had been coughing badly. He cannot expect to keep it from you any longer.'

She looked up at him and he noticed the pinched, narrow look of strain on her face.

'He needs plenty of rest and as much good food as we can get down him to keep his strength up. That is all we can do for him.'

She laid a gentle hand briefly on his shoulder, a swift light touch, but a reassuring one. He was unable to reply, his throat constricted.

He lay now, staring at the early morning light filtering through the shuttered window.

He was also anxious for Lucie.

She and her young charge had spent a night, maybe two now, out in the forest. He knew Lucie to be familiar with the surrounding area, but his main concern was that no harm should befall them. Thankfully, except for the storm two days since, the weather for October had remained fine and hopefully would remain so at least until he knew her safe. Whitelawne had sent out a search party, but finding them would not be easy. He felt unchivalrous because he really ought to be out there actively helping with the task, but he now had more pressing commitments at home. He turned over, groaned into his pillow and thumped it. He knew where his priorities lay.

He got up, washed, dressed and crept into his father's bed chamber. He went straight over to the window and opened up the shutters to let plenty of fresh air into the room. He would make sure to coddle his father against any draughts. The curtains had been pulled around the bed, so it was not until Guy approached and drew them back that he saw his father was awake and trying to rise.

'And what do you think you are doing?' he asked sternly.

'I cannot lay here, I have things to do,' his father replied, but as he tried to stand he caught his breath and with an abrupt snort, launched into a violent fit of coughing.

Making a grab for a linen napkin on the bedside coffer, he put it to his mouth and promptly sat down again.

'Lie back, Father,' said Guy, gently lifting his legs up and around to enable him to recline back against the bolsters and pillows.

His father was quite unable to speak as his chest heaved and spasms wracked his body. Guy could only look on in horror as the napkin started to turn dark red. Deciding it might be better for his father to sit up, he reached from behind and, slipping his arms through and under his armpits, raised the frail body to a sitting position. Thinking to make him more comfortable, he pulled him forward to place another pillow against his back. This was a mistake, for as Guy was burrowing and fussing around him, his father's head tipped back and, having very little strength to lift it again unaided, started to choke. Realising this, Guy tried to remedy the situation, but in his haste, he became clumsy and heavy-handed so that the fragile body slumped sideways this time. The coughing had ceased but his father lay motionless on the coverlet, blood trickling from the corner of his mouth. Guy gently lifted him back again, making sure that he was settled comfortably and securely. Anxiously, he watched the deathly pale and sweat-glistened face. After what could only have been a few heart-stopping seconds but seemed like an eternity, Guy was relieved to see his father's eyelids flutter. When a couple of deep breaths were taken that did not result in any further coughing, he knew the attack had subsided. He wiped the last trickle of blood from his father's trembling mouth and chin and, tenderly taking his hand, knelt by his bedside.

Alisoun found them thus when she came into the chamber a few moments later with a brew of horehound and feverfew syrup.

*

By mid-morning Guy ventured out, mainly to clear his head. In this restless mood, he decided to do a tour of the estate and pay a visit to the tenants' village. It was quiet down in the undercroft as he passed through, no doubt all going about their own business. Alisoun had made his father comfortable and reassured him she would stay close at hand inside the house. A bell was placed by his bedside in case he needed her.

As Guy stepped out into the yard, Angus loped over to him, wagging his tail in welcome and hoping to keep his master company today. He was not disappointed.

'Come, boy.' Guy gestured for him to follow as he made his way to the stable. On passing the dairy he spied young Tom inside. His mother, always intent on keeping the lad occupied, had given him the task of churning the milk and, unaware of Guy's presence, was singing and dancing around the churn as he worked. Guy had to smile to himself. He could hear the familiar sound of Matthew chopping wood in the wood hut at the far end of the yard.

In no time at all, Felix was saddled up and they trotted out of the stable, his hooves stirring up the summer's dust and autumn leaves.

With Angus in tow they made their way up the lane, flanked on either side with the woodlands edge of oak, elm, crab apple and hazel. It was a warm, bright autumn day and the sunshine lit up the ambers, oranges and reds of the foliage, which made a pleasing contrast to the deep blue of the cloudless sky. A flock of starlings chattered together amongst the thickets of buckthorn and holly, entwined with old man's beard and ivy, the latter climbing down to carpet the lane's verge. Crows cawed loudly in the treetops and the squirrels rustled and chittered happily in their twiggy drays. Emerging from the lane out into the open, Guy drew rein at the top of a knoll and gazed over the land and their flocks. Shading his eyes against the low sun's glare, he regarded the familiar landscape in front of him. It sloped gently down and away from the forest ridge high above him. The buildings and roofs of the abbey were just visible, nestling amongst the trees lining the ridge road.

Starvecrow's borders ran adjacent to this road ending at the bottom of Stumble Hill and then down the valley to finish at the line of willows that marked the border stream at the bottom of Starvecrow Hill. This stream carried on through to Dachurst, eventually meeting the River Medway and making it one of the many streams that crisscrossed the valley floor.

In the far distance he could make out two figures working in the lower pastures. A jay called harshly, a soft, fresh breeze ruffled his hair. He kicked Felix into a canter and headed down the track that would take him across the estate and on to the tenants' homes. With harvest over, it would be mainly the men now out on the land ploughing, making ready for next year's crops of wheat, oats and barley, and undertaking general maintenance work such as repairing boundaries and clearing ditches in readiness for the rainwater and melted snow, which would inevitably run down from the forest in the wet months to come. Taking advantage of the dry weather, he could see that Grainger and a team of men were doing just that. They were clearing a long, deep ditch that ran below a bean field. His father's idea of growing beans in quantity this year had paid off, and they were growing well and in abundance. He was hailed and cheerily greeted by every one of the workers as he stopped to pass the time of day with them.

'Such an October day is rare, is it not?'

'Aye, that it is,' they all replied in unison.

But Grainger spoke of his concerns about the continuing dry weather.

'The pastures are parched and tinder-dry, the stream barely a trickle in some places. Let us hope we get some decent rainfall soon for the sake of the flock and the winter crops.'

'Do not worry yourself too long and hard,' replied Guy, 'I am sure it cannot continue for much longer. Give it a sennight and I guarantee we'll be wishing it were back thus!' he said, raising his eyes to heaven.

'You're probably right, sir. Never satisfied aye,' Grainger replied, his worried frown turning into a sardonic smile.

And sure enough, within the exact amount of time predicted by Guy, the weather did change and gave cause for the reeve to hark back on this conversation.

'Anyway, gentlemen, I must away. I am on a mission to visit your good wives!' With a wave of his hand and a swish of Felix's tail, he rode off down the bean field's margin with Angus lolloping after them.

'Oh, aye, sir, they'll like that!' they shouted after him merrily, laughing, winking and nudging each other before bending down to continue their back-breaking work.

Heading down into the lower pastures, he passed and acknowledged the two tenants busy mending a weak spot in the boundary hedge with a couple of hurdles before any of their small herd of cattle managed to break its last vestige of resistance.

Cutting through a small wood, Guy entered a pasture of sheep, who nonchalantly looked up from their grazing.

He decided he would do a random inspection and, after a contest to determine who was the nippiest and fleetest-of-foot, he tussled the first ewe into submission. The Cotswold were a long wool breed of good stature, standing square with straight legs and strong, wide shoulders. He checked the udder for lumps, and then the teeth, to see that the incisors and the upper pad met correctly and that there were none broken. Finally he checked for blowflies, which could be a problem in the summer months especially, but as the fleeces were still quite short and clean, he found none. He was pleased with the results and, smacking the last one's behind, sent her packing.

He cantered past the tithe barn, which stood on the greensward where all the celebrations took place. The huge oak doors stood open and he could see it was full to the rafters with sacks of cereal crops. He raised a hand in greeting to all within who were bringing in the last of a bountiful harvest of apples. Very soon the tenants would be celebrating the apple harvest by enjoying a few days of leisure after all the hard toil.

The tenants' homes on Starvecrow were a good size and in a good state of repair. The inhabitants were allowed to do as they pleased with their own living space. Most separated it into two – one to live and sleep in, the other for livestock and storage for their produce. All households had their own small plot attached. Some used it for vegetables, herbs and fruit, others for a few chickens or pigs. Additional outhouses were used as a brewing shed, a dairy and a bake-house. They really had free rein to do whatever they wished and they all took full advantage of it. A bartering system enabled everybody the opportunity to share all the produce available so nobody went without. They were also lucky enough to have a master who was not one to bow too much to convention. They had never known him to make a father pay a fine if his daughter left to get married, or a son to become a monk or lay brother, and upon the death of a tenant, he never expected to be compensated. If they wished, and had somewhere else to go, the remaining family could move on or the eldest son, with the cooperation of his siblings, could succeed his father and stay on the estate. He would accommodate anybody as long as they were able to support themselves and worked hard towards benefitting the community as a whole. He had even been known to bail out tenants on occasion if he thought it warranted.

Guy knew that most of the women, apart from the few bringing in the last of the apple harvest, would be busy at home with their chores today.

They saw him coming.

'Aye up, 'ere comes the young master,' one announced to the rest of the group, who were sitting outside one of the dwellings spinning wool and darning clothes.

'E's a fine looking 'un ain't 'e,' said another, winking at her neighbour and smiling.

'Aye, that 'e is. 'E be in fine fettle, that one!'

'Coo, what would I give to be a score younger right now!' commented an old toothless granny, who then shrieked with laughter.

'Stop it, Ester! Be'ave yourself, you'll embarrass 'im,' scolded another.

On the contrary, Guy felt very comfortable with all these women; after all he had known them since he was old enough to ride out with his father. He enjoyed their teasing and easy banter and, much to the delight of them all, he could give as good as he got and it was all taken in good part.

Guy dismounted and put a hobble on Felix to stop him roaming too far, but he had to un-hobble him again when a group of boys came charging out from a copse of trees, wielding their wooden swords and asking if they could "'ave a go" on him. As on previous occasions, Guy had no qualms in letting them have a ride on Felix as he was a placid, even-tempered horse, but he did insist on keeping a firm hold on the reins.

Young Harry was first up.

'Remember what I told you. Hold on tight to the pommel, sit down hard and square in the saddle to let him know you're there, and a horse responds to the reins, your legs and most importantly, to your voice. Right, are you ready?'

'Yes, yes!' shrieked an excited Harry, waving his play sword above his head and jiggling backwards and forwards in the saddle.

Jabbing his heels into Felix's flanks, he shrieked, 'Giddy up, horsey!'

Thankfully, Felix, who carried on munching the grass, seemed untroubled by this.

'No, Harry, I have told you before, press in with your thighs and knees, tap with both heels once and say "hup". Let's try again, shall we?' Guy said patiently.

'He'd make a good father that one,' said one of the watching women, leaning close to another.

'Aye that 'e would.'

After reluctantly relinquishing his sword, Harry tried again with some success this time, and off Felix trotted in a wide circle, Guy holding onto the reins.

'Let me do it on my own!' he cried, trying to pull the reins out of Guy's grasp.

'I do not think so, young man. Your mother would not be too pleased with me if you ended up headfirst in the stream down there!'

Harry whooped. This was great fun! So much so that when the time came to give up the saddle for the next in line, he was very reluctant to do so. It took all Guy's skills of persuasion to get him off and Dickon on.

When Guy had finally quelled the children's demands, he made his way over to the women that had doubled in number since he first arrived. It had not taken long for his presence to be known about the village.

'Good day, ladies,' was his greeting as he made his way towards them, taking off his riding gloves and tucking them down between his leather jerkin and belt.

He received a genuinely warm welcome from the coterie who willingly offered him a seat within their circle and a mug of freshly brewed ale. Guy soon concluded they had a happy, contented and prosperous population in residence. It was not long before the conversation turned to the 'goin's on' at Whitelawne. They voiced their disgust at the treatment of Joanne and Will and the way in which their equals were being forced to live and work. Finally Geoffrey's murder and the plight of Lady Eleanor was raised.

'Don't fancy 'er chances much if they got 'old of 'er,' was one doleful comment.

'It's all 'appening a bit too close to 'ome for my liking,' was another.

But they were greatly dismayed when they heard Lucie was involved.

'Aye, of course, she's lady's maid up at the big house now. No doubt ye be especially worried about her?' inquired a perceptive Emily Grainger, the reeve's wife.

She watched Guy's face intently.

'Indeed I am,' he replied.

'Ah, but she be a feisty one that one!' exclaimed Ester, feeding a strand of wool from her distaff to the spindle.

'Anyone who tries to mess with 'er will get what for, I can tell ya!'

Everyone agreed.

'Well, let's hope so,' said Guy, remembering Lucie was a headstrong girl who could undoubtedly look after herself.

'How goes the master? We have not seen him for a while,' asked young Beth, picking up her two-year-old who had toddled over for a cuddle.

Guy had no idea how much anyone knew, if anything, about his father's condition, but had already made up his mind to lay bare the situation. He owed it to all the tenants to disclose the news personally and, with respect, he knew that the quickest and most efficient way of getting any news around the estate, would be to tell the women.

Hence, Guy left a somewhat disconsolate bunch as he bade farewell. He apologised for distressing them so, but they told him they would rather know than not.

*

Soon after, gifts started to arrive at the house for the master; a lavender scented cushion to help him sleep, a tonic to build up his strength, posies to lift his spirits, and someone had crudely whittled what appeared to be a crow from a piece of wood.

It transpired that the horse dealer was telling the truth. Not only did he eventually convince Percy that he was ignorant to the demise of the palfrey's previous owner, but the gatehouse received a visit from his wife with five snotty nosed children in tow, pleading his innocence and loudly weeping and wailing for his release. A frazzled Percy dispatched them all to the hall kitchens for a well needed bowl of pottage each whilst he finished his interrogation.

'I would be pretty stupid to steal a horse and then try to sell it on my own doorstep, wouldn't I?'

'Aye, you would, but someone 'as done just that! Who was it? Who did you buy it from?'

'Don't 'member 'is name,' Amos Smewing mumbled evasively, lowering his eyes to the ground.

'Look,' said an exasperated Percy, 'whoever sold you the palfrey might not only 'ave been involved in that violent robbery, but maybe many more to boot!'

'Well that ain't my concern, is it? I didn't do it!'

'Aye, that might be so, but if you don't tell me who sold you the beast, you could be 'anged for 'arbouring a criminal!'

A look of disquiet passed over Smewing's face.

'That ain't right 'cause I wasn't meant to know, was I?'

'Look, just do yourself a favour and tell me 'is name, will ya?' shouted the deputy, clenching his teeth and bearing down menacingly over Amos' stooped body.

Amos had spent most of the previous day and all of last night locked in the cage, spending most of that time trying unsuccessfully to avoid the attentions of aggressive drunks and being vomited over by the grossly inebriated ones. He had a bruised and cut right eye, his tousled and tangled hair had twists of dirty straw sticking from it, and the front of his leather jerkin and hose had something quite questionable adhering to them. He stank. Percy recoiled and walked over to the arrow slit window of the guardroom to inhale a breath of fresh air. Turning, he faced the now subdued and apprehensive Amos, who was bound and seated on a low stool in the centre of the chamber.

He spoke in a more conciliatory tone.

'Look, Amos, I do not want to 'ave to send you down to Striggar in the vault and leave you to 'is gentle powers of persuasion, do I?'

More often than not, just the mention of the ugly, brutish gaolers name made even the most foolhardy sing like a lark.

Amos realised he was damned if he did speak out and doubly damned if he didn't. Undoubtedly in his time as a dealer he had traded horses of dubious origins, not asking any questions, but this time he had come unstuck. Resigned to the only path left open to him, he reluctantly started to blab.

''E only 'ad the one 'orse. I thought it strange 'cause I know 'im to be a pot man at the Castle Inn. 'E's never dealt in 'orses before but said 'e could get me more if I wanted.'

'Just 'is name, Amos.'

'Cyril Fuller,' muttered Amos sullenly.

'Who?' shouted Percy, cocking his ear to indicate he repeat the name.

'Cyril Fuller!' he repeated louder.

'Now, that wasn't so 'ard was it? Those two little words 'ave just saved your neck!' said a relieved Percy, walking behind to untie his wrists.

Thank goodness for that! He had never relished abandoning anyone for the grotesque Striggar to slake his perverse predilections on, and left that course of action as a last resort.

'Before you skedaddle, a few words of advice. Be more careful who you 'ave dealings with in future and I suggest you move on pretty sharpish!'

Amos didn't need telling twice – he couldn't move fast enough. He was up and halfway through the door before Percy called after him, 'Oh, and your brood are in the kitchens. Get yourself something to eat and then 'op it!'

*

Percy, accompanied by two burly constables, headed for the Watergate, which gave access to and from the wharf through the southern town wall, below the bridge archway and barbican. The huge gates stood open, allowing a procession of labourers with large bundles of fleeces on their backs to make their way down the wooden ramp onto a level platform, to load up a vessel moored at the wharf side. There were a number of other vessels moored mid-river, waiting their turn to be unloaded and reloaded again.

They wove their way through the clutter of coffers, casks and sacks. The wharf was bustling with the activity of sailors, labourers and merchants going about their business. Percy narrowly averted a collision with a young potboy who, his face contorted with concentration, was intent on delivering two fistfuls of quart pots, filled to the brim with ale, to a group of labourers taking a well-earned rest on a pile of ropes. He was told if he managed to deliver them without spilling a drop, a tip was in it for him.

The Castle Inn stood over in the farthest corner abutted to the town wall. It was a ramshackle affair that had started life as a single taproom and had been added to over the years, a cookhouse being one attachment with a lean-to wash house being another. It was mainly frequented by the labourers and sailors who navigated the busy commercial Medway waterways reaching up to North Kent, and served not only the town's corn and tallow chandlers, wool exporters, timber merchants and anyone who needed supplies transported in bulk, but also the river-edge industries such as the potteries and iron works. The proprietor generally kept an orderly house and apart from a few scuffles now and again, and these being no more frequent than any other establishment in the town, was left to conduct his business as he saw fit. Therefore he was more than surprised to see the town's deputy sheriff striding into the taproom in the middle of the day.

Being well rehearsed, they had dispersed in three directions, Percy heading straight for the taproom while leaving Winter and Skinner to each stand guard directly in front of the cook and wash house entrances. Winter kicked out at two kites scavenging around a discarded animal carcass, and with his sword stabbed at a rat, which chittered off down a hole beneath the cookhouse.

A silence descended on the taproom as Percy entered. The patrons all knew who he was and had a distinct advantage over Percy, who didn't recognise any of them.

'What do you want?' barked the gruff, grossly overweight landlord who was in the process of collecting empty pots.

'Cyril Fuller. Is 'e 'ere?' asked Percy, scanning the room.

When nobody moved and no answer was forthcoming, just ten pairs of suspicious, unfriendly eyes staring back at him, he decided not to linger and backed out again with his hand resting on his sword hilt. Outside, looking from left to right at his henchmen, Winter placed a forefinger to his lips and pointed over in Skinner's direction. He indicated that Fuller was in the wash house. Skinner had peeped through a rip in the filthy hessian curtain that hung over the doorway and, knowing their quarry, had identified him.

There was certainly something going on in there, but it was most definitely not pot washing. They all looked at each other as a series of grunts and groans, something being knocked over and a muffled giggle could be heard coming from within. Smirks of amusement flew between the two constables. They were going to relish this.

Percy stood foursquare, loudly cleared his throat and in a very precise and authoritative voice shouted, 'Cyril Fuller. As deputy to the town and district sheriff, I demand that you stop what you are doing and show yourself!'

The noises from within abruptly stopped. A string of curses followed. When nobody appeared, Percy repeated his demand at the same time as gesticulating to Skinner that he draw back the curtain. Stepping forward, Skinner tentatively placed the blade of his sword halfway through the opening and briskly snatched the curtain back to reveal the bare buttocks of the pot man desperately trying to pull up his hose. A slatternly maid, with whom he had obviously been enjoying a covert liaison, screeched as she propelled herself from a table, clutching her unlaced bodice together and hurriedly pulling down her skirt. By this time, an inquisitive crowd had started to gather in the yard, just in time to see a red-faced Cyril being manhandled from the wash house, trying to hold up and tripping over his dishevelled clothing. Most found the spectacle very amusing and the laughing and finger pointing only added to Cyril's embarrassment and total humiliation. The landlord was furious.

'You lazy, good for nothin' tyke! You're s'posed to be washing the pots, not tupping the serving wench!' he yelled, shaking his fist.

The potboy, having delivered the four quarts of ale successfully without spilling a single drop, deposited his tip down the back of his shoe. Fighting his way through the throng of people, he was curious to see what the raised voices and hilarity were about. Having manoeuvred his way through the crowd on all fours, he scrambled to his feet to see Cyril being dragged away by two constables and Betsy in the wash house trying inconspicuously to lace up her bodice. Well, he knew what that meant – he'd have to do all the washing up! He glowered at her. Feeling eyes boring into her, Betsy stopped mid-lacing and looked up to see an expression of scorn written across her younger brother's face.

'What are you gawping at? Shog off!' she shouted.

'Oh no you don't!' interrupted the florid-faced landlord. 'Get in there an' start washing the pots!' he yelled, directing a well-aimed clout at the lad's ear.

*

This one was a tougher nut to crack, but then he had more to lose than most. If he was to confess all, he would certainly be a dead man. If he didn't hang by the neck first, Baldwin and his cronies would kill him, that was for sure. Taking the horse and selling it to

Amos Smewing had been one big, stupid mistake. He had not only risked his own neck, but that of the outlaws as well.

Cyril's older brother was an associate of Baldwin's. He did not get involved in the actual robberies, as indeed Baldwin did, his job was to spirit the pilfered horses well away from the area and sell them. He was always on the move between horse fairs and markets and, luckily for him, was probably miles away by now.

When he was able, Cyril helped his brother out, but being discontent with the measly spoils from the robberies, he occasionally deigned to throw his way, he had made the erroneous decision to keep one of the horses back to sell and pocket the money himself. The rest is history. He was history.

Percy had made Striggar's day.

His victim hung shackled to the dank, slimy wall of the vault. A brazier sputtered motes of red hot ash as an iron bar was placed into the glowing lumps of charcoal. The only light came from a shaft cut diagonally down from ground level through the thick wall of the gatehouse. Rusty bars were the only barrier between the fetid, oppressive atmosphere in the chamber and the fresh air of freedom outside. In the dim murk, a stretching rack took pride of place. Implements of torture adorned its framework. A grotesque iron mask hung there, glinting menacingly in the brazier's glow and a pair of thumbscrews lay discarded upon it.

The last thing Cyril Fuller remembered with any clarity was the oafish, distorted features of his tormentor, exposing his obvious delight in the tasks he was about to execute.

The low morning sun shone through the high un-shuttered window. Alisoun had lit a fire for Sir Robert's benefit, and father and son sat companionably together at the hearthside discussing a rota for the next year's crops. Their first yield of beans had been very successful and, deciding to repeat the same next year, were debating which field to sow them in. All the time Sir Robert did not over exert himself; he remained stable and, although he was happy to relinquish most of the responsibility to Guy, he still wanted some input into the running of the estate. Matthew appeared at the top of the undercroft stairs.

'Excuse me, Sir Robert, Guy,' he said, nodding to each in turn, 'but young Jake, the stable lad from Old Soar, has just rode in with a message from Sir Thomas.'

'Then please send him up, Matthew,' replied Sir Robert, looking quizzically at his son.

'We have not heard from my brother-in-law for a while. I wonder what has prompted this occasion.'

Their curiosity was soon allayed.

Jake, a strapping young fellow of seventeen, ran up the stairs two at a time. His ruddy complexion, contrasting with his fiery red hair, was alight with excitement. This was the first time the master had sent him on an errand and he felt very grown up.

He stopped, nodded his head in greeting and took a crumpled missive from a pouch on his belt.

'For you, sir,' he said, stepping forward.

Sir Robert took it and broke the seal. Before reading what was written, he sent Jake downstairs to the undercroft for refreshment and to await any further instructions. Scanning the short message first before reading it in its entirety, Lucie's name sprung out the page at him.

Hearing the sharp intake of breath, Guy enquired, 'What is it, Father?'

'It is Lucie and Richard's betrothed. They are at Old Soar, found their way there yesterday.'

'Thank God,' was Guy's immediate response.

'Any mention of Eleanor?'

'No, there is not.'

'I should go to her, Father.'

'Yes, of course you must...' Guy was already striding from the room. 'And fetch them both back here,' shouted Sir Robert after him.

The Manor of Soar lay about three miles north of Starvecrow. Guy and Jake travelled up onto the Plaxtol Road through the forest. They ascended to meet the top crossroads. From here the roads ran west through the forest to Shipbourne and east down the more open road to Hadlow. Continuing over the crossroads onto the crest of the land, they came to Dunks Green, a tiny hamlet where several dwellings stood around a small triangular greensward. Many of the occupants were busy in their neatly fenced-off yards and gardens. An alehouse stood a little way off. Two men who must be the local blacksmith and his apprentice given the scorched and scarred thick leather aprons they both wore, were taking some respite from the heat of their furnace and supping a thirst-quenching quart of ale. Hearing the approaching horses, they turned to acknowledge them. Some of the villagers going about their business recognised Guy and bade him a good day. All of them knew Jake. One villager mending a broken tailboard on his cart called out to him.

'Does your Amy know you're out gallivanting? Make the most of it while you can boy, she'll be layin' on your nightshirt tails soon enough!'

Another laughed at the jest.

'Aye, 'e'll not know what's 'it 'im, will 'e!'

Jake laughed good-humouredly, the colour rising in his cheeks.

'Is Amy your sweetheart?' enquired Guy.

'Aye, sir, she is. We are to be wed in the spring.'

'Well, congratulations, young man.'

'Thank you, sir.'

They rode on and from this high open ground Guy gazed northeast over Old Soar. He could just make out the manor house in the far distance. It sat on high ground overlooking its well-tended and fertile lands. Fields were being ploughed in readiness for next year's crops and herds of cows grazed in well-grassed meadows, though a little dry and parched due to the lack of rain. Flocks of sheep nibbled on sparser grass growing on the lower pastures.

The meandering lane leading to the manor house took them down off the Plaxtol Road where they forded a shallow stream. This usually wet, boggy area was now baked hard, the trampled grass, sedge and rushes flattened by the many hooves of cattle and sheep that made their way to drink there.

They travelled up again, the lane narrow between the high tree-lined banks. Startled rabbits zigzagged about in front of them, disappearing down the many burrows dug between the exposed interweaving tree roots. Down this dark, dank corridor, fungi and lichen grew in abundance. Tiers of the grey and white oyster fungi cleaved to birch, beech and elm and the parasitic black knobbly King Alfred's cake had attached itself to the branches of a fallen ash tree. The strong smell of the garlic parachute wafted around, captured within the confines of the canopied lane. After emerging from the covered way and travelling more dips and bends, they finally reached the manor house.

Old Soar Manor was a relatively new building. His Uncle Thomas had built it, mainly to gain more privacy for himself and his wife Elvera. Times were changing and to live with the whole household in one big hall was not the requisite any more. Made of Kentish rag stone, it had been attached to the much earlier built great aisled hall, which, being the principle entrance, had required another door to be knocked through for the family to gain access to their private solar via a spiral staircase. Underneath the first floor solar was the undercroft, used for storing goods and personal possessions. A chapel had also been attached to the solar with the under-chamber being used as a granary store. A wooden staircase and landing running along the outside chapel wall gave public access without intruding on the solar and family.

It was a peaceful, tranquil site and from this summit the occupants could see for miles around, Ightham being three miles north and Tonbridge five miles west. Guy breathed in the pure, fresh and somewhat cooler air. A chilled breeze ruffled his hair and, looking out over the low, grey horizon, he could see dark clouds amassing. After the continuous warm weather they had enjoyed up until now, a cold wet winter ahead was not a prospect he was overly eager to embrace, especially taking into account his father's ill health.

'Looks like the weather is about to break,' he said, indicating the skyline.

'Aye, sir, it does,' replied Jake, dismounting from Scallywag, his roan of many colours and holding Felix's bridle for Guy to do the same.

He led the horses away and Guy made his way to the far end of the hall and around the back to its entrance. As he turned the corner he found the courtyard to be a bustle of activity. Heavy oak trestles had been scrubbed and left to dry. Servants were sweeping and shovelling the old and soiled floor rushes from the hall and barrowing them away to a midden heap. Winter was coming and this was probably the last chance to change them before the wet, colder months, when trying to sustain some warmth, layer would be laid upon layer. The hard stamped earth underfoot was first being purged with lye, a caustic cleaning solution of wood ash mixed with water. This would then be left to dry before quantities of fresh green rushes were scattered, together with toadflax and lavender to keep the fleas and bad odours at bay. Everybody was too busy to take much notice as he walked in. The central hearth fire had been lit, but the huge black cooking cauldron was empty, hanging on its iron trivet away from the flames. A cold repast would be served today.

Eager to ascertain the situation regarding Lucie and her young charge, Guy quickly made his way over to the door in the farthest corner of the hall, but as he put a hand to open it, he hastily had to retract it again. It was already opening up before him. They stood staring at each other.

The first sight of him after so long stuck Lucie a blow under her heart and took her breath away.

'Guy!'

She wore a head rail, a linen cover held in place by a band around her head, and although the light was dim here, Guy could still see the bruising around her left eye and tiny, livid scratches across the bridge of her nose and cheek.

'Are you all right?' he enquired, resisting the urge to raise a hand and caress the swollen cheek.

Instinctively, Lucie put her own hand up to her face. As she did so, more scratches and welts were exposed on her forearm. Guy winced.

'My, you have been through the mill,' he said gently, taking her hand.

'I'm fine. Just a few scratches, that's all,' she said, followed by a self-conscious giggle.

Even though she knew him summoned, to see Guy suddenly standing there had been a shock.

She had not seen him since before Owen's death and had forgotten how close they had once been. The quiet stoicism of recent years, weakened by the horrors of the last few days, suddenly crumbled. The brave smile dropped from her face and, overwhelmed, she launched herself at him. She buried her face into his neck and shoulder and a muffled sob escaped from her throat. Guy engulfed her in his arms and held her close, cradling her head in his hand.

'Hush, you are safe now,' he whispered.

After a while she composed herself and drew away from him.

'I forget myself, I do apologise. I hope I have not embarrassed you,' she said quickly, brushing aside a few stray tears with her fingertips.

'Not at all. It has been a long time since a woman threw herself into my arms, I had forgotten how delightful it felt!' he quipped, trying to lighten a moment that he actually had found a little disconcerting.

Holding her at arm's length and looking upon the face he had worn ragged in his daydreams over the years, all he could manage to say again was, 'Are you sure you are all right?'

'Yes, thank you,' she said with a hint of uncertainty. 'I... I was just on my way to gather herbs from the garden to make a tisane for Heloise. She is not recovering very well from our ordeal, poor child.'

She stepped away from the doorway leading to the staircase.

'Your uncle and aunt are upstairs in the solar. I am afraid we have caused some upheaval. They have been very kind to accommodate us, but space is limited and I cannot expect them to continue with the disruption we have caused for too much longer. Your uncle has been sleeping in the hall and Heloise has taken the only bed available, so your aunt has also been inconvenienced, although she emphatically denies it. We must return to Whitelawne as soon as Heloise is able to travel.'

'When do you think that might be?'

'Tomorrow I hope, but I see the rains are coming.'

'Do you think it wise to return to Whitelawne with all that has happened? I presume you have been told of Geoffrey's murder?'

'Yes, I have. Do you think it is connected to Eleanor's plight, whatever that might be? We do not know if she is alive or dead.'

'That does not concern me at this moment in time; you and Heloise are my main priority. I think you should consider returning to

Starvecrow with me, until the situation calms down, at least. We have sufficient room, *and*,' he said, holding up a hand in a bid for silence as Lucie was about to protest, 'nobody will be inconvenienced.'

'If that is what you think best, then so be it,' conceded Lucie. Under the circumstances she felt quite relieved knowing a return to Whitelawne was not yet imminent, and she also felt Heloise needed some respite before facing a grieving family who were, after all, strangers to her. She did not think either party would appreciate or benefit from meeting their prospective in-laws at this present time.

She hesitantly went to go their separate ways.

'Lucie…'

She stopped and turned to him.

'How do you fare… really? It has been a long time…'

She smiled a soft, almost sad smile.

'I do well enough,' she replied, nodding her head slightly.

She took in the concerned, familiar features of his kind and handsome face before reluctantly turning to continue her quest for herbs.

*

When the dust had settled, dinner was served in the hall. It was a cold affair. A variety of pasties, meats, cheese and bread were laid upon the trestles where all the household had gathered to eat. A pottage had been put to the fire for supper. Thomas, Elvera and Guy sat on the top dais, with the household below. Lucie stayed with Heloise in the solar where Elvera had instructed one of the serving maids to take up a platter and attend them.

As they ate, the hall grew dark and a squally wind got up, blowing leaves across the threshold into the hall entrance, followed by large spats of rain. A young boy scuttled over to close the doors.

Once it had started, the rain did not stop. First torrential, then easing off to a steady incessant downpour, which showed no signs of letting up. Guy asked to stay overnight if it was not too much trouble. He would have to sleep in the hall in any case, and being as he hoped to escort Lucie and Heloise home the following day, it made sense.

Replete with meat pasties washed down with cider made from the fruit of many large apple orchards, they made their way back to the solar. Guy gazed around his surroundings.

The manor house was designed to be defended. Cross loops, through which arrows could be fired, covered all approaches, and if attackers did manage to break into the hall or undercroft, the staircase provided the last means of defence for the family sheltering upstairs in the solar. It spiralled clockwise so a defender had free play of his right sword arm. At the top of the stairs the door opened outwards to fit into a recess, and the retreating defender could pull the door closed behind him.

The solar was comfortable although smaller than Guy was used to, with three great windows, two of which faced east and west. The third in the southeast corner, looked down over the roof of the hall. Although the great hall still had the old fashioned stone ringed hearth at its centre, the solar had a fireplace and chimney. The fire had been lit and the shutters closed against the rain giving a warm, cosy atmosphere in the late afternoon gloom. Braziers were placed in the draughty areas near the windows and doors, which would be lit later if necessary. Oak benches lining the room, a large carved wooden coffer, an aumbry with silver flagon and goblets, and a bed were the only furniture. Comfort came from soft furnishings such as wall hangings, coverlets and cushions. Thick woollen curtains decorated with red and gold stitch-work enclosed the bed, and big plump embroidered cushions were scattered on and about a built-in window seat finished with gleaming Bethersden marble.

The chapel wing was attached to the corner of the solar, and in the opposite corner was the garderobe and latrine.

Outside, the sky was a scudding mass of ash-grey clouds. The rain slammed against the shutters, making them rattle with every gust. Inside, the candles fluttered in the draughts and braziers were eventually kindled for extra warmth. Industrious with her needlecraft, two enormous candelabrums burned either side of Elvera where she sat in her marble throne. Guy and Thomas, having pulled up two benches to the fireside, played chess on a small table retrieved from the garderobe. Lucie sat with Heloise who lay on the bed, seemingly oblivious to her surroundings. The ordeal of previous days had taken their toll, resulting in her retreating into herself. Lucie hoped this to be a temporary healing process.

Guy tried to concentrate on the game in front of him but found himself frequently glancing over at Lucie. The soft candlelight at the far end of the solar accentuated her arched dark eyebrows, high cheekbones, thin nose and wide, full mouth. The head rail covered her hair, but he knew it to be thick and glossy, the colour of chestnuts. He glanced over again and found himself transfixed by a pair of clear grey eyes fringed with dark lashes. Her wide mouth smiled readily at him, and he was mesmerised.

'Check!' Thomas shouted vigorously.

'You must learn to concentrate on the game in hand, my boy,' he laughed, winking and slapping him on the back.

*

Much later, and feeling a little light-headed from the wine he had consumed, Guy retired to the hall and lay down on the pallet supplied for his use. The wind and the rain outside and the restless stirrings of the household, all went unheeded as he drifted off to sleep experiencing, for the first time ever, a tiny flutter of excitement in the pit of his stomach.

Sir Hugh and De Clare's constable, Hugo Corbiere, gathered together all the available men between them. There were two separate outlaw camps somewhere between the old ruin of Castle Hill Fort and the quarry, within the vast dense woodland of the Wealden Forest. Two scouts had been sent forth in the guise of woodmen to pinpoint the exact locations. A plan had been inaugurated that needed to be executed as soon as possible, firstly because outlaws were known to move camp frequently and secondly, the weather was about to break and Sir Hugh did not want to be hampered by wet weather. They had managed to muster together approximately thirty men, which they divided into two groups. One was headed by Sir Hugh himself, the other by Hugo Corbiere.

They set off in their separate posses as soon as it was light, foot soldiers and archers first, followed by the mounted personnel in hauberk and aventail, which hung from their basin-shaped helmets. Sir Hugh was to advance into the forest from Castle Hill, while Corbiere travelled straight up the quarry hill to the ridge and headed down from South Frith. All were to spread out into the forest with the intention of encircling the unsuspecting outlaws. Not knowing how many they would be dealing with, Sir Hugh hoped they had sufficient men. He was under no illusions that there could well be casualties on their side. The outlaws would not succumb without putting up a fight, so an element of surprise was imperative. Timings had to be meticulous and selected from each group were scouts well practiced in communication skills.

Sir Hugh made his way to the old fort, which overlooked the low ground, between Castle Hill and the quarry. The only features left to show there had been any fortifications here was a wide ditch hewn from the natural rock and a few scattered boulders buried deep into the ground covered in moss and lichen. It was thought to have been built by farmers to keep Celtic and other marauding invaders at bay and had been immensely strong in its construction.

He knew they would be the first in position. From there, three archers, one a scout, not wearing armour, were sent on ahead. Once the other posse was in position, they would do the same. Separating and moving forward, they would communicate with each other when either camp was sighted. This exercise would indicate how far apart the camps were, and how many men were in each. Two archers would then remain while the scout returned with the information to his commander.

'No more than ten men camped in a clearing, four hundred paces ahead,' he panted.

'What about the other camp?'

'About a dozen men, roughly same again apart.'

'Right men, we are to spread out but stay in sight of each other. The one at each end, make sure you can see the last man of the other party. On the signal, stop and await further command. Quietly now.'

Silently the foot soldiers padded forward between the trees with the scout archer ahead of them, their bows, pikes and swords at the ready. Sir Hugh and the three other horsemen hung back slightly as they would be more conspicuous through the undergrowth. After a while, the scout nearing his coequal put his hand up to stop. This was repeated along the line. The trees were starting to thin out here so extra precaution was needed. He pointed to indicate a thin, scraggly column of smoke rising up in front of them and sunlight from a clearing could be seen through the trees. They slunk forward as he waved them on just that little bit further and again raised his hand to halt the proceedings. They were very close. Sir Hugh's heart was in his mouth. Any noise now would surely alert the enemy of their presence. A few of the outlaws could be seen moving about the camp. The scout looked round expectantly at Sir Hugh, who nodded. This had been well rehearsed. The scout raised a cupped hand to his mouth and made a sound that, to all but the trained ear, was the yodelling song of a woodlark. A reply was heard in the distance. Everyone was in position. He looked at the sheriff again for the final command. Sir Hugh placed his hand upon his sword hilt and nodded for the last time. The line of soldiers were poised for attack. The archer loosed a single arrow high into the sky. At the same time, Sir Hugh unsheathed his broadsword and held it aloft.

'Forward, men!' he yelled at the top of his voice.

Even before they were off their marks, arrows fired by the two front archers zipped through the air and felled two outlaws with deadly accuracy. A roar resounded through the clearing as the men-at-arms stormed forward. Pandemonium ensued. Half asleep, exposed and vulnerable, the outlaws were no match for the soldiers. Most of them having no weapon to hand were either cut down scrambling for one, or making a run for it in the opposite direction, thus steering them into the path of the encompassing assault. The soldiers had been ordered not to take any prisoners. They had been declared outlaws so would hang without trial anyway. The onslaught was swift and fierce. The contained outlaws that did have weapons put up a courageous fight but were cut down with lethal proficiency. Jumping unsuspecting travellers from behind was the limit to their skills; to engage with a fighting force such as this, there was no contest. There were no serious injuries in the ranks thanks to their mailed hauberks and helmets. While the men sat down to rest, Sir Hugh and Corbiere prowled amongst the dead lying bloodied and still in the clearing and further afield in the undergrowth and fern. There was nobody they recognised as they kicked them onto their backs to get a good look at their faces. Sir Hugh had been right to suspect them of being strangers. He had no idea who Baldwin was, but hopefully he was among the dead. Suddenly a shout went out and Sir Hugh looked up to see Percy emerging from the trees, holding a struggling youth by the scruff of his neck. His fawn tunic and brown worsted breeches identified him as being a forester's page and groom.

'Well, what have we here?' he enquired, sheathing his broadsword.

The youth returned a glowering expression before lowering his eyes to the ground.

'Found 'im 'iding back there,' said Percy, indicating a thicket of trees behind him.

'An' there's somethin' else I want to show you,' he said, dragging the boy back the way they had come.

Sir Hugh and Hugo followed. Back under cover again, Percy led them to a spot where the ground dropped away significantly. Peering over the edge, they saw a body spread-eagled below them, an arrow protruding from his chest. He wore the same distinct colour of uniform as the youth, plus a badge, sewn onto the tunic's breast. The badge displaying a horn established the body being that of a forester, and one that they recognised.

Sir Hugh turned to the page and demanded he tell them what he knew of the forester's involvement. The youth started to squirm.

'I don't know, I'm just a page!' he howled.

Percy shook him violently and threw him to the ground. Taking out his sword, he placed the tip of it under the youth's chin, making him blanch.

'You're in deep trouble, lad. Tell the sheriff what 'e wants to know.'

The youth's defiant demeanour suddenly crumbled and he began to blurt out what he knew.

'That horse dealer was always turning up, handing over pouches of chinking coins and mumbling in the forester's ear!'

It soon became apparent that he himself had played a reluctant part in the conspiracy; it was just unfortunate for him that he had been chosen to serve a crooked officer. The forester had often met with Baldwin, the outlaw-cum-horse dealer. For payment he had murdered the warden to get him out of the way, and had led the other foresters and Sir Hugh's and De Clare's men a merry dance, making sure they were never in the right place at the right time. This did not come as much of a surprise to the page's audience. A forester was similar to a gamekeeper and was responsible for enforcing the forest laws. They received no salary to speak of, but some of them had actually been known to pay for the privilege of having the job, knowing the opportunity for extortion was bountiful.

'The double-crossing bastard,' muttered Percy under his breath.

'Is Baldwin here?' Sir Hugh asked the page.

'He was. He may have escaped.'

'Right, get up. I want you to identify him. Percy, take him round the bodies.'

Percy once more grabbed the youth roughly by his collar and pulled him to his feet. Pushing him forward they commenced the gruesome task.

It was confirmed Baldwin was indeed among the dead.

The outlaws had been a mixed bunch of varying ages, and some were dressed in little more than rags. Sir Hugh wondered what could possibly have driven them to eke out such a miserable existence in the forest. Before leaving, all the bodies were gathered together and left for collection. On returning to the castle, Hugo would instruct a party of men to take sufficient ox-carts up into the forest to retrieve them. They would then be displayed on the outfields and used as a deterrent for any aspiring outlaws of the future.

The journey back to Tonbridge was more light-hearted than the tense, apprehensive march out. Everybody was relieved that the exercise had gone according to plan, resulting with no casualties.

They assembled in the castle's inner bailey to disencumber themselves of their heavy mailed hauberks. A sudden gust of wind squalled around the compound, picking up dust and debris. Percy looked skyward. The already greying sky had darkened even further and large drops of rain started to beat down onto the dry, solid earth. Just in time, he thought, rubbing his hands together. He headed for the hall kitchens, looking forward to a bowl of pottage or two, and a sizeable jug of ale.

Gwen was not happy. The wind and rain that blew in yesterday had been so severe there had been no question of three merchants continuing their journey through to Rochester, so she had offered them shelter for the night. That had been beneficial from a monetary point of view, but what was not good was the fact that Ewen had been up most of the night drinking with them, which inevitably resulted in him still being abed this morning with a thick head.

She sat on a milking stool, a long paddle at hand, stirring the ale mash stewing in a large wooden mash tun. She stirred more vigorously than was necessary, muttering aloud to herself and imagining it was her husband's head she was mashing. She had been up since dawn, had seen to the pigs and let them out, as well as providing a breakfast and seeing the guests on their way, all of them looking a little green around the gills.

'Serves 'em right,' she said spitefully, 'jogging up and down on those 'orses will soon sort 'em out!'

It was still raining this morning, although the wind had dropped and it was a finer mist of rain that fell from a heavily leaden grey sky.

She was suddenly surprised to hear the sound of many horses' hooves. This in itself was not unusual as many parties of horsemen, usually rich, well-mounted men who, having the King's permission, came to hunt in his forest for deer and boar. But to be hunting so early, especially on a day like this, and to ride into their yard, was.

She sat listening for a while at the disturbance outside. Then, still holding the paddle, she made her way tentatively to the side door that led out onto the yard where the pigs roamed. In quick, rapid succession, squeals of alarm from the creatures could be heard. Gwen, never one to shy away from a fight, whether it be to protect herself, her property or a person in need of assistance, stepped out into the open. She stopped dead in her tracks and hesitated. There were more horsemen than she had anticipated, about seven in all, some still mounted while others, daggers drawn, pursued her terrified pigs around the yard. One had already been caught and slaughtered, she noticed. Its throat had been slit and it now hung bleeding from a saddle.

'Oh no, not my pigs!'

Any second thoughts of a confrontation were dispelled as she let out a scream of fury and a stream of invectives as, raising the paddle high, she flew at one of the assailants, hitting him squarely on the back of the head and sending him reeling across the yard. With the element of surprise now lost, another blow aimed at a second fellow was fended off with a raised left arm, and this time it was Gwen who was sent staggering backwards to land, winded, in a heap on the ground. After a second or two she tried to get up only to be kicked down again, the perpetrator laughing at her feeble attempts to repel them.

'Stay down, you stupid bitch!' he growled through his kerchief and flashing a dagger menacingly in front of her face.

There she decided to stay, resigned to the fact that there were far too many of them for her to handle on her own. So as she sat there, she furtively took in as much detail as she could of the marauders and their mounts in the short space of time that it took them to finish off two more of her pigs and make away with them. These were certainly not a hunting party. Their faces were concealed behind kerchiefs and their clothes dirty and ragged. They were obviously common outlaws but what was unusual, she noticed, was that they all carried sheathed daggers and swords. The usual implements would be cudgels, axes, bows and lances, anything they could put a hand to, not the gentlemen's weaponry that this bunch carried. Most of the horses too looked of good breeding, and one in particular stood out from the rest. It was a small grey, a fine, elegant looking beast with its head held high. It looked like one of those, what do you call 'em – Arabians? In the back of her mind she was sure that she had seen it somewhere before…

She sat watching the retreating backs that had left her three pigs short and the others scattered in all directions. The puddle and the rain soaked into her clothes and the chill had started to penetrate. Her linen coif sat wet and askew upon her head, and her yellow-gold curls dripped cold rainwater down her face, neck and shoulders. She shivered and struggled to get up. As she made her disconsolate way back to the alehouse, a bleary eyed, dishevelled Ewen appeared at the doorway, yawning and scratching his head and backside.

'What was all the racket about?' he enquired.

Well, he never saw the paddle coming but he felt it right enough. He had the mother of all headaches on top of a headache, and one that he would never forget in a hurry.

*

By putting a mild sedative into her sleeping draught the night before, Lucie had ensured Heloise succumbed to a deep, sound and restful sleep. Seeming a little brighter, and taking more notice of what was going on around her this morning, Lucie decided her well enough to travel. Guy proposed they leave before the rains well and truly set in and make the journey too long and arduous.

Lucie rode Felix, and Heloise Scallywag, while Guy and Jake led them on foot. The leaves that had fallen from the denuded trees glistened underfoot as the small party made their meandering way down to the flat ground and the now swollen stream. The many deep hoof imprints on the shallow banks had puddled into sinks of rainwater and they stepped cautiously, taking care not to slip on the rapidly softening mud.

When they had arrived at Old Soar, Elvera had provided the women with clean garments and shoes from the household coffers. Theirs had been totally ruined in their flight through the forest. This morning thick woollen cloaks had been gratefully received, and were now wrapped around their bodies with the hoods pulled down against the chill flurries of rain.

As they journeyed, Heloise still stayed engrossed in her own thoughts, which did not overly bother Jake. Being quite a shy individual himself, he was quite happy to amble along in silence. Lucie and Guy, though, had much to talk about. Guy conveyed his condolences on Owen's death and explained he had not heard the news until his recent visit to the abbey. Lucie, after accepting Guy's sympathy, enquired about his time in the Holy Land. Conversation eventually moved on to his father's ill health, which she was sorry to hear, and then of Roger's slow recovery at the abbey.

'Heloise and I have much to thank him for. With his guardianship, we were lucky enough to survive with only a few cuts and bruises. The others were not so fortunate.'

She went on to relay in detail the events of the day that seemed so long ago now. She told of the ear splitting scream she had heard as they fled from the carnage.

'I fear it was Eleanor's scream I heard.'

'But if she had perished, surely her body would have been recovered at the scene?'

'Maybe they took her as a hostage?'

'Well, she has not yet been offered for ransom if that was their intention,' said Guy.

'I can only suspect she may well have come to a particularly nasty end.'

'Hmm,' concurred Guy.

'Did she treat you well?' he asked neutrally, holding back the prickly foliage of a hawthorn bush.

'Who? Lady Eleanor?'

'Yes.'

Lucie appeared to consider her words before she spoke, but, 'Well enough,' was her only reply.

Guy had to be satisfied with that, as she was obviously not prepared to elaborate any further.

There was a lull in the conversation. Guy had pushed back his hood whilst he had been talking to her, and Lucie took full advantage of this to regard his profile as he strode confidently along beside her. He was taller than average and held his broad-shouldered frame well. His body was muscular and toned from years in the saddle and on the battlefield, and the strong, clean line of his nose and full sensual mouth made him very striking indeed.

He still had the unruly hair of his youth, which now hung in wet coils around his face, the burnished gold tints darkened by the rain. She noticed he still had that habit of raking it back from his forehead. As always, she felt happy and at ease in his company.

They had been close as children, playing together with Ben, even staying under the same roof, sometimes at the cottage, other times at the manor house. The sentiments had always been there up to a point, but as they had grown older, the irrelevance of status felt in childhood had gradually veered towards the conception that he was the son of, and soon to become himself, a knight of the King's Realm. Once Guy was fully immersed in his squire training, she came to realise that a Norman knight, albeit half Saxon, was a hopeless prospect for a lowly shepherd's daughter. She had accepted the situation with good grace and moved on without any animosity. That was the way it was, she had told herself.

Coming up and out of the lane, they passed through the neat little village with the triangular greensward. Not a soul was in sight. The weather was certainly keeping people indoors today.

The rain had started to fall a little heavier now. As they descended from the top crossroads they took a slight detour from the road onto a track that disappeared beneath the trees, and provided them with a modest but welcome amount of shelter. Globules of rain dripped from the canopy above onto the deep leaf litter of the woodland floor. The smell of damp leaf mould filled the air. Lucie had always loved being out in the wild wood, whatever the weather. Since being in the employ of Lady Eleanor, she had missed the freedom and the opportunity to step out whenever she felt the desire to do so, and she inhaled long and deep, taking in the fresh, familiar fragrance of her surroundings.

Out from undercover, they arrived at the top of Starvecrow Hill. Lucie was starting to feel a sense of excitement at being so close to her childhood home. She might just as well have been living on the other side of the world, not only a little more than a mile away at Whitelawne, for the distance she had felt separated her from Starvecrow. The prospect of seeing Sir Robert, the manor house and being under its roof again really thrilled her. Guy, thankful for an uneventful journey and eager to be home and out of the disagreeable weather, gave Felix's muzzle a cursory pat and started off with some purpose down the hill.

Halfway down, a sudden cacophony of cawing and the flapping of many wings startled them to an abrupt stop. A murder of crows, disturbed from their treetop perches, took off and flew over their heads. The sky went momentarily black, casting a shadow over them and darkening what little gloomy, grey light there was of the day. Both the horses skittered. Guy cursed and was forced to pull down heavily on Felix's reins as he reared and sidled. Lucie clutched the saddle pommel tightly. Together they gently soothed him to a standstill. Jake, too, eventually managed to calm Scallywag, but not before Heloise, frightened of being thrown, had nimbly launched herself from the saddle. She landed on her feet to earn a surprised glance from Jake. They all stood listening to the harsh calls receding into the distance. The crows had gone. An eerie silence remained, a silence that had never been heard at Starvecrow. Whatever could have caused the mass exodus, and surely that was Angus Guy could hear barking persistently in the distance? It was just a sense at first, an intuitive feeling that something was amiss, but as they grew closer to the lane entrance, an indefinable anxiety impinged further into his consciousness and he recognised a need for caution. He reached for his sword and unsheathed it, the hiss of its withdrawal alerting his companions to the possibility of forthcoming danger, and seeing the grim line of his mouth and taut jaw, confirmed their concerns.

He turned to Jake.

'Anything untoward, get the women away.'

Jake nodded and took the reins of both horses. Lucie dismounted from Felix and went to stand back with Heloise, placing a reassuring arm about her shoulders and drawing her close. The rain had started to seep through their clothing, chilling their bodies and making their breath come in clouds, short and sharp, in rhythm with their thudding hearts.

Guy, every sense alert, turned into the lane and yard, his quick, keen and trained eye swiftly took in the scene. The yard was empty. The door to the undercroft was open, as was the door at the top of the stone steps. Outside the dairy, a bowl lay discarded, its contents spilt on the ground. The wattle fence, a barrier between the yard and vegetable patch and garden, had been trampled down, and the last of their root vegetables torn from their beds. He quickly surmised that they'd had intruders. Were they still here? As he skulked forward, not a sound could be heard. Where was Angus? Matthew? He moved stealthily over to the woodshed and peered inside. He became bolder, striding over to the stable and byre. Daisy, their milk cow, was there, nonchalantly munching from a manger full of hay, as were the oxen. More surprisingly, the pigs were still secured, but his father's chestnut mare was gone.

He was frantic now to find out what had happened to the household. As he ran towards the undercroft, Matthew appeared. He staggered to hold onto the door frame. He had been hit with some force, as a blossoming bruise was evident on the side of his face.

'We've had intruders!'

'Is everybody all right?'

'We're all right here, but they went upstairs!'

'Where's Angus?' Guy barked, already running up the stone steps.

'He chased after them.'

Guy ran swiftly through the open door and up to his father's chamber, with Matthew only a few paces behind him. He stopped suddenly in the doorway as if he had been struck motionless. His eyes could make no sense of all the confusion at first, and then he saw his father. He lay face down, sprawled across the bed, his dark and red-rimmed eyes staring into nothingness. The pallid and waxen hue of his complexion was in stark contrast to the bright red blood that could be seen on the coverlet. It had gushed from his nose and mouth in the final eruption of his lungs. Guy sheathed his sword and strode over to the bed.

'Dear God, have mercy,' he muttered in a cracked whisper before his throat constricted with distress.

Matthew, white-faced and swallowing convulsively to stop himself vomiting from the odious smell of blood, helped Guy to gently move his father onto his back. Guy sank down heavily next to the inert body and gazed disbelievingly around the chamber. His father's storage coffers had been disturbed and all his clothes and boots had been taken. The enamel trinket box that had sat forever on the wide stone windowsill had been prised open and left completely bare, the large gold pin and garnet, his mother's jewellery, betrothal ring and wedding band, were gone. The room had been completed ransacked.

*

It was dark and cold. The rain had ceased and between the scudding clouds the moon hung low and heavy in the night sky. A single candle burned on the coffer and the scent of incense filled the chamber. Guy knelt by his father's bed and gazed upon his ashen face. The candle flame guttered as Alisoun came into the room. She bought with her a flagon of wine and placed it upon the coffer beside the candle. Guy did not look up, but continued his vigil. He thought, hoped, that if he stared long and hard enough at his father's face he would be resurrected, returned to them somehow.

Alisoun stood someway off from the bed, her head hung in mourning and prayer. After a while the silence was broken by her soft weeping. It became too much for Guy to bear. He had held back for as long as he could and was unable to contain his grief any longer. The keening howl, the agony of it as it rose up through his throat was more painful than anything he had ever experienced in his life. It burst out of him, bringing forth a torrent of not only deep sorrow and anguish, but a sheer loathing for the bastards that had helped to put an end to his father's life.

*

It turned out that the small, fine grey Arabian Gwen thought she recognised had belonged to Geoffrey. She eventually recalled seeing it on occasion when he and his hunting parties had dropped in for refreshment. With this piece of information, Sir Hugh concluded that Geoffrey's and Sir Robert's killers were one of the same.

That night Angus had limped home wet-through and exhausted. Alisoun and Matthew had found him whimpering at the undercroft door. They had fed him, not that he ate much, and made him comfortable in front of the fire. He now lay at Old Matt's feet, his head resting on his outstretched paws, looking very forlorn. The humans did not fare any better. Young Tom lay curled up on his grandfather's lap staring into the flames, his thumb-sucking habit having returned. Matthew, Alisoun, Lucie, Heloise and Jake, who had decided his departure could wait, sat around the central table, and what meagre conversation they had was spoken in sombre, hushed tones.

They had just missed the raiders. Matthew explained how he had tried to fend them off, but single-handedly that had been impossible. After receiving the blow to the head, he had retreated back to the undercroft to protect his family. There they had tried to restrain Angus, but he had been so frantic to get at the intruders, he had broken free to pursue them. It could only have been a matter of minutes between the raiders riding off with Angus hot on their heels that Guy had arrived on the scene, and it had not been long after Guy had discovered his father's body that Ewen had appeared, out of breath, to warn them there were horsemen at large. Well, he was devastated to learn he had been too late and to hear of Sir Robert's tragic demise. It was a very sad, heavy-hearted Ewen who trudged slowly back up the hill.

In the deepest, darkest hours of the night, Angus crept upstairs in search of his master. He found Guy slumped in his chair before the dying embers of the fire. Through his misery and despair he had finally fallen into a restless, troubled sleep, in which his limbs twitched and jerked in sudden spasmodic contractions as if he were fighting off the intruders in his dream.

He had paced the solar all evening. Backwards and forwards, backwards and forwards. He had wept, he had raged. He was racked with grief and guilt, distraught that he had not been there to protect his father. Anger simmered within him at the thought of strangers daring to enter his home to plunder and wreak havoc, unknown lowlifes who would be miles away by now, reaping the boon of their spoils. But, by God, they would pay for it!

Angus, seeking affection, thrust his moist nose into Guy's hand, which hung over the chair arm. It woke Guy from his fragile sleep with a jolt. Feeling the familiar bulk, he let his hand rest where it was to savour the touch of warm, rough fur as Angus slowly passed under it to come round and lay at his feet. He rested his chin against Guy's leg and the dark, doleful eyes looked up into his. Guy leaned forward to caress his head. In return Angus gave a slow, half-hearted wag of his tail and emitted a long, mournful whimper. Guy reclined with a sigh but continued to stroke his companion's soft brow. He had always been indebted to the unconditional love and devotion Angus had faithfully awarded him, and at this particular time, he found it a great comfort.

'What would I do without you, Angus?'

*

Only Alisoun had seen Guy last evening. She had taken up food and refreshment and left it on the solar dining table. This morning she ventured up to find the solar empty and the food untouched. She guessed him to be still in vigil at his father's bedside so decided to leave him be for a while.

None of them had slept well last night. The women and Tom had shared the sleeping platform space whilst the men folk made themselves as comfortable as they could elsewhere. Jake had plumped for the stable where he bedded down with Scallywag. This morning they moved around the undercroft as quietly as was possible and talked in whispers. Matthew had asked Jake if he would afford him the favour of riding down to Tonbridge to fetch back the coroner and the sheriff. He readily agreed. His master would be mightily disappointed with him if he had not helped and supported his only nephew at this most tragic time. When he returned to Old Soar, he guessed it would be his duty to inform Sir Thomas of his brother-in-law's death. For him, what had at first started out as an adventure to bring about a happy reunion had turned into a mission with a very tragic ending.

With the departure of Jake, the household settled into a period of waiting.

Lucie had started to feel uncomfortable at being there, an intrusion, but Alisoun and Matthew persuaded her otherwise and that Guy would in no way want her and Heloise to leave. She was so very sad for Guy and she herself felt desolate. She had admired and respected Sir Robert very much. He had been such a fine, kind man. She blinked back tears.

When would Guy appear? Should she be presumptuous and go to him? Her dilemma was answered when she heard his heavy footfall descending the stairs. He looked dreadful. His eyes were puffy and red-rimmed with fatigue, and the stubble on his jowls and chin seemed more prominent on his pale, washed-out face.

Perusing the familiar faces assembled round the table, Guy's only thought was to thank God they were all safe and, he vowed, he would make sure they would always remain so.

*

'My deepest condolences on your loss, Guy. It is, of course, our loss too. Your father's passing is a dire shock to us all and his steadfast, generous and compassionate character will be greatly missed indeed.'

Percy had sent his commiserations via the sheriff. He was off following a sighting of the Turner brothers, who had been spotted lurking around the horse gate entrance to the town. Sir Hugh knew they now had bigger fish to catch, but the brothers were still suspects for Geoffrey's murder and they may well have valuable information about, or even be part of this gang that were currently operating in the area.

Guy had heard of Ewen and Gwen's misfortune, obviously carried out by the same gang who must have ridden straight down the hill to Starvecrow. Sir Hugh guessed that due to the bad weather and the time of year, they were preparing to go to ground, and these raids were to stock up on supplies and whatever else they could lay their hands on to help see them through the oncoming winter.

'No doubt there will be more,' he warned.

He was pleased to see Lucie and Heloise safe and verified the fact that nothing had been seen nor heard of Lady Eleanor. He also told of their success on Castle Hill and, as that had occurred the day before yesterday, it confirmed Guy's suspicions that there was more than one group at large.

'Baldwin was an outlaw from Tenterden way who had slipped back into circulation bringing others with him. He had bribed one of the foresters to kill the warden and manipulate our operations. They had also had the corroboration of the Fuller brothers, who helped spirit the horses away, the scoundrels!'

Sir Hugh left with the promise that Sir Robert's death would not go unpunished, and he would keep Guy informed of any developments.

*

Riding out in the early morning, Giles, Whitelawne's reeve, jogged along the ridge looking down on the mill-stream and sluice below. It was another foul day, but there were tasks to carry out that would not wait for better weather. Today he needed to check the sluice to make sure nothing had been carried down the swollen and fast-flowing stream to lodge in its gates. Running at an angle from the middle of the sluice to the riverbank was a palisade of stakes, a fish trap, and with any luck there might be a pike or a bream or two caught within it for the master's dinner table today. He dismounted and taking a net, a gaff and a cudgel from his saddlebag, walked over to the stream's edge. As he approached, he noticed a dark piece of cloth caught on one of the wooden stakes. Most of whatever it was, a piece of sacking maybe, was submerged in the pool. He knelt down on both knees and reached over carefully with the intention of unhooking the entangled cloth and removing it, but he had underestimated how far he would have to stretch. Not wanting to get any wetter than he already was, he decided to use the gaff. As he pushed himself back from his precarious position, his head automatically went down and what he saw under the surface of the water made him cry out in alarm. Sitting back on his haunches, he took a few seconds to recover himself. He must have been mistaken. Steeling himself for another look, he leaned forward again to peer over the bank's edge. No, he had not been mistaken. There it was, still staring wide-eyed up at him through the murky depths, a face so grossly bloated and distorted that it was impossible to identify whether it was male or female. The facial flesh had been nibbled to the bone in some places, making it apparent it had been there for some time. On closer inspection, he could see a rope had been tied around the neck, and because the body had stayed submerged, Giles guessed it had been weighed down with a heavy object, possibly a large stone. Using his gaff he hooked onto the rope as far down as he could see it, and having to muster all his strength, pulled up the anchor, which was indeed a very large weather-worn stone. On recovering the weight, the body ceased to stay submerged, and as it rose up and broke the surface, he half expected to hear it gasp and gulp for air. That was ridiculous, of course, but what could be heard was the gurgling and bubbling of trapped air as it escaped from the cadaver and the clothes it wore, erupting and blistering on the pool's surface. He turned the body and tentatively grabbed hold of its shoulders to manoeuvre it nearer to the bank. When it was in position, he dug in his heels, took the strain, and pulled out the saturated deadweight. He wrinkled his nose in disgust at the odious, putrid smell that was discharged with its recovery. Once the body was on the bank, he walked some distance away and vomited into a bush. He wiped his mouth on his sleeve and after inhaling copious amounts of fresh air, he returned to the body. By its attire, and the fact that strands of long dark hair had worked themselves free of its confines, made it obvious to Giles that it was female. Getting as near as he felt able, his features drawn in a scowl of concentration, he examined the face more closely. Water welled in the open mouth and dribbled from its corners. Due to the intake of water, and the fact that the pallid face and lips were tinged blue, he deduced drowning had been the actual cause of death and she had not perished beforehand. His suspicions as to the identity of the body were also proved correct. It was Lady Eleanor.

'By Christ,' he said to himself under his breath, 'more bad news for the master of Whitelawne.'

What had been a golden autumn had shifted into days and nights of gusty winds, rain and drizzle. The roads were all but impassable, and only a fool would undertake a long journey while the violent storms raged.

The braziers in the chambers were kept alight from early morning until people retired. It was the start of a season when folk stayed by their hearths, the men mending implements, the women with their needlework, and Starvecrow was no exception. The crows had gradually returned to their untidy twig nests in the trees, and after the burial of Sir Robert in the tiny Shipbourne churchyard, Starvecrow slowly settled into some semblance of normality.

The lower pastures had flooded, making in necessary for their beasts to be brought closer to home and for the sparse autumn grass to be supplemented with the stores of meadow hay that had been reaped in the summer months. The pigs were penned inside the warm and dry stable.

Many trees had been felled by the atrocious weather, keeping Guy, Grainger and the tenants busy until there was insufficient light to carry on with the clear up. Guy was happy to be kept actively occupied; it helped him to maintain a level of stability and sanity without which, he felt, he would drown in a bottomless pit. Every conceivable emotion – outrage, anger and frustration, desolation and despair – were all down there waiting to swallow him up if he dare to fall in.

The household had become somewhat extended, for which he was thankful. There had been no summons from Whitelawne for Lucie and Heloise to return so they remained at Starvecrow, both making themselves useful. Heloise, who excelled in stitch-craft, helped Alisoun repair old and stitch new garments made from homespun yarn, while Lucie helped with the everyday chores. Heloise also kept Tom occupied while the weather kept him indoors, and when he was asked to milk Daisy she would gladly accompany him to be shown how to milk and churn, tasks both of which she found very rewarding. Consequently everyone was relieved to see her gradually emerging from her languid mood. On a recent visit from Ben to see his sister, Guy had insisted that when Sister Hilda deemed Roger fit enough to travel, he fetch him back to Starvecrow to convalesce from his injuries. He did not want him to return to Whitelawne either; he still considered it not the best place to be at this present time, not only because of their double bereavement but he also understood the stand-off between Lord Charles and his tenants was still ongoing. If it was not for the flour, oats, beans and apples Starvecrow continued to donate to the Whitelawne tenants, the situation for them would be very dire indeed. Unfortunately some had resorted to poaching, only to be caught and prosecuted. Others had already left the estate, moving into towns, some travelling as far as London in the hope of finding a decent living for themselves and their families. Lord Charles was adamant William and Jack Turner were responsible for his eldest son's death, and possibly Eleanor's too, and was not willing to engage in any negotiations until the tenants, who he believed to be harbouring the pair, handed them over. He was vigorous in his belief that they were still in the area. They had been spotted by a reliable source whose name he was unwilling to impart fearing reprisals for the individual.

'Since when 'ad 'e been bothered 'bout anyone else?' Percy was heard to comment.

Today was the day Sister Hilda was begrudgingly allowing Roger to leave the abbey and her care. Starvecrow had received a message via a passing lay brother to expect him and Ben around mid-morning. Hopefully the rain would desist, if not for the day, for the journey at least. A two-wheeled cart with detachable sides was made available for transporting the invalid. Roger lay on a pallet, well wrapped up from the cold damp air under a patchwork leather canopy tied crudely to its wattle sides. Although being quite a short distance down to Starvecrow, Ben was aware how uncomfortable the cart would be for his passenger. The floor boarding was directly above the axles of the wheels so every stone, rut and hole in the road would be felt by its occupant. Sister Hilda, also knowing this fact, had administered a very strong pain-killing draught to Roger prior to the journey, giving it time enough to take effect. Sandals and cassock were out of the question for travelling in today. Ben was attired like any other in a plain brown serge tunic that reached to his knees, thick woollen hose, boots and a three-quarter length cloak with hood. Unfortunately as they commenced their journey a steady rain started to fall once more. Ben guided the abbey's only ancient brown cob slowly along the ridge and down the hill. A narrow stream of sludgy water ran down its centre, adding to the mire of churned-up mud and debris, which had been blown from the trees. They made slow progress as Ben tried to avoid as many obstacles as was possible. Roger lay semi-conscious in his sanctum under the canopy, knowing he was on the move but thankfully not feeling the consequences too much. The rain had not abated and started to trickle off the top of Ben's hood and drip off the end of his nose. His face tingled with cold and his exposed, wet hands turned to shades of blue and purple.

On entering Starvecrow's yard, Guy and Matthew appeared from the undercroft to untie the canopy and lift Roger into the house. Old Matt helped Ben to unhitch the cob and led it to the stable. Before he ventured inside, Ben scraped his boots on an iron boot scraper to remove as much of the caked mud as he could. Unfortunately there was not much he could do about his wet and mud-spattered clothes, other than take them off, he supposed, so he stood on the undercroft threshold full of apologies for the state he was in. Alisoun bustled over to him.

'No, no, don't be. Come in and let me take your cloak. Go and warm yourself by the fire.'

Ben was relieved of his wet, heavy cloak and was grateful of a chair offered to him by the fireside. Angus moved over to make room for him. Roger had been placed not too close to the hearth, where Lucie had made him comfortable and was in the process of fetching him a drink.

As Ben warmed his hands, he glanced around the room. The day might be cold, grey and miserable outside, but inside was warm and cosy, the glow from the fire and the lighted sconces adding to a homely atmosphere. It was nearly time for dinner, the midday meal and the main meal of the day. This usually took place between the tenth and eleventh hour in the morning depending on the season, and supper, a more modest affair, in the late afternoon between the fourth and fifth hour. People did not normally have breakfast. A householder might take some bread and cheese or whatever else was available upon rising, especially if he was planning to ride a long distance or be very active, but on the whole most did not eat until dinner time. Ben sniffed the delicious aroma of freshly-baked bread that flavoured the air and the pork and onions that bubbled away in the black cooking pot over the fire. Meat! What an absolute treat, he thought. Meals at the abbey consisted mainly of pottage, a vegetable broth, and although it was usually robust in its content – they grew all the vegetables they needed themselves – mealtimes could become monotonous and unexciting. Generally though, how much meat people ate depended on the day, the time of year, its availability and how well off they were. The church forbade the consumption of animals on Wednesdays, Fridays and Saturdays, and throughout Lent and Advent. Meat was more plentiful in the autumn. Feeding animals through the winter months would mean using vegetables, oats and corn, all the commodities much needed for human consumption, so many were slaughtered on or after Martinmas, the eleventh day of November. Some were roasted and eaten straight away, others were salted for preserving. Luckily for Ben it was a Thursday and obviously a pig had not long been slaughtered. He rubbed his hands together vigorously, more in anticipation of a hearty meal than in the need to get the blood flowing into the tips of his numb fingers.

The household was fully engrossed in their preparations. Alisoun stood slicing the large loaf while Heloise and Tom made ready the table. Old Matt removed the bung on a cask of cider standing in the corner, and filled a large earthenware jug with the golden liquid to place on the table. Both Matthew and Guy returned from the shed outside with armfuls of wood, enough to see them through until the following morning. Lucie knelt by Roger, gently lifting his head to enable him to take a drink comfortably. Roger's face, although still bruised, had started to lose the distended and inflamed puffiness it had first shown. The purplish-red discolouration had now turned a motley green and black, a sign of regenerative healing of the skin, and both his eyes were open and unobscured, enabling him to see about his surroundings, albeit a little vague and hazy in his drug-induced state. Sister Hilda had informed Ben that Roger's injuries were healing satisfactorily, though the break in his leg had rendered the limb twisted and forever damaged. A small price to pay, Roger had reflected later on in life, considering he could easily have ended up dead like all the others in the escort that day. It would take a few months yet of exercise and muscle building before he would even begin to regain anything like his former abilities, and there was a concern he may even fall short of reaching anywhere near them at all.

He lay back after he had quenched his thirst and relaxed in the knowledge that he was in a good place and with people who would take care of him.

Ben was not disappointed; the food was delicious and that, added to the hospitality shown him, made for a very pleasant sojourn indeed. Guy was a little subdued, he thought, not his usual self but that was understandable in the circumstances. His father had not long been taken from him, and he guessed it would be some time yet before he recovered fully from his shock and loss. He and Lucie had lost both their father and mother in quick succession some five years since, and he still missed them dreadfully. The death of a beloved parent left a hole that could never really be filled. But then he thought how lucky Guy was to have all these people rallying around who so evidently cared for him and his well-being. They were a companionable bunch, and when the time came he was sorry to leave.

He hugged his sister on departure and whispered in her ear how much happier he was to leave her there rather than at Whitelawne.

The King is dead.

King Henry III died on the sixteenth day of November in the year 1272. He had reigned for fifty-six years.

On his journey home from crusade, Edward heard that, on the death of his father, he had become King of England. At thirty-three years of age, he was the eldest son of Henry and Eleanor of Provence. He was in no hurry to get home and it was nearly another two years before he arrived at Westminster Abbey to be crowned King on the nineteenth day of August in the year 1274.

Edward was called 'Longshanks'. At six foot tall, he stood head and shoulders above his fellow Englishmen. He had black hair, which in later life turned pure white and was regarded as very handsome despite a drooping left eyelid, which he had inherited from his father. He could be a bully and was ruthlessly cruel with a violent temper. He once cuffed a page so hard around the ear that he agreed to pay damages, but all said and done, his reputation for chivalry and fearlessness remained unscathed throughout his reign. He was a brave fighter and, unlike his father, a very able administrator.

*

It was a cold and damp afternoon and the sky was overcast, suggesting more rain was on its way. The wind whistled and whined around the stable roof rafters.

The steady, regular motion of grooming Felix's soft, white hide and his warm, luscious smell was comforting for Guy. Since his father's death he had kept himself busy. If not, his thoughts were prone to deviate into the darker, more sinister recesses of his mind where there lurked sights and sounds he would much prefer to keep buried but were creeping imperiously close to the surface, the image of his father's death-stricken face being the most prominent. He pushed himself to exhaustion most days so that he could sleep deeply at night and not wake until morning. Each day dragged into the next and his mind only functioned on a pragmatic and indifferent level. He would become restless and irritable but knew that if he dwelled too long and hard he would not be able to function at all, and that would just not do. He was now master of Starvecrow Manor and duty was an obligation expected of him. It was a commitment to be undertaken wholeheartedly. He had long been a fighting man and for better or worse had always carried out his orders, conducting them with dedication, honour and dignity. He had seen many dead and had himself slain countless men. Of course he was not proud of that fact, but it had been a necessity in battle for his King and country, and in self-defence. He had never robbed anyone, even though looting in war was considered legitimate, and he certainly had never raped a woman. Luckily for him, willing ones had always been plentiful. But who were these unknown, faceless cowards roving the countryside, pillaging, killing, and raping defenceless women? Eleanor, he learned, had been raped before she was drowned, poor creature. What harm did she ever really do to anyone? Yes, she had on some occasions been bad tempered and rude, like some highborn women were, but why kill her? These men were devoid of any decency or honour, and the wanton nature of the crime had shaken him to the core.

He fondled the velvety soft muzzle and Felix whickered and nudged him back in return. He stooped down and started to groom the large furry-fringed hooves but was disturbed in his task by the jingle and clatter of horsemen approaching at speed up the lane outside. Angus, who had barely left Guy's side since the raid, leapt up and lunged through the stable door. In that same split second, Guy dropped the grooming brush and snatched up his sword, which he had kept close to hand and rapidly followed, his heart thumping in his chest. Four horsemen, their heads covered by their cloaks and their shoulders hunched against the cold, swept into the yard. Confronted with a bristling, snarling beast, followed by a maniac brandishing a broadsword above his head made both the horsemen and their mounts recoil in horror. One rider completely lost his balance and landed flat on his back in a pile of soggy straw that had been thrown down in an attempt to soak up the last torrential downpour. The fore rider ripped off his hood to reveal himself.

'Good God, man, what do you think you are doing!' yelled Sir Hugh, trying desperately to control his rearing horse.

Recognition registered, and Guy stopped dead in his tracks. Angus had also very quickly realised that this was not an invading force and refrained from his protective stance. Contrite, he lowered his head and ears and with his tail wagging tamely between his legs, started to gambol around the sheriff's now compliant horse. Guy lowered his sword but did not apologise, for although what might have seemed to the sheriff and his henchmen an overreaction, he on the contrary felt quite justified in his response. He swept his sword across the yard to indicate the figures standing primed at the undercroft door. Matthew and his ageing father had also rushed to the defensive, Matthew wielding an ancient battered sword, Old Matt holding aloft a pitchfork. Even the women had joined them, armed with hoe, broom and distaff. Their weaponry was scarcely impressive, but their intentions were brave. They were not about to be taken off guard again.

Guy fixed the sheriff with a cold, stony stare.

'I may well ask the same question of you; careering onto my property in such a manner and alarming my household!'

Sir Hugh was taken aback by Guy's hostility and took umbrage at his accusation.

'"Careering" was certainly not my intention as neither was "alarming" the household another!' he cried indignantly.

'I am sorry if we have caused any distress to you all,' he called over to the gathering at the undercroft door.

Once they had recognised and acknowledged the sheriff and his constables, they retreated back inside. Sir Hugh turned back to Guy and the two men regarded each other. The wind, which had now brought with it the rain, gusted around the yard snapping at their cloaks and hair.

'You had better come in then, all of you, get out of this infernal weather,' conceded Guy churlishly, lowering his sword.

Standoff over, he strode towards the house, leaving Sir Hugh and his constables to stable their own mounts. Once inside the undercroft, with its shutters closed against the inclement afternoon, the constables were given mulled ale to drink while Sir Hugh followed Guy's broad, silent and frosty back up the oak wood stairs to the solar, where at least a welcome blazed from the hearth, he thought wryly.

He took off his gloves and his damp cloak, which he hung on a hook on the wall behind a tapestry screen. Guy sat down and offered the seat opposite him at the fireside. Once seated, Sir Hugh scrutinised Guy's face. He observed the dark smudges under his eyes and the unshaven stubble covering his pallid cheeks.

'How are you?' he enquired.

Guy was frowning into the fire but managed a wry smile and a shrug. 'I do all right,' he muttered, immediately deserting the smile and continuing to stare into the flames.

Sir Hugh had always found Guy accessible and uncomplicated, quick to reassure and encourage, but these qualities seemed to have abandoned him. He perceived a reticence, a tension emanating from him. Sir Hugh sat forward in his chair and tried to make eye contact but Guy was to have none of it. Likening him to a sullen, petulant child, Sir Hugh gave up and reclined back in his chair, releasing a long, heavy sigh.

'Guy, you are probably the most good-natured person I have ever known. Please do not let what has happened sour your temperament.'

'Well, that greatly depends on what the morrow holds, does it not?'

He stood abruptly from his chair. 'I presume by your lack of any forthcoming disclosure you have not yet apprehended anyone?' Before Sir Hugh could reply, he continued. 'You must not forget that not only did those low-life's sack my home, terrorise its occupants and help themselves to all surviving links with my family – my mother's rings, my father's ancestral brooch – but worst of all, they took my father's life. They denied my father and I the opportunity to spend what little time we had left together. He died alone, frightened, choking on his own life's blood and what was left of his lungs, upstairs with nobody to hold his hand or comfort him in his last moments on this earth!'

His voice had become stronger and more agitated as emotion seized him. He raked at his hair while pacing back and forth across the solar.

'Of course I shall not forget that, Guy. I am as sickened and outraged as you are!' declared a somewhat affronted Sir Hugh. 'Please, Guy, sit down. I am concerned for you,' he pleaded to little effect. With more force he repeated his request. 'Guy, sit down! You are much troubled and are only distressing yourself further by behaving in this manner!'

Guy stopped in his tracks. He looked suddenly vulnerable, like a lost little boy, and Sir Hugh stood and went to him. He laid a reassuring hand on his arm and the now motionless Guy, allowed himself to be steered back to the fireside.

'Sit and calm yourself.'

Guy quietly obeyed. His friend stood behind him for a while with both hands resting affectionately and protectively upon his shoulders. Once he was satisfied Guy was sufficiently composed, he went over to the sideboard and poured each of them a generous cupful of wine. He took a much-needed gulp from one before replenishing it and returning to offer Guy the other. They sat in silence, Guy staring into the fire once more, while Sir Hugh watched him. He took another sip of wine.

'Will you allow me to speak openly to you?'

'Go on,' said Guy flatly, still preoccupied.

'I think this has more to do with your own feelings of guilt, as it does your anger at the injustice of it all. Am I right?'

These words made Guy's throat tighten. It seemed Sir Hugh knew him better than he realised. At last he turned to meet his gaze.

'Aye, I suppose it does. I should never have left him, I should have been here,' he said huskily.

'But you were on an errand of mercy, were you not, and you did not leave your father alone, you left him in the capable hands of Matthew and Alisoun, something you had done many a time without consequence. It was unfortunate you were not here when it happened, but if you had been, would the outcome have been any different, for your father, I mean? Nobody could have guessed what was about to happen and there could have been any number of you here to protect him, but the fact is, Guy, he was gravely ill and he was dying. Yes, those bastards with their opportunistic raid probably did hasten his death, so blame them, not yourself, otherwise you will never gain any peace of mind.'

'I cannot bear it,' Guy whispered to himself as if he had not heard a word of what had just been said.

'You can and you will – for your own sake!' cried Sir Hugh. 'I know it is hard but you must let it go. Your father is now in God's keeping and you must think on him as you remember him, as a loving and generous father. A father who nurtured a fine son any man would be proud to call his own.'

He stood once again and went to place a comforting hand on Guy's shoulder.

'Come now…' he coaxed.

Just when he started to think he may have spoken out of turn, Guy physically drew himself up and announced, 'You are right Hugh, I should not be indulging my emotions and wallowing in self-pity. I have responsibilities, a manor to run and people to care for. People who rely on me. And you, you will see justice done, that I do not doubt.'

'That's my boy,' Sir Hugh answered, patting his shoulder.

A wave of relief flooded through him. Hopefully this had shifted Guy from his melancholia. From thereon, and to Sir Hugh's continued relief, conversation became a little less fraught and stilted, with Guy gradually returning to his usual affable self. Before he touched on the other reason for his visit, the first of course being to enquire after Guy's welfare, he asked how the household was coping, especially with the extra numbers. Space was quite limited, admitted Guy, more so during the day as most of them tended to gather and eat together in the undercroft, though at night the only addition downstairs was Roger, as Lucie and Heloise shared his bedchamber, while he had since moved into his fathers.

'Yes, we are coping fine, I think. Nobody seems to get under anyone else's feet and to be honest I find it a consolation to have these people around me.'

'That is good then,' answered Sir Hugh.

'Mind you, I do not think I have been very good company of late. They have all been very tolerant and forgiving,' said a penitent Guy. Looking a little discomforted he continued, 'And I must apologise for my behaviour earlier.'

'Guy, please, there is no need to apologise. I, as well as your companions downstairs understand your grief. We all care and are anxious for you. You can rant and curse and be as ill-humoured as you wish, but just promise me you will keep that head of yours above water, will you?'

'Yes, I will.'

Guy was touched by Sir Hugh's concern and realised how blessed he was to have such a kind and dependable friend around who cared for his welfare and he conveyed as much.

'It is only what you deserve, Guy. Remember what your father always used to say – "you reap what you sow".'

Guy smiled to himself and nodded. Yes, he did remember.

They sat in mutual silence for a while, sipping their wine and listening to the rain peppering against the wooden shutters.

Sir Hugh decided it was time to disclose the other reason for his visit, but first he needed another drink.

'May I?' he asked, indicating his empty cup with a wish to refill it.

'Yes, of course. Help yourself.'

Collecting the flagon of wine from the sideboard, Sir Hugh brought it back over to replenish Guy's cup as well as his own. Placing it on a small three-legged table to one side of his chair, he sat down again and made himself comfortable. He cleared his throat.

'Guy, you were right, unfortunately. I have no new information to impart except there have been reports that the outlaws are getting increasingly bolder. They are often seen on the roads and lurking in woods, seemingly with no concern of being apprehended.'

'Have any been identified?'

'No. They always take a care to cover their faces.'

'Has Percy had any luck pinning down the Turners?'

'Ah, well, that is another matter I must talk to you about…' Sir Hugh fidgeted in his seat.

'I know you will admonish me for not informing you sooner…'

Guy was immediately attentive.

'What is it, Hugh?'

The sheriff took a deep breath before imparting the news.

'We have not seen Percy since the day he went in search of the brothers.'

'But that must have been, what, over a sennight ago!' exclaimed Guy. 'Why have you waited so long to tell me?'

Sir Hugh looked discomforted.

'Due to your circumstances I did not want to worry or trouble you, and Percy has always been capable of looking after himself and I felt sure that each day since, he would turn up. But it has been a long time now and he would have been in touch if he were able.'

'Have you searched for him?'

'We have made enquires, of course, but to no avail, and to be honest we have not a clue where to start.'

'Surely he did not undertake the venture alone?'

'No, he did not. He set off with the three constables that have accompanied me here today. Two he sent off to scout around the town's outer perimeter wall…'

There were many natural shelters and makeshift camps scattered around the town wall. These were used by the travellers who arrived after curfew, too late to enter the town and having neither the money, nor the inclination, to stay at the one and only ramshackle inn in the locality with its unsavoury clientele.

'…While him and Skinner went into town. Skinner thought it a futile exercise. As he pointed out, why would the brothers risk their necks venturing into town, knowing they were wanted men? But you know Percy, never one to miss an opportunity, he insisted they at least scour the alehouses and make some enquiries. Skinner explained they were making their way from The Bear and Ragged Staff when a young ragamuffin approached Percy and said something inaudible to him. Percy proceeded to follow him and

Skinner tried to keep up, but lost them in the usual market day crowds.'

'What do you know about this boy? Do you know who he is?'

'No, but he had very distinctive white-blond hair, not easy to miss. Our only saving grace is that the boy didn't know Skinner had observed the encounter. We have searched for the boy without success but we need to wheedle him out because until we find him, we are undeniably flummoxed as to Percy's whereabouts.'

They looked at each other sombrely, both realising the gravity of the situation. Not only were outlaws running amok and thumbing their noses at them, the Turners still needed to be apprehended, and finally, Percy had disappeared off the face of the earth! But, they both agreed, there was no question about it, finding Percy was now their main priority.

There was not much they could do today. The weather outside showed no sign of abating and it would not be long before the gloomy daylight began to fade. Eager to help and, if the truth were known, for adventure, Guy decided he would travel back to Tonbridge with the sheriff so he would be in situ for an early morning start on the morrow. In the meantime, after a much-needed shave, a quick light meal was eaten before they made ready for departure. Sir Hugh insisted that one of his constables stay behind at the manor whilst Guy was absent in the event of any unwanted guests, although he did emphasise that 'lightning never strikes in the same place twice.'

'Well, let us hope you are right,' was the sober reply.

The outer bailey was a swamp of puddles, mud and rubbish trodden in by the few chickens, pigs and goats that wandered freely, and the countless feet of the castle's occupants who endlessly crisscrossed it.

The solitary sentry, wearing a thick leather jerkin and a round helmet with nose guard, stiffened to attention as they approached the gatehouse. The sheriff shouted and beckoned over a valet to take their mounts for stabling.

They entered the guardroom to a buzz of conversation from a group of soldiers lounging at a trestle table with jars of ale and cider. They were using the guardroom for their off-duty recreation, which was preferable to the large dark and cold hall. With the majority of the castle absent, there was no need for the fire in the hall to be lit, and the use of candles and torches would be considered wasteful. The only time they would venture there was to eat and sleep.

Two guards, supposedly on duty, had obviously failed to hear the sheriff arrive. This was evident by the sight of one who, balancing on the back legs of his chair with his feet up on a table, was talking avidly to a woman standing in very close proximity to him. The other was being devoured by a serving wench sitting astride his lap. Seeing the sheriff suddenly standing there before him made the first whip his feet from the table, sending his chair toppling backwards. The jar of ale he had been holding was sent skyward as he flailed his arms about, windmilling frantically to try and right himself. The other was brought back from the abyss by a shower of the propelled ale, and a quick elbow in the ribs from his comrade. He stood abruptly, dropping the wench like he would a scalding lump of charcoal. He was mortified to be caught in such flagrant circumstances and by the sheriff no less, and swore under his breath. Both soldiers stood rigid and red-faced, ill at ease in front of the sheriff and his companion. Forgotten, the wenches quietly scuttled away back to the cold kitchens.

The sheriff's disapproval was apparent at having to witness such brazen behaviour. He loudly cleared his throat. The entire room fell totally silent and all eyes and ears fell upon him.

'Ahem… Soldiers. I shall be reporting this disgraceful incident to your commanding officer when I next see him… ahem… in the meantime carry on… with your duties I mean,' he blustered.

Titters of amusement at the sheriff's embarrassment could be heard. He knew he was mocked for his prudish morals and was visibly discomfited. Guy followed him across the room through a barrage of coarse laughter and crude comments, all of which he quickly silenced by sweeping the offenders with a ferocious scowl.

'You can deduce De Clare is still abroad,' said Sir Hugh scornfully over his shoulder. 'There is a lack of discipline and order about the place that he certainly would not tolerate if he were here. Corbiere ought to get a grip before his return or there will be hell to pay.'

A torch lit their way up the steep spiral stone staircase to the west chamber. At the top a thick curtain hung over the low doorway leading to Sir Hugh's office. Passing through this, he pulled aside another curtain at the far end to enter his living quarters. The room had neither tapestries nor hangings lining the rough stone walls, only the odd sconce here and there desperately trying to illuminate the dark interior. The two narrow unglazed windows were shuttered against the weather outside and a fire was lit in a small fireplace in the wall. Furniture consisted of a small table flanked by a couple of stools, a chest with basin and jug for ablutions, a bed with enclosing curtains, and a low truckle bed in the corner for Albert, Sir Hugh's steward. There was a rail attached to a bracket on the wall for Sir Hugh to hang his clothes and a small recess for a few possessions. To the left, a doorway led to the garderobe, which, after making his excuses, Guy made his way to. The boards of the latrine seat were covered with an ornately embroidered red and gold cloth, the opening plugged with a cushion of the same design and colours. This helped to prevent any odours or drafts rising up from the ditch and moat below. A neat pile of linen strips were provided for wiping one's derrière, and a bowl and a ewer of water was available for washing one's hands. Once Guy had relieved himself and washed his hands, he returned to the chamber where a flagon of red wine had been placed upon the table. Their journey from Starvecrow to Tonbridge had been a wet one and the late autumn chill had pervaded them to the bone, so the warmth of the small chamber, together with the wine, was very welcome indeed. Over a cold supper of bread and cheese, procured by Albert from the kitchens, Guy and Sir Hugh speculated on Percy's predicament and considered their strategy for the morrow. That night, Guy slept in Albert's bed while the disgruntled steward was relegated to the cold hall.

*

The day dawned chill, and a fine rain fell. The invisible roof of the castle sat wreathed in a silent, grey mist. The few people that were abroad had wrapped themselves in thick cloaks and hoods in an attempt to keep out the damp chill.

The search for the young lad started at the Horse Gate, and it was Sir Hugh and Skinner who first parted from the group to take the path[13] that ran behind the High Street and wound its way past the neat and cultivated back gardens of the two-storey dwellings that fronted it. These were the more attractive and prestigious houses of the town, situated on the cleanest part of the main street, leading from the principal gate into the centre of town. To the left of them an open expanse of common land stretched all the way to the wall and fosse, and from the pathway the town's small parish church of St Peter and St Paul could be seen. All was quiet; the only individual afoot was a servant discarding some vegetable matter onto a midden at the bottom of one of the gardens.

They made their way towards the church. Their intention was to explore Church Lane, then Swan Lane to eventually meet back at the market cross. Guy and Winter were to head for the Shambles, while Fellows and Wicks scoured the narrow streets and alleyways running off the High Street. Hopefully somewhere along the way their quarry would be apprehended.

'There are few people about as yet, but it will become busy enough when the working day gets started,' said Sir Hugh as they headed for Church House, a home for waifs and strays.

At the same time, Guy and Winter were entering the warren of lanes in the Shambles, by far the town's poorest and most densely populated area. It was a miserable, dreary landscape, made all the more gloomy by the weather. Some of the lanes were no more than

---

[13] Kinnings Row – running alongside the Ivy House.

seven or eight feet wide and the alleyways merely churned-up, muddy tracks. Water courses and shallow ditches that ran either side were little more than foetid open sewers to be urinated in and used as a dumping ground for any manner of human and household waste. Guy and Winter simultaneously lifted up their kerchiefs to cover their mouths and noses. Wattle fencing and crudely built stone walls, all of varying heights and conditions, separated the hotchpotch of small houses, rows of ramshackle wooden huts and semi-derelict shacks. Guy looked through the broken-down doorway of a single room dwelling. Even with his nose covered, his nostrils were invaded by the stench around it where the occupants came to urinate at night rather than venture any further to a midden or ditch. Through the gloom he could discern five small filthy faces, their hair tousled and matted with straw, staring wide-eyed and blinking at him over a wooden partition. Who was this stranger outside their door peering in at them? He raised a hand in greeting and then quickly in farewell when a gruff 'clear off!' was bawled from the dark interior. No white heads there, he determined. My, this was going to be a job and a half! There was no way they could effectively search every single dwelling, he realised. Not only were they too numerous, he also concluded that not all the occupants would appreciate their privacy being invaded, and that could lead to more aggravation than he cared to handle. He beckoned Winter over.

'I suggest we just comb the lanes and alleyways and then make our way to the market cross.'

Winter readily agreed. Many a time he and his colleagues had found themselves in a tight spot when the locals had accused them of 'snooping' around their neighbourhood.

The labyrinth of paths and alleyways were virtually deserted. The weather had kept many to their beds or huddled around a meagre fire. Only the ones fortunate enough to have any work, such as labouring on the wharf or in the tannery were astir, trudging their way through the grey-brown landscape, their pinched faces eyeing them up and down suspiciously. After a quick but thorough search, Guy and Winter made for the barbican and headed down the back lane to pass the parade of open-fronted stalls and workshops. The clang of hammer on anvil and the clunk of cleaver striking a chopping block indicated there were already tradesmen at work. A tawyer and his young apprentice, whose curly flaxen hair was covered with a tight fitting leather cap, were already diligent at their counter, softening pieces of leather by drawing them backwards and forwards over a blunt blade set in a block of wood. The air smelt of ripe raw meat as they passed a butchers shop. From the back yard a trail of blood trickled down to the central gutter. They kept their eyes to the ground as they dubiously picked their way through the discarded offal and bones that were strewn about. A mangy flea-ridden dog, having scavenged a pile of ox intestines, trailed them behind him as he skulked through a narrow gap between the shop fronts in search of a quiet spot where he could enjoy his spoils in peace. Two rats scurried from a doorway and ran down the lane, hugging the walls and chitchatting to each other as they went. Winter jumped back in alarm as the butcher's boy emptied a pitcher of blood in front of him, the splash narrowly missing his boots.

'Have a care!' he snapped at the lad, who hurriedly retraced his steps and called back after him, 'Sorry, mister constable!' in a high, pre-pubescent voice.

The jolly looking leather-aproned butcher lifted a large red, fat-fingered hand in greeting. He was laying out cuts of meat on his open counter. Joints and carcasses already adorned the façade, hung on iron hooks and displayed with great care in a bid to attract customers away from the competition, of which there was plenty. A gruff, bad tempered command sent a young boy scuttling from the smithy with a bucket nearly as big as himself to fetch water from the trough outside. With the doors wide open, several horses could be seen in the stalls patiently waiting to be re-shod. Beside them was the forge where the sweating blacksmith hammered horseshoes into shape at an anvil by a glowing furnace.

''Urry up with that water!' he yelled.

Once the leather bucket was full, the poor lad could just manage to lift it off the ground and spilt half its contents as he struggled back inside, leaving it to trickle and mingle with the blood in the gutter.

The others were already at the market cross. They looked a dispirited bunch standing hunched up against the drizzle, their search being as fruitless as their own. A dogged Sir Hugh endeavoured to rally his constables, telling them that by the end of the day they would have the boy.

'There are many hours yet until the day is done,' a dispirited Skinner muttered under his breath.

Sir Hugh heard the comment. Rattled, he suddenly turned on him.

'So, what do *you* propose we do, huh?' he demanded. He himself was frustrated by the lack of progress and did not appreciate Skinner's vapid attitude.

Skinner did not answer but deigned to look uncomfortable, staring down at and shuffling his feet. The sheriff continued.

'Should we forget about Percy then? Get out of this God awful weather, go back to the castle and sit by the fire? Is *that* what you want?' he asked, his eyebrows raised in query.

'No, of course not, sir,' mumbled the red-faced constable.

'Then keep your comments to yourself, you milksop!'

Feeling severely chastened, Skinner held his head in shame. He and the rest of the group were left in no doubt as to the extent of the sheriff's displeasure.

He addressed them all, looking from one to the other as he voiced his instructions.

'We will split into pairs again and find a discreet place to watch and wait. We will not go searching for him, he will make an appearance soon enough. We need to locate this lad and we will stay out here until we do. Is that understood?'

There were nods of agreement.

'Aye, sir, understood.'

'Good. The sentries on the wall and gates have all been instructed to keep an eye out too, so let's hope together we will get a result today.'

After pairing up again they set off in different directions. Guy and Winter headed for the wharf, pulling the hoods of their leather jerkins, which they wore under their cloaks, further down over their faces.

'Bloody accursed weather,' moaned Winter, shrugging and hunching his shoulders beneath his cloak.

'I 'ope we get the little bastard today.'

The weather had not lessened the river traffic and the unloading and loading of goods continued as usual. The pair settled themselves onto two empty casks in a corner next to the Watergate wall, below the bridge barbican. Looking up to the fighting platform above, Winter gave a whistle and a thumbs up to the man-at-arms stationed there to let him know of their presence. Large heaps of rope concealed them without obstructing their view of the wharf. It was a hive of activity, with merchants and sailors going about their business. Straw and sawdust used for packaging lay discarded, pulled from the many barrels and caskets by the merchants who wished to inspect their goods before taking possession of them. A column of labourers, each with a heavy sack upon his shoulders, jogged to and fro along two gangplanks appending a vessel to the quayside.

They sat bundled up against the weather, resigned to the fact that they could be there for some time. There was no telling where the lad might turn up, even if at all. One hour turned into two. Small talk between them had gradually dried up and keeping warm and alert became a priority. Every so often they would stand and jump up and down, or walk around their space, all the while keeping an eye amongst the busy throng. Just as Winter opened his mouth to bemoan that he was cold and hungry, a whistle sounded from above. The man-at-arms was looking down on them. He motioned and pointed behind the wall, on the river side. Immediately they jumped to their feet.

'What? The boy?' questioned Winter.

The man-at-arms nodded.

'What the devil is he doing over there?' he asked incredulously.

The man-at-arms shrugged his shoulders. Guy, too, was baffled. The lad had definitely not passed through from this side. If he had they would have spotted him.

'Maybe he came up the river?'

'Aye, maybe so,' answered Winter.

They made for the Watergate entrance. Winter reached to unsheathe his sword but Guy placed a restraining hand on his arm.

'No, I do not think that will be necessary. He is only a young boy.'

Winter gave him a cynical look, but removed his hand from the hilt.

'As you say, sir.'

They ventured through the open gates and stepped onto the wooden quay. Only the white head and shoulders of the boy were visible at the end of the platform as he hung by his elbows, struggling to scramble up from the path that ran along the riverbank and below the town wall.

He had managed to swing one leg up and was in the process of levering himself onto the quay when, much too soon, and much to Guy's chagrin, Winter shouted, 'Oi, we want a word with you!' and as Guy had expected, the boy looked up to immediately drop back down to the bank below and disappear from view.

Guy and Winter ran to the end of the quay and launched themselves from it. Guy landed safely on the path, which, although saturated with the recent deluge of rain, was still firm underfoot, but just out of reach of the lad, who twisted away from his grasp to continue his flight. Winter unfortunately had landed shin-deep in mud where a weak section of the bank had broken away to fall in the river.

'Argh, holy piles of shit!'

He stood there, stuck fast. Guy stopped and cursed, watching the receding back of the lad. He turned back in annoyance.

'Here,' he said impatiently.

Winter grabbed his offered hand. He slipped and slithered about haphazardly in the squelching mud until he was eventually recovered on the footpath.

The man-at-arms, who had been watching from his platform above, called down to them.

'He's almost at the bridge!'

They proceeded to jog along the footpath. The drizzle had since stopped but mist still hung like a curtain over the river. Through it, they could just make out the white-blond head dodging under the bridge's huge oak supports.

'Where is he going?' enquired Guy over his shoulder. Quite what the lad was going to do when he got to the bridge was a mystery as the riverbank ended there, with only the moat entrance and the river beyond it.

'Christ knows,' Winter replied between puffs.

He was not used to chasing anyone on foot, especially with what felt like half a ton of thick, sticky mud adhering to his boots, and was already worn out. They reached the bridge. The lad was nowhere to be seen. They stood perplexed, Winter puffing hard. They wondered whether he might have climbed up into the labyrinth of towering oak buttresses and was making his way along them to the other side of the river, but decided that would probably be impossible for a lad his size. They still checked out the possibility though, kneeling and crouching to look up and through, and seeing nothing.

'Well, I'll be…' said Winter, scratching his head.

All was still and quiet except for the slap of the brown muddy water as it softly beat the riverbank. The bank was much wider here, and a tangle of brambles and undergrowth grew against the town's sandstone wall. They both heard a noise from within. Winter placed a finger to his lips and stealthily made his way over.

'We know you're in there lad. Come out if you know what's good for ya,' he shouted brusquely.

The trapped boy didn't need telling twice. He stood up and, wincing in pain, tentatively tried to disentangle himself. In his haste to hide, he had carelessly dived into the thorny thicket, which had attached itself to his clothes and skin.

'Gotcha,' shouted Winter unnecessarily, grabbing hold of his dirty, ragged tunic and pulling him out into the open. The boy cried out as the last of the clasping thorns were torn from his skin. He made a sorry sight, standing there before them in his filthy, inadequate clothing. His feet were even filthier, bound into broken leather shoes, which had seen better days probably long before he was even born. Winter took no time in getting to the point.

'What do you know about the deputy sheriff's disappearance, eh?' he shouted gruffly, just inches from the boy's face.

The boy flinched but did not answer. He stood in sullen silence.

'Come on now. You were seen talking to him just before he went missing. You know where he is, don't ya?'

'I don't know nuffink!' exclaimed the boy in a burst of defiance.

'I'll give you nuthin, you little tyke!' Winter raised a back-hand to strike him.

The boy shrank away, but Guy had checked the expected blow.

'Go easy on him. Nothing will be gained by harshness here.'

'We'll see,' grunted Winter.

Just then Guy's eye was caught by something behind the bush and standing up against the wall. Striding over for a closer look, he found a paddle and a coracle hidden there.

'Well, seems he arrived in this and was about to make his escape in it,' he said, dragging it out.

He went back over to the boy, who returned a hostile stare. In a more kindly tone, Guy asked his name. The lad knew he was done for but supposed having this man as his interrogator was far preferable than the bullying constable.

'Robin,' was the surly reply.

'And where do you live?'

'Up the shallows.'

Guy raised his eyebrows at this. The area the boy spoke of was marshland, full of streams and bogs and not a suitable place to live at all.

'And who do you live with?'

'My father.'

'Just your father?'

The boy nodded, belligerently.

'Who cares who he blinkin' lives with!' shouted an exasperated Winter. 'Where's Ralston?'

Guy turned to face him.

'We first need to find out as much as we can from the boy.'

'Take 'im to the dungeons. He'll soon tell all when Striggar gets hold of 'im!'

On hearing the gaoler's name, the boy suddenly went pale and started to shake. Dismissing Guy's reproachful look and realising he'd found a weakness in the lad's tough exterior, Winter continued. He bent closer and gave a nasty smile, his thin lips parting over his yellow teeth.

'Do you know what 'e does to scrawny rag tags like you?' he whispered close to his ear.

The boy recoiled from the rancid breath, warm on his cheek.

'First, 'e 'angs 'em upside down by their ankles and flays the skin from their backs… then… he kindles a fire under 'em, banking and fanning the flames…'

Winter slowly and deliberately blew into the boy's face, making him grimace all the more and tightly close his eyes in terror. He stepped back but Winter grabbed the front of his tunic and pulled him close again.

'…Yer 'air'll catch first… then you'll start to cook… slowly… just like a pig on a spit, 'cept we kill pigs first, don't we. Yer skin'll melt off and drip…'

'That's enough!' shouted Guy, pushing Winter away from the boy.

The boy looked petrified. Letting out a howl, he dropped to his knees.

'Please don't send me to the dungeons!' he wailed.

'Start talking then!' snapped Winter.

The boy looked up at Guy. His ice-blue eyes brimmed and overflowed with tears and from his nose runnels of snot ran down his grubby face. Guy helped him to his feet.

'Come, now, tell us what you know and you will be spared that trial.'

Guy had some sympathy for the boy. In all probability he was an innocent party in all this and used merely as a means to lure Percy away. He untied his neckerchief and passed it to him.

'Here, wipe your face.'

The boy did so, but only managed to smear mucus and dirt further around it. He still stood there sobbing. Winter paced about, preparing himself for another onslaught if he did not spill the beans soon. The other gentleman looked on expectantly. It was time to tell all he knew.

His father had told him to tell the deputy, and only the deputy, mind, that the Turner brothers wanted to speak with him and that he could take him to them, alone, and he had done so in the coracle, back to where he and his father lived.

'Is he still there?' asked Guy.

'Yes.'

'Has he spoken with the brothers?'

'Dunno.'

'What do you mean, you dunno?' shouted an impatient Winter, striding over.

Guy placed himself between him and the cowering boy.

'I mean, I 'aven't seen 'em! They may 'ave come while I've been away, out getting food or somefin'.'

'Is he all right?' asked Guy.

The boy looked wary at that question and became uncommunicative again and stared down at the ground with an expression of mixed fear and defiance.

'Is he all right?' shouted Winter, poking him sharply in the ribs, making the boy jump and answer briskly, 'No! I don't think he is.'

'But he's alive?'

'Yes,' he replied in hardly a whisper.

The two men regarded each other, before Winter abruptly spun around and jabbed a stiff finger very close to the boy's startled face.

'You had better be telling the truth, boy,' he growled through gritted teeth, 'or there will be trouble such as you have never known.'

'I think we should forget about getting this lad to the sheriff first. We need to get to Percy fast, and I suggest we do just that. What do you say?'

'I agree, but all three of us won't fit in *that*,' said Winter, indicating the coracle.

'Well, you've got the authority… And the balls. Go and seize a boat from somewhere!'

The fine rain had stopped but mist still clung to the trees and rippled and swirled along the top of the town wall. Two men crouching behind a bush peered through a gap in its foliage to watch the guards on the wall walk. Tired of having to steal every morsel of food, sleeping in barns, ditches, and even resorting to pigsties on occasion, they had decided it was time to give themselves up. The atrocious weather of late, together with their inadequate clothing, had also been a deciding factor. But being innocent of any crime, they were not about to throw themselves at the mercy of the town guard to be subjected to the humiliation and the indignities a very public exhibition would bring. Their intention, if possible, was to surrender themselves straight into the hands of the sheriff, so avoiding the attentions of the guards and the gatehouse keeper was a priority.

A ripple of laughter drifted across no-man's land, a space of about forty paces between the bridge and the scrubland that hid them. All around the perimeter wall, an area of this width was harvested of any vegetation, keeping it open ground where nobody, especially an enemy, could hope to pass unseen. This, of course depended greatly on the vigilance of the guards. As they watched, the two men-at-arms turned their backs and disappeared into a small timber sentry box, which stood on the wide wall walk. The mist was on the move, making visibility changeable and, at that fortuitous moment, a wave billowed across in front of them, obscuring their view. William reckoned if he could not see them, then they would not be able to see him, and seized the moment.

'Quickly, Jack.'

Rapidly, and with a lightness of foot, they made their way across the open expanse of ground. William nervously glanced up at the wall still twenty paces away, and realised just how exposed they were. They reached the bridge that spanned the filthy waters but halfway across, they came to an abrupt halt. One of the guards had reappeared from the shelter. William laid a restraining hand on Jack's arm. Hearts in their mouths, they stood stock-still with their heads down, hardly daring to breathe. They were sure the guard above would spot them, but he was deeply engrossed in conversation and noisily enjoying the last mouthful of an apple. He discarded the core over the wall to land with a plop in the water. He then turned his back on them and, continuing his converse, disappeared from view. The brothers both breathed a sigh of relief and continued their silent dash over the bridge.

Now for the gatekeeper. Being the canny old soul that he was, he might prove more difficult to evade. Not many, if any at all, got past him. But luck was on their side today, for as they skulked past the huge open iron-studded doors, they spied the old man's back disappearing into his house.

They had made it inside the town unseen. Now to find the sheriff.

*

Sir Hugh, oblivious to what was happening on the riverbank or at the Horse Gate, drew his cloak closer about his body. The fine rain had stopped but a mist still hung over the town. Judging by the height of the watery sun, he guessed it was mid-morning. His knees were stiff from sitting too long on the stone steps of the market cross, but his discomfort eased when he stood up and walked slowly around it. Skinner stood some distance away. He was in a sullen mood, still smarting from the tongue-lashing he had received earlier. He stood idly, his scowl sweeping the High Street. He watched the few people abroad going about their business. A young packman, leading a pony laden down with panniers full to bursting with hanks of distaff-spun yarn, headed up Swan Lane to the weavers' cottages where it would be woven into cloth on the looms. A teamster and his draught horses lumbered past, the wagons axles creaking under the weight of its heavy load of oak timber. His eye was caught by a young woman who appeared in the doorway of the apothecary's shop opposite. Skinner recognised her as a maid from a local dignitary's household. She pulled up her hood and furtively looked left and right before scurrying from the doorway, clutching something to her breast under her cloak. Head down, she rapidly walked in the direction of the more presentable houses at the north end of town. Skinner speculated on her clandestine behaviour and cynically came to the conclusion she was probably with child and, it being the master's, needed to be rid of it. He tutted and shook his head. He glanced at the pillory that stood by the market cross and grimaced. He thought on last market day when a yeoman had been caught trying to sell rotten oats. Any trader found trying to deceive the unwary customer would expect to be punished here. Trade was regulated, and all guild merchants were well aware their position was open to challenge from other local traders and other town markets, so they were keen to protect the good name of their own. Likewise, Lord de Clare would be eager to ensure that nothing impaired the large income he accrued from the market day tolls. After grievances had been addressed in the courthouse, the man had been dragged unceremoniously through the streets to this place. Once his neck and wrists had been secured between its wooden boards, there had been no escaping his shame or the insults of the crowd, plus anything else they cared to throw at him. Skinner hawked and spat on the ground. That would make him think again before mixing rotten oats with good, he thought maliciously. His attention was drawn to the tavern. He watched as Mistress Ralf's voluptuous backside appeared wobbling from side to side as she swept the top step. As she moved down to the next one, her pendulous breasts made a welcome appearance. Feeling suddenly cheered, a salacious leer spread across his face. Mistress Ralf, feeling eyes upon her, stopped and looked about. Spying Skinner watching, she smiled and winked at him before shaking her besom over-vigorously and disappearing back inside. Distraction over, Skinner straightened up and with a determined effort tried to look attentive. Looking north he spotted four men-at-arms marching down the High Street towards them. They penned in two individuals, flanking them on all sides with their pikes.

'Sir!' he exclaimed and pointed in their direction.

Sir Hugh turned on his heel to receive the approaching company and scrutinise their captives. They were ragged and dishevelled, their dirty faces pinched and drawn with fatigue and hunger, but it did not take him long to recognise them as William and Jack Turner.

Unfortunately, the brother's attempt had been thwarted by the very same person they thought they had successfully eluded. The eagle-eyed gatehouse keeper, glimpsing movement over his shoulder, had alerted the guards.

There was no mistaking they were brothers although Jack, the younger, was more muscular bodied than his taller, longer limbed sibling and his hair mousey-brown and straight, whereas William's was a curly reddish-brown thatch. Both wore typically adolescent, straggly beards and their unkempt hair hung lank and dirty over their shoulders. Coming to a halt, the guards stood rigid to attention.

'Sir! The Turner brothers, caught entering the town,' one of them declared in a brisk, staccato fashion.

'Well, stone a crow…' Skinner exclaimed.

The sheriff, standing with clenched fists on his hips, frowned with displeasure, his grey-green eyes glittering under his bushy black eyebrows.

'Well, you two have led us a merry dance,' he huffed.

Two pairs of tawny-grey eyes stared levelly back at him.

'You know you are both wanted for murder and consorting with outlaws?'

If he expected to hear declarations of innocence or pleas for mercy he was greatly mistaken for the brothers continued to fix him with their steady gaze.

Sir Hugh looked from one to the other.

'Well? Do you have anything to say for yourselves?'

'We've killed no one,' William eventually replied coolly.

'Then there are coincidences that need some explanation,' retorted Sir Hugh impatiently.

'Take them to the castle,' he instructed with a dismissive gesture, and without any protest the brothers allowed themselves to be led away.

*

Once seated around the guardroom table, William endeavoured to convince Sir Hugh they had no involvement in Geoffrey's murder.

'Granted, when I lost my temper I could quite easily have thrust a knife into the bastard, I'll not deny that, but all I wanted was Joanne back. When I was thrown off Whitelawne I went to ground, later to be joined by Jack here. We had planned to rescue Joanne and go far away to start a new life, but we returned to learn that Sir Robert had already secured her release. That was when we heard we were wanted for Geoffrey's murder and had no alternative but to disappear again.'

'Why did you not take Joanne and go away as you had planned?' quizzed Sir Hugh.

'Because I did not want her to live a life where she would be forever looking over her shoulder and a future severed from her family.'

Sir Hugh could see his point.

'Please believe me when I say we were on our way to you. We are tired of sneaking around. We have also learnt that the master has informed the tenants of Whitelawne that if they were to hand us over to him, he will think again on his new proposals. He knows they are desperate and is using blackmail to contend for their loyalty. In their dire circumstances their memories might become a little hazy, so lest they forget he is a man who they should not invest their trust too heavily in, we decided to remove ourselves from any temptation they might be harbouring.'

He scratched at his beard.

'And not wanting them to suffer any more unnecessary hardship at our expense, we thought it best we come to you, hoping you will help us put an end to all the misunderstanding.'

Sir Hugh thought on this.

'And what about Lady Eleanor?'

William gave him a quizzical look. 'What about her?'

'Well, since Geoffrey, she too has been murdered...' he coughed. 'Raped and murdered actually,' he corrected.

He deduced from both William's and Jack's reaction that they genuinely had no knowledge of this. He continued, closely watching their faces.

'There is also the matter of the raids, one of which resulted in the death of Sir Robert...'

William baulked. 'What?'

The brothers looked at each other in disbelief. To reaffirm that he had heard correctly, William looked back at the sheriff. His grim expression confirmed he had. He paled with shock. Jack too was mightily upset.

'He was good to us... he...' His voice broke mid-sentence.

But once the initial shock had passed, it was replaced with outrage. William's control broke in an explosive oath.

'By, Christ! Was it not enough to be outlawed for a crime we did not commit? To know you thought us guilty of that and to now discover you thought us capable of more such savage deeds is insufferable!'

He stood up abruptly, making the chair clatter backwards to the floor. Sir Hugh sprang to his feet, his hand reaching for his sword hilt. The two guards stationed in the doorway leapt forward, their pikes poised at the ready. The atmosphere in the room suddenly turned very tense indeed, but unperturbed by the hovering spearheads, William paced the guardroom floor, his face now suffused with anger and indignation. His fists were clenched so tightly that Sir Hugh could see the whites of his knuckles.

'Sit down, Will,' spoke Jack nervously. 'This won't help.'

Although not normally aggressive, his brother had a hot temper. This usually cooled as quickly as it erupted and he hoped that would be the case in this instance. He understood Will's anger, but this was not the time nor the place to exert himself. Hand still wavering over his unsheathed sword, the sheriff looked decidedly edgy.

'Yes, your brother is right, William, sit down,' he urged.

In a more consolatory tone, he added, 'I am sorry I bestowed the news to you so bluntly, but I have to be sure that neither of you had any involvement in these incidents.'

'Would we have turned ourselves in if we had!' cried William incredulously.

Suddenly he was struck by the seriousness of the situation. It hit him like a thunderbolt. They had come here of their own free will to attest their innocence. Little did he know they would find themselves embroiled in a tangle of brutality and murder, and one of which they might not be able to extricate themselves from.

'Oh, my God!' He paled once more and suddenly felt sick to the stomach. What had he led his brother into here? Jack stood and guided him back to the overturned chair, picked it up and sat him down. Sir Hugh relaxed his stance slightly and nodded for the guards to retreat. They went back to stand in the doorway, their pikes once more crossed before them.

'I will have to keep you here in the cells for now until I – *we* – have decided how to proceed. Do you understand?' asked Sir Hugh.

Quiet once more, their heads down, the brothers nodded miserably. The sheriff's decision was taken without wrangle.

Hopefully they had made the right decision in coming here today and that their faith in him had not been misplaced. It seemed, though, that the outcome would not lay solely in his hands. The sheriff stood to indicate dialogue was over and ordered one of the guards to fetch them some food.

*

After a substantial meal and a much-needed shave to rid themselves of their unwanted facial hair and its occupants, the brothers were led to a cell of fresh straw and clean blankets, made ready by Striggar.

The sadistic gaoler had been hugely disappointed. He had been looking forward to an afternoon of inflicting misery and pain. Torture was his speciality, he grumbled to himself, not good bloody housekeeping!

They travelled upstream as the veil of mist began to lift. The main river followed the contours of the land along the valley floor to then meander off and nestle beneath the gradual incline to the High Weald above.[14] Flanking their right-hand side was a narrow strip of trees through which they could glimpse the outlying floodplain stretching out over the horizon. The deluge of recent weeks had drained off the Kentish hills and poured into the valley's basin, and many of the tributaries that wound their way across it had broken their banks. The main river itself was very high, and in some places the swirling undercurrents that eddied and stirred were nearly on a level with the water meadows.

The tapered prow of the flat-bottomed boat cut silently through the water. The ripple of oars and the patter of moisture dripping from the river-edge trees were the only sounds to be heard. Close by, a pig-like squeal from a water rail startled them all, making the boat wobble. Winter, positioned in the middle with Guy behind and the kneeling boy in front nervously made a grab for the sides.

He had secured the boat from a hapless tallow stick-maker and although its load of candles had been removed, the reek of mutton

---

[14] Running parallel to Barden Road.

fat still lingered, imbued deep into the wood after many years of transporting its cargo up and down the river. He sat moaning at the foul smell but was told to shut up; after all it was he who had chosen to procure that particular boat.

They passed a quarry[15] to reach the part of the river where winding water courses branched off in many different directions. Reeds grew thick in the shallows along the banks and Guy saw a water snake skimming across the surface, ripples spreading out behind it. The shallow channels forked and re-forked, but the boy knew where he was going and, veering off, he took them away from the cover of trees to advance onto the flood plain. The banks became shallower and the water deeper in some places, dispersing onto the flat terrain. This made it difficult to determine the deepest part of the water's course and before long they could feel and hear the hull scraping along the bottom. A few moments later the boat gave a shudder as it ground to a halt.

'We will have to walk from here,' said the boy.

He grabbed hold of a clump of sedge and pulled the boat into the bank. Rope in hand, he deftly clambered up the bank and waited for the others to disembark. All three then pulled the boat from the water. The ground underfoot was saturated but they stepped up a few feet onto slightly firmer ground, and from here Guy looked back and, under the curtain of dispersing mist, had a clear view of the castle in the distance. The waterlogged meadows gave way to uncultivated marshland, brown and dreary with high green reeds and cotton grass standing amongst deep stagnant pools. On the far periphery of the marsh stood a knoll, which was topped

---

[15] On Alders Meadow – behind the bungalows. Possible source of sandstone for Tonbridge Castle.

with a jumble of low, broken down ruins. People had tried unsuccessfully to settle in this boggy, foggy place, but most parts had never been drained or cultivated, and in its wildest regions only water birds flocked. Tales of waylurkers that lit flickering marsh fires at night to tempt careless travellers to perish in the black bogs and mires were rife, and kept the locals away. There were only a very few people who knew the terrain well enough to safely venture onto it, and this boy was one of them. He confidently led them along a well-trodden track, his companions following very close behind.

'How far?' asked Guy.

'Over by those trees.' The lad pointed.

Ahead, a line of horny gnarled osier trees and willows crowded close to a shallow stream.

'My home is behind them.'

They stopped in their tracks and unsheathed their swords. Caution was needed now, and hopefully they had not already been spotted. Winter grabbed hold of the boys arm and roughly pulled him to him.

'You keep your mouth shut, right?' he snarled into his face.

The boy nodded and hung back. He was fearful for what might happen next.

His father had not been well of late, not since his mother had died, anyway. He had got progressively worse, talking to himself and acting strangely. He had become increasingly worried and frightened of him. He had no brothers or sisters to share his burden, no other family in which he could confide, and what he was doing to that man was not right. He had told his father so and had received a wallop around the ear. Since then he had kept quiet and did what he was told.

Guy and Winter furtively continued to skirt the willows, stepping over several narrow leats that drained the water from the land into the stream. A way off, there stood a solitary shack on a piece of ground cleared from the surrounding reed beds. The shack leaned dangerously to one side and the roof was thatched with reeds on which grass and weeds grew. Next to it sat a large patch of mud and what looked like a pigsty and shelter, although there was no sign of any pigs. The white feathers, guts, and the severed head of a chicken lay discarded on the ground nearby. Guy told the boy to stay where he was, and he and Winter made their way stealthily towards the shack with its broken and rotting door. No sound came from within. Guy was just about to give Winter the nod to kick it down when they heard a series of groans and mumbles coming from the wooden pig shelter. Abandoning their quest, they went to investigate. An iron grille had been placed across the front of it, which was secured with twine passed through two iron eyelets, one on the grille, the other on a standalone iron post. As they listened no more groans came from within, only what could be described as a strange rattling sound. Guy crouched down to look through the crosswork of bars into the long, tunnel-like shelter. He could not see much, just a heap of filthy, grimy blankets. The odious smell that came from within made his eyes sting and his stomach retch. When his eyes had become accustomed to the dimness, he realised what, or rather who, was wrapped in the filthy blankets inside.

'Jesus, its Percy!' he cried.

'Quickly... Get him out!'

Guy put down his weapon and fumbled with the knotted fastenings. Eventually the grille gave way and together he and Winter carefully pulled Percy out from his filthy, fetid prison. As they moved him, he was taken with a sudden fit of coughing, the sound of which Guy was all too familiar with. When it was finished, Percy lay in a feeble, torpid state. The rattling they had heard came from his chest as he breathed with torturous effort.

'Who did this to ya?' asked Winter.

Percy could not say much, just mumbled something incoherent, but his relief at seeing them both showed in his stricken face and his gratitude at being released from the stinking hole was evident when he grasped Guy's hand and weakly squeezed it. It was apparent that he had been kept captive in the shelter for the duration of his disappearance. He was dirty, stunk and, judging by his emaciated appearance, had been starved of food. This factor was obvious when trying to get him to stand; he was unable to do so. His legs were too weak to hold him up due to the lack of use and sustenance.

'Lie down,' instructed Guy, and he and Winter lowered Percy gently back to the ground.

He looked around for they needed somewhere for him to lay, up and out of the cold and wet.

Suddenly there came a warning shout from the boy who had stood looking on from behind a willow tree.

Then, all hell broke loose.

The shack door was thrown open with such force that it was nearly ripped from its rough frame, the rotting planks splintering into pieces. With a bull-like roar and wielding an axe, a grizzled toothless man of an indeterminate age, ragged and dishevelled with long unkempt grey hair and beard, fell upon the two of them. Grabbing his sword, Guy sprung to his feet and, being an experienced fighter, easily parried a blow aimed at his head. He turned and gave the man a hard shove in the back with his foot, sending him sprawling. But he recovered immediately to swing round and cast a swipe at Winter who, caught off guard, received a hard blow to the top of his arm, just below the shoulder. He howled in pain and fell to his knees, dropping his sword to clutch the injured arm to his chest.

Towering above him with wild, crazy eyes, his assailant made ready to strike again but Guy was quick to respond and with another hard kick, in the kidneys this time, sent him reeling again to the ground. He landed winded and in pain, but still struggled to get up.

Please, Father, no!' screamed the boy, who was absolutely distraught.

But his father was not listening. The florid and dirty face was cracked in a ferocious grimace as he hurtled himself towards them once more. With Winter now incapacitated, Guy knew it was up to him to resolve the situation. He did not want to kill this man, especially in front of his son, but seeing the determination etched upon his face, he gauged he might have to. After many years of learning and applying his survival skills, he would not hesitate to inflict a fatal wound to save his own skin, as well as that of his fighting companions. Watching him carefully, Guy perceived that the man had now focused his full attention on Percy, who lay exposed and vulnerable on the ground. Realising his purpose, Guy rapidly stepped forward to place himself between him and his potential victim. The madman skidded to a halt before the tip of his sword.

'Drop the axe,' he demanded.

Eyes bulging and breathing heavily, their attacker shifted from one foot to the other. Spittle foamed in the corners of his mouth. Becoming increasingly agitated, he tried to dodge the weapon aimed at his chest. Guy jumped back and, with a quick lunge, swiped the blade across the fellow's upper arm. He winced momentarily but did not make a sound as blood spurted and started to trickle down his ragged and dirty sleeve.

'I said, drop the axe,' Guy repeated calmly but firmly, once more taking a four square stance.

He did not drop the axe, just gritted his teeth resolutely and gripped the handle more tightly, the stringy sinews in his skinny arm working all the while as he played with it in his hand. His eyes were still on Percy and in them was a fixed resolve to lay hold of him.

'I should've finished off the double-crossing rat when I had the chance,' he spat, once more trying to sidestep Guy, who successfully held him at bay.

It was becoming obvious that in this manic state the man held no fear of any reprisals, and most probably none for his life either, and this made him very dangerous. Guy was poised, ready to lunge again at any moment. Winter, also realising they had a madman on their hands, hauled himself to his feet and painfully took up his sword. He stood behind Guy and in front of Percy, just in case.

'But I wanted to see 'im suffer, suffer like we all did when he snitched on my father!'

He raised the axe once more and bellowed.

Robin, his son, screamed and ran forward. His father was about to get himself killed.

'Nooo!' he shrieked. Too late. He fell across the now crumpled body of his dead father.

He had raised the axe high and feinted a blow at Guy's head. As Guy ducked to one side, it left the way clear for his intentional strike. With lightning speed, he had thrown the axe, and before Winter had even seen it coming, it zipped past his ear to land with a thunk in the ground, two inches from where Percy rested his head. He was fast, but leaving himself open for a split second, Guy had taken the opportunity. Twisting his body, he had lunged forward and thrust his blade up under the raised arm and into their assailant's exposed chest.

The boy was beside himself. He implored and pleaded with his father to get up. Guy was overwhelmed with pity for the lad, but any remorse he felt was mingled with some relief. The outcome could so easily have been different.

He went over to the boy and gently lifted him off his father's prostrate body.

'Come now, let us get you inside.'

Robin allowed himself to be lifted and manoeuvred into his ramshackle home. He should have hated this man, but he didn't. He had realised a long time ago that his father was not well and on the pathway to self-destruction. He was eaten up with hatred and the need for vengeance, a combination that in the end had hastened and resulted in his own death. He could not blame this man; after all, if his father had not been stopped, he could have had three deaths on his hands.

Winter was in pain from his injured and bleeding arm, so they managed with some difficulty to lug Percy into the shack. Skirting a small unlit fire pit in the middle of the floor, they placed him on a broken down truckle bed in the corner. The only other furniture was a stool and a rickety table and a tiny cupboard. One shelf slanted perilously on the wall, which held a blackened cooking pot.

'Have you anything for the deputy to drink?' asked Guy.

The boy nodded and, going over to the cupboard, took out a cracked and chipped jug. Pouring weak ale into a well-used mug, he brought it back over to place it on the table. Gently lifting Percy's head, Guy held the mug to his lips. The first gulp made Percy start coughing again, so Guy pulled him up to rest his back against the wall. Once the coughing had stopped Percy resumed sipping the ale slowly. Whilst still holding the mug, Guy looked across at Winter, who sat on the stool still clutching his arm. He was losing blood and had begun to look unwell.

'We need to bind that arm. Here, take this for me.' He indicated to the boy, who took the receptacle and continued to hold it for Percy.

Guy examined the gash. It did not look deep, but it was still quite a serious wound.

'It probably looks worse than it is. As luck would have it, the axe was blunt,' he said.

'That's some consolation then,' replied Winter with a hint of sarcasm.

Guy took off his damp cloak and removed his jerkin. Pulling off his tunic, which was old but clean – he knew the importance of keeping a wound clean – he tore off the sleeves, then ripped the side seams, the front and back. He helped Winter remove his own outer garments as carefully as he could but a bolt of pain shot through his arm, making him curse out loud. Guy then skilfully bound the arm and shoulder and made a sling with the larger pieces of linen. Once finished, the patient blew a deep sigh of relief.

'That feels better, thank you.'

Guy grunted as he dressed himself. His mind was already mulling over his next task.

'We need to get you and Percy out of here as soon as possible. Luckily there are a few hours left of daylight, but first I must bury the lad's father.'

Outside on a patch of earth where a few scraggly vegetables had tried and failed miserably to survive, a shovel stood, stamped deep into the ground. He teased it out from its resting place and, because the earth here had been dug over more than anywhere else, Guy thought it the easiest place to dig a grave.

As he dug, he gazed across the flat, dismal landscape. A watery sun peeked through, only to disappear again behind a grey cloud. A wind gusted and on the horizon black clouds were starting to gather in the voluminous sky. Overhead a heron called its harsh cry and flew in circles, employing its slow, lazy wing beat. Guy wondered how anyone could survive in this godforsaken place. Maybe they didn't, he mused. If having to endure the loneliness, the enfolding greyness and the endless soughing of the reed beds didn't send you mad first, then the dankness and mist would likely kill you off instead. Poor Percy, he must have found himself immersed in his own worst nightmare being back on the marsh, starving and with the damp air invading his lungs.

He looked across to where the boy's father still lay, now covered with a blanket. It was not difficult to deduce what had happened here. This man's father had been one of the gang members Percy had informed on all those years ago, and he was wanting to settle a score. He had obviously heard that the Turner brothers were wanted men and had used them as bait. Robin, who most likely was ignorant of what lay in store for the deputy, had helped to lure him here. The lad could only be what, ten years old? Any blame must be laid squarely at the father's feet. Just then, Robin appeared through the broken-down doorway. He went over to his father and knelt by his side, tucking the blanket in around him. He then bowed his head and placed his hands together in prayer. As Guy witnessed this intimate moment, he was suddenly struck by the thought that the boy's grief would be no less tangible than his own. They had both lost a father and he himself knew how devastating that could be, but the difference here being it was his hand that had dealt the death-dealing blow, leaving this young lad an orphan. Dear God! He drove the shovel with some force into the ground and left it there. Standing motionless and consumed with guilt, he stared down at his now empty but slaughterous hands for a very long time…

*

His throat was parched and he licked his cracked lips. Sweat trickled down his forehead to runnel along the top of his eyebrows and drip down the sides of his face. The white linen coif under his half-helm went someway to help soak it up. His head was boiling like a turnip in a pottage pot, but to go without any hard head protection would be suicidal. His body too, encased in chainmail, cried out to be released. Oh, what bliss to feel a fresh breeze on his skin, a splash of cold water on his naked flesh! The fierce light made him squint as it bounced off the white sun-flashed rocks of the foothills. They were passing through a chasm in the rock – dangerous, but the only way forward for them other than skirting miles out of their way around it. They were on their way back from a scouting patrol. Two days since another of their reconnaissance patrols had been attacked by a band of Arabs and all of them slaughtered.

Scanning the surrounding hillsides a glint of metal caught the corner of Guy's vision. At the same time, the standard bearer leading the train stopped in his tracks. His bellowed 'My Lord!' was terse with sudden warning and made the hairs on the back of Guy's neck stand erect. Felix flattened his ears and skittered sideways, making him change his wet-palmed grip on the reins. Alerted, the party came together to tighten up their formation. Guy brought his shield across in front of him and drew his sword. The tension amongst the men was palpable. His own breathing became light and shallow. Setting his sights on the foothills rising high and wild around them, he sought out the enemy.

They came with a roar, sending up clouds of choking dust and wielding huge curved sabres and Saracen daggers. All were black-eyed and copper-skinned. Some had skin as black as ebony, with black beards bound in bronze and gold rings. Flourishing his sword above his head, Guy wheeled to meet the foe. A heartbeat later they were upon them. He heard the screams of frightened horses dancing around each other, their eyes bulging and their nostrils flaring with fear. He heard the clash of metal on metal. Ploughing through the fray, he slashed from left to right. Arrows hissed past his ears. One found its target. Sir Willis fell from his mount, an arrow sprouting from his throat. Sir Raymond was cut down from behind while he sliced at a man in front of him. Several had been unhorsed. One had claimed a redundant sword and stood fighting with one in each hand. Another was struck down, his head sliced clean off. All was chaos, the air scented with blood. Guy lashed out, opening an arm here, a leg there. A wounded black devil fell forward from his horse in front of them. Felix reared, kicked out and trampled him. His screams stopped when his skull cracked open like a walnut and his brains spilled out. Guy took a blow to his shield to counterstrike with a backhand at his opponent's right knee. The man screamed, his limb shorn right through to the bone. He quickly had to duck beneath the swipe of another aggressor, but as he jabbed his shield up under the man's chin, knocking him senseless, a sabre blade bit through a gap in the chainmail beneath his arm. He cried out in agony and took a sword hilt in the face. He fell. That was the last he remembered…

*

Together, Guy and Robin buried the body. After brief formalities conducted by Guy over the grave, he led the boy back to his home. There, he and Winter prepared for departure, deciding to use the broken bed pallet as a hurdle to transport Percy back to the boat.

As they made ready outside, Robin stood in the doorway looking on. His skinny frame shivered as the dark clouds gathered closer and a cold wind murmured eerily through the reeds. He realised he was about to be left all alone. More tears threatened and he tried desperately to hold them back. He couldn't. He heard the sound of a sob and realised it had come from his own throat. He prepared to re-enter his cold and lonely home.

Guy turned to address him.

'Right, ready?'

Robin hesitated.

'Come,' he said, reaching out his hand. 'We cannot find our way back without you.'

Uncertain for a moment, Robin sniffed but then wiped his eyes with the heel of his hand and took a few timid steps forward.

As he came nearer, Guy encircled his shoulders and drew him in closer. 'And anyway, you do not have a bed to sleep on.'

A chill, easterly wind blew across the Medway Vale. Winter was definitely on its way.

Lucie stood behind the screen in the bedchamber, washing herself over a basin of lukewarm water. In an age when common people considered personal hygiene to be of little importance, she was fastidious in hers. She washed herself daily and her hair regularly. Alisoun also made sure that the household always had a plentiful supply of fresh, clean linen. Once finished, Lucie put on a clean chemise and stepped out from behind the screen to dress herself. Since losing their belongings, she and Heloise had been most grateful to accept, first from Lady Elvera, and then from Alisoun, any spare or old clothing they were able to provide. Hence, both wore a combination of elegant-cum-practical attire. Over her linen chemise Lucie pulled on a dark green full-length coarse woollen tunic. It was cold, so another layer was necessary. She added a side-less long grey woollen surcoat. She then tied a leather belt loosely around her hips. Finally, bringing her hair from behind and over her shoulder, she proceeded to comb it through. Parting it in the centre, she wove a single plait on each side to then secure each one with a thin leather thong. Had she been at Whitelawne she would have wound each one round and round into a bun or 'rams horn' to cover each ear and fasten it in place with a hair pin. But she was not at Whitelawne, and in any case, she liked her plaits down. The homely nature if the outfit she wore also comforted her and reminded her of happier days gone by. She finished off by placing a short veil, secured with a head rail, over her hair to signify she was married, albeit widowed.

In the double bed someone stirred.

'Morning sleepy head. Up thee get, maid, there are chores to be done,' she said cordially.

Heloise smiled, stretched and yawned luxuriously. Although being high-born, she was not averse to helping the women at Starvecrow. She was such a sweet girl, they all thought so, not at all idle or full of airs and graces and had taken on the chores with relish. Lucie speculated that she was probably grateful for a reprieve, however short-lived that might be, and anything was better than marriage to Richard de Coulances. But after washing and dressing herself similarly to her companion, Heloise was happy to continue with one indulgence, and that was to have her hair combed and dressed. Being unmarried, she could have worn it loose but she expressed a wish to have plaits exactly like Lucie's.

Making their way downstairs and through the undercroft, they picked up two pails, one empty for milking Daisy, the other full of discarded vegetable skins and bean pods for the pigs. Another day at Starvecrow had begun.

*

Chores over for the time being, the household settled down to a meal of rabbit and onion stew, cabbage, peas and beans. Afterwards they either sat at the huge centre table or by the roaring fire, all engaged in easy conversation and keeping their hands occupied with either needlecraft, mending, or sharpening farm implements. The constable left behind by the sheriff sat with Old Matt at the table, thoroughly engrossed in a game of draughts. Lucie, after massaging an ointment of comfrey and solomon's seal into Roger's leg, was encouraging him to walk the length of the undercroft.

'That's it… On you come… Good. You should do this every day, a little further each time. It will build up your muscles and promote movement,' she said reassuringly.

Roger winced as a biting pain shot through his leg every time he put his weight upon it. The break had healed well, but had set badly, leaving the limb twisted. His progression was slow and lopsided and he could not walk far without stopping for respite. Lying abed for weeks had caused the muscles to waste, leaving them with little strength to support the damaged limb and making it necessary to use a walking stick. Guy had made Sir Robert's available to him. It was made of ash wood and had a beautifully carved ram's head for a handle. He stopped and leaned heavily on it. He closed his eyes, his face was pale and sweat-beaded. He breathed deeply.

'Phew. You know, if all the demons in hell were after me, I'd give myself up willingly,' he said good-naturedly, wiping his brow. Lucie laughed.

The thunder of hoofbeats could be heard turning into the yard. Angus, who had been lying at the hearthside, suddenly lifted his head. Everybody looked at each other. Lucie's heart leapt. Maybe Guy was back? A growl rumbled up from the depths of Angus' throat. Maybe not. This was not his usual response when the master came home.

At the same time, there was a sudden clatter of wings. Like an ill omen, all the crows had taken off again. They abandoned their nests and perches and cawed noisily high above, tossing and turning in the wind.

'What made them do that?' asked Roger in puzzlement.

The window beside Lucie overlooked the yard. She stood, went over to it and peered out. As she did so a shadow passed, startling her. Immediately Angus sprung up and stood stiff-legged. With hackles up and ears back, he continued to growl deeply. Matthew went to pacify the hound but, uncharacteristically, he snapped at his hand. They had only ever seen the like once before and that had been during the raid. Eventually Matthew managed to grab him by his collar while the sheriff's man strode over to open the door. The same shadow that had darkened the window now darkened the threshold, before it ducked and entered through the doorway. Angus, still making his low guttural rumblings, suddenly snatched himself free from Matthew's grasp. Snarling, his teeth bared, he launched himself at the visitor who, raising his arms up to protect himself, stumbled back with a shriek of alarm. There were cries of shock from the onlookers, but thankfully Angus did not reach his target. With lightning reflexes, Matthew had seized hold of his collar again and jerked him back. Grabbing his muzzle tightly, he swung a leg over to entrap him between his thighs. After a desperate struggle, he managed to drag Angus across the room and, with Old Matt's help, shut him securely in a cupboard underneath the stairs. Back in the kitchen, everybody was shaken by what they had just witnessed and none more so than their visitor, Richard de Coulances, who, once he had regained his composure, was not happy. He shushed away his steward and escort, who had rushed forward to protect him. They re-sheathed their swords and reluctantly melted away.

'That animal should be taken outside and slaughtered!' he raged, pulling his cap, which had been knocked askew back into place.

Matthew could only apologise and reiterate that he did not know what had come over the animal.

'Well, keep it away from me or it will find itself skewered, roasted, and fed to the peasants!'

There was a ripple of shock and horror around the undercroft at such a suggestion. Young Tom started to cry. Richard looked down his nose with distain at the lad, who then buried his face in his mother's apron.

He scanned the gathering.

'Your master is not here?'

At Matthew's confirmation that he was not, he seemed to relax a little.

Richard de Coulances held himself well, was of average height and quite handsome in an effeminate sort of way, but his dark eyes had a harsh, watchful look. His narrow-shouldered frame was richly dressed in a damask tunic with silver fastenings and a cloak lined with fox fur. His hair was not long but not too short either, with dark shiny curls framing his matching fox fur-lined cap. There was something unpleasant about him, and this was a man Lucie had mistrusted from when she had first laid eyes upon him at Whitelawne.

'I have come to retrieve my betrothed,' he said, continuing to look around.

They had only met once when there had been a betrothal celebration at her family home in Suffolk, but he would recognise her anywhere. She was a timid, witless looking creature, tall and gawky, who always looked like a doe-eyed deer poised ready for flight. Then he spied her.

'Good God, girl, what do you look like?' He eyed her up and down with contempt. 'Rescue is probably a more apt word,' he sneered, curling his lip. 'You're dressed like a harridan! Have you forgotten who you are?'

Heloise stood rooted to the spot, her hands clasped in front of her, uncertain of what to say or do. She shook her head and stared down at her feet.

'No, my lord,' she whispered.

She looked crestfallen, all the growing confidence and blossoming personality gained of late was dashed in an instant. *The boorish, loathsome man!* thought Lucie.

'Me thinks you have been here too long. Get your things, we are leaving!'

Heloise, rooted to the spot, continued to stare at the ground.

'Well, make haste!' he shouted severely. 'And you!' pointing at Lucie, 'you're to come too.'

Heloise was roused from her uncertainty by Lucie tenderly leading her off towards the stairs.

Richard then noticed Roger in the centre of the room, leaning heavily on his stick. He pointed again.

'Not you. You'll not be much use to me by the looks of it. You can stay here.'

He was picking and choosing as if they were livestock at a cattle market. Roger met his gaze with a cold challenge. Richard frowned at his insolence.

'What are you looking at? Watch your manners, churl!' he growled.

Although Roger would have liked to walk over and swipe the arrogant sneer from this popinjay's supercilious face, he had little option but to lower his gaze and hobble, utterly humiliated, over to a vacant chair by the fireside. A smirk of satisfaction creased Richard's lips at the groom's discomfort, the spurn was not lost on the assembled household.

'Well, am I not to be offered refreshment while I wait for my delightful bride-to-be?' he cried, pulling off his riding gloves with a flourish, one finger at a time.

Matthew and Alisoun, suddenly mindful of their duties, set to work making their guest comfortable. Matthew, after helping Richard divest himself of his outdoor wear, led him upstairs to the solar, while Alisoun hurriedly decantered a bottle of Guy's best red wine. Once sure their guest was sufficiently catered for, she climbed up to the bedchamber, where Lucie and Heloise were packing their paltry wardrobe. Lucie was fortunate in the fact that she had not packed all her clothes for the journey to Suffolk, whereas Heloise had travelled with all her attire, which was now lost somewhere between here and Oldbury. There had been a tunic too, a wedding gift for her prospective husband, exquisitely stitched by her own fair hand. Her skills as an embroideress were untouchable. She was now sitting on the bed, immersed in thought. She had returned to the day when she had first met Richard de Coulances.

The marriage had been actively encouraged and pushed along by Gilbert de Clare on behalf of Lord Charles. Sheep were her dowry, the main reason for the arrangement, and Lord Charles wanted more of them, first to pay for the upkeep of his ancestral home and lands, secondly to help sustain his family's lavish lifestyle.

She had been twelve years old and had met his gaze with a hollow feeling in the pit of her stomach. But it was more than anxiety that had tensed her, it was fear. There was a coldness in the way he looked at her. She knew, because he had told her so in a flat detached tone, in a dark corner and out of earshot, that the marriage was a necessity, far from welcome now and anytime in the future, and was an intrusion into his life, which, from what she could gather, was full of roistering, hunting, and more roistering. The feeling was mutual. She fervently wished she was marrying anyone other than him.

She heard her name being called from a distance. Lucie, sitting down beside her on the bed, considered Heloise's finely chiselled features. She had a fair complexion, a high forehead and a full rosebud mouth. Her eyes were a deep rich cornflower blue, and she had gloriously thick golden hair, the colour of wheat. She was a lovely looking girl, a girl any appreciative man would feel fortunate to have for a wife. What a shame it was to be him.

She gently called her name again and Heloise turned her immense, preoccupied eyes upon her.

'It will be all right, Heloise,' she said with compassion, clasping her cold hands resting in her lap.

'It might be difficult for you at first, but you will adjust, you'll see.'

She wished she really believed what she was conveying to the girl, but sadly the truth of it was she was just trying to make her feel better and probably without much success at that.

Heloise nodded stiffly and stood as Alisoun entered the room. She had come to bid them a sad farewell and help prepare them for departure.

Downstairs Richard sat contemplating, tapping his fingers on the side table. At fifteen, though her body was not yet fully ripe, she should be more than ready for marriage, he thought resolutely. He had been told she would make him a fine wife, would be devoted to her domestic duties and furnish him with many children. His mind, nor his body, had been set astir by the prospect. The marriage was a business arrangement, agreed three years ago. They had only met the once, at their betrothal celebration and he had seen her then as an awkward, ungainly child who could barely string two words together. By the sound of her today, she had not matured much, but he must admit, she was more pleasing to the eye than she had been then. Even through that awful peasant dress she was wearing, he had noticed high, rounded breasts, a slender waist and the hint of a lithe and supple body in the making. His imagination was roused and his breathing started to quicken, much to his surprise.

'Um, maybe there will be good sport to be had there after all,' he decided out loud to himself, a lecherous leer passing over his face.

His musing was interrupted by the sound of footfall on the stairs and down from the upper floor came his bride-to-be. She stood on the bottom step, again not making eye contact with him. She had changed the homespun tunic for a dress Lady Elvera had given her, and although it was a little short and generous around the bodice and waist, she looked well in it. Richard rose from his chair and, for the second time, swept her with his condescending gaze.

'That's a little better. At least there is some semblance of a lady now.'

Reaching for his gloves, which were on the table, he called for attention. 'Serf!'

Standing behind Heloise, Alisoun and Lucie glanced sideways at each other under lowered brows. He was deliberately being offensive.

A bristling Matthew ascended the undercroft stairs to stand before the blatant deflationary.

'Get my cloak, we are leaving.'

Not trusting himself to speak, Matthew only managed to nod his head in obedience.

Richard then turned to Heloise.

'Come, it is time for you to come back with me. Back to where you belong, away from this dingy and draughty little manor house!'

The Priory of Saint Mary Magdalene was founded in 1124 by Richard de Clare and was the home of an Augustinian order known as the Black Canons. The land for the priory was given to him by William Rufus, William the Conqueror's son, and was part of the Lowry of Tonbridge. The small community of black-clad figures were very popular and would often be seen out preaching in and around the town. Like many religious houses, they relied very much on charity from beneficiaries and the many travellers who sought shelter and hospitality there.

Contained inside its walls were a chapel, vestry, chapter house, refectory, dormitory and a library. There was also a small infirmary where local people and travellers who, finding themselves ill or injured, would be admitted for treatment.

Percy was taken straight there. Between the three of them they had managed to carry him to the boat, and after mooring on the riverbank opposite the town wall, had made the arduous journey up to the huge oak doors.

On knocking, they were attended by a porter who accompanied them to the infirmary block, which was set back from the main buildings. Winter was immediately led away to have his arm cleaned and dressed.

'You may need a few stitches,' he was told by a short stocky monk of about fifty, with white hair circled around his tonsured head.

Apprehensively, Winter followed him to the treatment room. Another younger monk, who introduced himself as Brother Peter, helped carry Percy to the hall. He had a serene face that almost bordered on the imbecilic, but he became quite animated with pride when he showed Guy their facilities.

The main hall was well lit, with a blazing fire at each end. There were five beds, each with clean linen sheets. The floor was swept out most days and washed down regularly. Medicinal baths, hair washes and beard trimmings were administered weekly.

Being considered a good aid for recovery, mutton was dished up three times a week, as well as the usual pottage, and all would be washed down with a daily quota of ale.

'All in all, the standard of care is very high indeed,' he finished off, looking very pleased with himself.

Guy was impressed.

'It certainly looks that way. I can't imagine anywhere better for Percy.'

Percy seemed to be asleep until a series of racking coughs shook his thin frame. Phlegm gurgled in his chest and his breath came harsh and tremulous.

'It is congestion of the lungs. He is very ill and must be allowed to rest. I must prepare some herbs. A brew of horehound and feverfew is the order of the day, I think.'

Brother Peter leaned over the hurdle and pulled back the filthy blankets as Guy explained the circumstances of Percy's plight. He wrinkled his nose in distaste and stepped back.

'With plenty of care and sustenance he will recover quickly enough. First though, a good wash down and a change of clothing is needed.'

Reassured, Guy helped move Percy into a side room where Brother Peter would clean him up, ready to be put to bed. Guy then collected Winter from the surgeon and young Robin from the kitchen, and together they made their way back to the castle.

It was almost dark when they reached the bridge, and curfew was almost upon them. It had not rained after all. A chill wind had blown the amassing clouds away, and the castle and town now stood silhouetted against a clear but rapidly darkening sky. Lighted torches on top of the wall reflected across the now quiet, still waters, and the muffled sounds of a town settling down for the night could be heard, carried across on the evening air. They made their way over the bridge to where three guards stood warming their hands over a brazier outside the guardroom. One of the guards doubletook. He had just finished all day sentry duty and he recognised the constable and gentleman as the pair who had pursued the young lad along the riverbank.

'You got 'im then,' he gestured towards Robin. Seeing the constable had his arm in a sling, continued, 'And got 'urt in the bargain.'

Winter gritted his teeth as he recalled the needle being pushed through his tender flesh. He'd had ten stitches.

'As you see. About your business, man,' he growled, dismissing him irritably.

He was weary, his arm was sore and it throbbed terribly. The guard shrugged at his uncivil manner and stalked off into the guardroom, leaving the others to attend the last three people that would gain entrance to the town that night, before the double portcullises were lowered and the drawbars on the huge gates hauled across.

In the gathering dusk, Guy, Winter and Robin made their way to the castle gatehouse. On enquiry of the sheriff's whereabouts, the solitary guard pointed his lance in the direction of a small stone building that stood beneath the south curtain wall. This was the county courthouse. Much of the business dealt with by the sheriff here was routine, such as the swearing-in of officers, the ordering of inquiries into trespass and the announcement of royal proclamations. It also served as a small claims court and where men would be declared outlaws. Any serious crimes such as rape, murder or arson would be presided over by local justices of the peace or judges sent down from London.

Ducking his head through the doorway, Guy saw the sheriff sitting at a huge oak table set on a low dais to one side of the hall. Large candles set on spikes protruding from the walls and an iron chandelier, raised to its position by a rope pulley, lit the chamber. Around the hall hung swords, shields, spears and other paraphernalia of past campaigns, most likely put there for no other reason than to decorate the bare, cold stone walls. Rough wooden benches sat piled up in one corner. These would be laid out in regimented order for witnesses, jurors and the public when any proceedings or hearings were in progress. With Sir Hugh sat Hugo Corbiere in chainmail, his round metal helmet and gauntlets sat on the table in front of him. He had been drilling his 'idle' soldiers in the outer bailey that afternoon. Also at the table sat Godfrey Bartholomew who was accompanied by two noblemen, both being business partners, major landowners and important members of the county elite. Sir John de Courcy owned manors at Penshurst and Chiddingtstone, and Reginald Soulsby had a number of manors on the fringes of the Kent and Sussex border. On seeing them, Sir Hugh stood from his chair and came forward, concern etched upon his face. From the description, he had recognised the young boy immediately. He had also noticed Winter's injured arm, but was deeply disappointed to see Percy was not with them.

'Where have you been?' he asked as he ushered them to the table.

He waved for a serving attendant to bring more wine over from a huge coffer with the De Clare coat of arms emblazoned across the front of it. They all settled themselves around the table. Young Robin stood someway off, looking on awkwardly. His eyes flicked between the sheriff and Guy, who glanced across and beckoned him over. The boy looked quite presentable after having bathed at the priory and given a clean set of clothes, a serviceable pair of shoes and a cloak to wear. He reluctantly came forward.

'This is Robin. Robin helped us find Percy.'

In the process of sitting down, Sir Hugh's head came up abruptly.

'You found him? Where? Is he alive?' were his barrage of questions.

Guy held up a placatory hand.

'Yes, we found him, and yes he is alive, although not at all well…'

'Where…'

Again Guy raised a hand to pacify the impatient sheriff.

'He is at the priory where I can assure you he will be most diligently taken care of.'

A look of relief passed over Sir Hugh's face.

Guy and Winter gave a full recount of their day while their audience listened on intently. Robin, thankful to be forgotten for the moment, sat down on the edge of the dais with his back to them, hugging his knees and staring forlornly into space. Guy, knowing full well that he would probably be listening, made every attempt to be tactful when mentioning his father. But not so Winter.

'A bloody possessed lunatic, that's what 'e was!'

Guy cringed and, catching his eye, glowered at him.

'What?'

Winter was completely oblivious to his lack of sensitivity and wondered what had warranted the black look. Glancing around the gathering and deciding that nobody was about to enlighten him, he shrugged and gulped down a good measure of wine.

'Anyway,' said Sir Godfrey, breaking the silence that had descended around the table, 'I am sure Percy will make a full recovery *and* I am in no doubt his insatiable appetite will certainly survive the ordeal,' he chuckled.

Winter puffed out his cheeks. He looked and felt exhausted and just wanted to go back to his quarters. When Sir Hugh suggested he do just that, he gratefully and swiftly took his leave.

Sir Godfrey, his mood suddenly becoming serious, glanced around at each of them in turn.

'Now, let's get down to business. In the absence of De Clare,' he rolled his eyes up in silent exasperation, 'we,' indicating the two men sitting either side of him, 'have summoned the sheriff to discuss the current situation and where we are to go from here.'

'And what is the current situation?' Guy asked.

'Hugh?' He turned enquiring eyes on the sheriff.

There was a moment's hesitation while the sheriff contemplated how to announce this, when Sir Godfrey spoke again.

'Come on Hugh, spit it out!' he bullied.

The sheriff cleared his throat.

'Ahem... Whilst you were away on your rescue mission, William and Jack Turner turned up. They surrendered themselves this morning and they emphatically deny any involvement in Geoffrey's or Eleanor's murder.'

Guy leaned forward, his interest immediately whetted.

'And do you believe them?'

Sir Hugh continued. 'They knew they were suspects for Geoffrey's murder and came to profess their innocence. When they were informed of Eleanor's, they seemed genuinely nonplussed.'

He then turned to Guy.

'Yes, I do believe them because if they were guilty they would not be here now.'

Without any preamble, Godfrey Bartholomew interrupted, his harsh voice echoing around the hall.

'Then, if they are not guilty, who is?'

Agitated, he slammed his fat beringed hand hard down on the table making the goblets shake and his flaccid jowls wobble. Young Robin jumped and looked up in alarm. He had heard enough raised voices today to last him a lifetime. He stood and moved across the hall to perch on a bench in the corner.

Godfrey turned to the sheriff.

'You are the King's representative and yet you are allowing anarchy to reign in his forests! What are you going to do about all this? We have received little satisfaction on the matter and it is the concern of many more than just we three.'

There were mumbles of agreement from his two companions.

Sir Hugh guessed Godfrey Bartholomew and his associates were really only looking after their own interests. They conducted their trade in the county of Kent and beyond, frequently travelling as far abroad as Wiltshire to conduct their lucrative business. There had always been danger travelling the highways, but unfortunately once word got out about specific hotspots potential clients would avoid the area like the pox, and he guessed that anything interfering with their business would be greatly resented.

'Anyway, firstly *we* want to be sure they are telling the truth! Get them both up here,' demanded Sir Godfrey, his eyes bulging in his frog-like face and the long scar standing out livid on his cheek.

Sir Hugh, his expression grim for he did not appreciate being spoken to in such an abrasive manner, turned to Corbiere.

'Bring them here to us please, Hugo,' he asked politely but with a hint of irritation.

Hugo nodded and left the hall.

The Turner brothers finally appeared. They looked subdued and apprehensive as they shuffled into the court house, accompanied by Corbiere and two guards who were then dismissed to wait outside.

'Well, what do you have to say for yourselves?' asked Sir Godfrey, stonily.

'There is something I would like to say first to Sir Guy, if I may?' William requested, nodding his head in Guy's direction.

'If you must,' was Sir Godfrey's impatient reply.

William stepped forward.

'Jack and I would like to convey our deepest sorrow at hearing of your father's death. Sir Robert was a good and a fair man and we shall be forever in his, and your, debt. If it had not been for you and your father…' He did not finish, but Guy knew to what he referred.

'We only did what we had to do,' he replied. 'We could hardly leave the situation as it was.'

'Even so, we owe a debt of gratitude,' William said, including his younger brother who nodded his affirmation.

'We were just glad to have helped,' said Guy graciously.

William gave a short, sharp half-bow and stepped back again to stand shoulder to shoulder with his brother.

'It seems you have convinced the sheriff here that you are both innocent of any crimes, but now you need to convince us,' bellowed out Sir Godfrey.

He sat back with a look of derision and expectation.

'I can only repeat what I have already told the sheriff. There was an argument between myself and Whitelawne's reeve. My only crime was to lose my temper. As a result, I was evicted from the estate. Jack here followed soon after. He too has done no wrong.'

This was all the explanation William was willing to give. He was not prepared to disclose that the reeve had been attempting to stop him from attacking Geoffrey, and for what reason.

'When we heard we were suspects for Geoffrey's murder, we stupidly decided to lie low. We realise now that was a mistake and we should have come forward immediately to proclaim our innocence.'

'What was the argument about?' regressed Sir Godfrey.

William seemed reluctant to answer.

'Well?'

'What was happening on the estate,' he eventually mumbled, dropping his gaze.

'Which was?'

'Things were changing.'

'He is telling the truth, I can vouch for that,' stepped in Guy.

'How so?'

'Lord Charles told my father he had plans to review Whitelawne's management. Passions were running high all round. It was pure hot-headedness on William's part.'

'Are you prone to moments of ill-temper then, moments of such pique that you strike out? Should I go as far as to say that you could lose control enough to stab somebody?'

'No, you should not,' was William's clear reply.

Everybody could see where this was going.

'I must stress,' put in Sir Hugh, 'that what happened to Geoffrey was not in the heat of the moment. It was a calculated act where persons had lain in wait to commit the crime.'

'Who's to say it was not these two who had lain in wait?' challenged Sir Godfrey, who watched William and Jack's expressions carefully to try and determine whether they were concealing anything.

Their faces remained constant.

William sighed heavily.

'Look, although we do not mourn the deaths of two De Coulances family members, I would fervently urge you to believe that we had no involvement whatsoever in them.'

'I believe he is telling the truth,' spoke up Guy, turning to look at each individual sitting around the table.

He'd held fast his conviction that they had not been involved in any foul play, and for all Godfrey's posturing, there was no evidence to suggest otherwise. John de Courcy made a disparaging remark under his breath. It was now Guy's turn to bring his fist down hard on the table.

'Now look here! I know these two to be hardworking, honest and trustworthy and I would willingly place a noose around my own neck if it were to be proved otherwise!' he said vehemently.

Sir Godfrey was taken aback by Guy's ferocity. The rest of the company sat in silence until the sheriff cleared his throat to concur.

'Hear, hear. I second that.'

There were audible sighs of relief from both brothers.

Sir Godfrey leaned on the table, steepled his fingers and brought them up to his mouth as if to pray. He tapped his pursed lips rhythmically.

'Well, rather a rash statement to my mind, but nonetheless it seems you have two advocates here willing to defend you, and as they are both men of impeccable integrity, it would be churlish of me not to give some credence to their recommendations.'

'Thank you, sir,' said William.

'But we are no closer to knowing who the perpetrators are and, it seems, no closer to finding out!'

Sir Godfrey turned accusing eyes on Sir Hugh.

The sheriff disliked Godfrey Bartholomew; he thought him overbearing and his only saving grace, in his mind, being he had been a loyal supporter of King Henry.

Well, he was not about to be intimidated by him. He was the sheriff and could be credited for many successes over the years.

'What can I do, Godfrey? There is probably an army of these ruffians spread out over miles in the North Frith wilderness. Even if they could be found, we have no military force here big enough to send against them. All we have is a depleted garrison, left here to defend Tonbridge, and God knows if they would even be able to do that if it was necessary!'

He glared across at Corbiere.

'All they seem capable of is prancing around the bailey waving their weapons about,' he said spitefully.

'That is most unfair!' was Hugo's indignant reply.

The courthouse erupted into a series of squabbles. Accusations and recriminations flew back and forth, accompanied by much head shaking, finger wagging and table thumping. Passions, and tempers, were beginning to run high.

'I appreciate the ones left behind are not the most experienced but they soon put paid to those horse thieves, did they not?' said Hugo Corbiere defensively.

'What about my business? I am losing money hand-over-fist!' wailed Richard de Courcy. 'And we have received little satisfaction on this matter,' repeated Sir Godfrey, yet again, 'terrorising every homestead in North Frith... in the alehouses... cocksure... laughing at us!'

'There is very little I can do unless...'

Suddenly losing patience with the bickering assembly, William shouted loud enough to be heard above the melee.

'But there is something we can do!'

An immediate silence fell around the hall. All turned to face him.

'Jack and I had already decided that if we got out of these,' he rattled the chains on his wrists, 'somehow we would repay our debt to Sir Robert. We want to help you find these murderers.'

There was a murmur of surprise around the table.

'And how do you propose to do that?' enquired Sir Godfrey with a hint of ridicule.

'Nobody knows we are here. Everyone thinks we are still hiding out in the forest. We could return there, seek them out and infiltrate if necessary. Winter is here and they would most definitely have gone to ground. We know the area well. There are many caves and other such places where these outlaws could be sheltering.'

It was now fully dark outside and the flickering light from the candles danced around the dim hall, playing with the shadows and glinting off the rows of armour and weaponry adorning the walls.

Robin was asleep curled up amongst the pile of benches, his cloak wrapped tightly around him and his white-blond hair sticking out in tufts from beneath his new cap.

'You are prepared to do that?'

'Yes, we are.'

'Um, very commendable,' said Sir Godfrey toying with his chain of office.

He turned to Guy. 'Their loyalty to you and your late father is clear to see.'

Guy felt humbled. 'Yes it is.'

She was with him again, as beautiful as ever, her long ringlets of yellow hair whipping behind her. Together they had spread their unseen wings to soar high over a landscape of snow-peaked mountains and white-cloaked forests. She laughed out loud when a sudden squalling up-draught snatched them higher, sending them wheeling and tumbling in the chill, clear blue heavens. Reaching out, she lovingly caressed his cheek. It was the lightest of touches.

'Take care,' she whispered.

He went to take her hand but his fingers slipped through hers and he found himself falling, plummeting down to earth through wispy grey clouds, her words echoing over and over again in his head, the hard unyielding ground spiralling up forever closer…

He woke with a start and sat up. He touched his cheek where he could still feel his mother's warm, lingering touch. Reclining back against the bolster, he sat to savour the moment. After a while, a soft pattering infiltrated his concentration and he looked up to see pellets of snow bombarding the window pane.

The weather had turned bitterly cold in recent days. Winds had swept across the countryside, cutting through towns and villages to pervade every single nook and cranny. There had been no escaping its voracious appetite to seek out and breach every shelter, every corner and crevice to leave violation in its wake. The wind had lessened overnight, its earnest mission to deliver and dump the snow on them had been accomplished.

Getting out of bed, Guy went to the casement window and opened it. The rush of cold air was crisp and clean. He leaned out as far as he could, his head just clearing the eaves. He twisted his body to turn his face skyward and closed his eyes against the cascading snowflakes. They landed on his skin to sting momentarily before melting away. Blinking them from his eyelashes, he twisted back round to scan the courtyard and garden below. A light blanket of snow covered every surface. All was white, still and quiet. Even the usually loquacious robin sat silent atop the open wicket gate that led to the apple orchard, his red breast fluffed up against the cold. Dotted here and there were bird tracks, the larger crow's feet being easily recognisable. He stood for a while and studied the spectacle before him. He had not seen snow for a good few years, but then the arid sands and scorching heat of the desert also seemed an eternity ago.

As he washed and dressed, he reflected on the developments of recent weeks. He had brought William and Jack back to Starvecrow with him. It had been decided that their offer of help in finding the outlaws was probably the best and only option left open to them. They had stayed long enough to regain their strength and make provision for at least three days at a time away in the forest. Guy and Grainger had helped them stash food, extra warm clothing and woollen blankets for their convenience at two locations in and on the edge of the forest, one being an old portable shepherds hut hidden from sight at the end of a deep and narrow defile, the other an abandoned roundhouse. This was sited on the edge of the forest, but because of its vulnerability, they reasoned it would be of little interest to the outlaws and therefore, if necessary, made it a safe haven for the brothers.

He wondered how they would be faring now the weather had turned, and expected them to be back very soon for respite.

Finding Lucie and Heloise gone had been a great disappointment to him, but then they would have returned to Whitelawne sooner or later, he reasoned, though he would have preferred the latter option. His absence at the time of Richard's visit had probably been fortunate. From what he had heard, his arrogance had surpassed itself, the mealy-mouthed snake-in-the-grass!

An aroma of freshly baked bread filled the undercroft as Alisoun paddled two loaves out of the oven. The household sat around the table, breaking their fast with bread and cold salt beef. Only young Tom and his granddad ate porridge. They both smiled their toothless smiles at him as he sat down amongst them. Roger sat at the end of the table, his place secured since Guy had offered him residency after being rejected by his former employer.

'How is your leg faring?' Guy enquired between mouthfuls of bread and beef.

'Better every day,' replied Roger.

He was still carrying a slight limp, despite the many hours he had spent exercising, but it had much improved.

'There is a little pain still, though not much.'

'Good. Do you feel up to riding out with me to check on the flocks today?'

Roger was well pleased. It was time he got back in the saddle again.

'Yes, I do, sir. I am more than ready,' he said enthusiastically.

'Right then, wrap up well,' instructed Guy after he had drained his cup of ale.

Three days since Guy had purchased a black mare, Bess, for this very reason.

Roger had to be boosted into the saddle by Matthew. He winced as a shaft of pain shot through his leg, but once seated, he settled with ease. His twisted leg made his foot sit at an awkward angle in the stirrup, pointing it towards his mount's stomach, but that did not hinder his riding in any way, and as they rode out of the yard, he soon began to enjoy the feel of the horse beneath him.

Muffled against the cold they made their way up the lane with Angus loping alongside them, the fresh snow crunching underfoot. Above in the stark and naked trees, crows squawked and quarrelled over a piece of carrion, probably the only piece they might find for a while, any other being covered over by the fresh layer of snow.

Emerging from the lane, Guy drew rein at his usual vantage point on top of the knoll to gaze down through the swirling snow, to the lower pastures and his flocks. The breath of man and horse mingled together, steaming in the cold morning air. On the misty horizon the snow covered roofs of the abbey could be seen peeking through the bare treetops.

'We should have a good clip next year,' he informed Roger, 'and a good few more lambs if the new ram has performed the duties expected of him. Come, let us see how they fare.'

He tugged on the reins and pressed his heels into Felix's flanks, who harrumphed and started forward. They headed down towards the gap in the border trees and entered the lower pastures. Guy pointed to a small dwelling a few hundred yards away.

'That is Joseph the shepherd's hut… And there is Joseph bringing in the flock.'

271

On spying the shepherd, Angus raced off, eager to help. Across the white winter meadow, Roger could see the small stone hut with its nearby sheepfolds and Joseph methodically counting and herding sheep into them. Angus pranced a little way off, just in case they had any other ideas. As they drew closer, Joseph looked up from his task to raise a hand in acknowledgement, but as he did so, something caught his eye down in the bottom pasture. Standing abruptly he pointed, but whatever he shouted was snatched away by the wind. Angus stopped his cavorting and, crouching low, had also honed his attention on whatever it was. Guy looked to his left, but his view was obscured by a narrow strip of woodland. Sensing some urgency, he and Roger spurred their mounts on. Passing the obstructing trees, they squinted down through the curtain of snow to where a scrubby willow coppice sat on the lower wet, boggy ground where the runoff collected. There they could see two horsemen harrying the last straggle of sheep. Guy reined in to take measure of the situation. One of the horsemen had dismounted and was struggling to lift a dead sheep up to the other still seated in the saddle. As Roger came up to stop at Guy's side he heard his sharp intake of breath.

'God's teeth!' he hissed.

A bitter taste of gall filled Guy's mouth and an implacable rage surged through him. He tightened his grip on the reins, and Felix sidled.

'This is just too much!'

Guy put his stirrups into Felix and they broke into a gallop. He had no sword on his person, only a small dagger sheathed in his belt, but he was not about to stand by and watch this brazen act. Roger, who was completely weaponless, started in hot pursuit. Angus, taking this as his cue, swiftly followed.

The wind blew the snow into their eyes and it froze on their faces as they raced down the field. Spying the distant but swiftly approaching riders, the intruders abandoned their booty. One swung himself back up into the saddle and, intent on a quick escape, they both turned their mounts and fled back through the willow coppice. A big mistake. A few paces in and their horses sank well over the fetlock in the thick glutinous mud. It sucked and squelched, slowing their progress. They struggled to reach the other side, hampered by the grey brown silt and layers of rotten leaves. But reach the other side they did, and they took to the wooded slope. Guy, knowing the problems the bog could pose, skirted around it, and ploughed into the wood close on their heels.

It was a dangerous game, weaving through the trees at speed. Luckily the woodland had been managed so it was not too densely populated, but the gill streams, ditches and occasional rocks scattered here and there were a challenge for any, even the quickest and most sure-footed of horses. Guy could hear Roger thundering along behind him. Branches whipped at his face. One snagged on his hood and snatched it back off of his head. Felix leapt a fallen tree and swung wide of a huge dead and rotten log with broken and jagged branches. Two startled deer leapt from their path, and a flock of sparrows exploded from the branches of a birch. A grey blur flashed past as Angus cut across to catch up with the first fleeing horse. Snarling, he leapt and snapped at its rider's calf. He missed but came rushing in again, this time his jaws clamping around a forearm. His fangs bit into flesh and the man shrieked in agony as Angus swung from it. The horseman brought his leg up and kicked out, hitting Angus squarely in the stomach. He yelped and let go, dropping to the ground to roll over and over. Guy was almost upon the second rider. He was a rough-looking fellow with a tangle of dirty black hair. He was dressed in little more than rags, his cross-gartered beeches were dirty and ripped, and he noticed he had odd boots on his feet. He had pulled back the hood of his tattered short leather cape to glance over his shoulder, and Guy was close enough to see a ragged scar running down one side of his face, almost closing one eye. He was also close enough to see panic turn into fear when the pursued realised his pursuer was closing in. He snapped the reins to urge his steed on harder. This one was riding bareback and Guy reasoned he must be a very experienced rider. He also had the benefit of a sturdy short-legged pony under him, ideal for the wooded terrain. A steep-sided gill loomed up in front of them and the pony cleared it without breaking stride. Guy was not so fortunate. Felix caught a hoof in the tangled roots of a tree as he was about to launch himself over, and stumbled. Bringing his head down, he tossed Guy forward from the saddle. Arms flailing, Guy sailed through the air, almost to land on the fleeing horse's crupper. He landed on his back with a thump and a loud, 'Oof!' Winded, he lay unmoving, wedged between two fallen tree trunks. He had hit the back of his head hard on a tree stump and he could taste blood in his mouth where he had bitten the inside of his cheek on impact. When he tried to get up, he felt dizzy, so decided to stay put for a while. Through the fuzziness, he could hear the approach of footfall. He imagined it to be one of the outlaws and struggled to get up, only to feel nausea overwhelm him. He sank back down again. He was next roused by wet fur and a cold nose sniffing around his face and ears. He raised a hand to ward off Angus' rough warm tongue rasping over his face.

'Guy.'

He opened his eyes and blinked to find Roger standing over him.

'Are you all right? Can you stand?'

Slowly the fog started to clear.

'I think so,' he said, although he was not at all certain.

'Here…'

Roger leant over one of the tree trunks and helped haul him to his feet. He too was struggling, his breathing coming quick and laboured.

'Is Felix sound?' enquired Guy.

He anxiously scanned the woodland and found Felix a little way off taking a drink from the gill he had not managed to clear. Grimacing, he rubbed the back of his head as he climbed out from between the trees.

'They are not so brave in small numbers, are they?' he said, as he gingerly and painfully brushed himself down.

Roger winced as he took a step towards his horse.

'No, they are not,' he replied.

'They ran like the cowards they are, only good at dispossessing the unwary.'

'I can see you are in pain. I should not have compromised you. God only knows what would have happened if we had caught them. It was rash of me, I apologise for putting you at risk,' said Guy.

Roger gave a mirthless laugh.

'No matter. It was worth it just to see their faces. They looked like hapless rabbits fleeing from a fox. Still, we will get another chance, I am sure, and next time we will be ready for them, the craven scum,' he spat bitterly.

Cold, wet and mud-spattered they made their way back through the wood.

The snow was falling heavily now, almost obliterating their vision across the pasture. Guy scowled down at the two dead ewes that lay half-buried, the chill wind ruffling their woollen coats that stood out dirty against the pure-white snow. A deep, red, bloody gash lay open the discarded ewe's throat. The other lay crumpled where it had been bludgeoned to death. The remaining sheep had long since gone, all scattered in a bleating panic.

He thought on Roger's words. Yes, they would definitely be ready for them next time.

They learnt later that they had not been the only victims. On that same day, other factions had struck out raiding and pillaging even the most vulnerable of targets, the Whitelawne tenants being one of them. Guy had given a derisory snort when he heard that. They would probably have been mightily disappointed with the meagre provisions to be had there, he thought.

*

William stopped suddenly in his tracks.

'Shhh! Quiet now,' he exclaimed in a hushed voice, holding out his hand to still his brother.

'Quickly, hide!'

Both men dived for cover just in time, before two horsemen appeared around a bend in the narrow track, which was scarcely wide enough for two riders to pass abreast. Either side of the track, thick trunks crowded close together, their twisted and tangled branches interlacing to give them some welcome shelter overhead. They crouched silently behind the towering sentinels, listening to the sound of the approaching riders. They passed so close that he and Jack could hear their conversation.

'Cor, that was a close shave. He nearly 'ad me. I thought we was done for!'

'Yeah, we still might be yet when… sees we're empty-handed!' was the grumbled reply.

Neither William nor Jack heard the name. Unfortunately one of the horses had snorted at that inopportune moment.

William and Jack glanced at each other. Both their minds were working in the same vein. This latest unsuccessful expedition had taken them as far as Chiddingstone and they were now making their way back to Starvecrow. Although they could not see them, it was obvious by what they had heard that these men were outlaws and most probably members of the gang they were seeking. William quickly made a decision and when they were out of earshot turned to Jack.

'You go onto Starvecrow, I will follow these two.'

Jack went to protest but his brother silenced him.

'If I don't go now, I may lose them. You go back, tell Guy we will soon know where they are concealing themselves.'

Jack was allowed no further time for argument and even before he had the chance to wish William Godspeed, he was gone, silently and expertly following the two unsuspecting outlaws.

They seemed to be in no hurry, their pace slow enough for him to follow comfortably. Nobody could move through the forest as silently as William. His lean frame was graceful and quick and his footfall light and cautious. He kept at a distance but could still hear the riders ahead in animated conversation, although what was being said was inaudible. They penetrated deeper and deeper into the tangled forest, but William knew their exact location. They were crossing Dinas Dene valley at the foot of the Greensands Ridge, and two miles further north over the ridge lay the small hamlet of Ightham. Suddenly they diverted onto another, even narrower track. Snakelike, it wound back and forth and had many other trails crisscrossing through it. Sometimes William would lose sight of them as it twisted and turned, only for them to reappear again. He concluded that in the summer months, the fern and bracken that could grow taller than any man would make this trail's very existence undetectable to the unknowing traveller. Their pace had dropped to almost a crawl. Twigs brushed against William's face and caught on his cloak, and it was becoming more and more difficult to proceed through the undergrowth with caution. As well as keeping his quarry in sight, he also had to be careful where he placed his feet. Roots and tangled bramble stems threatened to trip him up, and there were holes aplenty where he could easily twist an ankle. The track began to skirt the edge of an evergreen forest and, for cover and easier progress, William decided to move into it. It took him further away from the track and the outlaws, but with all the noise the two were making, he did not think he would lose them in a hurry. But the evergreen soon gave way to an oak wood, and he became a little more exposed again, the outlaws needing only to glance back, and the game would be up.

Feathers of snow floated down through the naked branches to land crystal clear on his cloak before melting away. His breath misted in the chill air. Thanks to Guy, they had prepared themselves well for the weather this time. He was pleased of the sheepskin jerkin belted under his cloak, and the extra layers he wore under that. A leather sheepskin-lined hood kept his ears toasty warm and two pairs of thick woollen hose and a pair of lined and sturdy calf-length boots did the same for his legs and feet. He moved through the silent ranks, feeling the rough bark beneath his fingertips. He could feel the ground underfoot, the soft crunch of snow, the crack of acorns and the rustle of dry leaves under the soft white crust. A small piece of a broken branch rolled underfoot as he put his weight on it, but thankfully he did not fall. The incessant jabbering of the outlaws covered any sound he may have made. The trail must have doubled back on itself as suddenly, in a heartbeat, the two riders were heading straight towards him. In three quick steps, William flung himself against the bole of an oak tree. Still engrossed in their conversation, they had not seen him. He waited for them to pass.

'Stop, I need a piss!'

They stopped. One of the riders dismounted and William heard the crunch of footfall on snow as he walked over in his direction. He settled his breathing. When he sensed the man to be close, he pressed himself even further into the rugged, scratchy bark. Out of the corner of his eye he glimpsed the toecap of a boot.

'You don't need to go any further, do you? S'not as if I ain't seen you piss before, is it?'

William stood motionless. The outlaw was only the other side of the tree. He would only have to reach around the trunk and he could touch the man. He heard the trickle and hiss and the sigh of relief as he urinated up the trunk.

'Come on, 'urry up!' shouted his companion, sounding utterly morose.

'I'm freezin' my balls off 'ere!'

'I shouldn't be so keen if I were you. We'll sure as hell get a kicking on our return with nothin' to show,' was shouted back as clothing was readjusted.

'Maybe we ought to try and find summink on the way?'

'Like what? I ain't seen so much as a poxy squirrel! Anyway, it's too bloody cold to hunt!'

They moved off, leaving William weak-legged with relief.

The trail meandered away again from the oak wood, and only when the pair were well out of sight, did he advance more slowly to stalk them once again. They travelled through a maze of shallow wooded valleys. Big flakes of snow were now beginning to fall. They drifted down to lay heavy upon dry and shrivelled bracken fronds and arching bramble. White hummocks and hollows hid stones and roots, and very soon he realised all their footprints would be covered over too. He bundled himself up and pulled his hood tight against the snow and a chill wind that had started to blow. He was becoming a little concerned and sincerely hoped they would reach their destination soon. He looked on the horizon to see the ridgeline stark against the grey, snow-laden sky and reckoned if he kept this in his sights, he would not get lost. But instead of climbing the Weald's gentle undulating landscape to bring them to the ridge's pinnacle, they skirted a hillside of ash trees and moved into a deep wooded cleft at its foot. Undercover again, this wood grew wilder and thicker than ever but gave William a welcomed respite from the wind and the swirling snow. He looked up through a tangle of hawthorn and guessed it was about noon, yet the wood was as dark as evenfall. Two fluffed up crows sat side by side in a great oak, silent and miserable, watching him. The sound of horse and rider had diminished so he put a spurt on to catch up with them. He came upon a stream rippling through the wood, where he knelt and plunged his cupped hands into the icy cold water to take a drink. He looked up to see the back end of his quarry wending their way up a slope to disappear over its brow. He could smell woodsmoke in the air. Cautiously making his way forward, he concealed himself behind a holly bush, which bore a very heavy crop of red berries. Peering over the rise revealed to him a clearing enclosed on three sides by a sheer, half-exposed rock face and bank crowned with beech, alder and oak.[16] At its centre stood a longhouse surrounded by a deep earth ditch. Around the ditch, a wooden palisade was in the process of being erected and a half-built outhouse sat neglected nearby, with logs and tools laying scattered around it. Constructed from split oak trunks, the longhouse was, he guessed, over thirty yards from end to end, and its high roof was covered with a mixture of thatch and sod. From this, a smoke hole sent forth wisps of grey smoke. Two huge wooden pillars supported an overhang of roof, which stood over a stout oak door studded with huge iron nails, and a giant stag's skull and antlers ornamented a low lintel above it. The compound consisted of a midden heap, an empty pigsty and sheep fold. There were a few scrawny chickens pecking around and in the far corner, Will could see a large enclosure where there roamed what could only be described as a 'mishmash' of horses, all being of varying heights, colours and breeds. He looked on in amazement. This was a holdfast in the making and its location had been chosen with some consideration. Hidden in a well-protected site at the foot of the ridge, the wooded and tangled banks behind made it virtually unapproachable from any direction other than the way he had come.

'Well, I never…' he muttered under his breath.

He watched as the two men rode over a roughly-made oak bridge into the compound. They dismounted and led their mounts towards the horse enclosure, disappearing from view for a while only to reappear again and make their way to the hall's entrance. Scarface lifted the latch, shouldered open the heavy door and they both entered, stooping to pass under the low lintel. William needed to get a closer look. He followed the perimeter of the ditch through thicket, brambles

---

[16] On the site of Ightham Mote.

and briar until he was nearly opposite the rear of the hall, which was bare of any windows. Now to negotiate the ditch. He looked down into it. He needed to be careful here. The snow covered whatever lay discarded in it, and there was no telling how deep the frozen run-off would be at the bottom. As he scrambled down the snowy slope, his foot dislodged a rock, sending it cascading down. He lost his footing and followed it, sliding the rest of the way and landing with a crack as his boots broke through the ice at the bottom. Luckily the sludge underneath only reached his ankles. He clambered up the other side, making a grab for an exposed root to pull himself up the last few feet. Creeping up to the hall, he remained vigilant. He listened for any sound. The horses whinnied and snorted, and raised voices could be heard coming from within. He skulked around the building to where two flaps of deer hide screened a small window and crouched beneath it. The smell of something roasting over the fire wafted under his nose and his stomach roiled so loud he feared it would be heard, but the argument raging inside would certainly eclipse any noises he might make outside.

'You do realise food is in short supply? That is our last pig on the spit!'

'Sorry, but we 'ad to dump 'em cos we was caught red-'anded. We just managed to get away as it was!' one of the men explained in their defence.

'You pair of lackwits!' the faceless voice spat.

'Get out of my sight, *now*, before you feel the toe of my boot up your arses!'

The harsh voice was raised even further. 'Listen, all of you! You're all out again tomorrow, do you hear?'

Bawled assents echoed around the hall as well as some disgruntled moans and groans. This was a voice whose commands were made to be heeded, William decided. It was crisp, authoritive and well-spoken. He edged round to tentatively peer through a slither of a gap in the hides. A fire pit filled the hall with a pale smoky haze. Over it a huge pig was being roasted. A youth laboriously turned the spit, and as it rolled over fat ran off it to splutter and hiss into the flames. The firelight revealed the faces and bodies of those sitting at trestle tables assembled around it. William guessed there were probably about twelve to fifteen men. This concerned him as there were not as many as he thought there should be. Maybe there were more, out of sight at the other end of the hall? Scones had been lit around the walls at this end, but the rest of the hall and its lofty rafters were obscured by the smog from the fire. Those who he could see were a mixed bunch of rough, unkempt looking individuals who looked like they would sooner slit your throat than look at you. The two closest to him were leaning over a trestle top, their heads close together, deep in conspiratorial conversation. They were travel stained and mud speckled, their clothes patched and repatched again. On the trestle in front of them sat a wood axe, a small bow, and a quiver full of arrows. One, with a bald head and an ear missing drank from a chipped stone cup, the other – a horn. He too was an evil-looking fellow with thin lips and a sharp nose. He kicked out at a dog prowling around their feet. It yelped and slunk off with its tail between its legs. His abuser gave a cruel laugh, showing a mouthful of brown broken teeth. William craned his neck to locate their leader. He found him sitting on a raised platform in a large throne-like chair above the fire pit. No common bench for him. He could make out, but not in great detail, what looked like a coat of arms occupying a space on the wall behind him. William judged his age to be somewhere, but not too far beyond his thirtieth year. He had a mane of jet black hair swept back from his forehead and reaching down past the nape of his neck. Heavy eyebrows hung over deep-set eyes, and his nose was long and slender. Lean-cheeked and under a tightly trimmed black beard he clenched a square, jutting jaw. His expression was dark and stern. He lounged back in his chair brooding, drumming his fingers on the armrest whilst jigging his crossed-over leg back and forth. He wore a studded leather jerkin over a green quilted doublet, and his breeches looked of good quality as did his long knee-length brown boots. A longsword and a dagger hung from a leather belt at his hip. This was a man of some bearing.

A chicken came pecking around at his feet. Deciding he had been there long enough and suddenly aware that there may be others yet to return, William took one more good hard look at the man before retracing his steps back to the holly bush. Once there he went down on one knee to peer again through prickles and berries to take in all he would later need to recall. Something wet and cold touched his nose, and he realised it was still snowing. The cold was starting to penetrate and a shiver ran through him. He shrugged under his cloak and looked up at the grey sky. It was time he started back. He only hoped he would reach Starvecrow before the light faded; if not, he might have to take shelter elsewhere for the night.

Stealthily he retreated from the hidden wood in the ridge and headed south, down in the general direction of Tonbridge. He had a lot to think about as he trudged back through the snow, which was nearly two feet deep in some places.

He was in no doubt that the person responsible for that bolt hole meant serious business and had no intention of being found easily, and who was this man that spoke like a lord but skulked around in the middle of nowhere with a bunch of outcasts?

'I have had talks with Richard, and I gather nothing is certain now. We may have been a little hasty.'

'Oh, you do, do you? Well, maybe if you *had* applied some restraint, our son and his wife would be here dining with us this evening.'

Lord Charles, his face flushed with too much wine, sat hunched over and picking at his venison pie. He looked up abruptly.

'Don't be ridiculous!' he spat at his wife.

Undeterred, Lady Isabelle continued.

'But then restraint has never been one of your strong points, has it?' she said, her voice level, though dripping with bitterness and contempt.

The barb was not lost on Heloise who sat opposite her, though what it referred to only husband and wife were privy to.

Lord Charles glanced back at his wife to find hard, dark eyes boring into his. Lady Isabelle had a way of staring fixedly, unblinking, until the recipient felt compelled to drop their gaze. Lord Charles did just that.

'Don't talk such flummery, woman!' he blustered, reaching for his wine goblet.

'Only the murderers can be held responsible for those deeds!'

'Revenge can take many forms, for slights that may well seem trivial in some people's eyes, but not so in others,' was the cold reply.

Lord Charles looked away, crestfallen.

*

Stopping at the window, Heloise looked out to see the snow had stopped at last. It lay deep and even, glowing white under a full moon and a sky littered with many glittering stars. A soft light filtered through the coloured diamond-shaped glass in the windows across the courtyard, shedding subtle shades of pink, yellow and green over its surface. The scene was so beautiful it should have gladdened her heart, but it only served to add to her melancholy, and made her feel more trapped and isolated than ever. She huffed, puffed out her cheeks, and rested her forehead on the frosting window pane. She hated it here. She hated the huge freezing cold house, and hated the just as cold Richard. If he was not treating her with indifference, he was talking to her in a tone that suggested she was quite the simpleton. She had also seen firsthand his harsh and brutal treatment of the kitchen and stable boys. She also hated Lady Isabelle, a totally selfish creature who cared for nothing and nobody but herself. Maybe she ought to practice more of what she preached, she thought wryly, recalling the comment made to Lord Charles, though she had been told her legendary tongue-lashings had been somewhat curbed of late. Heaven knows what she must have been like before! She cringed as she recalled witnessing the utter humiliation of a young serving maid at the dining table this evening. She had been scolded so viciously, and she herself had been that embarrassed, she had wanted the floor to open up and swallow her. The poor girl's only crime was to spill a drop of soup on the tablecloth, for God's sake! And as for Lord Charles, the cantankerous and pompous old windbag! She had heard he had not always been so disagreeable, that he had changed since his son's death. She might have felt some sympathy for him if it were not for his condoning of such behaviour. It was true she had never seen nor heard him physically or verbally abusing anyone, but turning a blind eye to the unnecessary deeds meted out by family members made him as guilty as they were.

She closed her eyes and rolled her head from side to side. She did not want to be a part of this family; she just wanted to go home. She had hardly seen Lucie. Lady Isabelle had appropriated her since their return from Starvecrow and had kept her busy elsewhere. She missed her so much.

Her forehead suddenly pained her. She withdrew it from the windowpane and progressed along the corridor, the walls of which were hung with thick woollen tapestries and from where flickering candlelight cast shadows into its dim recesses. She stopped at the bottom of the staircase, which would take her up to her bedchamber. From here, the corridor also gave access to the old hall. Behind a wooden screen, Heloise could hear loud guffaws and rowdy horseplay. Richard was playing host to his clique of friends. They had intended to hunt, staying at the hunting lodge, but being loath to venture out in the bleak weather conditions had decided instead to make their own entertainment at home.

Curiosity getting the better of her, she crept over to the screen and quietly moved behind it. She knew she would not be seen as curtains were always drawn across the entire width of the hall to keep out any draughts. This hall had once been the centre of everyday life where the whole household would eat and sleep together, but expansion of the house over the years had since provided private rooms and bedchambers for family members, and dormitories for the servants. It was now used mainly by the latter to gather and eat, and for administration purposes where, once a week, the tenants would come to pay their dues.

Peeking through the curtains, her eyes were immediately drawn to the high and architecturally complex vaulted roof. This hall had clearly been built for someone of great wealth. The three main oak timber arches that supported it were carried on the backs of carved crouching and snarling bears, wolves and wild cats, all of which seemed to spring out from the oak panelling, which finished at collar-level around the walls. The rafters were smoke-blackened after many years of exposure to the central fire pit which was no longer there. It had been replaced by a huge fireplace in the west wall. Here she found her adversary and friends, lounging across oak settles and benches in front of a blazing fire. They were all drunk, regaling each other in their wine-thickened and slurred speech of past conquests in every lurid detail. As she watched and listened, Richard stood up from the settle, which he was reclining on and walked unsteadily to a nearby table. He put down his wine goblet with a bang and reached for a flagon to refill it. Teetering on his feet, he concentrated hard as he lifted it up and tipped it slowly and carefully. When he had tipped it all the way without a single drop of wine decanting from it, he upended it and shook it vigorously. Annoyance etched across his face, he slammed the empty flagon back down on the table.

'Wine!' he shouted at the top of his voice. 'We need more wine, and be quick about it!'

From behind a wooden partition in the corner, which screened off the kitchens, a young serving maid appeared, carrying replenishment. She was a comely girl, probably no older than herself, thought Heloise, with a heart-shaped face, a button nose and full, plump lips. Russet curls strayed from her linen coif. The shapeless tunic she wore could not disguise the shapely figure beneath it, and Richard double took when he saw her. His gaze grew suddenly alert and assessing. A leer crossed his face when she passed him to place the flagon on the table.

'Well now, who do we have here?' he slurred.

The girl stood still with eyes downcast. Heloise did not hear the whispered reply.

'Rose, what a lovely name,' said Richard disparagingly, circling her and lifting a stray lock of hair. 'Is it not a lovely name?' he repeated louder, turning to his companions whose attention was now fully roused. Cruel sniggers could be heard across the hall, and Heloise felt a pang of pity for the girl.

'Where's the old crone that served us earlier?'

'She has duties elsewhere, my lord,' replied the girl, sending him a quick sidelong glance before averting her eyes again.

Richard lifted her chin but she would still not look him in the eye. She snatched her face away and turned to retreat, but Richard firmly grasped her arm and pulled her back towards him. Nobody, but nobody, turned their back on Richard.

He grasped her jaw tightly and held her head to *make* her look at him. She winced in pain.

'Stay where you are. You go when I tell you to,' he demanded in a tone devoid of any empathy.

He released her roughly. Agitated, the girl glanced behind in the direction of the kitchen, hoping upon hope that someone would come to her rescue, but she knew she was alone. After a long, hard day the others had taken the first opportunity to nip off to bed.

Richard, his aggression seeming to subside as quickly as it had flared up, pushed his face close to hers. As he did so, the petrified girl stiffened and a whimper escaped from her lips.

'What's the matter, my pretty? Don't you like me?' he simpered, breathing his wine-sweet breath over her.

'Yes… Yes, of course I do, my lord,' was the only reply left open to her.

'And the others?' he asked, nodding in their direction.

'Yes, my lord.'

'Good, then you won't mind having a bit of fun with us all, will you?'

He stepped away.

'It's playtime, boys,' he called, turning and rubbing his hands together.

His smirking, loitering companions moved in closer and started to circle like a pack of wolves surrounding their prey before a kill. Heloise's pity quickly turned to concern.

'I beg you, please…'

Before the girl could finish, Richard lunged at her and laid a hand hard across her face, left, and then right again, splitting her lip. Blood ran down her chin and she cried out as her legs buckled beneath her. Aghast, Heloise brought her fist up to her mouth to quell any sound.

'Raphe, Gerard, get her up!' demanded Richard, hostility returning in his voice once again.

For someone seemingly deep in his cups a few moments ago, he had certainly recovered sufficiently to aim a volley of sure and solid blows.

The two men approached and, taking an arm each, pulled the distressed young serving girl back on her feet, but there was no pity in the looks they gave her, even when she started to plead again.

One of his drink-fuddled guests slapped Richard between the shoulder blades so hard that he winced and staggered.

'Go to it, my man. You can start off the proceedings,' he slurred.

With a look of relish, Richard grasped the front of the girl's tunic and gave it a hard yank. She cried out in protest as it ripped from neck to waist, baring her breasts. Desperately wanting to cover herself, she struggled to free her restrained arms, but she was no match for her captives. Five pairs of cruel, hard eyes were fixed on her, the intent plain to see in their salacious, gloating faces and Heloise knew beyond any doubt of what she was about to witness. She looked on in disbelief and horror, her heart pounding in her chest. What was she to do? She was frightened but she could not stand by and let this happen, or walk off and pretend it had not. Suddenly, as if her brain had no control over her body, she stepped out from behind the curtain. One of the circle spied her as she moved towards them and indicated her presence to Richard who, about to launch the next stage of his attack, turned to face her. At first his eyes widened in surprise at seeing her, to then narrow with contempt.

'What are you doing here?' he spat savagely.

He showed not a morsel of embarrassment or shame at being found in such circumstances, just irritation at being interrupted.

She said nothing. Her throat was too tight and she felt sick with fear.

'What is the meaning of this?' a voice boomed across the hall.

Heloise breathed a sigh of relief. She never thought she would be so pleased to see Lord Charles.

Suddenly the serving girl was free. She stumbled to her knees and was finally able to cross her arms over her exposed chest.

Lord Charles spoke again as he stormed across the hall.

'What kind of men are you that attacks a helpless maiden?' he demanded angrily.

As he looked from one to the other, they all condescended to hang their heads and stare at the floor in shame. Richard turned a dark shade of red and gave a petulant shrug under his father's scrutiny. His house guests melted away into the shadows, leaving him to stand alone before him.

'Well, have you nothing to say for yourself?' Lord Charles challenged, his jowls wobbling with indignation.

'I was punishing her for insubordination,' replied Richard.

His father raised an eyebrow at that.

'*That* is what you call punishment is it?' he said pointing at the half-naked girl curled up on the floor. 'Wanton brutality is what I would call it. Did you not learn any lessons from your brother's exploits?'

Richard did not answer, just gave his father a defiant look.

'And... And have you no regard for this girl's honour?' Lord Charles spluttered incredulously.

'She is only a serving wench, Father,' replied Richard, his lip curling in a sneer of arrogance.

'How dare you, you witless, spoilt brat!'

Lord Charles, appalled by his son's conceitedness slapped his flushed, supercilious face and sent him reeling.

'Go!' he croaked, choking on his anger and pointing towards a door in the far corner of the hall.

Richard, holding his stinging face, sloped off, but not before giving Heloise a dark, sullen glare. Lord Charles watched him leave and, for what seemed like an age to Heloise, said nothing at all, just stood and stared blankly at an empty spot on the far wall, his face bereft and his shoulders slumped.

He felt utterly weary and full of... what? Shame? Yes, that was what it was, not only for both his son's behaviour but also for his own. He had always been too lenient with them and had become practiced at closing his eyes to things he did not wish to see, so he should share some of the blame, he supposed. Well, he had always been a weak man, had he not? His wife frequently took great delight in telling him so. How could he have sired such offspring? First Geoffrey, now Richard too. Boys will be boys, he realised, but how could they behave thus? In his younger days, he himself had been lustful and unreserved in his carnal activities, but all his couplings had been consensual. He had never forced himself on any woman. He sighed heavily. He pressed fat, stubby fingers into his throbbing temples. His head was in a whirl and he could not deal with this right now.

'Lord Charles?' spoke Heloise hesitantly.

He turned to her with flat, dead eyes.

'See to her please, Heloise,' he said, and left, his footsteps slow and heavy.

Silence filled the hall.

*

Heloise woke with a start. The night candle was still burning on its pricket and the embers in the hearth were still glowing red. Somebody was outside her door. Alarmed, she sat up and quickly scrabbled the tangled bedcovers down with her feet. Keeping a watchful eye on the door, she scrambled out of bed. The latch hasp lifted and dropped, then lifted again, and in fell Richard. Heloise exclaimed and made a grab for the coverlet to cover herself. Richard lay on his back, resembling a beetle trying to right itself. It was obvious he had continued drinking well into the night, and finding herself alone in a bedchamber with him drunk was not a situation she wished to find herself in. Managing to roll onto his side, Richard kicked out at the door to close it with a slam. He searched the room through a blurry drink-fuelled haze to find Heloise backed up against a large chest in the corner.

'Ah, there you are,' he slurred as he pulled himself to his feet with the aid of the bedpost. He stood rocking backwards and forwards, watching her. The fire crackled and spat in the hearth, but Heloise felt no warmth from it and shivered under his gaze. She wrapped the coverlet tighter around her, not only to cover herself but also to try and disguise her quivering body. She was frightened and a sob threatened to escape from her throat, but she swallowed hard. Her pride would not let her break before this detestable man. Richard continued to study her.

'What do you want?' she asked, trying to keep her voice level.

'You,' he said slowly, pronouncing his lips and looking like a pouting cod fish.

Releasing the bedpost, he took a step towards her but had to grab it again to steady himself. In his inebriated state, Heloise thought she might stand a good chance of evading him, and felt slightly emboldened by this.

'Why? You look at me with loathing and treat me with contempt. You do not like me, you just want to humiliate me. What makes you think I would give myself to you willingly, or even unwillingly for that matter?'

Suddenly Richard burst into laughter, making her start.

'My word, such eloquence! I never thought you had it in you.'

Just as quickly he stopped laughing and narrowed his eyes. They caught the candle light and glinted wickedly.

'I will have you with or without your consent, it bothers me not.'

'Well, it bothers me, *my lord*,' she emphasised.

Although her heart was pounding with trepidation, Heloise raised herself to her full height and looked disdainfully down her nose at him. She had to show she could stand up to him. Richard, not gaining the cowering response he craved, resorted to verbal abuse.

'You are ugly, a clodpate, a simpleton and a slut, and I have reservations about your suitability!' he spat, his face screwed up with repugnance.

'If you think to hurt me with your cruel names and aspersions, you are greatly mistaken.'

Overcome with frustration in the face of her steadfastness, Richard rushed towards her, but Heloise was ready for him. She promptly sat down on the edge of the chest, put her feet up and adeptly kicked out at him, sending him sprawling back across the bed. She made a dash for the door but Richard, having recovered quickly, grabbed her arm and with one fluid movement swung her round to land beside him. Before she knew what was happening, he was on her. She found herself flat on her back, straddled and pinned down. Heloise realised he may well have exaggerated his drunkenness to deceive her. She struggled against the hands clamped around her wrists, but with little effect. She thrashed until her limbs ached with fatigue. Spent, she lay motionless and panting.

'That's better. Now you are being more accommodating,' he said, his breath warm and sour on her cheek.

Heloise averted her face, trying to get as far away from him as possible.

'What's the matter? Am I so abhorrent to you?'

'Yes, you are!'

She struggled again, thrusting her hips upwards trying to buck him off.

'Steady now. Save your bucking for later.'

His voice was low and thick with gloating pleasure. He rasped his stubbled chin across her face.

'You thwarted my intentions earlier this evening... Now it is up to you to sate them,' he panted.

My God, he was about to rape her! He was going to commit the ultimate act to assert power and control over her. Heloise's head spun in panic. How was she going to escape from this?

'Keep still,' he hissed, releasing one of her wrists to pull up her nightgown and to fumble within his own garments.

Heloise took her chance. With a screech of outrage, she grabbed a comb from the bedside table and viciously raked it down the left-hand side of his face, from eye, down his cheek, to chin. Bellowing in agony, Richard let go of her completely, and, feeling a momentary release of pressure from his thighs clenched around her body, Heloise, with the last vestige of strength left in her, bucked again. This time the manoeuvre was successful.

Running out of the door, she looked back to see Richard, writhing about on the bed, holding his bleeding face in his hands.

'You bitch!' he sobbed. 'You've ruined my face!'

The snow had started to fall heavily again in the small hours and the near blizzard conditions had caused drifts to bury some of Starvecrow's flock. During a break in the snowfall, Guy, Matthew and Roger struggled down to the top pasture to help Joseph and Grainger dig them out. Thankfully there had been only a small number of fatalities, these being the timeworn stock less able to survive their freezing incarceration.

In the still, hushed and crisp morning air the snow sparkled a pure dazzling white. Their breath hung in clouds as they trudged home back up to the knoll and along the snow-choked lane. Once back in the yard, and looking forward to breakfast and a mug of warmed ale, they kicked off their boots and brushed down their snow-encrusted legs before entering the undercroft.

'Helloooo.'

Guy turned to see Brother Benjamin, dressed only in his habit, waving his arms above his head. He had made the laborious journey down the hill, stumbling many times on the frozen snow-covered furrows, deep holes, rocks and roots. He was fortunate only to have cut his knee open; he could so easily have broken an ankle.

Stepping over the last furrow, he made his way over to them as rapidly as the conditions would allow.

'Guy!'

Puffing heavily, he had to stop to gather his breath. His face was mottled red and blue from exertion and the cold.

'What is it, Ben?' asked Guy with some concern.

'It is Lucie and Heloise?'

Doubled over, Ben gulped and gasped.

'Tell me, man!' Guys concern increased with every second.

'They arrived at the abbey in the early hours…Heloise had been attacked… she sought Lucie out and they fled… She says she will never return…'

'Attacked? By whom?'

'Richard.'

The men looked from one to the other.

'How does she fair?'

Ben straightened up.

'Shaken but no harm done… physically, anyway.'

Guys gorge rose. It left a bitter taste in his mouth.

'The craven dullard! He needs to be taught a lesson,' he hissed through gritted teeth. He was outraged. His aversion to this man was growing steadily.

He was brought back down to earth by Roger placing a hand on his shoulder.

'They will be safe where they are.'

That was true. Reassured and once again composed, Guy caught sight of his friend shivering from the cold.

'Come inside, Ben. You must be frozen to the bone.'

*

The snow was starting to recede. Rivulets of melt-water ran down Starvecrow Hill to gurgle into the bottom stream. Felix and Bess stepped carefully over the furrows and sinkholes, which were still slick with ice. Guy and William had taken this first opportunity to travel down to Tonbridge. Will needed to relay his observations regarding the holdfast near Ightham to Sheriff Breton and the town's council.

They travelled down and then up the narrow lane, where leafless branches brushed against them, leaving diamond droplets of melted snow to sparkle momentarily, before soaking into their clothing. They met nobody on the way, only encountered a small herd of fallow deer, which, when startled, jumped the lane in front of them. Cresting the plateau of open ground, they reined in to view the surrounding high ground of the Wealden Forest and the low ground beneath the Ridgeway. Stretching far out into a misty horizon, the River Medway cut like a ragged scar across the white and grey landscape. The low sky had settled into a still milky white, but dark clouds roiled in the distance.

'Do you think the weather will hold?' asked Guy.

'At least until we reach Tonbridge, I think,' replied William, drawing his hood closer about his ears to ward off the chill.

Plumes of mist erupted from their mounts' nostrils as they started forward and rode on towards Dry Hill.

*

Trotting across the empty tiltyard, their heads bent against the sleet hissing into their faces, they thundered across the drawbridge. After being relieved of Felix and Bess, a lone wet and wretched man-at-arms with water dripping off his nose guard, informed them that the sheriff was in the hall.

'Along with everybody else, I take it?' muttered Guy, looking around the deserted inner ward.

He was right. They could hear the noise even before they reached the building that stood next to the gatehouse against the inside wall. It was time for midday victuals, and the whole of the castle's occupants were crowding the benches and trestles, their voices raised to be heard above the din. The air was hazy with wood smoke and heavy with the smell of unwashed bodies, damp boiled leather and wool. The serving maids were busy carrying trays of ale and baskets full of bread, which, by the time they reached the tables, were nearly empty as hands dived in and snatched it as they passed.

They spotted Sir Hugh and Percy seated closest to the roaring fire. Beside them sat young Robin, happily tucking into a hunk of bread, his cheeks flushed from the heat and his blond hair sticking out from beneath the cap he constantly wore. Guy was pleased to see him and Percy sitting side by side and to see a sparkle in Robin's eyes that had not been there before.

'Well, young man, you seem to have settled in nicely. Are these two ne'er-do-wells looking after you?'

'Yes, thank you,' answered Robin, flashing him a row of perfect white teeth before popping the last mouthful of bread into his mouth.

'Guy!' exclaimed Sir Hugh, swivelling round on the bench.

'William too! I had expected to hear from you sooner. Come, come and join us,' he invited, moving up to make room for them both.

Guy and William threw off their cloaks and swung their legs round to sit next to him.

'We would have been here sooner if it were not for the weather,' Guy informed him.

Percy returned Guy's smile of greeting with genuine pleasure. He reclined in a standalone chair at the end of the trestle table, his long stork-like legs stretched out before him and crossed at the ankles. He rested his elbows on each arm of the chair and, locking his long bony fingers together, rested his hands on his stomach. He had gained some weight since Guy had last seen him; his cheeks were rounder and there was a distinct paunch weighing on his belt.

'It's good to see you recovered, Percy. You're looking in much better shape than the last time I saw you.'

'You're not wrong there, sir. Coo, I thought I was a gonna, and that's the truth!'

A line of serving maids emerged from the kitchens to then disperse in all directions around the hall. They watched as the most slovenly and sullen one of the bunch headed their way. She was built like a man, her pulled-up sleeves revealing thick muscular arms, and she had the face of a horse, the poor, unfortunate creature. She lifted the heavy black pot she was carrying as if it were no heavier than a feather and placed it on the end of the trestle with a thump. Picking up a wooden bowl each, they held them up to her in turn, whereupon she ungraciously ladled the onion broth into each, dishing out unequal measures and slopping it everywhere. Robin could not care less how it was served; his face became alight with anticipation and he licked his lips as he watched the golden liquid and silver slithers of onion plopping into his bowl. Lastly, William, who had been meted out a raw deal, tried to hold out for more. Still holding it aloft, he looked from his bowl to the girl and back to the bowl again. Seeing the look of expectancy on his face, the girl scowled, snorted and promptly chucked the ladle back into the pot.

'That's your lot,' she said gruffly before picking it up and flouncing off to the next table.

'It was worth a try, I suppose,' shrugged William, and, with an air of nonchalance, commenced his meagre meal.

Guy was surprised to see Percy still foodless and strangely unperturbed by the fact. Knowing his insatiable appetite, he wondered why. No sooner had he thought on this when he got his answer. From the kitchen came a handsome auburn-haired serving woman. She bustled towards Percy, carrying a tray and a bright smile. Seeing her, Percy sat up straight, rubbed his hands together and planted his feet firmly on the floor. Taking the offered tray, he placed it on his lap. On it sat a huge bowl of mutton stew and what looked like half a loaf of bread! What was it about Percy, Guy wondered. He was a tall, gangly individual, stooped-shouldered with long straight and thinning hair, and a hooked nose. Let's say he was not the shiniest apple on the tree, and yet he was always being fussed over and given preferential treatment by all the best looking women!

'Mutton. Good for aiding my recovery,' he informed the flabbergasted faces of all seated around the trestle. He then picked up an enormous horned spoon and proceeded to shovel it into his mouth.

'Ta, Mary, this is lovely,' he gobbled through a mouthful.

'Oh, tis no trouble, Percy,' she replied, fussing at the loose strands of her hair and tucking them back behind her ears.

'But slow down, or thy guts will complain,' she warned him, standing with her hands on her hips. She smiled on indulgently as

Percy chose to ignore the remark and carried on regardless. She left him engrossed and attacking his half loaf of bread.

After they had all eaten, Sir Hugh beckoned young Robin over to stand at his side.

'Run along, will you, to Burgess Bartholomew's house and leave a message to say we, meaning Sir Guy Guiscard'—he emphasised the *sir*—'William Turner and myself, will be along shortly to speak with him.'

Since his arrival at the castle, Robin had fallen into the role of messenger and attendant to the sheriff and was enjoying every minute of it. He was ready and eager to be away on his quest, but Sir Hugh lay a restraining hand on his arm.

'You know where he lives, do you?' he said, leaning closer to the boy.

'Yes,' replied Robin.

'And where is that?' checked Sir Hugh.

'The big house at the end of Swan Lane, opposite the gatekeepers lodge.'

'That is correct, but have you forgotten something?' asked the sheriff, regarding him closely.

The boy stared at the ground thoughtfully for a while but nothing came to mind.

'I don't think so.'

Sir Hugh bent his head even closer.

'Given our respective stations, do you think "sir" would be appropriate when addressing me?'

The boy looked contrite. He so very much wanted to please.

'Yes, sorry… sir.'

'But you are right, that is where the burgess lives,' conceded the sheriff, straightening up and back to his usual disarming manner.

Smiling at the boy he stood up, his intention being to leave the trestle. But as he turned and lifted a leg to step over the bench, his foot caught it and it was only Robin's quick reflexes that stopped him from taking a tumble.

'Do you need help… sir?' he asked, using his left shoulder as a bolster.

'No thank you, Robin, I can manage. Off you go.'

Robin scampered off.

'He is a good lad but needs reminding of his manners now and again,' said a red-faced Sir Hugh as he extricated himself from the trestle table.

'I hope you have much to report, William. Might I suggest we retire to my chambers? Matters would be better discussed in private, and before we visit the honourable Godfrey Bartholomew.'

*

It was a short walk to Godfrey Bartholomew's house at the end of Swan Lane. It was a newly built two-storey gentleman's residence, timber framed and elevated on a sandstone base.[17] Two huge windows on each floor overlooked the lane not far from the Postern Gate, the eastern gateway into the town. They climbed the steps cut into the sandstone base and Sir Hugh rapped on the front door. A small wizened face appeared at the side window to smartly disappear again. A few seconds later, the heavy oak door was opened by the same man. The hallway was small and a little gloomy, a sconce of candles on the wall was lit against the dark afternoon. After giving up their cloaks, they were ushered into the front room, which by comparison was very spacious and, owing to the huge bow window,

---

[17] On the site of Port Reeves House, East Street.

very light. It was dominated by a large desk where stools stood in front of it and a cushioned chair behind, positioned in the alcove of the window. A good vantage point for Sir Godfrey, Guy imagined, who, needing only to glance to his left, would have full view of the comings and goings at the tollgate.

'Sir Godfrey will be with you shortly,' said the servant retreating from the room.

A great log fire roared in the wide grate, and as soon as the door had closed behind them, the three visitors took themselves over to stand before it to warm themselves. William glanced about the room awestruck.

'I never realised people could live so well,' he said more to himself than to anybody that might be listening.

Colourful Flemish tapestries hung around the walls and a pair of oak settles covered with thick sheepskin rugs stood either side of the great hearth. A shelf of a few books and many parchments lined one wall, and a long table bearing a set of silver cups and a wine flagon lined the other. On a tray next to the flagon lay a block of sealing wax and a gold seal. William picked it up for closer inspection.

'That is the seal of Tonbridge, used to authenticate any correspondence the towns council might make,' the sheriff informed him.

William turned it over in his hands, but had to replace it quickly as the door opened and Sir Godfrey strode into the room. He wore a fine full-length green robe with a fur trimmed collar. Without a word, he swept across the room and, gathering its many folds before him, sat himself at the huge desk. His chain of office, which he wore around his neck, clinked as he waved for them to do the same opposite.

'Gentlemen,' he finally muttered.

Normally full of cheerful self-importance, he looked sombre today.

'So,' he commenced without preliminaries, 'you have some news for me?' he said with a slight edge to his voice. As there were only two stools, William stood stiffly behind Guy.

'Yes, William here has detected a stronghold. It is well hidden, still in the process of being built and sited deep beneath the ridge this side of Ightham,' Sir Hugh began, also without any preamble.

'How did you find it? Did you just happen upon it?'

'No, I followed two of the outlaws,' said William, who went on to explain this undertaking.

'How many men are there at this location?'

'I saw up to about fifteen men, but somehow I do not think that was all of them.'

'Do you think this is the same lot who murdered Geoffrey and Eleanor de Coulances and are responsible for all the disorder of late?

'Yes, I do.'

'Tell me about the ringleader,' he ordered.

William relayed his observations of the dark and brooding stranger.

'I think we have found our man,' put in Guy, tapping the table.

'What do you mean?' questioned Sir Godfrey.

'There was a purpose behind those murders, and for whatever reason, the De Coulances were targeted. Someone put the outlaws up to it to try and cover their own tracks and, not averse to doing somebody else's dirty work, especially if they are dependent on that person, the outlaws carried out the deeds. He may not have struck the fatal blow to Geoffrey's heart or put the noose around Eleanor's neck, but I guarantee it was on this man's say-so.'

Sir Godfrey made the usual steeple with his fingers and fixed Guy with his brown, protuberant eyes.

'Guy, was there a reason, a purpose, why your father died? No. The poor man just happened to be in the wrong place at the wrong time. Reasons, I do not care for. We cannot mitigate any crime because of a 'reason!' he snapped.

His jowls wobbled in indignation and for a fleeting moment a look of genuine distress passed over his face at the mention of his dearest friend and business partner. Guy was taken aback.

'I wholeheartedly agree with you, but I think you have misunderstood my point.'

Sir Godfrey's scowl deepened. He was not used to being spoken to in such a forthright manner. But unperturbed, Guy continued.

'I am not aiming to lessen culpability, just trying to establish what we are dealing with here. My father's death may well have been the result of an indiscriminate act, but regarding the murders, I fear something more sinister was going on there, maybe still is. We should not ignore the fact that other members of the family could yet become victims.'

Godfrey raised his eyebrows at that.

'Do you think that possible?' he asked anxiously.

'Yes, I do.'

He turned to William.

'Will you be able to find this place again?'

'I could not retrace my steps fully. The tracks and game trails they used were too complex, but I left markers on my return journey.'

'Good. This needs to be resolved quickly and time is of the essence. They need to be flushed out before they are ensconced in this stronghold of theirs.'

Sir Hugh could see where this was leading. He shifted in his seat.

'I want you both to take control of this situation,' demanded Sir Godfrey looking from him to Guy.

'But as I said before, we do not have enough men to make a determined attack, and even if we had, the approach is too narrow and there is no way to deploy,' argued the sheriff.

'Would this task be better suited to De Clare?'

Sir Godfrey looked at him impatiently, irritation in his face.

'Dear God, man! We cannot wait for De Clare! No, in his absence, I am granting you full authority and offer any resources you may need to seek out and obtain the heads of these outlaws and their leader.'

Guy suspected that Sir Godfrey was developing political ambitions way above and beyond his administrative duties and, wanting to impress the county elite, who were pressing him for results, felt compelled to take the initiative.

'But without De Clare and his men-at-arms…'

Godfrey drummed his fingers restlessly on the edge of his desk, his heavy features frowning.

'I know I can depend on you and have every faith in your ability,' he interrupted with stern resolution.

There was to be no argument. The interview was over.

The day was grey and the weather had turned bitterly cold again. They had assembled in the courtyard as the first watery rays of the sun brushed the rooftops. Wisps of mist still threaded lazily between the trees and lingered over the pastures. It was not the ideal weather for hunting, but he was restless and needed to get out of the house, for his own sanity if nothing else. All his father and mother seemed to do these days was bicker and irritate each other. His father had been like a bear with a sore head since his 'betrothed' had absconded to the abbey. Life had become a continual round of either oppressive silences or angry reproofs. He had 'disappointed' his father 'terribly', and his mother kept reminding him of how they had lost a most valuable commodity and probably the last chance of making any suitable marriage alliance. With his fingertips he traced the crooked pink tracks running down his cheek. What vexed him most was there was no disguising they were gouged by a comb and therefore inflicted by a mere woman!

Anyway, a pox on her, the stupid, frigid bitch! She could not be in a better place, he thought viciously, snapping up on his horse's bit and making it snort and rear in pain.

'Come on, hurry up, boy!' he snarled at the young kennelhand who finally appeared, his arms almost being pulled from their sockets by the hounds straining at the end of their leashes.

It had been a while since their last hunt and they were baying for blood. The kennel master cracked his whip over their heads to quell their excitement. He released them from their restraints while the boy looked on miserably, his arms crossed over his chest and his hands tucked up under his armpits. Not only were his fingers frozen, his hands had been painfully pinched by the leather straps wrapped around them and were now tingling back to life as the blood started to flow through them again.

Richards hunting party were as eager to be away as he was. They were not his usual companions – they had sloped off home after the last embarrassing fiasco. Today he only had Cuthbert, the young son of a neighbouring manor lord; a groom; and Marcus, their steward, for company. He did not like Marcus. He had not been with them long and Richard could not understand why his father kept him engaged in the household. His pale blue and deep-set piggy eyes were never still and would never meet yours. If, by chance, they did, his gaze would very quickly slide away. Yes, there was something decidedly shifty about the fellow.

On foot was the huntsman, four kennelhands and not far off a dozen dogs, four of which were lymers, a scenting hound and the rest being alaunts, the heaviest and most vicious of the hunting breeds.

King Henry had granted the family a chase in his forest. This gave them private hunting rights, which allowed them and their friends to hunt his roe and fallow deer. Wild boar was also available to them and was a favourite of Richard's. It was a dangerous quarry, its tusks could rip a man in half with just one swipe – but it gave good chase and took a lot of courage, and skill, to bring down.

Passing under the arched gateway, they travelled down the very aptly named Stumble Hill to then cut across Whitelawne land into Dinas Dene. Gobbets of mud flew up to spatter them and their mounts as they splashed through the deep ruts. One of the hounds took a tumble to end up completely covered in the dark, sticky stuff. Richard took the lead, kicking his horse to a steady trot until the trees closed in around them. Here he kept them moving at a slower pace. It would be treacherous to ride any faster. The soft ground was littered with half-buried roots and hidden stones. They followed a steep incline, a deer track so narrow they had to duck and shoulder branches away from their faces. A panicked rabbit fleeing in the wrong direction ran straight into the jaws of a bitch who grabbed its head, shook it and devoured it there and then, its bones cracking and splintering between her teeth. An owl, not afraid to be out in the daylight hours, perched on a bough, hoping to take advantage of any small creatures that might be flushed from their homes. It swooped down, a white ghostly shape, soft feathered and silent to carry off a squealing vole. They reached the brow of a hollow where they stopped to look down into its bowl filled with layers of leaf mould and dead, fallen trees. It was very quiet. Their mounts' hooves made hardly a sound on the damp earth and the hounds were too engrossed in sniffing out a scent trail to make much noise. Richard glanced back over his shoulder to make sure Cuthbert was not lagging behind, but he was right behind him, his young, fresh face bright and alert to everything around him. As they moved down into the hollow and up the other side, dogs and riders spread out. Back on level ground again, they moved into an oak wood where they weaved their way between grey-green trunks speckled with moss, some gnarled and ancient. They splashed across narrow gullies flicking up black mud and leaves, the dogs becoming more and more animated the deeper they penetrated. The deer tracks were getting difficult to follow now, the better trodden paths left way behind them. Then they heard it, a blast on the hunting horn, long and deep. Richard pulled up on the reins and his horse slowed to a halt where it whickered and tramped the ground. He held forth a restraining hand for Cuthbert to do the same and then stood up in his stirrups to get a better view through the trees. They would not be too far away, and he soon spotted the flicker of dog and the glint of spearhead behind the misty trees ahead. A flurry of crows suddenly exploded from their perches amongst the trees. Alarmed, Richard looked up to watch as they wheeled and screeched above their heads. A look of distaste puckered his features. He hated crows – the ugly, big black beg… One of them must have read his thoughts – it defecated mid-air. The propelled excrement just missed its target and landed with a splat on the ground, making Richard flinch.

There was a second blast. The dogs had found a scent. Crows quickly forgotten, Richard turned to Cuthbert, his eyes ablaze with excitement.

'Ready?' he enquired.

Cuthbert nodded, his facial expression a mixture of bloodlust and trepidation. This was not his first hunt, but he was not about to admit that his father had always kept him well away from witnessing or dispensing the final and fatal blow.

'Keep with me!' Richard shouted over his shoulder as he sat back down in the saddle.

Setting his sights to the trail, he kicked his horse into an easy canter to catch up with the rest of the party. The hound's innate instinct to seek out and pursue was evident as they bowled along, their mud-caked muzzles skimming over the ground's surface. There also appeared to be an element of organisation and teamwork amongst them when the rest of the dogs closed in behind the bitch that had detected the trail. The four horsemen remained a distance behind the pack with the huntsman and kennelhands loping alongside them. They divided up to travel around and regroup again once they had passed a massive rotten log, which had fallen across their path. The trail brought them to a stream where the dogs momentarily lost the scent. Heads down, they ranged up and down the far bank, before once more charging off a little further downstream. Spying their quarries' tracks, the huntsman knelt on the muddy bank to inform them that it was indeed a boar they were pursuing. It was not long before they caught up with the hounds and got a glimpse of the beast in flight. Once spotted, two more blasts were blown on the horn and, with their prey close to hand, the dogs started to bay. They travelled as fast as they dared, knowing that as long as they kept up with their target, it would tire soon enough. But they were led a long and determined chase. The boar crashed through tangled undergrowth and made them climb hillocks, up and down again the other side. It slowed them down by nipping between tree trunks, the gaps so narrow they had no alternative but to swing wide. Branches whipped at their faces and snagged their clothing. A flock of starlings burst from the dense foliage of a yew tree, one of which narrowly missed Cuthbert's face. Startled, he raised an arm to swipe it away. Another stream barred their way. Some dogs splashed through while others leapt over it without breaking stride. Eventually the pursued started to tire and, realising its pursuers were closing in, panicked and stumbled down a deep defile. Terrified and unable to scramble up the other side, it turned to make a stand. Some of the pack jumped the ditch to mill around looking down, while a few of the braver ones slid down to encircle it. The horses were lathered and the men on foot flagging by the time they caught up. All were breathing hard, the riders too. The boar nervously turned this way and that, looking through one little eye and then the other, but being afraid of its power and strength, none of the hounds were eager to be the first to move in. They hung back and barked sharp, persistent barks. The boar threatened each one with the sweep of its tusks. One brave hound rushed in. The boar turned, kicked out with her back legs and sent it sprawling. Unguarded, another darted in to bury its teeth into a haunch. She screamed and rounded to rake it across the face. The hound yelped, shook its head and moved away to dab at the wound with a forepaw. Although now injured and weakened, the boar managed to keep its tormentors at bay until the butt of two spears beat them off, while two more struggled to pin her down. The dogs had worked themselves up into such a frenzy and, being deprived of their kill, started to snap irritably at each other. Their master whacked the backside of one bitch who persistently worried at the boar's leg. She turned and, baring her teeth, lunged at him, narrowly missing his face, and making him stumble backwards. She got a trouncing for that.

Richard swung down from his horse and handed the reins to his groom. Cuthbert stayed seated in his saddle looking on. His eyes had widened to the size of finger bowls. He had never hunted boar before, and now it came to it, his excitement had turned to consternation at having to butcher the squealing and squirming beast before him. Richard made an impatient sweeping gesture.

'Come now, Cuthbert. Your first kill awaits you,' he said expelling clouds of warm breath into the chill air.

Slowly, apprehensively and with his breakfast churning in his stomach, Cuthbert dismounted. His inexperience showed as he licked his lips nervously and made a visible effort to work up his courage. Richard slyly chuckled to himself at this shaveling's obvious discomfort. He remembered dispatching his first boar rapidly and with great relish. Cuthbert unsheathed his sword, made his way to the bank and tentatively sidled down.

'Slice its throat and then drive down hard into its heart,' advised Richard casually, looking on with his hands on his hips.

He had re-sheathed his sword. If necessary, the spears would be used to finish off the job. Cuthbert swallowed hard, drew himself up and strode forward. But his posturing became excruciatingly prolonged and the kennelhands began to really struggle to hold their writhing captive down. They exchanged frantic sidelong glances, which told each other that they would not be able to hold on for much longer. Eventually and sufficiently, although not wholly primed for the task, Cuthbert brought down his blade. As he was about to rake it across the beast's exposed throat, there was heard a hissing sound and a thunk. Alarmed at Richard's howl of pain, Cuthbert turned to see him down on one knee, holding his shoulder-blade. Through his fingers protruded an arrow shaft. Momentarily stunned and taken completely off their guard, the kennelhands released their hold on the boar. Not missing the opportunity, the creature sprung to its feet to make a getaway, but not before gouging a huge slice out of her would-be killer's thigh. With a blood-curdling scream, Cuthbert too went down. Seeing their catch racing off into the distance, the hounds turned tail and followed in hot pursuit. Thinking they were under attack, and intent on their own welfare, the huntsman and kennelhands also made a run for it. The groom too. The scene was chaotic. The only one who held fast was Marcus the steward who, blaspheming under his breath, calmly dismounted and went to his master's aid.

Charles de Coulances sat slumped in a chair, cradling a goblet of wine, his tunic front stained red where his unsteady hands had spilt it. He was unkempt, his face was sunken and grey with stubble, and his eyes were red and sore. Deep shadows draped the walls and his mind. So deep in thought was he, he had not noticed that half the candles had guttered out and he was sitting in semi-darkness.

He looked down at the blood red liquid, nearly black in the dim light, and swirled it around. Sitting back in his chair, he sighed heavily and closed his eyes.

As he settled, his mind began to wander and after a while, a slow smile spread across his face.

God, she was so beautiful. His breath caught in his throat like it always did when his eyes rested upon her. She had the same dark features as Isabelle, but they were softer – warmer he would say. Her eyes were rich, deep and inviting and she had a smile that could lighten the dullest of days. He could feel her fingers fumbling for his, and he instinctively closed his hand around them. They wandered beneath the summer sun, through pasture and forest glade, far from anyone who might disturb them. He caressed her cheeks, neck and breasts, kissed her mouth that tasted of honey and cloves and buried his face in her unbound gloriously thick, softly perfumed hair…

He had loved her with all his heart and she was to have been his bride, but his parents had other idea and he had buckled under pressure and married Isabelle instead. He should have defied them, but he had always been cowardly and weak! His mouth twisted in a bitter grimace. She had been carrying his child but they still insisted he abandon her, and to his shame, he had. In the early days of their marriage, it had come to Isabelle's ears that he had fathered a son and it had cut deeply. Many men fathered illegitimate children, many of whom would be acknowledged and even brought up in the family home, but she had insisted the child's very existence be denied. His first, true-born son was Geoffrey. The shadow of the nameless woman who had borne him his bastard son still, to this day, lay between them, and he had resigned himself years ago that a man could not always be where he longed to be.

He opened his eyes where moisture glistened in each corner. He felt guilty now. He should not be thinking thus, not at a time like this. His oldest son was barely cold in his grave, with his wife lying alongside him, and upstairs his youngest lay desperately clinging to life. A father should not lose sons before him. It was a cruel thing to bear for any man. And Isabelle, for all her cold, hard exterior had not borne her grief well. Sometimes he heard her weeping quietly, but he could not bring himself to go to her. They should be grieving together, giving each other comfort, by God! His wife, his sons; he had let them down abysmally. He placed the empty goblet down on the table and his hand shook as he reached for the flagon to refill it.

*

Richard had lost a lot of blood. Dosed with syrup of poppy, he shivered and moaned feverishly. His breathing was harsh and he was still conscious. His mother sat by his bedside. She brushed his sweat-matted hair back from his forehead.

After the excruciatingly painful removal of the arrowhead, he had been put to bed and made as comfortable as possible. They had then sent for Sheriff Breton, who had questioned Marcus the steward and the huntsman and kennelhands who had eventually straggled back, minus a handful of the dogs. They all told of the arrow being shot from the cover of trees behind them. That was it. There was no evidence to associate anyone with the crime, and he could only come to the conclusion that it was probably perpetrated by the same person or persons that had murdered Geoffrey. Sir Hugh recalled Guy's concerns at their meeting with Godfrey Bartholomew. He had been right to fear for the rest of the family, and the sheriff had relayed this to Lady Isabelle, emphasising that she and Lord Charles should stay vigilant. It was then that she had become very afraid indeed. He had tried to calm her and had intimated that all would be resolved shortly, but he would not elaborate any further.

'Richard, can you hear me?'

Her son groaned and rolled his head from side to side.

'Do you know who might have done this to you?' she implored.

Richard opened his eyes. They wandered vacantly around the room until they rested on her concerned face.

'An arrow from nowhere... from the trees...'

His voice cracked and trailed off. Suddenly his eyes lit up and in a split second of clarity he whispered, 'Marcus.'

'What do you mean? Marcus did not do this to you, he brought you home,' replied his mother, nonplussed.

But Richard was not to be deterred. Back in his febrile state again he mumbled thickly 'Marcus, Marcus…' over and over.

'Marcus?' Isabelle mouthed to herself.

Her mind raced. Why was he so intent on the steward? Suddenly, as if she had been struck by an arrow herself, she gasped. Her eyes grew wide with alarm. It all fell into place.

'Judith,' she called to one of her maids, 'get Giles here, quickly!'

'Yes, m'lady.'

It was no good calling upon her husband; he was too engrossed in his own self-pity. No doubt he was downstairs now, drowning his sorrows in a flagon of wine, or two, she thought maliciously. He was such a weak man. She had always been the strong one and greatly resented the fact. She promised herself that one day she would allow herself the luxury of not being the dependable one. But that was for the future, not now.

It was not long before Giles entered the bedchamber. The door had been left ajar. He knocked and nervously stepped over the threshold into the candlelit room, wringing his cap in his hands. He wondered why he had been summoned by the mistress of the house, and at this late hour. Walking towards the bed, he looked down on the young master lying there. Even in this dim light he could see he did not look too well at all. When the mistress turned to face him, she looked tired and drawn, and her usually well-groomed hair was tangled and in disarray. Even so, she still fixed him with that unblinking, cold gaze of hers, her thin mouth set tight and her chin projecting contemptuously. She got straight to the point.

'Who could have known where and when Geoffrey and Richard were going hunting that day?'

Giles thought for a bit.

'The huntsman and kennelhands, I suppose, and those in the party.'

'Who could have known the whereabouts, albeit vague, of Eleanor and her escort returning from Suffolk?'

Giles thought again.

'Somebody from within the household?'

There was a pause while Lady Isabelle's eyes bored deeply into his. It made him feel uncomfortable. He shifted from one foot to the other and wondered where this was leading. Then she raised her eyebrows questioningly.

'What conclusions have you reached, if any, of Marcus' integrity?' she asked.

Significantly, at the mention of his name, Richard stirred in his bed.

'Marcus?'

'Yes, Marcus, the steward,' she said impatiently.

Although Giles' expression remained unfathomable, a wave of relief swept through him. He thought he himself was under scrutiny for whatever the mistress was alluding to. He did not actually have an opinion on the steward. Since arriving at Whitelawne he had kept himself very much to himself, and just got on with the job in hand.

'Come now, you must have a sentiment?' said Lady Isabelle coldly.

Giles cleared his throat.

'To my mind, he lacks character.'

'Please be more explicit.'

Isabelle gave him a hard, measuring look. Giles swallowed.

'Well, I say that, but in truth he has not allowed anyone to get close enough to him to find out what he really is like. Whether that is intentional, I do not know. But to me, he has always seemed elusive, staying in the background and not drawing too much attention to himself and yet having his eyes and ears everywhere.'

'Aha, I see.' It was as she thought.

Giles saw Lady Isabelle nod to herself as if what he'd said had confirmed something.

'Giles, my belief is that our enemy, whoever that might be, has an accomplice, someone from within this household, and I think that person is Marcus.'

Giles looked shocked. 'You mean Marcus was involved in the murders of Geoffrey and Eleanor, and this attempt on Richard's life?'

'Yes, I do. How else would their whereabouts have been known?'

Giles could not quite believe what he was hearing.

'But for what reason?'

'Oh, for any number of reasons. Which specific one, who can say? All I know is, someone is intent on destroying this family. Where is Marcus now?'

'I saw him riding out of the courtyard earlier today, alone. He is yet to return.'

Isabelle's intuition told her that he would not return. He probably knew he was on the brink of discovery and had decided to make a break for it while he still had the chance.

'Thank you, Giles. You may retire now as there is very little we can do tonight. The rat has scurried away. We will have to ferret him out another day.'

*

321

He was a bastard. He knew nothing of his father; only who he was. His mother would not speak of him, he had found out by lurking in the shadows and listening at cracks in doors, a practice he had become very experienced at over the years. He had asked her once for the truth of it.

'Never ask me about your father,' she had replied in a voice flat of any emotion. She would not even look on his face when she spoke to him.

And that was it, he never asked again. He tried to convince himself that it really did not matter, but it continued to eat away at him and, in the end, he really did need some answers. Swallowing his pride he plucked up the courage to ask his ancient grandmother. He did not fare any better there, it only served to teach him a new word, 'bastard'. She had spat it out with such vehemence, her face twisting with disgust. She never spoke to him as a rule but once she had started the tirade, there was no stopping the vile words that tumbled from her lips. She told him he had been born out of lust and deceit. He had run from the room, frightened and humiliated. From that day forth, any eyes that rested upon him made him cringe with shame. He imagined them looking deep into his soul and finding him corrupt and unclean. As he grew up he became rebellious and troublesome and would disappear for days, staying out in the forest alone. Nobody missed him. He would build camps in the hollow of huge oaks and pretend to be a great lord who owned all that he surveyed. He had a secret training ground in a clearing where he hid a sword and where he would practice his swordsmanship on a dummy made of cloth, stuffed with straw and hung from a tree. He would lunge, thrust, pivot and parry, hour after hour. He taught himself to use his sword with his left hand until he was nearly as proficient with it as he was with his right. Sometimes, if his mood was dire, he would climb the tallest oak, swinging himself up to move easily from one limb to another to perch morosely, watching over the household from afar. He would see Old John the manservant chopping wood in the yard, and the cook picking herbs from the kitchen garden. He would watch the young serving girls lounging and gossiping over the well and spy Flora, the very young kitchen maid, slyly being led away to the stables by Old John's son, Roderick the groom. Bet his mother didn't know *that* was going on under her nose! He would wander for miles, getting to know every game trail and every inch of the forest. One day, he came upon a small dwelling built of whitewashed cob, surrounded by a beautiful garden where an old lady lived alone. She asked him in for refreshment and he found out her name was Eadyth. He told her his name was Godric and where he lived, and she told him she knew of his mother and grandmother. Hungry for details, he lapped up anything she could tell him. He was told how beautiful and full of life his mother had been. She'd had many suitors come a-calling, and her mother too enjoyed a reputation as a great beauty and a fine hostess. Not now they weren't, he thought. Now they were sour faced and dour. The house, she said, was always full of guests, fun and laughter. Nobody called at the house any more either. Then along came his father. They fell deeply in love and desperately wanted to be wed but, unfortunately, his family had other plans for him and she was not to play any part in them. He left her with child, and minus her suitability. The ladies' fortunes took a downturn. Everybody shunned them. Extended invitations were ignored, and none were forthcoming.

Godric and Eadyth were to become firm friends and he would visit her often. She called him her 'little lord'. He liked that. She gave him the attention he craved, and in return he afforded her his company. She mothered him as much as he would allow and her affection was tolerated up to a point, but he shrank from her if she ever tried to hug him.

When he was fourteen, his mother had thrown him out, telling him he was old enough to take care of himself. He went to live with Eadyth.

She tried to convince him that bastards had honour too, but he could not, would not believe it. He would never forget what he was, but over the years he learnt to armour himself against the shame and the stigma it had brought him. It had hardened his heart, and he knew it. He had contemplated long and hard over the years, lying abed at night, and vowed that one day he would find this man who had abandoned him and his mother, and he would crush him and the like who had cast them aside.

When the old lady died, he had buried her under a blossoming apple tree at the bottom of her beautiful garden, left the little house and gone to Rochester. Why Rochester? He did not know really; probably because he knew he would be anonymous there. He became a soldier-at-arms at Rochester Castle, eventually becoming master-at-arms. Even a bastard could rise in the military. There was no denying he was very accomplished. In a very short space of time, he transformed a garrison of rabble into an army of sorts. But he worked them hard. After a particularly gruelling session where he had kept them out in the cold and wet bailey far longer than was necessary, one of the soldiers had called him a bastard under his breath and he had heard him.

'Who called me that?' he roared, turning to sweep the line with his broadsword and his bitter, dark and sharp eyes.

The offender did not own up, but then he did not have to. All eyes turned on him. Godric beat him to a pulp, finishing off by slamming his heel down hard on his nose with a sickening crunch. The assault had cost him his position. He was immediately discharged, being told that while brutal, unrestrained violence might be acceptable on the battlefield, exerting such a lack of control and discipline with one's own men was totally unbefitting of an army officer.

Yes, he was a bastard all right, in more ways than one. He was cold and hard, and mean.

The wind howling around the hall broke into his thoughts as did the whinny of a horse outside. A log shifted in the fire. He sat on his chair, oiling the razor-sharp edges of the sword that lay across his lap. The hall was hazy with smoke and heavy with the sweet, sickly smell of roasting horse. They'd had to butcher one today. No more chickens roamed the yard and he guessed that, by now, they had acquired all that there was to be had from local larders. A tun of ale had been fermenting for a few days and tonight it had been deemed ready to drink. Cups and goblets were being drained at a rapid pace. His head came up as he heard shouts and a bench being overturned. A scuffle had broken out. He'd not had the same level of success training this bunch of animals. Thieves, poachers, rapists and killers, the lot of them. They were all ignorant brutes. There was not one amongst them who could think for himself. They all needed to be led, told what to do, and the more time he spent with them, the more he despised them. He stood up and peered down through the gloom. He could see two men pacing a circle, eye-balling each other, one reaching down to pull a blade from his gartered sheepskin greaves. Surrounded, they were being egged on by others whose eyes were alight with excitement at the prospect of seeing some entertaining violence.

'Enough!' he shouted stridently down the hall.

That stopped them in their tracks. They all subsided with ill-grace, crestfallen at being denied the chance to liven up the monotony of their miserable existence.

Godric sat down again where he fixed his spiteful black eyes on Whitelawne's steward sitting at the trestle nearest the fire. He looked at ease, sipping from his cup of ale and conversing with his one-eyed, boil infested neighbour. No doubt he *felt* at ease too, being out of harm's way, the gutless scut, he thought malevolently.

'Things were getting a little too close for comfort,' he had whined and, 'I had a sense my time would soon be up and that I needed to leave.'

In other words, he had got the wind up and bolted. That was a grievous error. By doing so, he had jeopardised his cover. He did not profess to like the fellow. He was a quisling, a sneak, and a coward. All the traits he despised. He probably had a loose tongue too. To him, he was just a means to an end, and he had served his purpose. It was near time he got rid of him.

*

Guy was pleased to reach the outskirts of Tonbridge just before curfew. It was nearly dark and the temperature had dropped again. Snow threatened in the wind and despite his fur-lined hood, his ears were aching with cold.

As he crossed the bridge over the fosse, a lone sentry emerged to challenge him.

'Halt! Who goes there?' he barked as he walked towards him, the patches of refrozen snow crunching beneath his boots.

Plumes of mist erupted from his mouth and nostrils as he breathed in and exhaled the frosty air. Guy snatched off his hood and thrust out his arm to identify himself.

'Sir Guy Guiscard from Starvecrow, here to pay attendance on the sheriff of Tonbridge.'

The cold and miserable guard scrutinised his armband. He then nodded and, without a word, moved to one side to let him pass.

Felix plodded past the grander two-storey houses on the High Street where the rich merchants lived. The air was heavy with woodsmoke belching out from the chimneys and, from one house in particular, flickering candlelight filtered out through all of the windows. Guy surreptitiously looked in to get a brief glimpse into the occupant's warm and cosy life. A roaring fire burned in the grate, its flames glinting on the silverware set on a well laden table. He heard laughter and the chink of glass. Carrying on down the street, he looked over to his right, where the mean dwellings of the Shambles lay and, by contrast, all was in darkness. There was no flickering candlelight and only a few woeful wisps of smoke rising from a handful of chimneys. He shivered and huddled further into his cloak. He was cold and hungry. He needed something tasty to eat, a warmed mug of ale and a comfortable seat before he ventured into the stone-cold castle, so he headed for The Chequers. He made his way round to the stables and left Felix with young John, who was happy to take charge of him. As he turned the corner of the tavern, he nearly bumped into a drunk who, propping himself against the wall with one arm, was urinating up it. Making him start and stumble, the drunk then proceeded to pee over his own shoes. He staggered away, fiddling with the laces of his hose and grumbling to himself. Guy shook his head as he took to the tavern steps.

As much eye-smarting smoke filled the taproom as made its slow escape up and out through the high, central roof vents. The popular tavern was never empty. He nodded to half a dozen old men seated around a table playing dice. Alys, standing behind her counter drying pots, recognised this handsome gentleman from his previous visits. She looked him up and down appreciatively.

'Good evenin', sir. What can I get you?' she called over to him.

There was more than a hint of suggestion in her voice, and her look was as predatory as a dockside cat primed to pounce on an unwary mouse. Guy had never been one to court female attention; even so, he got more than his fair share of admiring glances from the fairer sex.

'Good evening, Mistress Ralf. Ale, warmed if you please, and a serving of your mutton stew would be most welcome,' he called back, giving her one of his disarming smiles.

'Right you are, sir.'

He made his way over to the huge fire, where the two resident dogs lay sprawled out in their usual place before the hearth. They both lifted their heads to inspect the stranger who dared to encroach on their space, only to yawn noisily before flopping back down again to resume toasting their snouts in the glowing warmth. It was not long before he heard the hiss of a red-hot poker, taken from the same glowing embers, and plunged into a pot of ale. With a blush and a shy smile the young serving girl placed the foaming liquid in front of him.

As Guy sat thawing out and waiting for his mutton stew, he reflected on all that had happened since his return from the Holy Land. After three years of fighting abroad, he thought he might have found himself at a loss, but he had not of course reckoned on the events that had materialised over the last four months. For a decade or more, he had flourished the Three Lions over the King's lands and followed the red crossed banner across Christendom. He had fought in winter and summer, in rain, snow, and in the scorching heat. He had killed more men than he would care to admit, but each and every one of them had been an enemy of either his King and countrymen, or his religion. He had come close to death on a number of occasions and had the scars to prove it. He sighed heavily. It all seemed a lifetime ago now but his fighting days were not over yet. He had to admit he was feeling both excited and apprehensive about the forthcoming campaign. It was not going to be straightforward. The route was complicated and it was certainly not the ideal weather. He was broken from his quiet introspection by Alys bustling over with a tray to place a steaming plate of stew before him.

'That looks delicious.'

The land lady scooped up the money Guy had left on the table for her.

'You are most welcome, sir,' she said, holding his gaze as she provocatively placed it down between her very generous breasts.

Guy's eyebrows lifted.

Had he been there, Hugh would most certainly have been mortified to see the spectacle, but it did not phase Guy. Well, only a little bit. He raised a fist to his mouth to clear his throat and compose himself.

'Yes, well, thank you, Alys,' he said, picking up his ale to take a sip.

As she swayed back to her counter, he had to chuckle to himself. My word, she was a tease. And certainly all woman!

As he ate, he turned his mind to Lucie. She and Heloise were still safely ensconced in Dene Abbey, and that was where he wanted them both to stay – at least until all this mess was over and done with. Heloise had repeated her vow never to marry Richard, even if it meant staying there forever. He hoped that would not happen, and in any case, it was touch and go whether Richard would actually survive the recent attempt on his life.

He then thought back to earlier times when, in childhood, he and Lucie had become firm friends. As they had got older, that friendship had grown into something deeper – for him anyhow – and he had dared to hope that Lucie's regard for him was mutual. When his squire service was completed, he had every intention of requesting his father's permission to ask for her hand in marriage. Without doubt he knew it would raise a few eyebrows – after all etiquette dictated he should marry a female of equal eligibility – but his father had never been a traditionalist and always did have a penchant for pushing the boundaries just that little bit further. But he had never given Lucie a sign of his true feelings, and on one of his visits home, he was to learn that she had become betrothed to Owen. On hearing the news, he felt his grief swell so strongly he thought that he might vomit. He felt absolutely bereft. His first instinct had been to go to her and beg her to marry him instead, tell her that they were born to be together forever, but Sir Robert had fervently forbade him to do so.

'You cannot. It is only your pride that makes you feel thus. She has had no inkling of your true feelings towards her, and you will only succeed in spoiling the young couple's blissful attachment.'

So he had taken his father's advice, concealed his disappointment and wished them both well.

'You will learn by this,' his father had told him rather sternly, though with some sympathy when he found him one night deep in his cups before the fire, drunkenly berating himself for dragging his feet. 'This will teach you to listen to your inner convictions and to voice or act on them without delay.'

It had been a good lesson and held him in good stead for the coming years, and he was now determined not to let a second opportunity slip through his fingers. Starvecrow needed her and he needed her, and when all this was over, he had every intention of declaring it.

Thoroughly thawed, replete and resolute, he made his way to the castle.

The inner bailey lay shrouded in river mist. The men had rose well before light and were making ready, loading two ox-carts, one with provisions, an assortment of spare weapons, helmets and aventail, the other with newly-scoured hauberks and shields. Torchlight shone on the helmets and played across the rivets of the mail shirts piled high in the cart. These were deemed too cumbersome and impractical for the men to march in and would not be donned until it was necessary. It had also been decided that due to the nature of the terrain, all were to travel on foot. Once everything was loaded, Sir Hugh turned to inspect the garrison of fifty personnel assembled there. Weapons had been honed and bows restrung. Boiled leather jerkins had been cleaned and mud brushed from boots and cloaks. He was satisfied to see that he had some semblance of an army, although it was a small one. Hugo Corbiere had gone to Rochester to collect reinforcements and had returned with Constable Herbert Meakins, four knights, and twenty foot soldiers and archers. As well as the Tonbridge contingent amounting to twenty of their own soldiers, combined with the few archers they had, there was Percy, Guy, Corbiere, himself and, of course, the two Turner brothers. Apart from Guy and the knights from Rochester, who had experience of fighting on the battlefield, they were all far from being the best swordsmen, but what they lacked in skill, hopefully they made up for in determination. He then turned to Guy.

'Ready?'

Guy nodded, saluted him, smiled and returned his hand to rest upon his sword belt. Sir Hugh then turned to address Percy.

'And what about you? Ready to go back to work?'

'Too right I bloody am. Let's go get these arse'oles!' Percy replied eagerly.

Sir Hugh abandoned his attentive expression and gave his usual withering look, but Percy did not care; he just wanted to get on with the job. Turning to the ranks, there were nods and 'ayes' of assent. Sir Hugh held up a thick leather-gloved hand.

'With me then!' he called, and the double-file column set off at a steady marching pace under the portcullis, over the drawbridge and across the outer bailey, the frost making the ground shine whitely in the grey darkness that marked the approach of dawn.

The horsegate keeper, having been raised from his warm bed so early to open the gate, looked on groggily, shivering and yawning as the small army marched out over the frozen fosse. They made their way up Dry Hill, travelling past the lane where the manorial windmill sails sat black and silent. The rhythmic din of boots, hooves from the oxen, and the carts creaking and swaying under their loads, reverberated around the quietness of the pre-dawn. As the first pale light broke through, they could see the trees and pastures around them still frozen white, as they had been for weeks. It was an unusually harsh winter but mercifully the snow had stayed away for the time being. Progress was slow, the ruts in the road were deep and frozen solid. It was tough going for the men, and every so often they had to stop to allow the ox-carts a chance to catch up. They travelled the main route, passing Starvecrow Manor, up to the junction to bear left along the ridge, past Dene Abbey and down to the lane that marked the end of Starvecrow's border and the start of Stumble Hill and the small hamlet of Shipbourne. They stopped by a little wooden bridge that crossed a babbling ice-rimmed brook. At its edge, a few ducks sat huddled together with their beaks tucked under their wings. It was too cold for them; none dared to venture into the clear, ice-cold water. A bitter wind gusted from the east, piercing through the men's cloaks and bringing with it a light flurry of snow, which spiralled and danced through the air. This was their last opportunity to break fast before entering the forest. Sir Hugh dismounted stiffly from the first cart. At the bottom of Starvecrow Hill, he had really started to struggle, so much so that Guy had suggested he sit up with one of the drivers. He had readily accepted and allowed himself to be man-handled up onto the cart. He now paced about, trying to get some feeling back into his cold limbs and he rubbed at his lower back, nursing an ache, no doubt resulting from the bumpy ride on the hard wooden seat. He ordered the bread, cheese and costrels of ale to be taken down from the cart and distributed amongst the men.

When they had finished their fast, the command was given to 'berk up!' They helped each other don the heavy chainmail and to adjust the aventail attached to each helmet. Because the ox-carts were to remain by the roadside, the extra weaponry was shared out amongst them. As well as carrying swords, lances and shields, maces, axes and knives were tucked down behind belts. The archers too were expected to carry two quivers of arrows, each slung across their backs instead of only one.

'We move on!'

William and Jack led, and officers and knights came next, with the foot soldiers following.

They weaved their way in silence, north-west across the wooded valley. The going got even tougher. In some places the men had to make their way in single file. Guy no longer recognised the landscape and he was not the only one. None of them had ever ventured this far into the forest, as there had never been a reason to. Fortunately William, being the most competent of trackers, was confident he knew their location. He and Jack had since gone over the outgoing route again, retracing the markers William had lain down on his way back from the holdfast. They had also re-routed in places where the terrain would be less of an impediment to them. But they had no idea how long it would take to reach their destination. A lone man travelling through the terrain as William had been was very different to an army of about fifty men, hampered by heavy battle dress and weaponry.

After marching for just over an hour, they came to a halt just inside the ash wood, where the tree line curved around the hillside. Here the men were told to rest, and they gratefully sank to the ground, their faces red with exertion and their shoulders and arms aching under the weight of their hauberks.

'That's the wood we are heading for,' pointed out William.

Guy followed the curve of the trees into the distance and saw the dark tangled opening.

'You can see the steep wooded bluff behind it. At its foot is the holdfast.'

Guy could see the bare patches of rock and the ragged silhouette of trees on top of the ridge.

Last night they had discussed variations of a plan, but a visual on the holdfast was needed before finalising any strategy of action, so William, the sheriff, Percy, Corbiere and Guy set off on a reconnaissance mission.

'You stay here with the men until we get back,' Meakins was told.

They moved through the ash wood and then threaded their way through the dense, dark thicket to come to the now frozen stream. Most managed to cross it without mishap, but as Percy tentatively stepped onto it, his boots could not get a purchase. Putting his arms out to steady himself, he bent over to place both hands down on the ice. Bottom up, he propelled himself across the surface. Muttering curses, he came to a stop on his knees in a clump of tufted grass.

'Shhh! Stay down,' hissed William, looking back and waving his hand up and down.

'The holdfast is just over this rise. Once on the brow we will be exposed, so slowly does it.'

Crouching low, they took to the slope. Halfway up, on William's gestured command, they lay flat to edge their way forward. They stopped to crouch behind a tree that had fallen, quite conveniently, across the top of the rise. Guy laid a hand upon the rough bark and slowly raised himself up to furtively peer over the trunk. He got his first glimpse of the holdfast. It was exactly as William had described it; the narrow timber bridge spanning the deep ditch, the longhouse, the outhouse, the still unfinished palisade, which was a Godsend, and the horse enclosure. How many horses were in there he could not see from this vantage point. There were no lookouts posted, but then what reason would the outlaws have to think they might be attacked at any time? It had continued to snow and was beginning to settle. A light dusting lay upon the ground and over the thick thatch and sod roof of the longhouse. Icicles hung from the overhang where snow had started to melt, only to freeze again. Wisps of smoke rose from the roof vent, and all was quiet. It was still early, so hopefully all of them, including their leader, were still in there asleep. Reconnaissance over, they returned looking grim faced and determined.

'What's the final plan then?' asked Meakins.

They put their heads together and quietly discussed final tactics. When they had finished, it was Guy who addressed the troop.

'Right, men, gather round and listen up! We are meeting an unknown quantity here. There could be as many of them as there are of us, maybe more, so we need to hit them hard and fast. There is only one way into the camp, that being the same way out, over a narrow bridge, which will only take two abreast. The bridge spans a deep ditch. *Try to keep out* of the ditch! You will be sitting ducks down there. The palisade is only half finished, the finished section being to the left. Backed up against a wall of rock too steep for them to use as an escape route, we shall be meeting them full on, and by advancing in a broad arc, hopefully will keep them contained. But first we need to flush them out. This is what we shall do.'

The men listened intently while Guy went over the plan of action. It was not the most sophisticated of plans, which initially relied greatly on surprise. When he had finished, Sir Hugh stepped into his place and scanned the faces before him. There were men of all ages; some young and fresh-faced, and others as old as himself. Some had seen active service, others had not. Because of the obstacles they faced, he knew there would be casualties, and that saddened him.

'Whatever lies ahead, I trust that God will see us through safely,' he told them sombrely.

Heads were lowered and there were mumbles of 'amen' and 'God have mercy on us'. Sir Hugh then turned to Guy and placed a hand on his shoulder.

'And God be with you, my friend.'

The familiar gesture and the sincerity of his words brought a lump to Guy's throat.

'And you,' was all he could manage to say.

He stalked away to stand alone for a few moments and hold his head in silent prayer, before making his way back to the company.

'Line up!' he called out tersely.

For all their sakes, he wanted to get this over with.

'Stay together, stay with me and from now on, *not* a sound!'

They trod carefully, taking care to hold their weapons close against their bodies. They moved into the wood and up onto the brow as quietly as possible. Guy gritted his teeth, praying that no noise would betray them. They then quickly spread out around the perimeter of the ditch. The longer they spent organising themselves, the greater the chance they would give themselves away. Once in position, the aventail flap was hooked over throats and chins, and forearms were passed through the leather straps of each shield to grip the topmost cross in hand. First, the front line knelt down on one knee, their lances pointing obliquely from ground to sky. Amongst the line, William and Jack knelt side by side. Both felt ill at ease. Jack's heart thudded in his chest and his hands trembled. William closed his eyes, suddenly feeling sick.

'Stay close, little brother,' he whispered.

Their eyes locked. God, what were they doing here, he asked himself. They were farm labourers, not soldiers. Neither of them had ever held a weapon before this day. Then, in his mind's eye, an image of Sir Robert appeared. *That* was the reason. Jack, as if he knew his brother's thoughts, nodded in acknowledgement. He then dropped his gaze, swallowed hard and faced front. For justice or for vengeance, they were here to settle a score.

Behind them, intermittently, stood the archers, their arrows notched and ready to fly. Five paces further back were the swordsmen, shields held in front and swords already unsheathed. A stone bounced down into the ditch, disturbed by one of the lancers. Guy turned his head and winced at the sudden sound. His heart thudded in his chest and his sword hand opened and closed around its hilt. Two archers, one at each end of the arc, proceeded to make fire with bow-drill and char-cloth, assisted by a soldier passing over tinder and dry brushwood from a sack. They all worked skilfully and quickly together, and in no time at all, a flaming arrow was notched and drawn back by each of the archers. They looked on Guy and waited for his signal. He nodded.

The two arrows were loosed, quickly followed by two more, and two more after that. They flew through the morning mist and light snow, trailing pale ribbons of fire to land on the roof. The snow was not deep enough to snuff out the flames, but they took a while to take a hold. Thin tendrils of smoke rose up into the sky and then the dryer thatch underneath started to crackle and spit. They all watched, waited and listened on the crest of the wooded ridge that overlooked the holdfast.

*

Something had woken him. Godric lay fully awake, listening. He sat up and pulled the thick curtains back from around his bed in the far corner of the dais. Swinging his legs round to sit on its edge, he immediately felt the chill air, and the rank odour of unwashed bodies, stale ale and urine started to invade his nostrils. He wrinkled his nose in disgust and pulled on his boots and studded thick leather jerkin. The fire had burned down to embers and the haze of smoke

339

around the hall was not unusual, but when he heard the crackle of thatch and noticed smoke starting to swirl down from the roof, he looked up into the rafters with alarm.

The sharp toe of his boot woke half a dozen men.

'Get up you lazy, low-born scum!' he growled.

Some woke up with a start and a grunt; others rolled over groaning, holding their heads and feeling the effects of excess from the night before. One muttered a sleepy complaint only to be kicked again even harder.

'Wake up, the roof's on fire!'

This roused them into action. Headaches forgotten, some made a mad panic for the door, and one made to clamber out through a window.

He did not know why but Marcus made his way over to peer through the deerhide flaps. Godric heard his sharp intake of breath.

'What is it?' he hissed.

'There's men outside.'

'What do you mean, men outside?' he questioned irritably, buckling his sword belt around his waist.

'Armed men. Soldiers with lances and swords.'

'How many?'

'Too many to count!'

'Then we're dead men!'

As if in affirmation of Godric's portent, Marcus watched in horror as the man clambering out through a window fell back inside with an arrow sprouting from his throat. When he opened his mouth to cry out in agony and horror, no sound came, only blood bubbled forth. In that same instant, the three men who had pushed open the heavy door went down, their bodies pierced with the first volley of shafts. Suddenly everyone was moving, reaching for their weapons. A surge of terror had lent an urgency to their posturing. The fire had taken a hold and there was no other option but to flee the hall.

*

Flames were creeping all over the roof now. The horses in the enclosure panicked first. As the smoke reached their nostrils they became skittish and started to blow and whicker. Just when Guy was beginning to think that maybe the hall was empty, three outlaws burst out through the oak door, coughing and spluttering. Two died instantly, but the other took a shaft through the shoulder. He staggered, but a second found him so quickly he probably never knew what had hit him. Another outlaw was climbing out through a window but when he saw what faced him, tried desperately to get back inside again. He took an arrow in the throat with one leg still dangling over the windowsill. He fell back into the hall without a sound. Smoke started to swell out from between the deerhide flaps and from the doorway. Still they looked on and waited.

Then the holdfast erupted. After all the chaos and confusion, the outlaws must have gathered their wits. They poured from the hall, boiling out like a nest of ants, clutching all manner of weapons; swords, daggers, maces, clubs, some of which were spiked, axes, and even a scythe.

'Lancers, hold!' Guy commanded.

Some of the outlaws bunched up in their panic, helpless and yelling curses as arrows continued to be loosed into them with deadly accuracy. Howls of agony echoed around the compound. From the corner of his eye, Guy glimpsed a notched arrow being raised and loosed in his direction. He and others around him lifted their shields. He covered his face a split second before the shaft thwacked into it, sending a shuddering shockwave down his arm. The perpetrator did not stand long. Two arrows thudded into him. He fell backwards, hands clawing at the feathered shafts. There were some anxious glances from the ranks, and Guy could feel their resolve starting to slip away.

'Stand firm!' he ordered.

The outlaws looked around desperately, trying to see a way of escape only to find there was none. They were trapped between a burning building and a deep, tightly surrounded ditch. Seeing the hopelessness of their position and resigned to their fate, the most heroic of the bunch surged forward, roaring and swearing ferociously. Some of them ran down into the ditch, others tried to leap it. Whichever way, the move was suicidal.

Guy flourished his sword high above his head.

'On, for justice!' he bellowed.

Lances were grabbed with two hands and brought down in unison. Two outlaws were impaled on the spearheads before they had even landed, one's weight snapping a shaft in half. Clearing the ditch, another landed, only to stumble and fall face down in the snow. As he struggled to get up, Jack made his first kill. He thrust the lance he was holding into the outlaw's back. His screams of agony would be something Jack would never forget for the rest of his life. It took some effort to pull it out again, he had driven it in so deep. He used his foot as leverage on the man's back to twist and pull the head free, whilst all the time his victim writhed and howled beneath it. With its release came silence and a fountain of warm blood, which sprayed up into Jack's face. He promptly doubled over and was violently sick.

The ones in the ditch were dispensed of quickly, the long reach of the jabbing lances picking them off easily before they managed to scramble up the other side. Outlaws were still pouring from the burning hall. A second wave followed the first, some managing to breach the ditch while, the lancers were still busy with the ones in it, only to come up against the knights and soldiers who were ready and waiting for them. Swords flashed and the sound of metal upon metal rang out in the chill, early morning air. One desperate man charged at Guy with a sword, but he parried easily out of reach before thrusting his own between his adversary's shoulder blades. Guy cut the next man down and traded blow for blow with another until he took the advantage. He swung at the back of a man's calf as he ran past him, axe in hand, intent on Sir Hugh's exposed back. He felt the blade slice down through to the bone, and the man crumpled to the ground in a welter of blood and agony. A calm came over him, and time itself seemed to slow in motion. His mind closed to the surrounding carnage as he thrust, cut and stabbed, every move instinctive, ingrained in his subconscious through many years of practice and actual man-to-man combat. He looked around for his next victim. Having neither friend nor foe close, he stood a while drawing air in deep, harsh breaths. A dull pain throbbed in his side where a sword hilt had butted his ribs, and his sword arm ached with the strain of sustained use. He surveyed the scene with grim satisfaction, at the damage wrought upon what he understood to be one of the largest and most brutal outlaw gangs operating in the area for many a year. Already, many of the enemy lay dead or terribly injured. The ditch was strewn with corpses twisted and tangled together, torsos impaled, limbs severed, blood and guts spilt. So far as he could see only a few of their own men were wounded. Cumbrous lances had been discarded for knives, axes and mace and he saw that many had successfully fought their way across the ditch to tighten their hold on the remaining outlaws. He searched for Sir Hugh and became concerned when he could not see him. Then he spotted him standing over a corpse, but clutching one hand to his side. He looked beyond the fighting. Flames were licking down the sides of the hall now and smoke was pouring out of the open door like a writhing snake. Grey and white ash fell from the sky, mingling with the swirling snow. He could hear the screams of the horses inside their enclosure, shrieking with terror. He caught the glint of blade to his left and turned as an outlaw rushed at him, a giant of a man, bearded and wild-eyed with tufts of red hair sticking out from beneath a tight-fitting helmet, which was rammed down over his head. Guy easily fended off the untrained sword thrusts with his own. Catching the wild man off balance, he pushed him with his shield to follow through with a hard strike across the back of the neck, ripping through flesh and bone. Gasping, his eyes wide with surprise, the big man went down onto his knees to then topple facedown, never to move again. Guy heard the thunder of hooves and turned to see the terrified horses stampeding from their enclosure, trampling over and scattering men in all directions. Whilst being granted another moment's breathing space, he watched in amazement as a man sprung up from nowhere onto the bare back of one and, clinging onto its neck for dear life, make a break for the woods, his cloak billowing out behind him. He also witnessed one of the soldiers from Rochester turnabout and shout something after him and, with wrathful force, hurl a lance at his back.

*

As the men swarmed out of the hall, Godric crouched down low amongst them to block out any sight of himself. It would not do for him to be identified. He slid into the outhouse, where he would wait for an opportune moment to escape. Two were already cowering inside. He kicked them out.

'Get out there and fight, you craven lickspittals!'

He knelt down and, with one eye closed, peeped through a gap in the rough timber panelling. Men were falling all around. He saw Black John, thus named after his thatch of thick, black hair and the eye-patch he wore, go down with an arrow to the chest. A lance came hurtling across the ditch. It was Fingers Dick's turn to go down. The spearhead entered his throat to explode out the back of his neck, red and wet with blood. He fell like a boneless corpse, broken and lifeless before he hit the ground. To Godric's annoyance Marcus had followed in after him.

'I'm a steward. I want no part of this!' he spluttered, panicking and grabbing at Godric's shoulder.

Godric shrugged him off and batted him away like a troublesome fly. 'You may have no choice in the matter,' he answered, delighting in the look of pure terror on Marcus's face.

The heat from the hall was becoming unbearable and he knew he would have to make a move soon. Burning thatch floated and danced through the air. A kiss of wildfire landed on a horse's hindquarters. It screamed in terror and reared up, its hooves pawing at the air. Back on all fours again, it turned and lashed out with its hind legs, kicking down the wooden stakes that fenced it in. All the horses, maddened by the noise, the smell of smoke and the slaughter, converged onto the opening and charged through it. Seeing his chance, Godric elbowed Marcus out of the way and darted out through the doorway. Amongst the confusion, he run alongside the last bolting horse. Somehow he managed to grasp its mane and vault up onto the animal's back but, not to be easily cast aside, Marcus was right behind him.

'You can't leave me here!' he shouted desperately, making a grab for Godric's ankle.

Godric's black eyes fixed on him with loathing. If he thought he was going to get up here with him, he had another thing coming! He kicked out, hitting Marcus squarely in the face and knocking him to the ground. The horse reared and lashed out, catching another man in the temple with a sickening crunch. He too fell to the ground with a howl of pain. Without harness and reins, Godric had no way of controlling the runaway horse. He lay low along its back, wrapping his arms around its neck as it ploughed through the mayhem to jump the ditch and crash headlong into the tangled wood. A lance whipped past, very close to his ear. It took all his skill and strength to hang on, and how he managed to stay mounted he would never know. Branches and foliage zipped past his head and snatched at his clothing, until eventually the noise and turmoil behind him receded into the distance.

The last of the outlaws on their feet soon died. The wounded lay moaning, but not for long. Meakins and Corbiere prowled amongst them, performing the coup-de grace until all was still and silent, their anguish over. Guy looked around at the savage slaughter. The ground was littered with the slain. He had a momentary stab of conscience before he recognised that any survivors would be hanged anyway. They had lost seven men, three from Rochester and four of their own. Sir Hugh had been wounded by a spear thrust that had somehow found its way up and underneath his aventail, grazing his neck. He had also been battered hard in the side with a cudgel. He sat on the tree trunk that lay across the rise, looking utterly exhausted and holding a linen coif to the superficial but very sore wound. The heat from the burning building was hotter than any blacksmith's furnace and had driven them all back to the perimeter of the clearing. Once there, they realised that snow had continued to fall steadily throughout the morning, but the radiating heat from the holdfast had melted it before it had hit the ground. The men were dead on their feet. Some sat or lay scattered around the tree line, resting their aching, bruised bodies and nursing a wound or two. Others were still driven to a frenzy, pacing backwards and forwards with the battle-madness in their eyes, reliving the carnage over and over again in their minds. It would take a while for them to calm themselves sufficiently to rest up. Only then would they start to feel their battered and aching bodies and reflect on their good fortune at still being alive.

William and Jack Turner sat alone, slightly apart from the rest, both deep in their own thoughts. They were not seized by the bloodlust, never had been. All they had done was fight for their own survival and were lucky enough to get away with a few cuts and bruises. Jack felt sick to the stomach and could taste vomit rising in his gullet as it still spasmed and heaved. William looked on his brother's sickly pallor.

'Are you all right, Jack?'

Jack lifted his troubled eyes to his brother.

'Aye,' he said, the uncertainly clear in his voice.

They both knew, in truth, he was not. He had wanted nothing more than to run away from the horrors he had witnessed *and* committed today. The terror and the disgust had overwhelmed him. He had skinned rabbits and deer when out hunting, and had helped slaughter many an animal on the farm at Whitelawne until he was completely covered in blood and gore, but, after today, that would all dim to insignificance.

'Just remember this, little brother. You may well have saved a lot of decent, honest people's lives today.'

That was cold comfort to Jack. He shook his head sorrowfully.

Exhaustion hit him like a hammer blow and he could not even muster the strength to remove himself from William's presence before he learned over to vomit once more.

*

Guy looked up, his expression darkening at the sight of Percy dragging forward a man he recognised to throw him down on his knees in front of Sir Hugh. The man's face was covered in blood and he dabbed at his nose with the back of his hand.

'The steward from Whitelawne.'

All heads turned and regarded the captive grimly and he visibly withered under their gaze. His body trembled from head to toe.

Sir Hugh puffed out his cheeks and slowly exhaled. He placed his sword tip down between his legs and sat forward to rest his forearms on the hilt. He cleared his throat and looked levelly into the blood-smeared face, trying unsuccessfully to make contact with a pair of eyes that would not comply. He too recognised him.

'What *were* you thinking of, consorting with a coven of murderous, thieving outlaws?' he asked in a disappointed tone.

Marcus did not answer and continued to look anywhere rather than at the sheriff.

'It sickens me to think that you, after being given a position of trust, should coldheartedly conspire against that same family who took you in.'

At least the steward had the grace to look uncomfortable at that.

'Was it you who killed Geoffrey de Coulances and his wife?'

'I have killed no one. Those outlaws did the deeds,' mumbled Marcus.

'On whose orders?' demanded Sir Hugh raising his voice.

'Don't know his name.'

'Speak up!'

'I do not know his name!'

Sir Hugh huffed loudly and shook his head.

'Caught red-handed in their very camp, you know your life is already forfeit. You may as well tell us all you know before you hang.'

'It's true, I don't... And before you ask, I don't know where he came from either,' he said sullenly, still staring at the ground.

With that, Percy, as quick as a flash, knelt down behind him and grabbed a handful of his hair. He yanked his head back with a violent jerk, baring his throat. Marcus cried out and flinched as he felt a cold blade against his skin.

'Shall I open his throat?' asked Percy, his face creasing into an evil sneer.

'You expect us to believe that?' carried on the sheriff.

Finally, Marcus made eye contact. 'You must believe it,' he implored, careful not to move or open his mouth too much in case he cut his own throat. All the while, his body continued to tremble.

'Was he the one who got away on the horse?' questioned Guy.

William would have been able to confirm the identity of the horseman had he witnessed the mad dash, but he had been somewhat engaged at the time.

Marcus did not answer.

To prompt him, Percy jerked his head back even further.

'Yes... but I still can't help with his name,' was the strangled reply.

Guy cursed under his breath, furious that they had allowed the main man to get away.

'I know who he is,' called an unknown soldier making his way over to them.

Guy recognised him as the foot soldier who had thrown his lance at the retreating back of the escapee. He was a Rochester man of some stature, with yellow hair and disconcertingly pale ice-blue eyes, a colouring that smacked of Viking ancestry. It was obviously clear that he had a broken nose, an injury sustained long before today, which lay splayed across one side of his face. His hauberk was splattered with blood, so too the double-headed axe, the handle of which was pushed down behind his belt. He had lost one of his heavy leather gloves, and a dripping red gash laid open his knuckles. In a loud, clear voice edged with a nasal twang, he addressed the listening company.

'His name is Godric le Farges. He was once Rochester's master-at-arms, and he is a bully, an evil bastard. He did this to me…'

As if anybody needed clarification as to what Le Farges had done to him, he pointed to his nose and pivoted on the spot for all to see.

'I am sorry, but that is all I can tell you.'

'Thank you, soldier, for that information. I will make sure you are well rewarded for it,' said Sir Hugh.

'The only reward I want, sir, is to see his head on a pole and I am sure there are many others who share my way of thinking.'

He then stood to attention, saluted, turned on his heel and stalked off.

Scrutiny returned to the hapless steward once more. Question after question was barked at him by his implacable interrogators.

'Why did he want members of the family dead?'

'Where and how did he recruit his criminal gang?'

'What were you hoping to gain from it all?'

It went on and on. Marcus' nose hurt, he was wet through, weary and frozen to the bone. He just wanted it all to be over with and it was not long before he broke down under the pressure.

'I don't know… I don't know… I don't know!' he cried, over and over again, shaking his head from side to side.

It was true. He knew absolutely nothing about the man, not even his name. He found it hard to believe himself, but he had never shared a confidence with him, or divulged any of his plans. He came and he went. His men had told him that he regularly disappeared, but he always returned after a few days, anytime, day or night. Where he went, they too were not privy to. He supposed that by not sharing his plans or whereabouts with anyone, nobody could betray him. To this day, he still did not know how he'd become involved in all of this and he most certainly had not gained from it in any way – quite the contrary! Suddenly, to everyone's surprise, he laughed bitterly.

'I wish I had never set eyes upon the blasted man!'

After a nod from Sir Hugh, and with a grunt of irritation, Percy roughly let go of him.

'You snivelling, miserable wretch…' he growled with a look of disgust on his face.

'There is one possible chance for you,' informed Sir Hugh. 'If you can tell us about all your dealings with this Godric le Farges, I just might be able to save your neck.'

Marcus swallowed and nodded his understanding.

'I can do that.'

He told them that Godric had taken a huge interest in the De Coulances family's affairs. He wanted to know absolutely everything about them – their whereabouts, where they were going and when, who visited them, what plans, if any, they had for the future.

'You were in his pay then, with instructions to inform?'

'Yes.'

'Did you not want to know why?' asked Guy.

'Yes, but he told me I should just do as I was told and not ask questions.'

'An arrogant fellow, then,' noted Sir Hugh.

'He is.'

'Where do you think he has gone now?' Guy enquired.

'I have never known his whereabouts before. Why should I know them now?' was the curt reply.

Marcus winced and hissed as the scornful Percy boxed him around the head for his discourteous manner.

Finally realising there really was nothing he could tell them, the surly steward's hands were bound together as he was informed he was under arrest and would return to Tonbridge to be held at His Majesty's pleasure.

'Or until we 'ang ya!' spat Percy, viciously pulling at his bindings so they cut painfully into his wrists.

He was then taken to one side and put under armed guard.

With an audible sigh, Guy sat down next to Sir Hugh.

'So they were both complicit in the family's demise, but I wonder what reason Le Farges would have to want to harm any of them?'

'*That*, dear boy, is anyone's guess,' replied the sheriff as he slowly and painfully attempted to stand up, but his legs started to buckle beneath him and he had to lock his knees to stop himself from crumbling to the ground.

He closed his eyes for a brief second and Guy sprung up to reach out and steady him. Sir Hugh groaned quietly to himself. God, he was getting too old for all this! Every muscle ached and sharp lances of pain shot through every bone in his body. It will be a long trek back to Tonbridge.

'Sit down, Hugh, you are exhausted.'

'Yes, I am not feeling my best, I must admit,' he gasped, as he allowed Guy to guide him down to his resting place again.

'You stay where you are, I will get you a drink.'

Guy made his way into the wood and the stream, where he filled his basin helmet with water through a hole in the ice, which had already been broken by others that had needed to quench their thirst and tend to their wounds. He took it back and passed it to the sheriff, who gratefully drank it down, the ice-cold liquid slaking his parched throat and going a little way to reviving his flagging spirit.

'Some good and loyal men have died here today, Guy,' he said, shaking his head sadly as he looked around the battleground.

'Damn! We were within a hare's whisker of seeing an end to all this, once and for all. It pains me greatly to know that man is still at large!'

'And I,' said Guy, his voice bitter.

The next job was to bury the dead, and every man that was able got on with the task. Making good use of the ditch, the bodies were thrown in with those already there, but the covering of the corpses would have to wait. Corbiere would send a party of men back at some point, with shovels enough to finish the job. Until then, they would be left open to the elements, wild animals and the crows to pick at. Not wanting to bury their own men amongst the dross, they were gathered together and made ready to carry to the ox-carts for transportation back to Tonbridge and a Christian burial. By early afternoon, the company were ready to move out. A light snow still flurried around and it was growing colder by the minute. It was imperative they left soon. Being midwinter, it would not be long before darkness descended upon them. As they were about to move off, a splintering crash rang out across the clearing, making them flinch and duck away as the longhouse collapsed in a ruin, sending out sparks and pieces of flaming wood. The holdfast would continue to burn and smoulder well into the night.

*

Amid all the commotion of departure, Guy slipped away.

He moved quickly through the tangled wood and skirted the hillside of ash trees. Finding the first discreetly placed marker, he forged his way across the valley. Woodland turned to forest, and for what seemed like hours now, he picked his way through it. Along the way he must have missed a marker, for suddenly he no longer recognised the shape of the hills or the curve of the landscape. He looked for any familiar landmark but found none. Where was the oak wood or the evergreen forest they had passed through on their way here? He cursed and remembered why he had never much cared for woods. Every direction looked the same, and it was so easy to find oneself lost. The watery sun had sunk low in the sky and brooding shadows had begun to lengthen and lurk between the trees. The wind had dropped and a deep silence settled in around him. He shivered as an uneasiness crept over him. He had a distinct feeling of being watched. His fingers twitched over his sword belt. He shrugged his shoulders beneath his cloak and pulled the hood further down over his head, trying to dispel the feeling. He heard the hoot of an owl in the distance. Maybe he had been a little too hasty to venture out on his own. This was a dark, primeval place, a great swathe of untouched forest full of ancient oaks, elms and beech whose trunks crowded close together. In the deepest parts it was as dark as night and a place where many would not venture for fear of what they might find, human or otherwise. He continued to pick his way through the undergrowth and climbed a steep incline, to where a low ridge would hopefully give him a vantage point. Under the crust of snow the ground was thick with leaf mould, rocks and roots. He cursed as his foot slipped and he fell into a thicket of brambles, bringing down a number of arched stems, which hooked themselves onto his clothing and hair. He fought to free himself. Thankfully his heavy leather gauntlets protected his hands, but each movement had brought lacerations to his face and his hair tangled with prickles and burr. Eventually freeing himself, he moved away. He reached the ridge only to find the same again, a mass confusion of woodland and undergrowth stretching out before him. Evenfall was fast approaching, and he needed to carry on if he was to hold any hope of getting out of the forest tonight. Finding a track would at least give him some idea of his location. The feeling of unease came over him again. He pulled off his hood and glanced around. He leaned into the silence and encroaching darkness, straining to hear any noise; anything that would tell him the feeling was warranted. He heard a flicker of sound. It seemed to come from a mighty oak with twisted, broken limbs and massive misshapen roots. He listened again.

'Who goes there?' he called.

Silence.

He slowly unsheathed his sword and cautiously made his way over to stand in front of its bole, which was easily wide enough to conceal any would-be attacker. As he opened his mouth to speak again, a squawk and a flutter made him look up in alarm to see a large crow staring down at him through tiny, black gimlet eyes. Guy exhaled and closed his eyes when he recognised his folly. Remonstrating with himself, he was about to move off when the crow stood, opened its stout bill and cawed loudly, a harsh scream, a croaking call that sent an eerie echo reverberating through the forest. Guy was forced to duck as it glided down over his head, flapping its wide black wings to land very close to him, and from where it proceeded to act in a very peculiar manner. Strutting back and forth, it bobbed its body up and down, to then skip along, all the while shrieking wildly. Stopping several feet away, it turned and started the whole procedure again before taking to the air to perch on a low branch in another oak further on. Flying down once more, it fixed him with its beady eyes, cocked its head, cawed and, continuing to look back at him, hopped on. Watching the spectacle, a thought struck him, but Guy immediately pushed it from his mind. How fanciful, ridiculous even, to contemplate the idea that the bird was enticing him to follow. He chided himself. It was more likely to be mocking him for getting lost! But the longer Guy watched the bizarre behaviour, the more convinced he became and, recognising he could not get any more lost than he already was, decided to follow it. When he stepped out to do just that, it did indeed seem to him that the bird was intent on leading him off somewhere.

Where the crow led, Guy followed. It beckoned him through the deep and frozen forest, over dead and fallen tree trunks, across shallow gills, up steep, treacherous banks and through bastions of holly and ivy. Then, bemused, Guy watched for the last time as it took flight over the tree tops and vanished into the gloom, never to return. In the near distance, a murder of crows noisily ascended. They wheeled and circled above in a shrieking menagerie of sound, to then coalesce into one black cloud and sink slowly down again to roost. Guy stood peering up at the moon through the shifting cloud. Its pale light served only to trace the outline of the trees silhouetted against a darkening grey sky. He saw quite clearly a pair of snowy owls sitting high in a beech. They sat huddled together and as he watched, one of them elongated its body and swivelled its head to stare behind and beyond. Guy followed its line of vision. The trees ahead were starting to thin. He heard dogs barking in the distance and headed off towards the sound. Through a break in the cloud, the yellowing bloom of the moon revealed a track in front of him. Relieved, he stepped out onto it, finding himself a few feet from the main road and halfway up Stumble Hill. Snowflakes tingled on his face and melted in his hair. He wrapped his cloak tightly around his body and with some purpose started the long, strenuous climb up to its crest on Greensands Ridge. Here, the road veered sharply to the left, leading off to Ightham and Oldbury, and from this point, on a clear day, one could look back across the dense Wealden Forest stretching down towards Tonbridge. He turned right onto a track that would eventually lead to the tiny hamlet of Plaxtol. Ahead, the twelve-foot high walls of Whitelawne House came into view. Guy made for the arched gateway that would take him into the courtyard. Luckily, the gate was still open, and he darted through it, glancing up at the intricately carved stonework depicting a hunting scene, where deer and boar ran from men with spear and blade, and a wildcat hissed down at him. The front of the house was in darkness. A plume of smoke rose from one of the chimneys. Taking a wide berth of the courtyard he loped across the snow-covered grass to one corner of the house and followed the wall around to the back. Here stood the usual outbuildings; stables, storerooms, workshops and the servants' privies. Not a soul was in sight. How strange, he thought. Being quite early, surely there would still be the hustle and bustle of servants going about their business? Where were the stable lads? Where were the household dogs that usually ran amok, barking and peeing up anything that did not move? A strange atmosphere unnerved him. Maybe his hunch had been right. He reached for and unsheathed his sword. All the ground floor windows that he could see were shuttered. That was unusual in itself. Lord Charles liked to show off his wealth when he was in residence by lighting up every single room. Candlelight shone from a top floor window only, casting a glowing light across the white expanse of garden, broken now and again by the black shape of an ornamental urn, or a statue in the distance. So, there was somebody at home. He furtively made his way back to the courtyard and up to the main door.

He worked the latch. It opened easily and he moved inside. All was quiet in the hallway. If he wanted to make his way upstairs, he needed to venture into the dining room first. As quietly as he could, he opened the left hand door and stepped in. The room was eerily quiet. From what he could see by the winter moonlight peeking through the shutters, two places had been laid for dinner. The table was set with the fine plates, cutlery and Flemish glass that he remembered from his last visit here, and a flagon of wine sat at its centre. Lord and Lady C were obviously expecting to dine at home tonight, he conjectured. But where were the servants? Where was Drake? He crept into the next room, like an animal, alert and suspicious. He glanced around the dim, shuttered interior. He jerked his head up and stilled his breathing. Someone was in the room with him. He heard a soft footfall. It came from behind the door he had just entered through and left wide open, almost flush to the wall. With infinite care, he made his way back over to it. He could taste nervous acid in his throat. He swallowed and, putting his ear close, could hear breathing on the other side. Taking a deep breath himself he stepped back and, with all the force he could muster, shouldered it. As he jumped back out of the way, he heard a startled yell, and a body crumple to the floor. With a wash of relief, mingled with a touch of regret, he saw Drake lying there, looking up at him, his face as white as a sheet and his eyes as large as two roundels of cheese. Guy lowered his weapon.

'Drake! What are you doing? Why were you hiding from me?' he hissed.

Feeling some pity for the quivering wreck, he put out his hand and helped him to his feet.

'Quiet, sir, he will hear you!' Drake whispered urgently, glancing anxiously at the far door that led to the inner hallway.

'Who?'

'I don't know who he is… He f—forced his way in… and drew a knife on me…'

Guy knew who he was. It was this Le Farge, and his intention was to harm Lord and Lady de Coulances, he was sure of it.

'Where are your master and mistress?' he urged.

Drake's nervousness made him stammer.

'U—upstairs in Lady Isabelle's room… I t—think. They were just about to have d—dinner…' he gulped, his prominent Adam's apple working up and down in his throat.

'I heard him tell the m—master to get r—rid of everybody… the kitchen staff an' all… Lord Charles did just that, and th—then they went upstairs.'

It was as Guy thought.

'Now listen, Drake. Your master and mistress are in grave danger,' he said in an urgent undertone.

The manservant's eyes widened even further. He was trembling like a leaf. This Le Farge had really put the fear of God, or the devil, into him.

'He is an assassin, a murderer.'

With a sharp intake of breath, Drake pressed the tips of his fingers into his bottom lip. He looked absolutely petrified.

'I need your help to show me how to get upstairs.'

Guy could sense Drake's reticence. He was more liable to run a mile than to do what he had asked of him. But the manservant took his hand away from his mouth, swallowed hard and nodded, though rather hesitantly.

'Good,' said Guy firmly, making to move away.

Drake shot out a restraining hand.

'B—be careful, sir… He is like the devil himself!'

'And I am the avenging angel!' Guy hissed back sharply.

'With me!'

Drake winced as Guy shoved his resisting back, pushing him with some force towards the far door. They made their way to the inner hallway, where the walls were covered with expensive tapestries and where another dark corridor led off to the old hall. At the far end, there stood a wooden screen. A couple of frightened servants stared out from behind it.

'Get back!' hissed Drake, shushing them away with his hands.

They hastily retreated. Guy was relieved to see that Drake looked a little calmer now, more earnest, because he could not do this without his help. Without a word, the manservant pointed up the wide staircase and, making sure to follow behind Guy, they both quietly mounted it. Above was another corridor, with several doors leading off from it. There was a strip of candlelight under one of them. Guy looked at Drake, who nodded affirmation. Guy reached the doorway and stood listening for a few seconds. He then grasped the handle and the door opened smoothly. He did not move from the threshold, just pushed it fully open. It was the master bedroom. On one wall, a fireplace was set and a fire burned brightly from it. Glancing around, he glimpsed a bed draped with rich hangings and bright tapestries, but his immediate attention was drawn to a long settle over in the far corner. On it, sitting facing him, were Lord and Lady de Coulances. They both stared straight ahead and, at first glance, looked for all intentions of welcoming him into their home, even though this was their bedroom and not the customary place to receive guests. But Guy noticed they were clutching each other's hands, and Lord Charles' mouth was working but no sound was coming out. Lady Isabelle looked white-faced with fright. Guy himself was about to speak, but his words too died in his throat. He had seen him. He sat in a chair a little way off and opposite the couple, looking quite relaxed, one leg crossed over the other and cradling a goblet of wine in his hand. A dagger lay on the small table by his side. He knew Guy was there.

'Good evening, Guy. Please, do come in,' he said, without looking round.

Guy moved into the room, his sword still in his hand, though pointing downwards and slack in his grip. His first concern was for Charles and Isabelle's welfare. He walked over to them. The look of relief in their faces to have him there with them was heart-rending to see. Poor Lord Charles; he looked so frail and vulnerable sitting there, his once robust frame wasted away to nothing more than skin and bone. Lady Isabelle sat with her usual erect carriage and her proud, narrow, aquiline face was calm, but her dark eyes were full of emotion and her stubborn chin wobbled when he looked her in the eye and whispered, 'Take courage. I will not let anything happen to you.'

He placed his hand over their clasped ones in reassurance and felt them tremble. He could sense Godric's scrutiny. He turned to face him. He was dressed from head to toe in black, wearing high leather boots, a wide, silver-buckled belt with a sheathed longsword. His slick hair was long, falling well beyond his shoulders. He was dark and sharp featured, and a heavy brow shelved a contemptuous frown. He wore an immaculately trimmed close-cut moustache and beard, and through it he smiled a smile that cut like a knife and did not reach his coal-black eyes. It was true, he did look like the devil himself. He emanated power and control, and Guy could quite see how he could evoke fear into someone such as Drake. Guy's eye was caught and drawn to a large round gold pin securing his cloak, which he had thrown behind his shoulders. At its centre was a huge deep red garnet. It looked familiar. His bemused expression turned to one of recognition. There was no mistaking it was his father's. Guy recoiled with shock and revulsion, and found a smirk playing across this unwelcome visitor's lips, the sight of which released in him an acute urge to smash his fist into the arrogant, sneering face. He resisted the impulse and took a deep breath to calm himself. As quickly as it has appeared, the smirk disappeared.

'Come, take a drink with me,' said Godric, now smiling and leaning over to fill another goblet.

Guy stayed immovable.

'I only drink with friends,' he replied coldly.

Godric's expression changed yet again and he downturned his mouth in mock misery.

Guy sensed this was a man whose changes in mood and expression came quickly and easily to him.

'You disappoint me. You would drink with Lord Charles and Lady Isabelle here, and I know, even with your servants, but not with me? What makes me so different?'

How strange, Guy thought, that he knew nothing of this man and yet he seemed to know such things about him?

'Because you are a rogue, a thief, and a murderer,' he said, barely able to contain his anger.

'You have hurt my feelings,' said Godric leaning back in his chair and taking a sip of wine.

'Do you know who I am?'

'Godric le Farges.'

'Ah, I see my name, and probably my reputation, precedes me,' he said, slowly inclining his head.

'Did you know Lord Charles here is my father?'

So that was it. There was the crux. It all fell into place.

'I am of spurious birth… A bastard, if you prefer that term.'

Guy's expression remained neutral.

'It happens,' he replied flatly.

Godric looked on him sharply, his eyes glinting as they caught the candlelight.

'That was a niggardly response. Is that all you have to say?'

'What did you expect me to say? If you were hoping to hear some words of sympathy from me, you are greatly mistaken. Since time immemorial people have been born outside of wedlock and had the misfortune of being abandoned. They just got on and made the best of their lives.'

'That is easy enough for someone like you to say.'

'And what *is* someone like me?'

Godric's jaw worked as he gritted and ground his teeth.

'Someone of privileged birth, someone who was raised and nurtured in a *loving* family. *I* was never given that opportunity. Do you know, I never even knew I had two brothers?'

'Yes, I was fortunate, but then I never knew my mother either; she died. I would have had a brother too if he had lived.'

'That is different.'

'How so?'

'He–' Godric hissed as he slammed down the goblet he had been holding and swept his hand over in Lord Charles' direction, '–did not leave my mother and I because he died, mores the pity; no, he just cast us aside. He coldheartedly turned his back and threw us to the wolves! As a consequence, my mother was shunned by society and she hated *me* for it! She would not speak of him; in fact, she never spoke to me about anything much at all. I have spent my life trying to forget what I am, but not so others. Oh no! Eyes would seek me out and fingers would point. "That's the bastard", they would say. Then, when I saw how they lived…' He nodded in the settle's direction, '…How they and my brothers wallowed in a life of luxury, I realised just how much had been taken from me and I vowed I would take something back for my trouble.'

It was quite a speech, but Guy was still not to be moved by it.

'So you decided to kill them.'

'I did not kill them!' spat Godric, his face now flushed and his eyes flashing like chips of black onyx.

'But it was on your orders! You are as guilty as if you had done the deeds with your own hands!'

'They all deserved it!' Godric shouted back, standing up now and turning the small table over with a crash, sending its contents spilling in all directions.

Lord and Lady de Coulances jumped and made a grab for each other. They lowered their heads to stare down at the floor, quaking in each other's arms. Guy hoped for their sakes that he had not unnecessarily provoked this highly volatile and violent individual. He stepped back and raised his sword. Godric was probably half a head taller than him, lithe, and built like a warrior. He had still refrained from unsheathing his own sword, even though his dagger had just been tossed across the room with the table. Guy could not believe this man's blatant arrogance and confidence in his own infallibility. If he wished, he need only to reach out and he could run the man through! It would be as easy as that. So why did he not do it? Instead, he stood his ground.

'Did they?' he questioned coolly.

'Did Lady Eleanor deserve to be raped and drowned? And what about Geoffrey and Richard? Was it their fault their father had sired a bastard? What about the others – the escort, the old nurse?'

At this point, Guy lowered his sword and walked right up to Godric to shout full in his face.

'And what about my father, huh? Did he deserve to die, terrified and alone, breathing his last agonising breath while your reprobates ransacked his home?'

He was angry now and did not fear this man, not one whit. They stood eye to eye for a brief moment, their breathing long and hard. Guy backed off to calm himself and his voice again.

'What do you propose to achieve tonight? What are your intentions towards these people?' he said, indicating the couple cowering on the settle.

Godric was silent for a while, frowning with petulance. Guy watched him intently, not knowing what his next move might be. If he was not dealing with a madman here, he was definitely dealing with a self-obsessed and ruthless one, and was well aware that whatever he had planned, he would endeavour to see it through to the bitter end. He was dangerous – very, very dangerous indeed.

'What I have wanted all along. Revenge,' said Godric, coldly.

There was a whimper from the settle.

'I do not think so. I think your only option is to give yourself up.'

'What, to be done by the neck!'

'*That* is no more than what *you* deserve! You are a coward and a…'

Godric had never had any time for gentlemanly conduct. Before Guy could finish his sentence, he pounced and slammed his fist hard into his stomach, driving the air out of him.

'So, you would make me a coward as well as a murderer?' he roared.

As Guy doubled over, Godric brought his knee up to make contact with his face. Dazed, Guy fell back.

Unsheathing his sword at last, Godric lunged, but Guy had recovered quickly and managed to parry the move. Their swords clashed. Godric pressed the attack; high, low, overhand, he rained down blows. Upswing, side-slash, attacking, moving into Guy, step and slide, strike and step, faster and faster until, breathless, he stepped back and dropped the point of his sword.

'Not bad,' he acknowledged.

Guy breathed long, deep breaths and stepped back, watching him warily. Godric raised his sword once more and flew at him again. Left, right, back-slash. The blades kissed and sprang apart, and kissed again. At one point Guy stumbled. There was a shriek of dismay from Lady Isabelle, but he went down on one knee instead of falling and never lost a beat. His sword came up to block the downcut, which would have seen him opened up from shoulder to waist. Then it was Guy's turn to take the advantage. He pushed Godric back stroke by stroke and pinned him against the bed panel, but Godric quickly raised his foot and kicked out, sending him reeling. He was on Guy as quick as a flash and again he had to fend off a downswipe.

'Um, not bad at all for a King's lapdog!' Godric sneered when he paused again to catch his breath.

Guy would not take the bait. To have any chance of survival he knew he would have to remain calm and focused. Both were breathing heavily. The dance resumed. Furniture was scattered and kicked from their path. It seemed to go on forever, and shoulders were starting to numb from the jarring they were taking, and the weight of their swords grew heavier with every blow. Godric's stamina was beginning to wane. He was not swinging swiftly enough nor raising his blade as high. His skills had also gone to pot since Rochester and the realisation discomforted him. He should have had this man skewered by now. This needed to be addressed fast, but the second's loss of concentration found him slashed across the brow. He felt a momentary sting and a trickle of blood ran down the side of his face. Then the cold tip of a blade pressed against his Adam's apple. He held his arms out in submission.

'Yield! Throw down your sword!' rasped Guy, but as Godric made as if to comply, he spun, ducked and darted out of reach.

Guy's response came too late and Godric slashed at his side, but not content with that, he kicked him hard in the ribs as he went down and a couple more times when he lay prone on the floor. Intent now on the couple who had left the settle to quail in a corner, he stalked towards them, his eyes blazing.

'This is *my* house and *my* land!' he shouted, his voice thick with gloating triumph.

Drake suddenly appeared from nowhere. He must have stayed lurking outside, and had seen and heard everything. He frantically glanced down at Guy, but he had hit his head on the way down and was unconscious, or worse. Godric had raised his sword and made to go for Lord and Lady de Coulances, but Drake was quicker. In a single fluid movement, he bent, picked up Guy's sword and, running at this unknown enemy, thrust it with some force. It pierced through the back of Godric's neck, the tip bursting out of his throat in a splatter of blood. In front of their very eyes, Charles and Isabelle witnessed astonishment turn to a frown. Momentarily, Godric looked like a thwarted child. Letting out a gurgling roar of rage and pain, he dropped his sword and brought his hands up to his throat. Blood oozed from between his fingers. Feeling the warm stickiness, he took them away again to confirm his fear. Looking on

Lord Charles, he tried to speak, but of course he could not. Choking on his own blood, his anguished eyes never left his father's face as his legs collapsed beneath him and he fell to the floor.

*

Guy did not fully regain consciousness for several days. His recovery took weeks, and his survival was largely due to Lucie's skills as a nurse. As he lay there, dosed with willow bark and poppy syrup, she had cleaned the wound and sewn it up. The scars of many battles and skirmishes puckered Guy's smooth, flat stomach and biceps, and Lucie was careful not to botch the operation like so many others had done before. She had then administered clean linen dressings, smeared with honey to prevent any festering. A fractured rib had been bound tightly and facial bruising, cuts and scratches medicated. Whilst recuperating from his ordeal, Guy had received an unexpected visit from Lord and Lady de Coulances. He apologised for receiving them whilst he was still abed, but Lord Charles flapped a hand dismissively and Lady Isabelle gave him a friendly smile before sitting in a chair beside his bed.

'No matter, Guy; we are just so sorry for what you have suffered in saving our lives. We are most grateful to you, and Drake of course, and will be forever in your debt.'

They told him how Richard had also made a full recovery and that they had decided to call off the new proposals for Whitelawne, had started a rebuild of their tenant homes, and were negotiating a new tenant farmer and landlord agreement. When they had left Guy felt a sense of peace, and he thanked God that the greatest of all human virtues, humility, had eventually won the day.

Lucie came into the room and sat by his bed.

'Tell me what happened, if you feel able to.'

She sat listening as Guy told her about the holdfast, the fact that Marcus, Whitelawne's steward, was Le Farge's accomplice, but for whatever gain was questionable. Also Le Farges escape, the crow leading him through the forest – yes, you did hear right – and the desperate time at Whitelawne.

'What was he, Lucie? He was not a normal human being. He wanted revenge but killed all those innocent people along the way and would have perhaps killed his own father. It chills my blood.'

'Some disturbance must have happened in his mind.'

'But I do not believe he was mad. He was a calculating and a manipulative creature, and I think he genuinely believed he was quite within his rights to act as he did. Maybe his circumstances just gave him an excuse to commit his evil exploits. I do believe, though, that Lord Charles and his family did not deserve the measure of spite levelled against them.'

'Come, you must rest now,' said Lucie, reaching behind him to fluff up his pillows and make him more comfortable.

He had not been the best of patients and was becoming more and more restless now that his health was restored almost to the full. He longed to be up and about, but Lucie stubbornly insisted he stay where he was for a little while longer. During this time, he took the opportunity to play chess and draughts, usually with Roger or Old Matt. He had taught Lucie chess but when he played with her, he could not concentrate, and she always beat him hands down.

'Not bad for a novice, am I?' she had laughed.

Guy was finding it more and more difficult having Lucie in such close proximity and not being able to touch her. Today, having her leaning over him, he was in pure agony.

'Are you hungry?' she asked.

A smile played on his lips, and he had to swallow down an inexcusable retort to really what was a very innocent question. Lucie caught the look and abruptly stepped back from him and the bed. A flush rose up from her neck to bloom across her cheeks, and she lowered her eyes demurely to the floor. Guy's heart sank. He had overstepped the mark; she had realised what was going through his mind and was offended. But to Guy's delight, when Lucie slowly raised her eyes again to meet his, stare for stare, her bashful expression had changed into one of mischief.

'With a blush like that, I think I could eat *you* for breakfast.'

'You need a shave first,' was the matter-of-fact reply.

'Are you going to do it for me?'

He held out his hand.

Heart pounding, Lucie took it and walked towards heaven.

Early August 1274

The sun shed a golden glow across the fields, catching in the thin mist that rose from the river. The air was languorous and smelled of lush, ripe grass. Swallows wheeled in the late summer sky and rosy-pink-breasted linnets warbled shrill and sweet. In the distance, sheep bleated in the meadows that were carpeted with buttercups and clover.

The tranquillity was intermittently disturbed by what sounded like thunder rumbling in the distance. It rolled in to then recede as it was carried back and forth on the gentle breeze.

The rumblings grew louder and eventually they came, leaving in their wake a cloud of choking dust. A great procession of knights, squires, lords and their ladies, councillors, advisers, physicians, attendants and servants, all escorting their King along the hard and dusty road to London. To avoid the dust, the King rode at the front of the train, surrounded by his royal guard, reclining in the royal litter and shaded under the crimson canopy of state. Beside him sat his beautiful dark-haired queen, Eleanor of Castille. Behind them, on sumptuous cushions and cradled in the arms of their wet nurses, sat their two youngest children. Eleanor, who had accompanied

Edward, on this last crusade, had given birth to them whilst they were abroad.

King Edward I had acceded the throne nearly two years earlier at the start of this long journey home from the eighth Crusade. Stepping onto English soil at Dover, he had found Gilbert de Clare waiting for him. Wanting to be amongst the first to greet the new King and offer his hospitality, he extended an invitation to dine at Tonbridge Castle. The invitation was graciously accepted by the new King and his Queen.

Bringing up the rear, and trundling along behind the King's escort were the wagons, one after the other, their axles creaking under the weight of their heavy loads and piled high with furniture and furnishings and trunks of clothes and linen. Passing through small villages, country folk ran from their homes. They looked up, shading their eyes against the sun to get a glimpse of the spectacle that was their King. They called out his name as he passed and held up their children for his blessing. They scattered rose petals on the road before him and threw flowers up to his radiant queen, who, to their delight, caught and covered the litter's interior with them. It took seven long, cumbersome days for the entourage to reach Tonbridge. On the way, the King slept and ate wherever he could impose himself. Honoured to receive him, his hosts put aside their concerns at how much it would cost them for the privilege.

Tonbridge town was alight with excitement. De Clare had ridden hard, returning ahead of the entourage in plenty of time to oversee the preparations for the most festive week in its history. He encouraged the masses to celebrate the King's patronage to the full. Brightly coloured pennants were flown and hung from eave to eave along the High Street. Flowers were arranged in pots and troughs, and stood on every windowsill.

They arrived with great ceremony at Tonbridge Castle, where the Royal Standard was raised from the gatehouse battlements to show the King and his household were in residence. First in line for accommodation in the town came the lords and their ladies, then the King's advisors and councillors. Every inn and lodging house was fit to bursting. With the entire Tonbridge garrison now back, the castle's outer bailey was also crammed solid. With such limited space those left over – the royal guard, lesser knights, their pages and squires and servants – all found it necessary to pitch tents on some of the outfields.[18]

The castle kitchens were inadequate for the proposed task, but luckily, since the weather was fine, the inner bailey had availed itself to be used as a preparation area. Servants toiled from the early morning. Benches and trestle tables had been set up for them to peel the many barrow-loads of vegetables and fruit, pluck the mountains of chickens and various wild fowl and skin the rabbits, all of which would be roasted in the ovens or, due to lack of space, on a spit. Two huge spits had been set up out of the way, next to the courthouse by the south curtain wall. The castle blacksmiths had been busy for the last few days, forging and hammering together sheets of iron to make two huge fire pans to house them. These would take whole deer and boar, while leaving the kitchen spits free for smaller fare, and the ovens for bread, pastries and pies. In the kitchens, fires blazed beneath huge cauldrons and braziers full of red-hot charcoal gave off a simmering heat, over which sauces and pie fillings were prepared. A young boy stood turning a spit laden with partridges, while another ladled the juices back over them. In the corner, a trussed up boar hung upside down from a

---

[18] Lower Castle Fields.

chain awaiting a butcher's attention. Batch after batch of loaves were paddled into the ovens and then paddled out again. Once cooled, a young serving girl cut them into hunks and threw them into huge wicker baskets, ready for consumption by the lesser classes who would dine in the common hall. For the Great Chamber upstairs, where the King and Queen would be entertained, small bread rolls were being baked, half being moulded as the Great Seal of Edward I, the rest as Gilbert's.

Everything had been thought out with meticulous detail. The heat was stifling, the overall workload phenomenal but everyone, from the lowly kitchen maid up to the Red Earl himself, wanted to make certain that their contribution to the programme of entertainment would stand up to comparisons with whatever there was to come for the King of England.

Whilst here, Edward was to take the opportunity to confer into knighthood a handful of squires from his household. Gilbert and other local lords also wanted to renew their oath of fealty, and swear their allegiance to the new King.

Up in Sir Hugh's chamber, he and Percy were preparing themselves for the ceremony. Robin was standing on a stool, helping Sir Hugh don his heavy chain of office. Kept in the treasury coffers under lock and key, it rarely saw the light of day. This morning Robin had polished it until he could see his face in it and was now making sure it was laying properly across the back of the sheriff's tunic and shoulders. He patted Sir Hugh's shoulder and jumped down.

'Yep, that's fine... sir,' he smiled happily.

'Thank you, Robin.'

Seeing the smiling face beneath his thatch of untidy white-blond hair, Hugh felt a clutch to his heart. Here was an orphan alone in the world outside of his wardship, and he felt wholly responsible for his welfare. He was a capable and a willing lad, a little ray of sunshine to be honest, who was always ready to do his bidding. He enjoyed having him around. Percy, too, had taken to him, although he would not admit to it. He was always telling him to get out from under his feet, and shooing him away.

Percy stood over a basin in his linen shirt and hose trying to have a shave.

'By Christ, you could ride bare-arsed to London on this!' he grumbled loudly, holding aloft a small blade.

'I'll sharpen it for you, Percy!'

Percy readily passed the blade to Robin, who took it over to a small whetstone in the corner, where he diligently started to sharpen it, his tongue sticking out in concentration.

'Mind you don't cut yourself,' Percy called.

Sitting down at the small table, he took a swig of ale and pulled a platter of bread and salt beef towards him and started to tuck into it. Sir Hugh regarded him thoughtfully. This was something new, showing a little concern for the lad. Was he mellowing slightly? He also seemed to be taking more care of late with his appearance, changing his linen on a regular basis and washing and shaving most days. He'd had a haircut yesterday. Still, maybe that was just as well, being as he would be attending the swearing-in ceremony today.

'Percy, you do realise that you won't be eating upstairs in the great hall with us.'

'Um,' replied Percy, holding his nose to one side with one hand and contorting his mouth while he ran the newly honed blade carefully down over his upper lip with the other.

He did not seem bothered about the fact.

'But, no doubt you will probably be well looked after... as always,' said Sir Hugh irritably.

'Um,' was again the only reply.

He obviously had his mind on others things.

Sir Hugh huffed and straightened his collar for the last time.

'Please do not be late.'

*

The castle's Great Chamber on the second floor boasted two huge south-facing windows. Outside, carved stone heads of the Earl himself, Lady Alice and his parents sat either side of each, gazing down over the inner bailey. Inside, tapestries lined the walls and a huge fireplace took pride of place, the stone canopy carved with the three chevrons of Clare.

Everybody that was anybody milled round the hall, awaiting the King and Queen's audience. Guy stood with Lucie, Sir Godfrey, Sir Hugh, and Percy. Guy had been so pleased to see his squire of arms, Adam Fitzgibbon, back with the royal household and to hear that he was one of the knights-elect to be knighted today.

Adam had spent all last night, the last night of his squirehood, in the castle's tiny chapel, kneeling before the altar in silent prayer. A sword and shield, both of which would be presented to him at the ceremony, had been placed upon it. Beforehand, he had prepared for the vigil by ritual bathing. The body needed to be thoroughly cleansed as a symbol of purification. The first stage of the proceedings had commenced that morning, when he joined others to hear Mass and a lengthy sermon on his duties and responsibilities. Then the sword and shield had been blessed by the chaplain.

*

Gilbert de Clare's eyes darted around the hall, making sure everything was as it should be. He sent Lady Alice over to inspect the layout of the dining table, and then went over to a small dais where upon sat a huge, carved solid oak imitation throne. He had commissioned the work especially for the King's visit. It was not sitting quite straight, so he called over two of his household to help him tweak it so. Sir Godfrey turned to Sir Hugh.

'That must have cost him a tidy packet,' he said crustily.

'What a waste of money, unless of course he is intending to plant his own scheming arse upon it afterwards,' he sneered.

Sir Hugh was taken aback, not only dismayed at Godfrey's vehemence but also by his indiscretion. He shot Bartholomew a warning look that told him he should hold his tongue. He hoped nobody else had heard the remark.

With a flourish of trumpets, the King entered with Lady Alice on his arm, followed by the Queen, escorted by Gilbert. Next came the Archbishop of Winchelsey, who would preside over the proceedings, and then the King's council.

The King wore a blue tunic with a deeper blue mantle wrapped around his shoulders and fastened with a huge sapphire and gold ornamented pin. A chain of linked gold rosettes inlaid with precious stones hung loosely around his waist, and on his head sat a slim gold coronet encrusted with sapphires.

The queen wore emerald green, cross-banded with threads of gold. Her dark hair was caught loosely at the nape of her neck, and encased in a lattice frame of gold thread and topped by a small gold circlet. She had a serene and calm countenance about her, but underneath there was no doubting the King had a stoic and faithful ally, all attributes any husband would welcome in a wife. Adored by her husband, whom in return she adored herself, they were to have sixteen children.

Edward waved a beringed hand around the assembly. He had changed little since the last time Guy had seen him some two years earlier. He was thirty-five years old, the same age as himself, but his jaw-length black hair, which was parted in the centre, had started to turn white, as had his short beard. He was a handsome man with heavy-lidded, vivid light blue eyes, one drooping significantly, but despite their sleepy appearance, they missed very little. Spying Guy standing in the congregation, he made his way over to him.

'Guy!' he exclaimed enthusiastically. 'How fare you?'

Guy bowed deeply. 'I am well, thank you, Your Grace.'

'I was sorry to hear of Sir Robert's death. My father had always regarded him with friendship as well as a great respect.'

'It was indeed a sorry day, Your Grace, as grievous as the day we lost your own father.'

'Yes, indeed it was.'

There passed a sad grimness in his expression, but it lightened when his eyes rested on Lucie standing beside him.

'Ah, now, who is this?'

'Your Grace, please allow me to introduce you to my lady wife, Lucie,' said Guy, proudly.

Lucie was with child and looked radiant in a deep burgundy gown. The colour brought out the chestnut hues in her hair, which was covered with a short silver gauze veil. The voluminous skirt that hung from beneath her breasts could not disguise how heavily pregnant she was. Being so close to her time, she really should have been confined to her bed, or to the house at least, and even though she knew some might consider her being there highly inappropriate, she was not about to miss this rare opportunity to meet the King. She gracefully curtseyed long and deep.

'Your Grace.'

Guy helped her up again by cupping one hand under one elbow and placing his other arm around her ample waist. She had worried that her weight and extended stomach would hamper the deployment and that she might topple over. She turned and gratefully thanked him with a nod and a smile.

'How wonderful,' smiled Edward.

Whether he referred to Guy's attentiveness, their marital union, Lucie herself, or her gravid state, nobody could fathom. Maybe it referred to all four?

Lucie and Guy bowed their heads graciously as he moved off and made his way over to the throne and sat down. Eleanor, his queen, sat to one side looking on. With everybody in place, the ceremony, a solemn and religious affair, began.

Adam Fitzgibbon was the first in line to swear the oath and be knighted. He was brought forward and presented to the King by two sponsors who introduced him.

'Adam Fitzgibbon, son of William Fitzgibbon of Rouen, Your Grace.'

Adam knelt before his King. He wore a white vest to symbolise purity, which was covered by a red robe, symbolising nobility. Black hose and shoes, which symbolised death, finished off the ensemble. He solemnly took his vows and swore his oath of allegiance. The oath was an expression of sincerity and fealty, and should he ever break it he would, according to the church, face divine retribution. Then came the important part; the dubbing.

Edward stood, and taking the proffered blessed broadsword from the Archbishop, rested it first on Adam's left shoulder and then on his right.

'Adam Fitzgibbon, I dub thee Sir Knight. Arise, Sir Adam,' he pronounced.

Adam stood up and stepped back, whereupon his sponsors girded on his sword and spurs. There were to be two more pronouncements before the assembled nobles could retake their oaths of fealty.

Gilbert de Clare stood before the King, who remained seated and, keeping his eyes downcast, recited the oath he had originally quoted to King Henry III twelve years earlier, when his own father, Richard, had died.

'My Lord, I came to you with nothing and I begged for your mercy. In your generosity, you gave me all the necessities of life and took me under your protection. In return, I pledge my devotion and services to you, and as long as I live I shall remain faithful and true to you in word and deed.'

At this point, Sir Godfrey made a moue of distaste and, leaning close, he hissed in Sir Hugh's ear.

'Look at him, the sycophant. He should stop his fawning, it will not serve him. If the King has any sense, he will remember how he changes sides more often than the wind changes direction.'

Sir Hugh pursed his lips and stared stonily down at the floor. He needed to distance himself from Godfrey Bartholomew. This was not the time or the place to voice his resentments, and he most certainly did not want to get involved or be seen to take sides. *That* could be a very dangerous game indeed.

'I shall never resign from my duty to you and I will pass the rest of my days as your true and loyal servant.'

De Clare then knelt before the King and, as an act of homage, offered his clasped hands.

He finished by saying, 'I swear my fealty to God and to you, my King.'

Edward took his hands in his own and stood, raising De Clare up with him.

'I accept your fealty and thank you for your loyalty.'

There was a quiet 'harrumph' heard at Sir Hugh's shoulder.

Letting go of his hands, Gilbert was able to step back. He paused, and bowed deeply.

*

It was a splendid banquet. The long oak dining table was set with plates and goblets of silver. Hands were washed and once seated, grace was said by the chaplain. Today, before the feast commenced proper, a surprise dish was set before the King. It was a huge pie, which he was urged to open. When the King removed the crust, to his delight, a flock of blackbirds flew out, to *tchak* and swoop around the chamber. The horrified Queen had to be assured that the birds had not actually been baked in the pie but the pie crust cooked first and the birds placed inside once it had cooled! Tureens of rich sauces and silver flagons of fine red wine from Burgundy were scattered around the table. Dish after dish laden with cold roast meats, fowl and pies were paraded in and placed before the King. He tasted all the dishes first. His favourite, roasted swan in a spiced wine sauce, like all the others once he had had his fill, was passed down the table.

In the common hall downstairs, the air was hazy with smoke and heavy with the smell of roasting meat and bread. Its walls had been draped with the arms of many great houses and, taking pride of place, hung the red and gold three lions of Edward I alongside the yellow and red chevrons of Clare. Serving boys and girls ran back and forth, carrying many dishes. Tuns of ale lined all four walls. The occasion had warranted the Lord's permission for everyone to take their fill. This was not an invitation to be missed, and full advantage was taken of it. It was very noisy; voices could be barely heard above the din of clanging pewter plates and cups, raucous laughter and the mutterings of drunken conversation. It was especially noisy at the far end of the hall next to the kitchens, where Percy, Mary and Robin sat. Mary, who had been working in the kitchens since first light, was taking some well-deserved respite. She sat very close to Percy, who straddled the bench with his long legs. He leant even closer to talk into her ear. Whatever he had said made her giggle and blush. Young Robin sat quite happily next to the canoodling pair, crunching on a plate of roasted onions and watching the antics of those around him. A couple of jokers were trying their hand at mummery and were mimicking the hunt, apishly prancing around the hall, one on the back of the other and chasing after their imaginary prey. He hooted when an ale-sodden retainer laughed so much he fell backwards off his bench, pulling his neighbour with him.

After the banquet, for the King's entertainment, there was jousting on the outer bailey and quintain in the tiltyard. Those relegated to the outfields had already put on their own entertainment to keep themselves amused. The meadows became a sea of colour.

Tents with silk banners rippled in the breeze, and outside each one, shields displayed the identity of its occupant. Pavilions had been raised by the river and the townsfolk, not to be left out of the merry-making, were invited to come and see the spectacle, watch the games and to sell their wares. The knights in their polished helmets, hauberks and silk tabards displaying their family coat of arms, and the destriers adorned in full battle dress, the splendour of it all took their breath away. The jousting would go on all day until dusk, the hooves of the great war horses tearing up clods of earth, which left a scar for months to come as a reminder of their presence. People screamed for their favourites and exclamations were cried out in unison as riders clashed together, their lances cracking and splintering on impact. One unfortunate knight was unhorsed so violently he flew backwards, his legs in the air, to land with a resounding splosh in the river. After the initial gasps of dismay from the crowd, they could not contain their mirth when he finally emerged from his dunking, coughing and spluttering with a circlet of yellow and white water-crowfoot adorning his helmet. But they cheered loudly when he bowed graciously to his conqueror.

Fires stayed alight all through the night, where bacon, eggs and onions were fried and huge cauldrons of meat pottage bubbled, supplied by the castle and stirred by the household servants. In the fire's glow, jugglers juggled, mummers cavorted and men gambled and got drunk. Carousing soldiers sang bawdy songs, local whores and camp followers vied for business, making the odd scuffle and cat-fight a consequence. In contrast, over the other side of the camp, singers and musicians filled the warm night air with sweet, melodious music, and lovers sneaked off to find a quiet place by the river to make love to it under a clear and beautiful starlit sky…

What a time was had by all! They talked about 'when the King came to town' for years, and how Tonbridge had never seen the like before, or since, and probably never would again.

*

The King was to go on from Tonbridge to Otford, where he stayed briefly with the Archbishop of Winchelsey at his home, The Bishop's Palace,[19] and where Thomas Becket, the Archbishop of Canterbury, had once lived.

Edward, eager to keep such a determinedly fierce and ruthless subject, albeit a suspect loyal one on his side, decided to entice Gilbert closer into his alliance by offering his daughter, Joan of Acre, in marriage. Gilbert, already being estranged from his wife for some years, declared the marriage to Alice invalid, and after disinheriting his two daughters, he remarried into the royal family. (What a cad!) Tonbridge Castle grew in status alongside its Lord, and when Edward embarked on a trip to Flanders, he left his son Edward, Prince of Caernarvon, and the Great Seal of England in the castle's care. This was an honour indeed for Tonbridge.

---

[19] Standing in ruins today – Otford, near Sevenoaks.

Epilogue

The window shutters had been thrown open, filling the chamber with light, and a gentle breeze wafted through, bringing with it the scent of late summer.

Lucie lay snuggled against Guy, her head resting in the juncture of his shoulder blade, her limbs wantonly thrown across his chest and lower torso. Guy pillowed his head with one bent arm, and lightly stroked her thigh and buttock as he cradled her with the other. They lay relaxed and contented in the aftermath of their lovemaking. With half-closed lids, Guy looked down on Lucie's flushed and upturned face, framed by her luxurious and tousled chestnut hair.

Starvecrow had prospered. By selective breeding, fleeces and surplus lambs had fetched good prices. They had also invested in a small flock of Lincolns, a breed being well-woolled to the knees and hocks. This produced a heavier and considerably more lustrous fleece than the Cotswold, and they were considering keeping some back for dyeing and weaving at Starvecrow. The cloth would be of a high quality, as good as any Flemish weave but would not accrue the added costs of transportation and would therefore mean less expenditure for the end customer. Lucie was confident that some of the tenant women had the skills for the task and, given the opportunity, would benefit hugely working from their own homes.

She gently fingered the ragged scar running down his side.

'Are we going to visit the women today?'

'Today is as good a day as any, I suppose,' replied Guy, tucking a lock of hair behind her ear.

The baby snuffled in his cot next to the bed. He was a good baby. He suckled well and, once replete, slept for most of the night but he always woke hungry, and after a while started to become quiet fractious.

Raising herself up onto her knees, Lucie leant forward and cupped Guy's face in her hands. She kissed him lingeringly. He responded by wrapping his arms around her and drawing her close. Her heavy and swollen milk-sore breasts brushed against his chest. She winced and drew away.

'Um, I must feed the babe.'

Getting up, she pulled on a robe to cover her nakedness and went over to pluck their screaming son from his bed. Guy propped himself up onto one elbow to watch Robert, his firstborn, being put to the breast. He guzzled furiously, a strand of his mother's hair clutched tightly in his tiny fist.

Guy swallowed hard. The sight had brought a lump to his throat. It was a shame his father had not been here to see his grandson born. He glanced over at the framed needlepoint on the wall across the room. His mother had sewn it when she and his father were first married. 'Love is foreseen from the beginning, and outlasts the end,' it read. He looked back at Lucie and his son, and his heart swelled with love and pride. Feeling his eyes upon her, Lucie looked up and smiled back at him.

*

Roger wandered into the garden, where an old fallen apple tree provided a comfortable seat. He sat and, placing his walking stick to one side, stretched his legs out in front of him. He leant back against a conveniently placed bough. It was a glorious morning. He closed his eyes and raised his face to bask in the already warm rays of the early morning sun. He heard a noise and opened one eye to see Heloise walking towards him. She was so beautiful, and he knew he was the most fortunate man in the world. They were to be married soon. If things had gone to plan and she had married Richard, they would never have had the opportunity, and that knowledge made their love for each other all the more precious. She sat down beside him, and he closed his hand over hers and squeezed it. They sat in silence, content within each other's company. Heloise had brought with her needle, thread and a half-finished linen shirt she was embroidering. This was her wedding gift to Roger, and she would often come and sit out here to take full advantage of the daylight. But for the moment, she sat idly, casting an eye over the beds of lilies, campanula, phlox and bergamot. Their heady scent hung in the air, and she breathed in deeply and closed her eyes. Bees droned as they drifted haphazardly from bloom to bloom, the resident robin trilled from a nearby tree. Somewhere, softly, across the valley, a cuckoo called…

Suddenly the peace was shattered by the sound of the new baby crying.

'The young master has a lusty pair of lungs on him, does he not?' chuckled Roger.

Opening her eyes, Heloise turned to look upon her betrothed.

'He most certainly does,' she laughed as she picked up her needlecraft.

*

As the crow flew over Starvecrow Manor, it heard, with some satisfaction, the baby crying. Through the open window she was pleased to see the trinket box containing the gold and garnet brooch sitting back where it belonged on the windowsill. Looking down, she spied a couple sitting companionably in the garden and, flying over the knoll, a shepherd reclining in the short, sheep-cropped pasture, chewing on a blade of grass as he watched over the flocks. She soared higher. All was very quiet; the air hummed softly past her ears and stirred the feathers on her long, broad wings as she glided over the lush green meadows and fields of pinkish-gold corn, which stretched up to a belt of oak and beech and, eventually, to a cloudless blue horizon. Only the sounds of a late summer morning obtruded; the murmur of scythes reaping the corn, the gossip and laughter of the tiny figures below, who walked behind forking the bales into rough stooks for drying. The gleaners, bending over the stubble, worked their way across the shaved strips, standing now and again to stretch their aching backs or to call to each other, squinting and shading their eyes from the brightness of the sun. Their offspring squealed with delight as they played leapfrog up and down the field's margins. To her right, the rooftops of the abbey came into view. In the lower orchard, cattle lowed lazily and munched on the sweet summer grass. A brown-clad lay brother walked into the stables with a dung fork and a bucket to hand. Others bustled across the maze of courtyards and outbuildings, from storerooms to kitchens, fetching water from the well in the cloister to fill the huge pots for cooking. Chickens squawked at the arrival of their breakfast and the chapel bell resonated, tolling on the still air, calling a procession of nuns to their devotions. They made their silent way along the stone cloister towards the Lady Chapel with its rose window, their heads bowed in reverence and their arms folded within the wide confines of their white robes. She continued on her course, over the stream where the fields of Starvecrow finished and those of Whitelawne began. Laundry was hung out to dry between the huddle of Whitelawne cottages. There was an enthusiastic bestirring about the place. Her eyes zoomed down on the busy scene. Men were up ladders hammering and sawing, re-lining and mending their roofs. A bakehouse was being erected, and a dairy. A table was being laid for breakfast in the shade of the alder tree. Laughter tinkled in the air as womenfolk walked across the worn grass track, carrying platters of bread, meat and cheese, jugs of milk, and two huge pitchers of ale. She coasted up to the crest of common land where children gathered wood, a small flock of sheep grazed, and a couple of pigs rooted. She could not resist diving down, cawing loudly to flush out the small birds and send rabbits scattering in all directions, to take cover under the ribboned yellow, spiky and green-black gorse. She swept up over the trees again to change direction, circling high and around to follow the ridge road, back to the top of Starvecrow Hill and over the deep thatched roof of The Starveling Crow. In the yard an unshaven and tousled man stood scratching his backside. Tipping his head back, he gaped an expansive yawn. As he opened his eyes, for a startling second, they met with the crow's, and then she was gone, down towards the willow-fringed hay-scented meadow speckled red, white and yellow with poppies and ox-eye daisies.

She headed for their favourite perch, an ancient oak, half of whose branches were dead and where moss and lichen clung to its bole, and creeping ivy hung heavily from its limbs. It was cool and dim in the wood. As she came to rest, there were flutterings from above and the occasional angry quork of complaint at being disturbed. She uttered a harsh, croaking call in response, fluffed out her glossy black plumage and, after preening her feathers, settled down, wholly satisfied that the future of Starvecrow was secured for the next generation.